Wicked Sunset

Book #4 in the Sunset Vampire Series

Jaz Primo

RUTHERFORD LITERARY GROUP

www.rutherfordliterary.com

Novels by Jaz Primo

The Sunset Vampire Series
Sunrise at Sunset: Revamped
A Bloody London Sunset
Summit at Sunset
Wicked Sunset
Sunset Rising **

** Additional Titles Forthcoming

* * *

The Logan Bringer Urban Fantasy Series
Bringer of Fire
Bringer Unleashed *

* Additional Titles Forthcoming

* * *

Gwen Reaper
(A Young Adult Paranormal Romance)
**Winner of the Paranormal Romance Guild's Reviewer's
Choice Award for Best Young Adult Novel of 2012!**

* * *

All titles published by Rutherford Literary Group

This is a work of fiction. Names, characters, places, and incidents either are the product of the author's imagination or are used fictitiously, and any resemblance to actual persons, living or dead, business establishments, events, or locales is entirely coincidental. The publisher does not have any control over and does not assume any responsibility for author or third-party websites or their content. Any trademarks mentioned herein are not authorized by the trademark owners and do not in any way mean the work is sponsored by or associated with the trademark owners. Any trademarks used are specifically in a descriptive capacity.

Published by:
Rutherford Literary Group
1205 S. Air Depot, PMB #135
Midwest City, OK 73110-4807

Cover art by Sharon Legg
Sharon Legg Digital Art

Edited by Lea Ellen Borg
Night Owl Editing Services

ISBN 0988569027
ISBN-13 978-0988569027

DEDICATION

This book is dedicated to the beta men in the world, who have strong and heroic hearts, majestic souls, and dedication to the women they love that's just as mighty as, or stronger than, any alpha men (who typically play at being heroes until it's time to do dishes, help with the laundry, give the children a bath, take out the trash, etc.). And for all the amazing alpha women in the world who love their beta men; strong women who recognize and cherish the valued daily commitment to thoughtful and supportive acts of love that honor them.

CONTENTS

ACKNOWLEDGMENTS

As ever, my love and thanks to my best friend and wife, Lori, who tirelessly supports and encourages my literary journey. My special thanks to our long-lived cat, Selina, who steadfastly interrupted hours of typing to remind me of the need for infrequent breaks; albeit for attention and treats for her, of course.

Thank you to my gifted and talented editor, Lea Ellen, whose mastery of prose and grammar and keen attention to detail has helped make me become a better author. Special thanks to my cover artist, Sharon, who has captured, and visually reflected, the spirit and emotion of the Sunset Vampire Series.

A heartfelt shout-out to my supportive friends and family for their wonderful and valued support and encouragement. And my sincere thanks to my beta readers, who are a constant source of thoughtful and valuable feedback for my novels.

Part I

Atlanta

JAZ PRIMO

CHAPTER 1

Caleb

Just as gravity perpetually held the moon in orbit, my heart was upheld by the sheer power of love.

My daily thoughts were focused upon not only the lovely vision, but the mesmerizing presence, of one woman; the most dangerous and beautiful vampire in the world.

* * *

A summer's day in downtown Atlanta was hotter than hell; the nights were merely purgatory.

Strolling through the evening streets, I looked up at the tall woman beside me who could easily pass for an Amazon stolen from ancient lore.

Her long red hair cascaded about her shoulders like a beautiful mantle and she carried herself with a poise suggesting royal bearing, though she'd scoff if I ever told her that.

Her name was Katrina "Kat" Rawlings; a vampire.

She's my vampire.

I held her hand as we proceeded down the sidewalk amidst a veritable fog of humidity.

She gazed down at me, her sharp emerald eyes piercing

into mine in striking fashion. "Looking forward to the concert, my love?" she asked.

"Yep, I'm ready to rock."

It'd only been a week since we returned home from the near-fatal vampire conference in Slovenia; scarcely time for us to unpack, really. And yet we were already fully engaged in new ventures.

That evening, our destination was a rock concert at the Philips Arena.

A passing car blaring Beastie Boys' "Make Some Noise" momentarily distracted me.

Kat tightened her grip on my hand to refocus my attention. "There's still time to cancel if you don't feel up to it," she said. "You have a lingering concussion, after all."

My concussion was the *lovely* parting gift I'd acquired back in Slovenia in the act of saving the lives of people, and a number of vampires, who I cared deeply about—including the woman beside me.

Kat's the love of my life. How could I have done any less?

"I feel fine," I replied.

"You look more than fine to me," she said.

Her intense gaze pierced through me, seizing me where I stood, and I felt the electric charge of desire permeating the space between us. Since the first moment I'd set eyes on her, she'd affected me in a chemical, almost feral, manner.

I felt inexorably drawn to her.

My pulse quickened as a carnal appetite grew inside me. The edges of her mouth edged upward in that I-read-your-body-and-know-what-you're-feeling manner. It was yet another of her innate vampire-related abilities that made me feel nearly naked, like some open book for her to consume.

I'm hers to consume; utterly and without reservation.

For as many times as she'd partaken in my blood, it felt as though she'd likewise injected her very essence into my bloodstream.

Kat was my only true craving.

She was all I wanted in life.

She guided us alongside the nearest building and towered before me. Grasping my chin between her fingertips, she titled my head upward and pressed her soft lips against mine in a passionate kiss.

And just like that, it felt as if the world around me ceased to exist. All that mattered was Kat and me.

"I want—"

She kissed me again.

"You want what?" she muttered against my lips, eliciting a tickling sensation.

I grinned. "You."

"I can arrange that," she whispered.

She kissed me deeply and I felt my breath practically being drawn from my lungs.

Heaven on Earth.

Then a fleeting pang of guilt washed over me.

"Paige and Ethan," I said. "They're waiting."

"I could text them to go ahead without us. Then it would be just you and me at home for the entire night."

Honestly, at that moment, I was half-tempted to give in to that idea.

"That'd be rude, given how Paige has been going on about Angelical Tears since she heard their tour was stopping here," I said. "Heck, it's like she's a part-time promoter for them or something."

Angelical Tears was a modern Goth-metal-alternative rock group that my dear friend, almost a sister, Paige Turner, had brought to my attention.

After listening to some sample tracks, I had to admit the group had a unique sound. They'd recently come into their own and had begun a nationwide tour, and I was looking forward to hearing them.

Kat nodded her head. "Paige has been rather insistent lately, hasn't she?"

"So, how about a rain check on some quality kissing until post-concert?" I asked.

"I'll seriously consider it," she said coquettishly.

She kissed me.

"Maybe just one for the road," she said.

"Hey, you lip-lockers!" called a familiar voice from across the street. "Hurry up or we'll miss the warm-up group!"

"Speak of the devil," Kat said.

We proceeded to the Philips Arena, and the building was at near-capacity level.

Angelical Tears sounded great, and the audience loved them. Their songs varied from pounding hard rock and visceral lyrics to sweeping romantic tracks that spoke of heartfelt passion, and on occasion, lamenting.

The lead singer was a beautiful young woman who had a powerful angelic-sounding voice. Additionally, her inclusion of Russian lyrics in some of the songs was exotic and visceral sounding.

The band played guitars and drums like extensions of their own bodies, pouring raw, heated emotion into their performance. Combined with synthesizers, their sound was both unique and enthralling.

It was no wonder they attracted such a large fan base.

They seemed liked an epic band that was destined for greatness.

During the concert, something odd caught my attention. Despite their obvious Goth elements, the lead singer and the bass player had other familiar qualities.

I wrapped my arm around Kat's waist and spoke into her ear. "Hey, two of them look kind of like vampires, don't you think?"

She merely nodded, but Paige tapped me on the shoulder and gave me an exaggerated wink.

"No wonder you love them," I said.

She merely smiled, swaying in time to the music.

After the concert, which included two curtain calls, Paige led us past a group of fans along a rope barricade to the area leading back stage.

"Paige Turner and company," she said to a muscular

man holding an electronic tablet.

He motioned with a nod for us to proceed.

"You know the band?" I asked.

"Hey, I know people," she said.

"And I bet they usually end up a pint shy of blood for that," I said.

"Oh, hush, snark-face," she said.

Soon, we were standing backstage talking with the band. Paige introduced us to Julia, the vampire lead singer, and her vampire mate, Glenn, the bass player.

"Great concert," I said. "Julia, your voice is amazing, and Glenn, you rocked that bass."

They were both very kind and gracious. I quickly felt comfortable around them, so it made asking my next question so much easier.

"Aren't you afraid of all the attention?" I asked. "I mean, people are going to notice your lack of aging eventually."

"No problem," Glenn said. "It'll take a long time before those things became an issue. Lots of bands like ours wear makeup, which helps."

"That's all it takes, a little makeup?" I asked.

"Dude, look at KISS," he said.

Julia frowned at him. "Really, Glenn, KISS? That's who came to mind first?"

He shrugged. "It is what it is. Hey, how about a beer?"

"Don't forget, honey, we're signing for fans in twenty minutes," Julia said.

He grinned. "Just one. Maybe two, tops."

I chuckled and followed him to a nearby cooler where we drank beers and talked about their nationwide tour.

I had a blast, and even Katrina seemed to enjoy herself. Without a doubt, Julia and Glenn had earned my vampire stamp of approval.

And they even signed our concert T-shirts.

* * *

By the time we'd finished visiting with Glenn and Julia, the crowd had thinned out significantly. Kat and I held hands while Ethan and Paige walked arm and arm behind us during the walk to the parking garage.

"Angelical Tears was great," Ethan said. "I have a feeling they're going places."

"Yeah, the next city," Paige piped up. "They are on a nationwide tour, after all."

I heard a growl and a squeal, and glanced over my shoulder to see Ethan trapping Paige in his arms and wriggling his face against her neck.

She squealed again. "Hey, no fangs!"

"Glenn and Julia seem really wonderful," Kat said.

"Yeah. And Julia's voice has amazing range, not to mention she's a beautiful woman," I said. "And it was nice of them to sign our T-shirts."

"Hey, vampires make great singers," Paige said, as she and Ethan quickly fell into step behind us again. "And, kiddo, don't forget that one of those shirts is mine."

"You know, if they make it really big, they're going to have to be careful being in the limelight," Ethan said. "Entertainers receive a lot of scrutiny from the media."

"Well, as vampires, at least they can devour the paparazzi," Paige said wryly.

Kat and I both glanced over our shoulders at her.

"What? It's only paparazzi; they're not like real people, right? Who'd care, really?" she countered.

Kat and I looked at each other and simultaneously shrugged as Ethan chuckled.

Standing in the parking garage elevator, I regretted that the evening had passed so quickly.

Isn't life just like that? The good times are so fleeting.

"Which floor?" I asked.

"We're on three," Paige said. "And it's a level, not a floor."

"It doesn't matter. There's a floor on each level," I said. "You know, that stuff made of concrete."

She gave me a look. "Whatever, college boy."

"Paige, maybe you and Ethan would like to come over for drinks?" Kat asked.

"Nah, me and my old man are heading straight home for some hot sex-capades," she said.

Ethan appeared quite pleased while Kat and I merely stared at her.

"What?" she asked. "We're all adults here, right?"

"Uh, maybe a little TMI," Kat said.

"I'm just sayin'," Paige said. "Hey, it's not like I said, 'we're heading home so he can bend me over and stuff me with his---"

"*Paige*," Kat interrupted.

She stuck her tongue out at Kat.

I couldn't help but laugh.

When the doors to the third level opened, only a sparse number of vehicles remained.

"Here you are," I said. "Kat and I are on the next floor."

"Level," Paige corrected.

"Whatever," I said.

Kat and I said our goodbyes to them and proceeded up to the next level.

Floor?

I looked at Kat.

"In a hotel or office building, it's called a floor," I said. "Why does a parking garage make it a level?"

"Please don't start," she said.

I shrugged.

"I had a blast tonight," I said as the elevator doors opened.

There were only sporadic vehicles parked on our— *elevation*—so I easily spotted Kat's Audi.

We scarcely walked twenty feet when the elevator doors opened behind us. We both turned to see Paige exiting.

"Hey, gimme' my concert T-shirt," she said.

As I reached into the bag I was carrying, strange popping noises sounded and two distinct holes appeared in the door of the car beside us.

"Wha—?" I said.

"Gun!" Kat yelled, pulling me down onto the concrete.

"Crap!" Paige yelled from behind us.

CHAPTER 2

Caleb

Two additional muted popping noises preceded more holes appearing in the side of the vehicle just above our heads.

Adrenaline surged through my body, awakening an acute sense of alertness that nearly overwhelmed my senses.

Kat jerked on my arm and literally pulled me across the concrete toward the opposite side of the vehicle.

"Stay down," she ordered, bodily pressing me against the rough concrete.

Yeah, right; as if I was going to be able to get up with a six-foot tall vampire practically sitting atop me.

"Are you hurt?" she asked.

I tried in vain to determine where Paige was as I heard the sound of someone yelling and then what sounded like a windshield breaking.

"Dammit, are you *hurt?*" Kat demanded.

"What? No!" I snapped.

"One down!" Paige's voice echoed from somewhere deeper in the parking garage.

"We've gotta' help her, Kat," I urged while trying to wriggle free from beneath her.

Her face loomed before mine, our noses almost touching.

"Stay!" she hissed in a tone that chilled my blood.

I could practically feel the harsh tone of her voice against my skin as her command reverberated through my body.

I lay stunned and immobile as my heartbeat raced, thundering in my ears.

She dialed her cell phone with one hand, and I noticed she was holding a small combat knife in her other.

"Gunmen on our level. Paige engaged. One down. Quantity unknown," she said into the phone.

Moments later, a vehicle's tires squealed, followed by the sound of a motor revving and accelerating.

"Go help Paige," I said.

"Shush. Not yet," she said.

What the hell was she waiting for?

"Clear!" Paige's voice echoed in the distance. "One's getting away!"

Kat moved in a blur and I felt the immediate absence of her weight from atop me.

Before I could begin to rise, she was already gone. All I heard was the muted sounds of rapid footsteps against pavement.

"You okay?" Ethan asked, seemingly from nowhere.

I thought my heart stopped as my head whipped around to stare at him. I was met with full-on nausea and the world seemed to spin for a moment.

"Whoa," I said.

Firm hands grasped me by the upper arms, solidly supporting me in place.

"Slowly, Caleb. You've got a concussion," he cautioned. "Remember?"

"Hey, *you* surprised *me*," I said with no small degree of irritation.

"You okay?" he asked.

Ignoring the sense of nausea rolling through my stomach, I nodded while pensively scanning the area.

Horns blared loudly followed by the sounds of two vehicles crashing together from one of the lower levels.

Somebody screamed once in surprise off to our left, followed by the sounds of people conversing in urgent tones.

Ethan cocked his head to one side. "I'll check it out. Stay put. Got it?"

I scarcely had time to nod before he disappeared from view as air swirled around me.

"Hi, ladies," his voice echoed a short distance away. "Listen; there's been some trouble here in the parking garage tonight."

"Oh, no," a woman said. "What happened? I heard a crash just now…"

"Well, I think there were some gunshots nearby, and then there's some sort of car accident that just happened a couple of levels down…"

The telltale sound of a heavy metal door opening echoed from somewhere nearby.

Maybe a stairwell door?

The waves of nausea abated as I crept back toward the elevator where I could find partial cover behind another pair of parked cars.

Seconds later, Paige and Kat reappeared. Kat carried a body over her shoulder while Paige held a large rifle.

"I'll go get the other body," she said, handing the rifle to Katrina.

In the time it took to blink my eyes, she had disappeared from view.

"Caleb? A little help here?" Kat asked, holding the rifle away from her body.

I grabbed the rifle by its stock and followed her in the direction of our car while glancing over my shoulder in Ethan's direction.

I didn't see anyone.

"We need to stow this guy in the trunk before someone sees," Kat said.

I stared at the prone fellow that she hefted over her shoulder. He was Caucasian and appeared to be in his mid-to-late thirties, if I had to guess. His neck had ugly-looking black and purple bruises around it.

He looks human.

"What about surveillance cameras?" I asked.

"The ones along the main route in or out of here were all disabled," she said. "Looks like our shooters took care of that before they set up."

"Wouldn't someone have noticed that by now?" I asked.

"Most surveillance systems are on autopilot," she said as she placed the body in our trunk. "Actually, you'd be surprised how few of those cameras are actively monitored. They're mainly forensic; helpful for looking back at what's already happened."

"That's not particularly reassuring," I said.

"Makes most people *feel* secure though, doesn't it?" she asked.

The irony in her statement wasn't lost on me. I had grown to feel secure surrounded by vampires, and yet, I'd nearly died tonight.

The entire situation felt surreal.

She snatched the rifle from my grip and stowed it atop the body in our trunk.

"Hey, you only had to ask," I said.

She gave me a cold stare that could probably freeze open flames.

"Don't even start," she said.

I wanted to snap back with something sarcastic. However, given her demeanor, I chose the diplomatic high road of keeping my mouth shut.

"I hope I don't have to torch my car after this," she said while slamming the trunk closed.

I hadn't considered the post-killing clean-up process. I fleetingly contemplated the merits of watching more TV crime dramas and forensic documentaries.

"Where's Paige?" Ethan asked, startling me.

I jolted and my heart practically stopped.

"Crap," I said. "You surprised me."

Get a grip, Taylor.

12

"Funny," Kat said sweetly, though with a smile that didn't meet her eyes. "I noticed he was there."

Oh, how I wanted to say something completely out of line.

Calm. Calm. Don't encourage her. Just shut up.

Ethan must've sensed my irritation because he shook his head ever so slightly at me in silent caution.

"I directed those women away from the area," he said. "But I heard more voices not far from here."

I noticed something moving out of the corner of my eye and turned to see petite-looking Paige effortlessly balancing a tall man's body over her shoulder.

"Get in the car, Caleb," Kat said.

"Ethan! Let's get this thug into our trunk," Paige said.

"You got it," he said, taking the body from her. "I parked over here."

"Ever the gentleman," she quipped.

The two of them quickly headed away just as a small group of people exited the elevator not far from us.

"Caleb," Kat said. "The car. Now."

I frowned at her, miffed that she was treating me like a child. I gave her a dirty look as I opened the passenger door.

She revved the engine at first, but then casually backed out and drove to the exit as if nothing unusual had just occurred.

I looked into the side mirror to see Ethan and Paige trailing us in their car.

I was beside myself with curiosity over what we intended to do with the bodies, but I simply felt too miffed at Kat to ask her anything. Instead, I silently fumed while staring out the passenger window.

Prior to our Slovenia trip, I'd have put up with such things. Now, I no longer appreciated people telling me what to do.

And I've killed two people since then.

Well, one person and one vampire, anyway.

And yet, that fact still hadn't quite sunk in yet. It also felt unreal, like a bad dream.

And I was surprised by how little guilt I felt over that recollection.

Baldar Dubravko definitely deserved to die, though perhaps not the limousine driver.

Kat remained silent as she drove us back to the estate. The only sounds were road noise and classical music playing over our digital radio.

I had to admit that the cessation of conflict between us was refreshing.

We'd no sooner pulled up in front of our garage when Kat turned bossy again.

"Go inside and lock the doors," she said. "Set the security system and don't leave the house until I return."

This is getting really old fast.

I folded my arms before me and stared back at her incredulously.

"Somebody's acting awfully bitchy and tyrannical all of the sudden," I said.

She stared at me with a wholly displeased expression.

"*Tyrannical?* Oh, don't even go there right now," she warned. "I'm not in the mood."

"Hey, I didn't choose for us to walk into an ambush, you know."

Her eyes flared bright green. "Oh, so I did?"

"Look, I never said----"

She held up her hand. "Stop. Just go inside like I asked. Please."

As I exited the car, I wondered, not for the first time, if female vampires could suffer from bouts of PMS.

Glancing toward the street, I noticed that Ethan's car was stopped further down the driveway just inside the gates. Paige was standing near the open passenger door watching me.

She mouthed a question. What?

I shrugged at her and threw my hands up in a questioning gesture.

Kat got out and promptly retrieved two shovels, an axe, and a container of lantern fuel from the garage. She glared at me on her return to the car.

"House. Now," she said.

Not wanting to create a scene, I marched into the garage and hit the button to close the overhead door.

Later, as I sat on one of our kitchen barstools drinking a cold beer, I contemplated the night's events.

Was tonight's attack intended for me, or for Kat?

Or maybe both?

* * *

By the time Kat returned, it was well past one o'clock in the morning. I was in the back living room lying on the couch watching television when I heard her enter from the garage, disable the alarm, and walk into the kitchen.

Well, Ms. Snippy's returned.

"That's done," she said, sounding quite a bit less sarcastic than earlier.

"Welcome back," I said neutrally.

I switched off the TV and got up from the couch to go take a shower. Between the late hour and my growing sense of exhaustion from my abated adrenaline rush, I'd had more than enough drama for one night.

"Don't you want to know what happened?" she asked.

I turned and looked into the kitchen where she was leaning against the island counter.

"I'm sure you handled everything just fine," I said.

"You aren't even curious?" she asked.

I inhaled a deep breath and let it out slowly.

"Honestly, it's easier not to ask," I said. "It'll probably just lead to an argument, and I really dread fighting with you."

I turned to walk down the hallway in the direction of our sublevel master bedroom. The air swished around me and she stood before me, regarding me with a gentle expression.

She grasped me by the shoulders. "I let my guard down tonight, and it might've cost me the man I love. That made me angry, and I apologize if I directed some of my frustration at you."

"I suppose that makes sense," I said, though I still felt somewhat annoyed by her earlier behavior.

She softly kissed me on the lips, and pulled me into an embrace.

Okay, this is nice.

She pulled away from me and gazed down into my eyes, all hints of her earlier aggravation gone.

"However, someone needs to be just a little less defensive," she said. "I'm looking out for your best interests; particularly your safety."

Okay, maybe not so nice, after all.

"And I appreciate that," I said. "But it's not healthy to order me around. It feels dismissive, as if I'm some kind of subordinate or something."

Though I felt her arms tighten around me, to her credit it seemed as if she was considering what I'd just said.

"Why do I end up feeling like the bad guy at times like this?" she asked.

"Listen, you're not the bad guy," I said. "I love you and I'm grateful for what you've done for me, including protecting me."

She frowned. "Where did this independent, self-sufficient streak come from all of the sudden?"

I shrugged.

"I dunno," I said. "Maybe I'm actually starting to feel a little less helpless for the first time in my life."

Slovenia changed a number of things for me, including my self-image.

Her eyebrows arched. "Oh, really?"

"Yeah, I think so," I said. "I realize I'm stronger than I thought I was. I'm not helpless anymore. You taught me how to defend myself, and helped me realize that, despite my past, maybe I'm not destined to be a victim."

She kissed me on the tip of the nose. "I won't let you be a victim."

"I know," I said. "Only now it's time for me to show you that you don't have to fight all my battles for me anymore."

"Caleb, I---"

"No," I said. "You have to let me prove it to you. If I finally believe in myself then why can't you?"

She sighed, shaking her head.

"I do believe in you," she said. "But I worry your self-confidence will overreach your good judgment, and I can't stand by and let that happen."

"Every bird falters when they first learn to fly," I said.

"Birds with concussions risk more than faltering," she said.

"Fair enough," I said.

She kissed me on the lips this time.

"But I'll consider being more lenient with you, moving forward," she said.

I resisted the strong inclination to roll my eyes.

"Gee, thanks," I said dryly.

"*Be nice*," she cautioned with a frown.

I bit my tongue and forced a conciliatory smile.

Geez, alpha vampires sometimes…

* * *

In the week following the parking garage event, the only mention on the local news was about the car accident that was brought upon by a 'man brandishing a rifle' who scared the drivers, thereby leading to a collision of vehicles.

Fortunately, there were only minor injuries reported. The news indicated that the local police were still investigating, though something told me that, given Kat's thorough nature, they wouldn't find either of the gunmen's bodies.

A shiver coursed through my body as I realized how close we'd come to being shot. For that reason alone, I pleasantly endured Kat's more protective nature since the event.

That's not to say I'd become a shut-in again as I had when Chimalma had pursued us. Instead, I merely had to accept that if I left the estate, Kat was coming with me.

While bearable, it was still like having a clingy girlfriend with fangs. I quickly gained an appreciation for shopping, if only to spend time away from the estate.

Admittedly, the new athletic shoes I purchased were working out nicely.

However, even the most patient person could only endure so much for so long, and I had no intentions of letting recent events rule my life.

I refuse to be ruled by either fear or fate.

An idea struck, and I immediately went into research mode.

Later, I peered into Kat's office at the back wing of the estate's first floor and found her rapidly typing on her notebook keyboard, which sounded like a small indoor hailstorm.

"Let me guess, you've hit upon the next great American novel," I said, casually leaning against the door jamb.

She paused and looked up with a curious expression.

"Got a minute?" I asked.

Her brow arched suspiciously.

"I was thinking about our parking garage event. I researched the topic of concealed carry firearms permits in the state of Georgia, and I---"

"No," she said flatly and returned to typing.

"Why the hell not?"

"You haven't mastered knife combat yet."

"I'm pretty good as it is. And just what do knives have to do with it?" I asked. "Come on, a gun is easy to use and doesn't require a lot of training. Instant protection."

She stopped typing and looked up at me. "Yes, and that's the problem. They're too easy; so easy that they give you a false sense of security. And if someone takes one from you, they can be used against you."

"But then, so can a knife," I said, feeling quite satisfied with myself for thinking fast.

"If someone takes a knife from you, there's still a good chance you can defend yourself. You might even be able to evade your attacker. Not so true with a firearm."

After pausing a few seconds to gloat, her gaze shifted smoothly back to her notebook screen.

Her logic was sound enough, though I hated to concede defeat.

"I don't actually *need* your permission, you know," I said. "I'm an adult, after all."

She looked up with a cool, commanding expression.

"Surely, that's very adult of you to say," she said, her voice thick with sarcasm. "And the answer is still *no*. Not yet, anyway. Keep practicing your knife techniques. Once you've mastered them to my satisfaction we'll talk about guns."

Her focus returned to her notebook and she resumed typing.

She's treating me like a damned child!

I was exasperated and a string of expletives flared my mind, ready for launch. However, I took a deep, deliberate breath and then slowly exhaled.

She paused from her typing and stared at the screen before her. "You're not going to let this go, are you?"

"Nope," I said.

"Tell me something. What happened to that agreeable mate of mine that used to be so much more…compliant?"

"He disappeared somewhere in Slovenia," I said.

She slowly looked up to stare at me with a probing expression.

I met her gaze and then calmly turned and stalked away.

* * *

A small cloud with a silver lining arrived later that week via a phone call from none other than Alton Rutherford, Kat's vampire mentor and our mutual good friend in London. Of the vampire powerbrokers in the world, he was not only leading the list, he was the poster child for it.

Following his investigation that was based upon information provided by Kat, including DNA-related evidence, the nature of which I had no interest in delving into, a number of significant developments had taken place.

First, both of our prospective assassins were identified, as well as the identity of who hired one of them. A vampire named Wasim Samara, a former associate of Baldar Dubravko, was identified as the one responsible for hiring the assassins.

Second, and much to my surprise, Alton personally headed up the detail that tracked down Samara. After all, he had an entire cadre of vampires to rely on to do those sorts of things.

Still, it merely reinforced the degree of affection and concern that he held for Kat, including perhaps for me.

Upon confronting Samara firsthand, Alton said that their interactions went poorly...fatally so for Samara, that is. As with Dubravko, I had a hard time conjuring any degree of sympathy for the vampire's demise.

He did order people to kill Kat and me, after all.

In the end, Alton assured us that word of the confrontation and its ultimate resolution was being actively publicized in the vampire world, which Alton estimated would result in a reduction in the number of threats to Katrina and me.

Well, in the near future, at least.

I, for one, found it quite reassuring, though Kat was decidedly less reassured.

Still, I admired how she wrestled with her misgivings and gave me her blessing to once more come and go as I pleased.

Never mind that it felt humiliating to need her blessing in the first place.

I celebrated by enjoying a daylong fishing trip at Mill Creek Lake just north of town.

It felt as if a degree of normality had finally been restored for the first time in months.

When I called Paige lakeside to brag about the development, she merely chuckled.

"Better revel in your newfound freedom while you can, tiger."

I didn't like the way that sounded.

CHAPTER 3

Caleb

During the final days of June, I felt the pull of my college office calling to me. It was still so hard for me to believe that, having only started my burgeoning career as a history professor the previous fall, I was already being let go due to budget cuts, effective the first of July.

Crap.

It made little sense that overly-conservative state legislatures would cut funding to colleges during poor economic conditions, since that's where people flocked to for vital job training and education that might get them back into the job market.

One conservative legislator said on the news, "People just need to pick themselves up by their bootstraps."

Yeah, but what were they supposed to do if those same people didn't even own a pair of boots?

Politics aside, at least Katrina had been very sympathetic and supportive since I told her the news of my layoff while in Slovenia. While I appreciated that, it did little to curtail the anger and resentment that I felt over the development.

Crap happens, right?

It still grated on my nerves. Badly.

"I'm going to the college," I said to Kat in passing, as

she reclined on the couch reading a book.

At first, she looked up with a concerned expression, but then her features softened.

"I understand," she said. "Be careful, my love."

Careful? I'm going to the college, not a bar.

I've had a horrible track record with bars.

"Will do," I said.

The drive to the college was laced with feelings of longing, as if I were savoring the acts of a routine that was counting down to dissolution.

In truth, that was probably a good analogy.

When I arrived, my good friend and colleague, Dr. Tanisha Browning, was in her office sorting through a large stack of old exams and essays left over from previous semesters.

Professors are packrats, really.

I chatted for a time with her, recounting a much safer and mundane version of my trip with Kat to Slovenia.

Oh, yes, peaceful days of scenic sightseeing, quaint Slovenian shopping, sleeping late, and romantic quality time with Kat.

There was no mention of vampires, terrorist plots, corrupt government officials that beat me within an inch of my life, or killing a human and a vampire using a briefcase full of explosives.

And, of course, no mention of my newfound and lingering concussion.

Essentially, no mention of any part of the reality that constituted the past few weeks of my life.

My life is nothing more than an endless litany of secrets…and lies.

I suppressed a heavy sigh.

Then the topic turned to my impending departure, including the need to clean out my office. Tanisha said she was shocked over the decision, and lamented that I had been selected rather than some other faculty members she knew who didn't put as much passion or effort into their teaching.

Too bad she hadn't been the person passing out the pink slips.

"Are you going to start packing up your office today?"

she asked.

I had intended to, but by the end of our conversation I'd lost my resolve. Besides, the division dean, Paul Wright, had given me the remainder of the summer to remove my things and turn in my key.

It wasn't as if they were hiring a replacement for me.

Downsizing really sucks.

"Paul said I have until mid-August," I said with a shrug.

She rose from her chair and gave me a warm hug, which I gratefully accepted.

Among other great qualities, Tanisha was a really good hugger.

"Well, don't rush things if you're not ready," she said.

She knew me better than I thought.

We chatted for a short time longer before I said goodbye. Afterward, I locked up my soon-to-be-former office and headed for the parking lot.

The late June Atlanta sun and humidity made for a hot, sultry drive home. Halfway to Mableton on the I-20, my car's engine suddenly sputtered and bucked. A glance at my dashboard indicated a sudden drop in oil pressure, followed by a heavy clunking noise coming from the engine.

Veering into the right-hand lane, I coasted off the highway and onto the shoulder, and promptly turned off the ignition. Though not a mechanic, it didn't take long to determine that I had sustained an engine problem that went well beyond some new plugs or a gasket.

To be honest, it was a relatively old Honda Civic, and I feared the worst.

Following a call to Kat for the number to our insurance towing service, and a wait of less than an hour, a wrecker finally arrived to tow my ailing car to a nearby auto shop. Fortunately, they were able roll my car onto the rack within an hour.

I patiently waited as a mechanic named Jeff evaluated my vehicle, during which time I walked next door to a burger joint to eat a late lunch.

Great. First no job and now car trouble.

Soon after returning to the shop, Jeff briefed me on the damage.

He said the engine had sustained a major cylinder failure; two of them had simultaneously seized. It would require at a minimum a complete overhaul, or better yet, a complete engine replacement.

Hell, the twelve-year-old engine already had well over a hundred and twenty thousand miles on it.

As fate would have it, the estimated cost of engine overhaul was more than I had left in my savings account. The wiser choice was to purchase another vehicle.

In my case, that meant used rather than new.

Okay, no job and now I'm planning to take on a car payment?

I wondered if Alton would be willing to electronically transfer some money to me from the vampire-donated funds that I had received at the conference.

My reverie was interrupted by a phone call from Kat, who called for a quick status report.

"I'm so sorry, my love. But don't worry, this isn't insurmountable," she reassured me in a kind, supportive voice.

Said the wealthy vampire to the cash-strapped human.

"It's still daylight, so I'll send a cab to pick you up, and we can talk more about it here at home."

I thanked her, and asked Jeff to park my car in their temporary holding area behind the shop until I called him back with a decision. Then, I nearly emptied my wallet to pay him a relatively generous cash bonus for his trouble; which was the least that I could do for his courtesy and quick assessment.

I ventured that I'd have just enough cash left for the cab ride home.

I texted Paige with the latest news while waiting for my ride to arrive.

Sorry about your POC car, she texted.

I replied, *POC?*

Piece of crap! she texted.

Hater. U suck.

Then she sent, *I do. Fang U very much, Mr. Yummy.*

That was quickly followed by a smiley face.

I shook my head, knowing full well that she was correct. The sad truth was that my car really was a piece of crap. Only it had become a dead piece of crap a bit too soon for my bank account's preference.

By the time the cab arrived, I felt physically and emotionally drained, both from the intense summer heat and my cascade of negative emotions. More than anything, I just wanted to go home and pop open a cold beer.

By the time the cab dropped me off at the gates at the end of our estate's driveway, I was only too happy to be back.

However, and rather unfortunately, I had also developed a splitting headache. My lingering concussion was acting up again.

Well, so much for a cold beer.

Undoubtedly, the equation was simple: a concussion plus a pounding headache plus prescription pain relievers equaled no beer for me.

As soon as I walked through the front door, Kat was waiting in the shadows of the front living area, well beyond the late afternoon sunlight that poured in past me. She must have sensed my condition, because as soon as I shut the front door, I felt a rush of air and she enfolded me in her arms, hugging me against her.

"I'm glad you're back," she said.

She disengaged from our hug and pulled away from me to stare into my eyes.

"Are you in pain?" she asked.

"Headache," I muttered.

She retrieved some pain relievers that had been prescribed for me by Ethan. I kicked off my shoes and meandered into the living room at the back of the house, where I lay on the couch.

What a totally crap-tastic day.

Kat dropped to her knees on the carpeted floor beside me and soothingly ran her fingertips across my forehead and through my hair.

Needless to say, that felt amazing.

Sometime later, the meds finally took effect and I drifted off to sleep.

CHAPTER 4

Caleb

I jolted awake to the sound of my cell phone ringing. I fumbled around for it on the end table and glanced at the display. I tried to gather my wits about me as I wondered why Katrina was calling.

Hadn't she just been next to me on the couch mere minutes ago?

"Kat? Where are you?" I asked.

"Sorry to wake you," she said. "But could you please come help me with something in the garage, my love?"

"Uh, okay," I said, glancing at my watch.

It was evening already.

I've been asleep for nearly five hours.

Fortunately, my headache had subsided and I felt decidedly better.

I walked into the dark garage, the only light coming from the dull illumination emanating from the security lights outside.

"Kat?"

I noticed a sport utility vehicle parked just outside the garage in the driveway.

I slapped at the nearest light switch on the wall.

The garage lights snapped on, casting a glow across the

shiny new midnight blue surface of a Chevrolet SUV. It was rugged looking, and yet had smooth edges, giving it a sleek appearance.

"Happy early birthday, my love."

Katrina stood outside the vehicle with her arms neatly folded before her, intently observing me.

"No, way. You—you can't—" I stammered.

She frowned at me.

"Don't you like it? You need a new vehicle, after all."

"Like it? It's amazing," I said. "But that's not the point."

It was probably the best gift that anyone had ever tried to give me.

It just seemed like too much; way over the top, in fact.

Besides, now that I'm jobless, the insurance premiums are going to be a killer.

I sighed with resignation and threw up my hands.

How could I make her understand?

"Look, I'm sorry, Kat. It's such a wonderful gift. This SUV's like something out of a dream. It's just that I can't accept it. Heck, I probably can't even afford the insurance on it."

Her look of concern transformed into amusement as she regarded me. "Caleb, my love," she began in a soft, patient voice. "It makes me happy to do this. And I don't expect anything from you, except to see you happy. And the SUV has been added to my Audi's policy, so don't worry about the insurance."

"But---"

"No," she interrupted me. "Just say 'thank you,' you maddeningly prideful man."

I sighed, appreciating my shiny new gift.

I should have the grace to be appreciative, I suppose. She means well, after all.

"You know, a lesser woman might feel greatly insulted right now," she said quietly.

I looked up at her with surprise. I certainly wasn't trying to be rude. "Oh, please, you're hardly a lesser woman, by anyone's measure."

Face it, other women pale by comparison.

"Perhaps," she said. "Just the same…"

"Kat, I'm not trying to insult you, of all people," I said. "This is all on me; I'm broken inside or something. I don't know…I don't fully understand it. I just don't feel deserving of such a wonderful gift."

She regarded me with a sad expression. "Caleb, my love," she said, holding her arms open. "Come here."

I slowly approached her, walking into her open arms and letting her enfold me in them. She rested her chin atop my head.

"You dear, sweet man," she whispered. "You deserve this and so much more. If only I could make you understand that.

"You were made to feel so worthless and undeserving during your childhood by a drunken reprobate of a father," she said. "If it hadn't stopped when you were eight, I don't know where you'd be now."

Eight…when you killed that son-of-a-bitch father of mine. How can I ever repay her for that?

"Yeah," I said. "But some of the damage was done by then; you merely kept it from worsening. I'm still a pretty screwed up guy, Kat."

"Don't say that, my love," she said, holding me tightly in her arms. "Don't berate and belittle yourself like that. Listen to me, if there's one thing I've learned during over five hundred years on this Earth, it's that we're all a little screwed up inside. It's really only a matter of degree."

I hugged her close; forever grateful for everything she'd done for me in my life, especially those things that I wasn't even aware of until just recently when my memories were freed.

Despite what she said, I realize I'm still damaged; that much is true.

I gave her a final big squeeze in my arms, determined not to ruin the happiness of this moment any further.

"Thank you for my birthday gift, Kat," I said. "You're unbelievably kind and generous. In fact, you're the best. And

I love you so much for that and more."

"You're absolutely welcome. And I love you, too," she said.

She pulled from our embrace slightly and craned her neck to affectionately kiss my lips.

I cherished her kisses, so sweet, and yet, practically charged with emotional electricity.

She disengaged from our mutual embrace and held my hand. "So, you won't mind driving this around town then?"

"As if," I said.

Driving an impressive piece of automotive machinery like that was going to be a dream. And it was definitely the vehicle of choice for when we went camping.

Camping in style!

"Oh, it's definitely over-the-top amazing," I said. "I better call Jeff at the shop and arrange to dispose of my old car."

"Oh that," she said. "Well, one of the documents you previously signed for me was a durable power of attorney, you see. So, I already signed the title over to a salvage yard on your behalf this evening while you were sleeping."

In a simple stroke of a pen, my old car had been relegated to a mere junk heap in its damaged state. I'd spent a lot of years driving it. In fact, I'd driven it from Ohio to Atlanta when I moved away from home to go to college.

My car is as broken as I probably am inside. Although, hopefully in my case, Kat will keep me.

Then something else she had said finally registered in my mind. "Power of attorney?"

"Mm-hm. Naturally, I'm able to help you with your personal affairs much easier that way," she said.

"When exactly did I sign that?" I asked.

Why was her revelation news to me?

She frowned. "Don't you remember? It was one of the papers that you signed along with the request to add you to my credit cards before our trip to Slovenia."

"Huh."

I'll be damned.

"You know, you really should read paperwork more closely before you sign it," she said dryly.

My mouth gaped open.

"Wait a minute. With durable power of attorney, you practically own me!"

Her eyes narrowed. "Nonsense. Your best interests are imperative to me, my love. You shouldn't question that."

I scoffed. "You've got to be the boldest, most unbelievably alpha-controlling vampire I've ever known."

She drew her body up to full height and towered over me somewhat menacingly, adopting a predatory expression as she gazed into my eyes.

She's ferocious.

She stepped toward me, her green eyes blazing with a feral glow, emanating her vampire nature in veritable, powerful waves.

Momentarily caught off guard, I stepped backward until my back pressed against the SUV's cool exterior.

Undeterred by my reaction, she slowly bent her head down to firmly kiss me on the lips.

"Face it. You *love* me like this," she whispered.

My arms encircled her slim waist and I smiled into her kiss.

True.

I pulled her against me and initiated a series of lengthy, passionate kisses.

God, she's a great kisser.

I could've stood there all night, in fact.

"So, how about taking me out for a spin in your new SUV?" she suggested.

I chuckled, and she sped around to the passenger side as I eagerly climbed into the driver's seat, which felt like it had been made just for me.

"This is so awesome," I said as I started the engine.

My fingers played across the dash to tweak the stereo and air conditioning controls like a pilot prepping an aircraft for flight.

"You can upload the music from your iPod into the entertainment console, as well," she said.

Oh, yes, gotta' have my driving tunes.

As we pulled out of the driveway, she reached out and lightly caressed the back of my neck with her fingernails, eliciting a shiver that ran all the way down my spine.

* * *

Less than an hour after returning from my maiden test drive and parking *my* SUV in the garage, Paige stopped by for an impromptu visit. I quickly took her by the arm and half-dragged her into the garage to see my kick-ass, though way over the top, birthday gift.

Kat watched with an amused expression as I pointed out the host of cool features to Paige.

She kept swatting at my hand. "Stop pointing at everything so fast, you country bumpkin."

I folded my arms before my chest. As I watched her I could tell she was at least mildly impressed.

"Are you crazy, Red?" Paige finally asked. "You don't give a man an SUV for his twenty-seventh birthday. That's more of a thirtieth birthday gift, at best."

Kat gave her a bland look. "And just what, precisely, should I have given him, then?"

"You give him what any twenty-something-year-old guy wants," she said, pausing for dramatic affect. "The latest game console and a renewal to his favorite porn subscription."

She gazed at me sidelong and offered an exaggerated wink. "*Dominatrix Monthly*, right?"

I glanced at Kat, noticing that her eyes nearly bulged from her head in surprise.

Then her intent gaze fell upon me.

Ooh, that's not good.

"What?" I asked. "Your gift is the best, Kat. And besides, we've already got of the newest game consoles and—"

My head swiveled to stare at Paige. "Wait, they actually publish that?"

Kat groaned.

"Oops, making your Dom jealous," Paige remarked.

My Dom?

I regarded Kat with a wide-eyed expression.

"Why are you staring at *me* like that?" she demanded. "I'm the one who's wondering what kind of porn you're into."

"Wha—" I gaped.

"Oh, so our boy likes a little leather and riding crop action, eh?" Paige grinned. "I don't mind saying, I'm a real kitten with a whip myself."

My head pivoted to glare at her incredulously.

Kitten with a whip?

Whoa.

My imagination quickly generated a vision of that, and I felt immediate arousal. Fortunately, I caught myself mid-thought and raced to push that aside.

Major warning bells! La, la, la…don't go there.

"I don't think so, missy," Kat said. "Just go practice your skills on Ethan, thank you very much."

Paige shrugged innocently. "Hey, I'm just sayin'."

Kat growled. "Well, stop sayin'."

I threw my hands up in frustration. "Okay, okay, everybody stop!"

Both women stared at me curiously, though Kat appeared a little too exasperated for my taste. In fact, she appeared quite put out.

The vision of a perfect Dominatrix, in fact.

I shook my head.

Don't go there!

I stared directly into Kat's still-animated-looking emerald eyes. "Just to be clear, I don't have a porn magazine collection."

"They come in online subscriptions, too," Paige said.

My attention darted to her. "Zip it! You're not helping right now."

I returned my focus back to Kat. "I don't need any porn, Kat. I have you."

Wait, that sounded better in my head.

"That's oddly romantic," Paige said with an arched brow. "Quirky, maybe even a bit twisted, actually. But romantic, nonetheless."

My shoulders slumped. "Okay, I give up."

Kat, ever the alpha, yet still sensitive, took control of the situation by wrapping her arm around my shoulders.

"I don't have any concerns about porn, my love," she said. "Your eyes told me everything I need to know."

"And everyone in Pleasantville lived happily ever after," Paige squeaked. "I think I need a tissue."

I looked at Paige with narrowed eyes, silently mouthing, 'shut up.'

She winked back at me and grinned.

"So, you bought him an SUV for his birthday, but where in the hell's his birthday cake?" Paige asked.

"You know, you're an absolute menace, shorty," Kat said.

"I do my best," Paige said.

Although, I had to admit that a cake sounded pretty good at the moment.

"Do I get a cake, too?" I asked.

Kat looked at me with a wry expression. "Your birthday's not actually until July 17, you know. I still have time. Your gift was merely needed a little earlier than planned, that's all."

I shrugged. "Cool. Just askin'."

Paige folded her arms before her and regarded Kat with raised eyebrows. "So, maybe a porn-looking cake then?"

"Oh, *shut up*, porn queen," Kat said.

* * *

I was on my second hour of playing the latest version of Halo on the game console in the theater room when Paige suddenly appeared by my side, plopping down upon the floor Indian-style next to me.

"Hey, tiger," she said. "Got another controller?"

I paused the game and fished another controller out of the storage cabinet.

"Damn, this is a huge screen for a video game," she said, taking in the projection screen mounted on the wall.

"Bigger is better," I said. "Hey, I thought you were chatting it up with Kat."

"Yeah, well, Alton called and the chit-chat shifted to him," she replied. "She motioned to me that it was a private call, so I hunted you down."

I handed her the spare controller and reset the game configuration for an additional player.

"What the hell are we playin' here?" she asked.

"Halo," I replied.

"Well, Halo to you, too, twerp," she chimed. "Honestly, what is it with you men and video games?"

"It passes the time until we get to have sex again," I said.

"You nerd. Keep playing this stuff and you can forget getting any more sex," she muttered.

"Oh, fun-ny," I said.

I showed her the controls and described the game for her. We had only played for about twenty minutes when she turned to stare at me.

"Listen, I don't know if you've noticed or not, but Red actually treats you just like a dominatrix does her Sub sometimes," she said. "It must feel very emasculating. But then, I realize that you seem to like that sort of thing for some reason."

"What do you know? And why are you still hung up on the porn topic?" I asked, annoyed over both her tone of voice and topic selection.

"Hey, don't get all defensive on me," she said. "I just call it like I see it. And you, my friend, are one whipping away from 'Yes, Mistress, may I have another?' That's all I'm sayin'. But hey, if that's your thing."

Oh, dry up.

I grumbled an expletive, ignored her, and continued to

play. Fortunately, she let the topic drop.

However, her comments struck a sour cord in me, and before long, my thoughts wandered.

I had never deeply considered the nature of what Paige had suggested, or even the structure of Kat's and my dynamic relationship for that matter; certainly not from that angle before.

Do I feel emasculated by Kat? Is a dominatrix really what I want from her?

It was true that the balance and nature of our relationship was quite different from other couples.

It's not as if that make me less of a man or anything.

Does it?

Those were all confusing prospects, as well as sort of emotionally overwhelming to consider all at once.

In fact, it made me feel aggravated.

"You don't like Kat's and my relationship, do you?" I asked.

Paige abruptly paused the game and turned to me.

"I never said that. And besides, Red's like a sister to me; I love her. But you're my friend, too, and I just want what makes you happy, okay?" she said. "It's just that Katrina is a powerful vampire as well as a powerful woman. She's a lot for any man to handle."

She's very powerful, for sure.

"Yeah, well, I definitely can't see Kat getting handled by any man," I said.

"My point exactly," she said.

"You don't exactly get handled by anyone either," I pointed out.

She tilted her head slightly. "True. Except when I want to be handled."

"Kat's probably the same," I said. "So what's with all the concern all of a sudden?"

She frowned as she stared at me. Actually, it was more like right through me.

"I'm just worried that you'll get lost in allowing her to

36

control you like she does. Although, that has to be somewhat tempting for someone like you, isn't it?"

"Someone like me?"

She reached over and patted me on the back.

"I love you, kiddo," she said. "But you're attracted to really assertive, powerful women, and that's something you have to be sure not to lose yourself in. I've seen it happen the other way to women who've lost themselves in a powerful man. Eventually, they just forgot who they were."

I didn't know how to respond to that.

"You've come a long way since I first met you, tiger. And I adore the man that you've become. I like you just the way you are, so I'd hate to lose you; what you are now, that is."

"Sure, but—" I said. "I mean, it's really all about maintaining a healthy balance, right?"

"But then, that's the challenge, isn't it?" she asked.

She resumed the game and I half-heartedly returned to playing. However, what she said kept replaying over and over again in my mind.

…a powerful woman.

…you'll get lost in allowing her to control you.

…tempting for someone like you.

…they forgot who they were.

Was I allowing Kat to swallow me up? Was that what I wanted?

Kat's and my relationship had developed so quickly in the nine months since we began dating that I'd hardly taken time to consider its evolution.

Hell, I'm already her mate. That's practically like "vampire married."

Was I getting lost in her? Was I relinquishing my independence to her?

I contemplated my desire for her; how passionately I loved her, and how I craved her body.

Was I giving up my independence in exchange for love and sex?

Perhaps, but I couldn't help feeling as though there might

be more to it than that.

It is more. I don't simply want her; I need her.

Was it because of my past; my abusive childhood?

I suddenly felt confused and filled with a host of uncertainties. It was exhausting to contemplate.

There's too much for me to digest right now. I need a quiet place to think; to work it all out.

"You all right, tiger?" Paige asked. "You just got blasted by a baddie, you know."

"Huh? Oh, crap," I said, breaking from my train of thoughts. "And they're called the Covenant, just so you know."

"Yeah, yeah, whatever. Ugly-ass, weirdie-lookin' dudes," she said. "Face it; you're still such a hopeless little nerd sometimes."

I nodded. "Yeah, but I'm your hopeless little nerd."

She gave me a mock-horrified look. "Hey, you stole my line, you little turd."

"*Psyche,*" I said, and restarted the level.

I forced our recent conversation about my relationship with Kat and its seemingly endless implications to the back of my mind while escaping back into the video game with my friend.

Somehow, fighting off an alien invasion felt much safer, and perhaps more familiar, territory.

CHAPTER 5

Caleb

The next day, I thought about what Paige and I had discussed. Her words kept replaying in my mind.

Determined to confront matters head on, I found Katrina in the sublevel room, essentially our grand subterranean bedroom, sitting at the station that supported the array of computer consoles and control center for the estate's security and surveillance system.

She looked so sexy sitting there barefoot and wearing a pair of satin lounge pants and matching camisole. Her hair was pulled back into a single, tight ponytail, giving her that authoritative, yet sexy, look that I loved.

Had I not been so focused upon my question at hand, I might have considered more amorous endeavors.

"Hey, Kat, got a minute?" I asked.

Her welcoming smile was epic. "Always for you, my love."

I gave her a quick kiss as I gathered my thoughts.

"What's up?" she asked with an arched brow.

"I'd like to talk about some stuff that's happened recently," I said firmly. "And about us."

The narrowing of her eyes was so quick that I almost missed it; her features quickly returned to a receptive expression. She rose from her seat and took my right hand in hers as she guided us to the edge of our bed to sit.

"Does this have anything to do with the parking garage incident from the other night?" she asked. "Or is it your birthday gift that's still bothering you?"

Damn. I'm being outflanked already.

"More the former than the latter," I said.

"Okay. Go on," she said.

Despite her encouragement, I still felt uneasy.

Well, here goes nothing.

"I think—" I said. "Rather, I feel like you frequently make decisions for me. I think it's better if we act as equals in our relationship, don't you?"

Okay, that came out more bluntly than I'd hoped.

One of her eyebrows momentarily arched before returning to its former position.

"What I mean is, I feel like you sometimes disregard my preference in matters, especially in front of others. You sometimes order me around instead of asking my opinion. Some people might call that emasculating."

"Emasculating? And by *some*, do you have somebody specific in mind?" she asked. "Do you think that I emasculate you, or is that something you feel pressured by others to believe?"

Realizing I was suddenly treading in potentially dangerous waters, I paused to consider her question at length.

"Nobody's pressuring me into this," I said. "But let's take right now, for example. You're challenging me just for bringing up the topic."

There. I said it.

But why do I feel like some overly-emo schmuck?

The look of shock on her face surprised me, and I watched as her expression morphed into something introspective. Her fingers lightly caressed the top of my hand in a soothing, yet mechanical, process.

Okay, this is going better than I expected.

Seconds later, her fingers froze in place and her eyes captured mine in a flat stare.

Strike that. This isn't good.

"So, you're saying anytime I disagree with your preference on something, even if I feel it's counter to your safety, particularly when I'm much more informed than you on the matter and you're willing to recklessly endanger yourself, I'm emasculating you?" she asked.

I swallowed, slowly digesting the multiple parts of her question.

"If I understand you correctly, that's it exactly," I said, chin held firmly up. "It's a control issue, essentially. It's how you demonstrate control in front of others, as well as to me."

Paige would be so proud of me.

"So, I'm too controlling, as well?" she asked in a cool voice.

Eerily cool, in my opinion.

"And I *emasculate* you? Make you feel inferior?" she asked.

With a swift pull of my hand, she rose from the bedside, hauling me to my feet.

"What the—?"

She foot swiped my legs from beneath me, using my arm to smoothly control my fall facedown onto the carpet. Then she held my arm straight upward behind my back as pain centered in my shoulder.

"Ow!"

I felt the pressure of her bare foot against my shoulder blades, pressing me into the carpet.

"Kat, what hell are you doing?!" I demanded, glaring sideways at her as I stared at her other bare foot.

"Now this is emasculating," she said coldly.

I was too stunned to say anything else.

I attempted to leverage my upper body strength to push myself up from the floor, to no avail.

Okay, this really sucks.

"Let go!" I yelled. "And get your damned foot off my back!"

"I have all day," she said.

"For *what*?"

"For you to see the difference, Caleb," she said. "What I'm doing now is undoubtedly emasculating."

"Fine, let me go," I said.

"Apologize first," she said.

"No," I said. "You're full of crap if you think---"

She lifted my arm ever slightly while maintaining the pressure of her foot on my back.

More pain ensued.

"Okay, okay. I apologize," I said.

I battled between the conflicting feelings of confusion and mortification over having to apologize.

Dammit, she was the one at fault, not me.

And like a swiftly passing storm, her right foot disappeared from behind my back and she let go of my arm, which flopped down beside me.

Before I could push myself up from the carpeted floor, she moved with that fast, vampire-like speed to perch on the side of the bed again, casually crossing one leg over the other.

My arm and shoulder ached as I rose to my knees, only to see her right foot hovering playfully in the air before me.

I fought against the sudden urge to bite her big toe, just for spite.

"I've never done anything like that to you, either privately or in public, and I didn't relish doing it just now," she said. "When I first met you, you were practically afraid of your own shadow, and I've worked so damned hard to help build your self-esteem and self-confidence. Why then, would I ruin your progress?"

I was too angry with her at the moment to give her question a passing thought.

"You accused me of emasculating you. What a low blow, Caleb," she said with narrowed eyes. "Oh, I'm sure your tender ego is bruised right now, but it's important that you truly understand what the hell you're talking about before you dare accuse me of harsh things like that. In fact, I feel very hurt and insulted that you've such a low opinion of me."

To say I was still furious with her was an understatement

of epic proportion. With one fluid motion, I rose to a standing position and glared daggers at her.

"Yes?" she asked. "Don't worry, I won't tell anyone else about this. It's just our little secret."

My mouth opened to say something but I was too pissed off to respond. I'd only end up saying something I'd later regret.

Instead, I stormed from the room.

Dammit!

Maybe there'd been occasional extremes with Kat but she had never done anything to me like that before.

She's way out of line this time!

I darted for the doorway to leave, reaching into my pocket for the keys to my SUV.

The air swirled around me and I felt my keys being snatched from my grip.

"Give 'em back," I said.

She held up my keys and jingled them.

"No, you need to cool off first," she said. "Take a walk if you have to sulk."

Screw you!

"Whatever," I said.

I barreled down the hallway, and on my way through the kitchen I snatched my wallet from atop the counter. Then I grabbed the SUV's spare set of keys from inside the cabinet.

Satisfied that I'd outwitted her, I stormed through the door leading into the garage. With door knob in hand, I heard Kat's voice calling after me.

"Leave me alone," I said, slamming the door behind me with one hand while slapping the button that opened the garage door with the other.

I jumped into my SUV and started it up with a flick of my wrist. The tires squealed as I pulled out of the garage and onto the sunlit driveway.

I pressed the remote to close the garage door and caught a glimpse of two pale feet inside the garage as the door lowered.

Revving the engine, I came close to scraping the edges of the SUV against the wrought iron gates at the end of the driveway as they slowly swung open before me.

My cell phone rang but I pointedly ignored it.

It's probably her, anyway.

Minutes later, I barreled down I-20 out of Mableton toward downtown Atlanta as Nine Inch Nails' "Survivalism" blared over the speakers.

Weaving in and out of traffic, I relished the freedom of the open road and letting my vehicle's tires grind away against the hot summer asphalt.

My cell phone rang on three separate occasions and I finally grabbed it and put it in silent mode before tossing it over my shoulder to the back of the vehicle.

That felt very liberating.

The bright sunny day ensured that no vampires, particularly one red-haired menace, would follow me.

Not yet, anyway.

By the time downtown Atlanta loomed before me, I was in the mood to get a beer. I wanted somewhere new and different, untainted by any previous experiences with Kat.

I needed somewhere where I could be alone to think.

To sulk, she'd said.

Whatever.

At the moment, I didn't care either way.

I pulled into the parking lot of the first bar that looked interesting, a large warehouse-looking establishment called Old Skools. The overly large parking lot was lined with pine trees, giving it a secluded appearance.

There were only a few vehicles in the lot.

I glanced at my watch.

Late afternoon; too early for the evening rush.

I slammed the door shut on the SUV and walked toward the main entrance as the chirp-chirp from the vehicle's alarm system sounded behind me.

The entrance to the place consisted of two large faded wood doors with blackened ornate crosses etched into them.

Old Skools? Surely this isn't some church or something.

Who knew? Non-descript churches seemed all the rage in the Bible Belt in recent years.

I pulled one door open with a creak, only to be presented with a small, dark entry area that hosted another set of brushed metal doors adorned with industrial-sized bolts and rivets.

I heard the subdued thrumming of music.

Pulling one of those doors open revealed a large, roomy interior interspersed with square black columns and a dark tiled floor. Alien Sex Fiend's "I Walk the Line" pounded over a speaker system.

Much like the parking lot, the place was devoid of patrons. However, I was somewhat surprised to see that the few customers present were dressed in leather, latex, PVC, and dark clothing like something from a fan gathering for *The Matrix* films.

Then it hit me.

Great, I'm either in a Goth rave or a dungeon.

Could I pick a place or what?

I half-considered turning on my heels and leaving.

"You've really gotta' work on that outfit," came a woman's voice to my left.

I frowned and glanced down at my faded jeans and black T-shirt.

My gaze shifted to a woman wearing a fitted black leather dress and matching stilettos. Her black hair was in a bob and dark eyeliner gave her an edgy appearance.

Great, probably a dominatrix with my luck today.

"You're no graver, but you could be a weekender with a little work," she said.

"Stop harassing the customers, doomcookie," the bartender called from behind a nearby black laminated countertop that looked like a narrow runway.

"Keep your smithing to yourself, Frankie," she countered and shot him her middle finger.

I sighed, fully aware that I had definitely chosen the wrong establishment.

That's what I get for stopping at the first place I come upon.

I turned to leave.

"Hey," called the bartender. "Gonna' have a drink?"

Glancing back over my shoulder at him, I reconsidered my options.

He seemed welcoming enough.

Aw, hell. Why not? The beer's probably as cold as the next place, and I'm not here to make friends.

I walked over to the bar, noting the bartender's nearly gray eyes and dark hair. His dark T-shirt was decorated with silver barbed wire imagery, which seemed strange for a bartender.

"What'll ya' have?" he asked.

"Whatever's on tap that's fully-leaded," I said.

"Didn't figure you for the light stuff," he said.

He turned to pull a glass of Budweiser for me while I discreetly surveyed the place using the mirrored wall behind the bar. It was a useful trick that Paige had taught me earlier that spring.

It didn't take long to assess where I was.

Yep, a Goth bar, for sure.

Paige would probably love the place.

My eyes caught the bartender's curious gaze as he turned to place the glass of beer before me.

"Thanks," I said as I placed a twenty-dollar bill on the countertop.

"No hurry. We'll settle up before you leave," he said.

I nodded and took a long swig from my glass. The cold beer tasted pretty good and felt soothing going down my dry throat.

"Nice place," I said for lack of something better to say.

"Thanks," he said with an amused expression. "Except you didn't know it was a Goth bar until you walked inside, did you?"

I shrugged. "Maybe not."

"Thought so," he said. "Well, everyone's pretty tame in here; no troublemakers or anything. I won't have that."

"Good to know, thanks," I said. "Colorful clientele."

The edges of his mouth upturned in wry amusement. "Takes all kinds in this world, doesn't it?"

Too true.

"We just opened the doors for today, so the really serious crowds haven't started coming in yet. But just wait, it gets more interesting. You already met Beth over there. She's a local attorney, but most of the others are local college students or weekenders."

I looked up into the mirror to gaze back at the woman who I'd met when I first came in.

I caught her stealing a glance at me, as well.

People will surprise you, I suppose.

"I'm Frank, but everyone calls me Frankie. You from around here?" he asked.

"Caleb," I said. "From around Mableton."

"Well, Caleb-from-around-Mableton, just call me when you're ready for a refill. And in case I'm not around, we have two beautiful lady bartenders who can also help you," he said before turning to line up bottles of liquor behind the counter.

"Sounds fine," I said. "I'll hang around a bit."

I took another swig of beer. Then my mind returned to stewing over my 'episode' with Kat.

What the hell had gotten into her all of a sudden?

CHAPTER 6

Katrina

As soon as I heard the tires on Caleb's SUV peeling out of the garage, I knew that I'd probably gone too far with him. But he'd really burned my ass with his insinuations over how I've injured his delicate masculinity.

Men are so damned sensitive when it comes to their egos.

Even so, Caleb had caught me off guard with his accusations.

How dare he accuse me of emasculating him, of all things?

I recalled how angry he'd been when he stormed out of the estate.

Just great. He probably thinks I'm a crazy bitch now.

I dialed his cell phone for the umpteenth time since he had left.

Voicemail again.

I sent him yet another text message and waited.

Minutes passed as I thrummed my fingernails against the granite kitchen countertop.

He's ignoring me.

I slapped the countertop, being careful not to hit it too hard. I'd already had it replaced once since I'd moved in.

It had taken decades to master my own strength, and there had been so many broken things to replace over the years.

Hell, so many broken people, as well. Humans are so very fragile.

But I had been careful with Caleb earlier. The only thing damaged was his ego.

I rubbed at my eyes with my fingertips as I sat down at my computer console in our bedroom.

Our bedroom…where we'll probably not be having sex for some time after what I did.

"Men," I said, tossing my cell phone over onto the bed. I'd just keep texting or calling otherwise.

A longing washed through me as I recalled the last time that we had made love on that big, soft bed; that glorious, wonderful location where I could spend a lifetime with him.

I sighed as our argument replayed in my mind
It had to be Paige that got into his head again.
Wasn't it?

I logged into the web-based environment that allowed me to track the transmitter in Caleb's SUV. Fortunately, I've never mentioned that technological aid to him or he'd probably have simply walked away from the house this afternoon.

I did tell him to take a walk, after all.

Then again, I could've tracked him by that chip that I placed into his shoulder back in Slovenia, too.

I absently watched as the miniature blip associated with his SUV moved across the on-screen map.

What am I going to do about him?

"I could always let him do something humiliating to me, if he wanted," I said.

I couldn't help but smile at that. The man didn't have a harsh bone in his body, which was yet another reason that I loved him so dearly.

A pang of guilt shot through me as I realized how my self-control had lapsed with him, allowing my own harsh side to come through a bit more strongly than might have been prudent.

He really knows how to push my buttons sometimes.

I queued up some music on the computer and The Lady

Lamb the Beekeeper's "Hair to the Ferris Wheel" started to play.

I recalled the angry expression on his face as he glared up at me from his prone position on the floor. A feeling of guilt washed over me as I realized how satisfied I'd felt at that moment.

Okay, maybe I'm an evil bitch, but it's really kind of hot to have a sexy guy at your feet.

I sighed with a bitter realization.

It's better when he actually wants to.

Dammit, I've worked so hard to bolster his self-image and self-confidence, sexual and otherwise.

The truth was that I'd finally found a man who knew how to please me, and someone who I loved more than eternal life itself.

In his own sincere way, he already worships me.

So what the hell is wrong with me?

Thinking back, all of those years of partnering with alpha males had been such an infuriating waste of time and effort. I'd spent more time fighting with them for dominance in the relationship or uncovering their ulterior motives instead of being able to enjoy an honest, open relationship with them.

Which was another reason that I'd killed all but one of them in the end.

But Caleb changed all that. He didn't challenge me for the alpha role in the relationship; instead he selflessly offered me kindness, honesty, and trust.

And love.

I smiled at that thought.

Then another realization dawned on me.

Truth be told, I know it really turns him on when I'm being assertive with him.

Then again, he is a beta male, after all.

Either way, I'd do most anything to please him.

It's all about him. Doesn't he realize that?

He still doesn't understand that he's the one who actually commands me most of the time, albeit subtly.

There's virtually nothing I wouldn't do to fulfill his needs.

Heaven help me if he ever realizes that in full. I may lose all influence over him then.

Except regarding issues involving his security and welfare.

I'll never relinquish those.

However, as with today, I'd let the 'bitch out of the barn' a little too much with him.

Still, it's a woman's prerogative to overreact on occasion, right?

I glanced up at the screen to note that Caleb's SUV had stopped, so I zoomed in on the location.

"Old Skools?"

A quick Google search revealed what I needed to know.

"A Goth bar?"

Okay, that confused me a little bit. I couldn't recall him ever going to a Goth bar before.

I glanced at the clock and sighed, realizing there were still a couple of hours of prime daylight left before I could do anything.

Well, kudos to him for making his grand escape in the afternoon. I can't go after him until after sunset or I'll be burned to a crisp.

I went back upstairs to heat up a ceramic mugful of blood in the microwave.

As I waited, a thought struck me and I raced to the phone near the counter, causing a stack of mail to flutter onto the floor.

I dialed with one hand while tossing the mail back onto the countertop.

"Hello, Sexy Blondes Incorporated," answered a familiar perky voice.

"Paige, I need your help," I said. "Caleb stormed off a little earlier."

"Another fight, huh? What up with dat', girlfriend?" she asked in a sarcastic tone.

"*Paige,*" I growled.

I had a sneaky suspicion she knew more about it than she was letting on.

Being careful not to reveal any details that might

embarrass Caleb, I quickly explained to her a little of what had happened.

As we talked, I went upstairs to the second floor master bedroom that was rarely used. I fleetingly recalled how Caleb and I had made love for the first time in that room.

"And you say he went to a Goth club?" she asked.

"Yeah," I said, while rummaging through the lesser-used clothes that I'd stored in the closet.

Suddenly, I spied an outfit that just might fit the occasion.

"Shorty, you're the only one of us who's currently equipped for a daytime mission," I said.

My limited mobility during daylight was something I intended to address in the not-too-distant future.

"Please, just talk to him and see if you can coax him to return home," I said.

"C'mon, Red," she said. "Let the kid blow off some steam; give him a little space. You smother him sometimes, if you ask me."

I didn't ask your opinion.

I calmed myself to avoid an argument, though it was challenging not to bite her head off.

"I understand what you're saying," I said diplomatically. "However, after what happened downtown the other evening, I'd rather he not be out on the town unprotected."

Given the subsequent silence, I thought that our connection had been lost.

"All right, that makes sense, I suppose," she said with a tone of resignation in her voice.

"So?" I asked, shaking my head in mild frustration.

"Yeah, yeah," she said. "But what if he doesn't exactly want to return home? I mean, from what you said, he was pretty pissed at you when he left."

I hoped that wouldn't be an issue.

No, he'll vent and then want to come back home.

"I have a backup plan, but it's no good until after sunset," I said.

Please, just come home, Caleb. I'll make it up to you somehow…

"Don't worry, Red. I'm on the case," she replied.

Then she giggled. "This should be good. I haven't been to a Goth bar in years."

"Uh-huh," I said.

Well, at least one of us was amused about the situation.

I just want him safely back home. Maybe if I can hold him and talk to him, we can try to heal the wound that's been opened between us.

Of course, I realized that in order to heal the wound, I'd need to understand what type of injury I'd be treating.

Bruised ego, or bitter resentment?

Or maybe a little of both?

I thanked Paige for her assistance and retrieved my mug of warmed blood from the microwave. As I perched on a kitchen barstool and took a sip, appreciating the warm liquid flowing down my throat, my emotions finally began to calm a little bit.

I quietly analyzed the events of recent days, including the unfortunate exchange with him earlier that afternoon.

Slowly, the logic of his behavior dawned upon me, like a morning sun peering over the treetops, banishing darkness in its wake.

Oh, my dear, haunted Caleb. I think that I finally understand what's really at play here…

I felt stupid for not seeing it already.

CHAPTER 7

Caleb

By the time I'd secured a small table in the back and finished my second beer, I was surprised to admit that the bar was starting to grow on me.

For one, the music was actually pretty good; it reminded me of a harder version of the alternative rock that I liked. For example, I considered that Angelical Tears' music would fit right in here.

My mind wandered for a bit before returning to my aggravation with Kat.

Sometimes she's just so damned overbearing.

I stared into my beer, searching for an oracle of some kind.

Unfortunately, I doubt any answers are coming from this glass of beer.

When I looked up again to survey the room, the place was starting to fill up, which kind of surprised me. I wouldn't have expected this kind of crowd to be prevalent in the Atlanta area.

Maybe New York or San Francisco, but not around here.

I rubbed at my forehead with one hand, trying to dispel the tension that had formed.

I removed my hand just in time to see a familiar blonde-haired woman walk into the bar carrying a pile of folded leather riding gear, along with motorcycle helmet and black boots, which she placed on a small table near the entrance. She took only a moment to take in her surroundings before boldly strutting into the bar.

No way.

Paige wore a little black leather miniskirt, sheer long-sleeved top that revealed a leather bra underneath, and high-heeled ankle boots. Black eye shadow outlined her smoldering blue eyes and a studded black leather collar accented her petite neck.

Oh, she's hot.

Her edgy, sexy look immediately caught every set of eyes in the place, and she rocked her hips like a dangerous vixen on the prowl to the sound of Razed in Black's "Oh My Goth!" blaring overhead.

She flashed a half-grin to patrons both left and right of her as she continued her trajectory directly toward my table.

Honestly, I felt the sexual tension quadruple in the room, affecting me in exactly the same way. Even the female bartender appeared mesmerized by her.

She stopped directly before my table and struck an alluring pose. "Oh-my-Goth, imagine seeing you here, kiddo," she squeaked.

My mouth opened but words completely escaped me.

She beamed at me with a feisty-look as she practically poured herself into an empty chair to my right.

"Oh, how I love your expression right now," she said with a tone of satisfaction.

I had to force myself to take a breath before speaking.

"You. Look. Amazing."

Good Lord, if I wasn't already spoken for...

She giggled playfully as she regarded me.

"Just so you know, I could eat you up right now, tiger," she purred.

Our eyes locked. A sly smile slowly dawned upon her features as I felt a spark of desire flare from deep inside me.

Dangerous territory…

Abruptly, she broke from our stare contest, and I thought that I glimpsed her quickly frowning as she looked away from me.

She made an overly-lengthy visual inspection of our side of the club before looking back at me with a decidedly more playful expression.

"You sure can pick the joints, can't you?"

In near record time, the bartender made a personal appearance at our table to retrieve Paige's order.

"Absolut and cran, please," she ordered. "And another beer for my boy."

When the bartender departed, Paige winked at me and said, "All the good Goths are drinking vodka and cran nowadays."

"How do you know so much about---"

"What, Goth? Eh, I lived in southern California for years; it's like second nature to me," she said off-handedly, while flashing a flirtatious look at two black-clad young men seated a table away from us.

"The real question is what you're doing here," she said.

"Kat and I had a bit of---"

"Yeah-yeah, I heard; the drag-down cat fight with your Dom," she interrupted.

My mouth dropped open.

Kat told her?

She frowned. "What's wrong?"

"I can't believe that Kat told you," I said.

"Told me what?" she asked. "That you had a big fight?"

I paused. "What *exactly* do you know about that?"

She appeared puzzled. "Not as much as I thought, apparently. But maybe you can fill me in now that I'm here."

Yeah, not gonna' happen.

She snapped her fingers repeatedly. "C'mon, dish. I want all the gory details."

I slowly let out a deep breath that I'd been holding.

She frowned at me. "Hey, is there something important I

should know here?"

"Nah, no big deal," I said.

Her eyes narrowed suspiciously. "O-kay, then. Back to my earlier question. Why did you end up *here?*"

I shrugged. "First place I came to."

She gave me a shrewd look. "Well, aren't you just Captain Adventure today."

"You don't know the half of it," I muttered under my breath.

The bartender returned and our drinks were smoothly placed before us.

"Thanks," Paige and I both said simultaneously.

We locked eyes and Paige grinned brightly.

"She's on my tab," I said before the bartender walked away.

"Why, thank you, kind sir," Paige said.

We sipped our drinks in silence as she swayed to the industrial music playing.

"How did you track me here?" I asked.

She shrugged. "Red did all the work. She sounded pretty worried about you, in fact."

Yeah, I bet.

I offered a sour expression in silent response.

"Oh, that look says it all," she said. "*Somebody* must have been really raging when they took off. Am I right?"

"That's about the size of it," I said.

"Good for you," she said. "My boy has some balls after all, it seems."

I nearly winced.

Yeah, well, I'm lucky Kat didn't step on those while she was at it.

"Penny for your thoughts," she said as she produced a cell phone from God-knows-where and started texting.

"What are you doing?" I demanded. "Aww, c'mon, don't text Kat already."

"Hey, chill. I'm only tellin' her you're safe and sound," she said.

"Well, you can tell her to stay the hell away and leave me

alone while you're at it."

She glanced up at me wide-eyed. "What? I don't think I've heard you servin' 'tude like that before," she said, placing her phone onto the table before her. "Just what the hell happened today?"

I took a long swig of my beer, and then told her about our argument, but without any mention of the 'floor episode.'

"And just where's your cell phone?" she asked with an arched brow.

"I left it in the SUV somewhere," I replied.

"Notta' cool play, dude," she said. "Bad Caleb; no biscuit."

I rolled my eyes. She always had a unique way of lightening my mood, no matter the circumstances. She was one of the best friends I'd ever had, and under different circumstances, I could see her as so much more.

She snapped her fingers before me. "Hey, stop broodin' over your old lady and perk up," she said with a playful expression. "You're in a Goth club all alone with Little Miss Dressed-to-Kill! How often does that happen, kiddo?"

I chuckled.

"I'm betting not often enough," she said.

"You are dressed to kill," I said. "In fact, you look absolutely hot."

She squealed an endearing laugh. "Good boy," she giggled. "Let's rave!"

Rave?

Before I knew it, she had grabbed my hand and practically jerked me out of my chair. I trailed behind her as industrial music blared from the overhead speakers.

I took comfort in the fact that a crowd of people were already dancing, so at least I didn't create a spectacle.

Paige's enthusiasm was infectious, and before I knew it I was thrashing about with her on the dance floor and having a great time. Between her and the rhythmic beat of the music, it didn't take long for me to banish my former gloomy thoughts in favor of some fun.

In fact, it felt really good.

I wasn't paying attention to how many songs we danced to, but I worked up quite a thirst.

We made a couple of brief trips back to our table to our drinks but always ended right back out on the dance floor.

Paige looked like she was having as great of a time as I was. I felt relieved to suspend my angst-ridden, depressing thoughts about my relationship with Kat, particularly everything that had happened earlier.

We returned to our table, and this time, Paige let me sit down to wipe my perspiring forehead with a cocktail napkin.

"Awesome dancing, tiger. I noticed somebody's been doin' their cardio," she said. "Good boy; we'll reconsider that biscuit."

I couldn't help but laugh as I looked past her toward the club's entrance.

As if following some cosmic script, "Stripped" by Shiny Toy Guns blared overhead at the moment that the newest entrant to the bar made her presence known.

Kat was attired in an alluring black leather halter dress with matching stilettoes, and she carried a small leather clutch wallet. Her red hair was pulled back into a tight ponytail, and her black lipstick gave her a dark, foreboding look.

Her penetrating gaze scanned the bar, flashing bright green as soon as she fixed her gaze upon me.

My breath caught in my throat as I watched her part the room while she approached me in a stalking, methodic fashion.

She looked like a beautiful but dangerous red-haired demon that had come to collect her next unsuspecting soul.

Me.

A number of people stopped dancing and simply stared at her as she passed, giving her a wide berth.

"Subtly was never Red's strong suit," Paige said.

Kat stopped just short of our table, her eyes never leaving mine.

"I'm gonna' snag a fresh vod and cran," Paige said,

smoothly slipping from her chair as she grabbed her cell phone and headed toward the bar.

"I hope you don't mind if I join you," Kat said, commandeering the empty chair immediately to my left.

"A lady wouldn't presume," I said.

"A gentleman would've offered," she countered reproachfully.

Okay. I didn't have a response for that.

"You haven't returned any of my calls or text messages," she said. "I was worried about you."

"And now you're here to retrieve me?" I asked.

"That's rather unkind," she said coolly. "Don't you want to feel wanted? Shouldn't I want to seek you out and show my love and concern for you?"

I hesitated and took a long swig of beer.

"Caleb, it's quite an interesting little place you've discovered here, but please, let's go home and talk things out," she said.

"I'm not leaving."

"Well, you can't camp out here forever, you know," she said.

"Ever hear of hotels?"

I got a small, perverse thrill over her resulting stony expression.

"Oh, please," she said. "Don't you think that's overreacting a bit?"

Oh, really?

I simply stared back at her.

Her eyes narrowed. "I see," she said. "At the very least, perhaps you'd permit me to sit with you while appreciating your new hangout?"

"Okay," I said with a shrug. "Actually, this place will grow on you if you just give it half a chance."

"I'm sure," she said. "But home would be more comfortable for us to talk, wouldn't you agree?"

"I'm not going home," I said. "Things are still a little raw with me right now."

A sad expression permeated her features, though it didn't alter either my resolution or my feelings.

One of the servers who had been making her rounds stopped by our table.

"Welcome to Old Skools. What can I get for you?" she asked, fully focusing her attention on Kat.

Maybe it was merely the lighting in the place, but I'd swear our server's skin flushed as I watched her.

"Dark and Stormy, please," Kat said.

"Right away, ma'am," the server crisply replied, making a beeline for the bar area.

The irony of Kat's drink order wasn't lost on me.

Fitting, actually.

In addition, I couldn't help but feel a pang of jealousy over how quickly she had commanded attention and responsiveness from our server.

Typical vampire allure.

Was I so different?

"I see you have a fan club already," I said.

"What?" she asked, taking notice of the attentive stares that she was receiving from those nearby.

As I watched, she swept each of the faces of onlookers with a flat, icy stare. Almost instantly, prying eyes averted to other locations.

Then, she calmly interlaced the fingers of both hands before her on the table and returned her full attention to me.

Jeez, she's in full-on alpha mode right now.

Though I wasn't about to admit it, I found it both intimidating and somewhat sexy.

"I realize and accept that you're upset with me, and I'm willing to concede that my little demonstration went too far with you earlier this afternoon," she said.

"No. The way that you treated me today was no less than downright cruel," I said. "I came to you to rationally discuss my feelings, just as you've suggested in the past."

She scowled at me. "To calmly accuse me of emasculating you," she said flatly. "Do you have any idea how that made me feel, Caleb? To think that after all the efforts that I've given to love, nurture, protect, and support you that it had all been in vain; because instead I've merely emasculated you? You seemed to throw that word out like it was some new toy to play with. That's a hard, harsh word; or at least to me it is."

I fought back a wince from the venomous tone in her voice.

She closed her eyes and clenched her jaw, as if in the midst of struggling against some hidden, yet intense, urge.

When she finally opened her eyes, she appeared composed and more relaxed, though I still noted a look of strain in her eyes.

"Please, go on," she said. "You were saying?"

"There's no point, really."

At that moment I didn't have the stomach to say much else. It seemed we both felt hurt and affronted at some level.

We looked away from each other for a time.

When I finally looked over at her again, she gazed into my eyes in a suddenly tender manner that threatened my firm resolve.

Never breaking eye contact, she leaned closer to me. "Please. Talk to me. Something else is bothering you, and I need to know what it is."

What was it about her that made her so maddeningly obstinate and hard one minute and then seemingly gentle and nurturing the next?

The server promptly arrived with her drink and carefully placed it on a crisp-looking napkin before her. The woman stared down at Kat like she was in a degree of awe.

"Thank you," Kat said with a polite expression.

"You're very welcome," she said with a lilt to her voice. "I'm Ellie. Please don't hesitate to motion to me if you need anything."

I nearly gawked over the way the woman was gushing over Kat.

Seriously?

Ellie was blushing, and honestly, I'd noticed in the past that Kat had that effect on a number people; men and women.

And me.

Kat nodded and waited for Ellie to depart before returning her gaze to me and gesturing for me to continue.

"It's very simple," I said. "The point is you were wrong to do what you did to me today."

She considered me at length before speaking.

"Unfortunately, and unless you haven't noticed, you have a tendency to require very direct methods of demonstration in order to bring errant behaviors or blatant misperceptions to your attention," she said. "For all your agreeable nature, you can be such a stubborn man sometimes."

I stared at her.

Why am I having such a hard time trying to explain to her how I feel?

"You don't have to be an overbearing dominatrix with me to make a point," I said.

Her momentary look of shock was priceless and I felt satisfied I made the impact I'd hoped.

She took a deep breath, closed her eyes, and slowly exhaled. Then, she regarded me with a tight-lipped expression.

"Oh, please. Do you actually know what being, much less serving under, a dominatrix entails? You know, for an intelligent man with a Master's degree, you're having an awfully hard time with your vocabulary recently," she said. "But then, perhaps my outfit and this environment contributed to your misinterpretation."

I frowned, not sure how to respond to that. Of course, it didn't help that she was very much looking the part at that moment.

"First of all, I've never asserted the role of dominatrix over you. If I had, you'd damned well know the difference," she said.

I didn't really know what to say to that.

"You mean, you've been a—"

"Not professionally, but you'd be surprised at the host of talents I've acquired over five centuries that I haven't revealed to you yet," she said. "Make no mistake; people have never paid to have sex with me. If you neither earn it nor deserve it, you certainly don't receive it, money-be-damned."

I stared wide-eyed as my mind reeled over her revelation.
A host of talents? Just how far out of my league is she, anyway?

"I have a pretty good idea what you're thinking, my love, and I recognize that look on you face," she said. "Stop doubting and belittling yourself. You've come a long way in the short time we've been together. You're neither as fragile nor inferior as you think."

She gazed back at me with a patient, knowing look.

Taking up my nearly empty glass, I finished off the remainder of my beer.

She arched one brow.

"It's only my third," I replied to her unasked question.
Jeez, I'm not some idiot alcoholic like my father was.

"And have you eaten anything?" she asked.

"Here?" I asked. "They were all out of goth snacks by the time I arrived. After all, we're in a club, not a restaurant."

"There's no need to be snippy," she said.

She glanced over her shoulder and motioned to a nearby server. It was then that I realized that the server and a number of other patrons were once again casting curious glances in our direction.

We always attract so much attention when we're out.

Of course, I realized that it was likely to be less me and more Kat; she commanded the attention of most eyes in a room.

She's got vampire allure on steroids.

We sat in silence as the server brought a fresh beer and a Dark and Stormy to our table. She cast a longing look at Katrina but offered me a polite smile before departing to check on some nearby patrons.

Kat frowned after her and returned her attention to me.

"Our server probably wants to ask you out for a date," I said. "As would a number of guys in the room."

"Not happening," she said. "Now, where were we?"

I smirked. "You know full well where you left off," I said. "You're just testing to see if I'm keeping up. I haven't had that much to drink just yet."

She appeared amused as she took a sip of her drink.

"I think we left off at my self-esteem issues," I said. "And your revelations about hidden talents. A dominatrix?"

She frowned at me. "Not a dominatrix."

Hopefully, the mood was lightening between us slightly.

"I bet you'd be a really good one, though," I said in a mock-conspiratorial tone.

The edges of her mouth curved upward slightly.

"Maybe I've never been an actual dominatrix, but I've known a couple of them over the years, and you might be surprised at how well I can fulfill that role for you," she said with a grin that looked half-menacing. "Interested? We could take things very slowly, if you like. It doesn't have to be conducted in a… How did you put it? Cruel manner."

While slightly scary, there was a forbidden allure to the idea of roleplaying with her.

Crap. What the hell am I thinking?

"I don't think that's a very good idea, after what happened today," I said. "Do you?"

"Caleb," she said. "What loving couples do together, or share together, is entirely between them. I don't care what other people think. They can all go to hell, for all I care."

Her eyes glistened. "Dammit, I love you, and I want to be whatever you need me to be. I want to fulfill your needs. You're all that matters to me."

Her admission hit me with full force; like a tidal wave of emotion.

I swallowed hard, feeling a lump grow in the back of my throat. "That means a lot," I managed to say.

The sudden emotional overload in my brain threatened to overwhelm me.

I deliberately glanced past Kat to see Paige obviously enjoying herself while dancing to the sound of Soft Cell's "Tainted Love" with a young man who was dressed in classic Goth rave wear.

I couldn't help but smile.

"That's your Paige look," Kat said.

"I have a Paige look?"

"Oh, yes," she said. "It's quite distinctive, actually."

"Does that bother you?" I asked.

"That you have 'a look' for her? Not as long as I continue to see the ones that you have for me," she said.

"Look, I'm not contemplating leaving you, if that's what you're implying," I said. "I'm just really disappointed, shocked, and still a little hurt."

God, how over-the-top-emo did that just sound? What the hell's wrong with me all of the sudden?

Her body language appeared more relaxed. "Well, at least we're finally talking, and you're being honest with me about your feelings."

The fact wasn't lost on me that vampires were the world's best lie detectors; not that I was trying to mislead her about how I was feeling.

We sat for a few minutes, sipping our drinks and staring at each other.

"So, where do we go from here?" I asked.

"You could start by telling me what's really bothering you," she said. "That is, if you're ready to talk about it."

What? Somebody hasn't been listening very closely, it seems.

"That's funny. I thought we've been discussing what's bothering me," I said.

"No, it's not about today. The heart of the matter isn't so much about me, neither my dominance nor your perceived embarrassment over your submissive nature, my love," she said. "Although the real topic of concern, the true culprit here, has affected your sense of masculinity."

I frowned.

Is there a psychologist in the house?

"This is about your recent job loss," she said.
I felt bewildered as I stared back at her.

CHAPTER 8

Katrina

The look on Caleb's face was nearly alarming to me.

On occasion, my intuition has failed me, but most of the time it has been rock-solid accurate.

Like right now.

At first, he sat stunned; almost statue-like. Then he rubbed at his forehead with a pained expression, and I knew that my revelation regarding his recent behavior had been spot-on.

"We've been home for a couple of weeks and you haven't even made a concerted attempt to clean out your office at the college," I said.

"They gave me all summer to do that. I'll do it soon," he said glumly.

"You know full well, my love, they're not likely to change their minds about your layoff," I said, though I took absolutely no pleasure in saying it.

He needs to accept the stark truth.

"Shit," he said. "I know that."

I wanted more than anything to hold him tightly in my arms and kiss him. But that's not what he needed at that moment.

Unfortunately, tough love often hurt the giver as much

as the receiver.

Besides, he needs to be the one to make the next move.

We sat in silence for a time, and I inspected my surroundings while sipping my drink.

Finally, he said, "I feel...discarded."

My head whipped around to stare at him as he looked at me with a weary expression. My heart sank, wondering what he was referring to.

"Discarded," I said.

"Yeah, being let go from the college felt like being casually discarded," he said. "Like my role as a professor was somehow optional. We're a college, for God's sake."

The relief that coursed through me was palpable.

For a moment, I thought he was referring to how I'd made him feel.

"That's a completely understandable emotion, Caleb," I assured him. "But you're not worthless because of what happened. And you're certainly no less of a man because of it, either. As I recall, you were more than enough man for me last night."

He offered a wan smile.

I reached out to grasp his hand in mine and gently squeezed it. Then I lightly caressed my thumb across his skin.

"There's no way I could have anything less than the utmost respect for all you've accomplished in your life," I said. "You should feel very proud of all of the crap you've overcome. I'll do anything I can to support you and help your dreams come true, including another teaching position if that's what you want."

He nodded. "I appreciate that," he whispered in a tight voice.

"And I'm so sorry if I overreacted earlier today, or humiliated you in any way," I said.

"*If?*" he asked.

I stifled a sigh.

"Fair enough," I said. "But you didn't exactly give me time to de-escalate the situation, either."

"I-I just needed to leave," he said.

I detected an elevation in his pulse and his pupils dilated slightly.

Tension. There's something else he's not telling me.

I pondered how to best broach the topic.

"You do have a maddening tendency for flight when you're upset with me," I said. "It worries me."

He looked up at me with a curious expression. Then his lips pressed together in a fine line. "And you have a tendency to pursue me before I can sort my thoughts."

"It's been hours since our spat," I said.

"Spat?" he asked.

Touché, I suppose.

I stalled for time by sipping my drink, which I had to admit, was tasty.

"We've argued before, but this time it was different," I said.

He rubbed one hand across his forehead.

"Was it only my overreaction?" I asked.

His jaw tensed as he raised his hand and signaled to a server for another beer.

He's so not driving home tonight.

"Look, it's moot," he said. "What's done is done. I'd rather not dwell on it. In fact, I'm already beyond it."

His response only made me insatiably curious. And I didn't have any intention of 'letting it go' until I understood it myself.

"No, you're not," I said.

He has a self-destructive tendency to repress his emotions and then later turn them inward on himself.

Risking another explosive reaction on his part, I stared at him with my best impassive expression, which, in the past, has normally done the trick.

Ellie delivered a fresh beer to him and then looked at me curiously. I nodded my head and she departed with the empty glass.

As he took a sip of beer, his eyes caught mine and widened. I continued projecting my thoughts.

I'm waiting...

"What?" he asked.

I continued staring at him, mentally nailing him in place before me.

"I can't go there," he insisted, visibly uncomfortable.

What the hell happened that he's so reluctant to talk about?

The music pounded around us, so I wasn't concerned about anyone overhearing our conversation. Still, I scooted my chair closer, my eyes never leaving his the entire time.

I slowly leaned forward until my face hovered before his; deliberately invading his personal space.

To his credit, he didn't move an inch.

"You no longer trust me," I said.

"W-What?" he stammered. "Yes, I mean, no. Dammit, of course I *trust* you."

I arched one of my eyebrows imperiously.

I'm no amateur at this game.

He swallowed, and I detected his body's mounting tension. His breathing increased and his eyes dilated again, and I was suddenly very concerned with what he might reveal.

Whatever it is, I'll be supportive. I'm not a completely cruel, heartless bitch after all. At least, not usually.

And, of course, I love him.

His face flushed. "The way your treated me earlier—"

He frowned.

"I felt so angry and embarrassed," he whispered.

Wait, he said something about that earlier.

"And I resented you so much," he said. "I didn't want to even be around you anymore."

Oh...anymore?

His revelation was certainly something that I felt we could overcome, or at least I could understand. I could temper my behavior.

Dominance was an art that I had long ago become innately skilled at.

I reached out to caress the side of his face and adopted a

sympathetic expression.

"There's nothing to be embarrassed about, my love," I said.

"No, it's pretty fucked up, actually," he said.

His strong language surprised me, but perhaps it spoke to the conflict that he'd been wrestling with.

"You can't treat me that way," he said, his words pouring from him like a floodgate. "I can't go there again. It's just too much…way over the top for me. It was just too demeaning; too cold."

Then he stopped but his eyes still brimmed with emotion.

"It's all right. I understand, my love," I said, gently patting his hand. "It was a harsh mistake on my part, more so given the abuse you endured as a child."

He merely nodded, visibly shaken.

A fresh wave of intense guilt hit me.

Shit.

He must've felt like I was an abuser from his past.

Once again, I was happy I'd killed the son-of-a-bitch, abusive drunk-of-a-father of his. Caleb might not have lived to see adulthood at the hands of that bastard if I hadn't intervened.

Enough of the past; move forward. He needs me now.

"I was wrong to mistreat you," I said. "It won't happen like that again. I promise."

He appeared relieved, yet I still sensed an underlying sense of anxiety in him.

"There's something else?" I asked.

"You know I accept how you are, don't you?" he asked. "I accept that you're an assertive woman. I mean, it's your alpha vampire nature, right?"

I nodded.

Then something else occurred to me. "But it's more than that, isn't it? You like it, don't you?"

I heard his pulse racing, even above the music blaring around us.

His eyes narrowed. "Sometimes."

I reached up to grasp his chin between my thumb and forefinger and nailed him with another penetrating, impassive look, my face only inches from his.

"You not only like it, you want it from me," I said.

His facial muscles visibly tightened. "Yes. Maybe," he said. "I don't know."

Better. Much better.

"To both, wanting and liking it," I said.

"Usually," he said in a wistful tone.

I smiled knowingly at him.

I know you better than you think, my love. I've studied your reactions. I've heard your pulse race and felt your desire rise on those occasions. I've seen your pupils dilate and heard your breath quicken.

You can try fooling yourself, but you can't fool me. I know what to give you…what you expect from me.

I'm more than prepared to give it to you.

"What I do to you…it's erotic for you. It arouses you," I said.

"Yes," he said intently, heat and passion lacing his voice.

I love this. He makes my heart sing.

Intimate recesses of my body ached for him. My hunger for his blood reached a crescendo that raged through me.

"You need this from me," I said. "You need me to handle you in this special way."

I need to handle you in this way, so very badly, in fact. The control and power; neither of which I'll relinquish to anyone.

He nodded, and his eyes still blazed with a kind of fervor that was delicious to drink in.

"Yes," he said.

Such a simple response; and yet, so satisfying to hear.

"Would it surprise you to know that I need to treat you this way? That I want to," I said. "It's exhilarating."

His pupils dilated and his breath caught.

Oh, yes, he understands.

"Why?"

His question intrigued me.

"You spark such strong feelings and hungers within me, Caleb," I said. "All the men who I've attempted relationships with in the past were so disappointing. They betrayed me; tried to manipulate me for their own designs. Over time, their greed was tiresome. Each time, they grew even worse; shallow and too risky to endure. Ultimately, my only satisfaction was the blood I drained from them.

His eyes widened.

"But then you came along; quite unexpectedly, in truth. Your innocence and earnestness was so honest and unexpected; not self-serving or manipulative, so unlike the others. Instead of setting your sights on what you could take, you focused on what you could give to me; your trust, your love, your blood, your body. You were the polar opposite of all the other men who came before you."

Except Samuel. But then, I was a human. Life was so different then.

Yet, that wasn't entirely true, either.

No…Caleb's more like Samuel. The two of them weren't all that different, really.

In fact, my feelings for them feel so familiar.

And satisfying.

His eyes gazed back at me almost worshipfully.

"You needed so much from me, my love, and yet you asked for nothing. You simply gave, wholly and unconditionally, with complete abandon, even to your own detriment and well-being," I said. "You're too embarrassed or self-conscious to demand anything of anyone. This might surprise you, but I'm not going to allow any of your needs to go unmet; especially the ones you're too shy to ask of me.

"I'm starting to figure you out, my love," I said. "It's taken some time, but I'm there. And tonight, this very moment, I know what you need, though even now you're too afraid to ask for it."

My eyes burned with desire for him; not only to meet his needs, but to compel him to accept them.

"I'm the woman you need," I said. "Regardless of your

self-imposed silence, I'm reading your body like a roadmap and drawing my conclusions from the look in your eyes. You'll revel in my accomplishment. You have no idea how prepared I am to be the woman you need. I'll shock and amaze you."

His breathing grew ragged, and his pulse raced, even over the loud music around us.

Then, a look of shame crossed his features, which completely surprised me.

Oh, no, you don't. I want this more than you now.

"Listen to me, Caleb. Don't fear what you want from me. Your needs are nothing to be ashamed of. You fulfill my needs in the same way that I complete yours," I said. "We need each other."

I've never admitted that to anyone before.

My own forthrightness surprised me.

I remained silent, allowing the impact of my words to settle into his mind.

His eyes met mine with something close to awe in them.

He understands me even better now, doesn't he?

I wondered why we hadn't sat down to have this frank conversation before; or at least, a hell of a lot sooner.

How many disagreements could we have avoided?

"I just don't want to lose myself," he said with a haunted look in his eyes. "I don't want to disappear."

That surprised me.

"You're not going to lose yourself," I said. "I love you too much to let that happen. I'll give you what you need, without erasing who you are. I love the man that you've become too much to lose you."

He took a deep, steadying breath. "I want you so badly," he said. "I don't care how other people see it; I can't be without you."

His words overwhelmed me, boiling my blood with desire.

The essence of his love courses through my bloodstream.

"You have me, now and for as long as you want me," I

said. "Now, my love, tell me why you need me in this special way that only I can fulfill."

I didn't know what prompted me to say that. However, it was something that I had mulled from time to time; something that I meant to ask but never found the courage to broach.

At first, he had a blank expression, but then appeared to be deep in thought.

Finally, he looked me in the eyes. "Before I met you, there was a desperation inside me; a place that scared me…a place that formed when I was young where I sought to escape," he said. "But you made me feel safe and you fulfilled something missing in me; something I couldn't provide myself with. And, over time, you've helped me to cope with that desperate place inside of me, helped me confront it.

"Your strength, your dominance, is sometimes intimidating to me. But it's also reassuring and protective. You make me feel safe and secure, and loved, and I love you for that," he said.

My dominance protects him. And I make him feel safe, secure, and loved.

My heart practically melted.

You have such a wonderful way with words, Caleb.

Of course, the irony wasn't lost on me that somehow a vampire like me, a predator who loved him yet craved the sweet blood running through his veins, could somehow make him feel safe and secure.

It touched me deeply, and in ways I couldn't have imagined just a couple of years ago.

Oh, God, how I love this man!

I kissed him softly on the lips, and ran my fingernails along the side of his face.

A visible shiver coursed through his body, which pleased me to no end.

"Today I abused my responsibility to you. And I overreacted," I said. "I'm so very sorry, my love. Please, forgive me."

"I'll forgive you," he whispered.

I closed my eyes with relief. When I opened them again, he was smiling at me.

What are you thinking now, my wonderfully sexy man?

"Yes?"

"Just so you know, I think you're absolutely ravishing right now," he said.

As if the priceless look on his face when I walked into this place didn't tell me everything I needed to know.

I reached out to cup my hand around the nape of his neck and pulled him to me, passionately kissing him. His lips were amazing.

"Thank you," I said. "It pleases me to please you; to fulfill you."

He appeared vastly relieved as I smiled back at him. He appeared reflective and sat back to take a big swig of his beer.

There, that wasn't so difficult, now was it?

Oh, hell, who was I kidding? I thought I'd lost him for a time there.

No, let's not repeat this kind of intensity anytime soon. It's far too exhausting.

Despite the unusual venue surrounding us, and the intensity of our conversation, I nevertheless felt relieved.

For the first time that evening, I sat back and took in my surroundings with a degree of appreciation.

It really wasn't such a bad little club, after all. Although I was amused at the notion of Caleb wandering into this place on pure happenstance.

He certainly has a penchant for the curious and unusual.

He ran into me, after all.

It was yet another one of the many qualities I loved and adored so much about him.

Ellie wandered over to our table with a look that bordered on embarrassment, as if she were intruding on our intimacy.

Any earlier and you certainly would've been intruding.

"May I get another drink for you?" she asked tentatively.

"Yes, another of the same, thank you."

Her eyes lingered on me, and I sensed a hint of arousal in her. Yet, she said nothing more and carefully retrieved my nearly empty glass before retreating back to the bar.

I'm flattered, but I've never had an interest in other women.

I glanced across the table at Caleb.

Now, him; he's another topic altogether. I simply can't get enough of him.

A familiar yearning rose within me.

Or his blood.

My gaze resumed its circuit, playing across the faces of the people gathered around me. I easily recognized a look of either subdued longing or desire, or both, on a number of faces who peered back at me.

Well, this place is teeming with the willing or the submissive. Alas, I only have eyes and heart for one, in particular.

I reached out to grasp Caleb's hand in mine and flashed him a playful look, which he responded to in kind.

Then I noticed Paige writhing on the dance floor with both a young man and young woman, alternating her attention between them.

She breaks a lot of hearts, too.

Her attention turned serious as she pointedly stared at the bartender serving some patrons.

Once my eyes targeted him, I understood why.

"A vampire," I said.

CHAPTER 9

Katrina

Caleb squeezed my hand, but I kept staring at the bar. The bartender looked at Paige with the unmistakable recognition of seeing his own kind. His eyes quickly scanned the room and settled on me.

"What's wrong?" Caleb asked, moving his face close to mine.

I spared him a sharp glance. "Why didn't you tell me there were other vampires in here?"

"What?" he asked.

"The bartender," I said.

My dear, oblivious mate.

He looked toward the bar with a surprised expression. "That's Frankie," he said. "I think he owns this place; seems like a really nice guy."

"Um, vampire? Pale features, penetrating gray eyes?" I prompted.

"Listen, Kat, I didn't even realize it at the time," he said. "Look around at everyone else. I mean, hell, it's a Goth club. Most everybody's got pale faces, and some are wearing those costume contacts. What was I supposed to think?"

Admittedly, he made a valid point.

"Stay here," I said, rising from my seat.

He gave me a cross look. "Seriously? More ordering already?"

I rolled my eyes. "Pretty please?"

"Oh, fine," he said, exasperation evident in his voice. "Go intimidate the friendly vampire."

I bent down until my lips nearly touched his ear. "We're doing so well, but my inner dominatrix is quickly surfacing, my love."

"Hey, you're supposed to be nice to me right now, remember?" he said.

"I'm only nice when you need nice," I said with a crafty look.

The satisfied look on his face was priceless.

Oh, I feel so powerful right now.

"Now, be good and I'll return for you shortly."

I playfully nipped at his earlobe and walked away.

On my way to the bar, I overheard a man's voice in the background, "Whoa, man, you are one lucky bastard."

"Thanks," Caleb said. "I couldn't agree more."

A fleeting smile crossed my lips before I replaced it with a steely expression, refocusing my attention at the vampire looming ahead at the bar.

Paige fell in alongside me and caught my arm to halt my advance.

"Just what have you been grilling our boy about over there? He looks spent," she said in a hushed tone. "And a little horny, actually."

"We've made amazing progress in a very short time. Right now, he's reconciling the balance of his needs against his previously self-imposed limits," I said, casting a side-glance at the bartender. "Ultimately, he's coming to terms with who he is, which is better for both of us."

"He can't do all that in just one hour," she said.

"Paige, this is a really bad time to discuss this," I said with a meaningful nod toward the bar.

"Okay, okay, Miss Dark-and-Snarky," she said.

I frowned at her.

"I'm just sayin'," she said.

As we approached the vampire, he regarded us with a sense of trepidation, but remained steadfast as he placed his hands on top of the bar. A young woman standing close to him looked at us warily as she reached out to place her hand at the vampire's back.

"Hello. I didn't see you when I came in," I said.

"I was in the back storage area receiving a late shipment and doing inventory," he said. "Frank Raven. Call me Frankie."

My eyes went to the twenty-something human woman standing beside him.

"My girlfriend, Heather," he said. "Listen, I don't want any trouble here. If I'm in your territory---"

I held up my hand. "I'm Katrina Rawlings," I said. "My friend is Paige Turner. And no, you're not encroaching on my territory."

He nodded with a frown and exchanged glances with me and Paige.

"Katrina…your name sounds kinda' familiar for some reason," he said. "But then, I don't really keep up with vampire politics."

He gestured with one hand toward the far, unoccupied end of the bar.

We obliged him.

"And the young guy over there that I met—Caleb?—is your boyfriend?" he asked.

"My mate," I corrected him.

He seemed slightly surprised by that but didn't press the matter. Instead, he turned his attention to Heather.

"Please go check on Caleb," he said. "Make sure that he gets our VIP treatment."

"Sure," she replied with a tentative glance at Paige and me. She proceeded out into the main area among the patrons.

"Thank you," I said.

"My pleasure," he said.

"How long have you been here?" Paige asked.

"I bought this place when I moved from Newark to Atlanta about six months ago," he said.

Paige looked at me. "Interesting. And just what're the odds of our boy wandering into the only vampire-operated place in town?"

I had to admit, it was ironic.

Frankie gave me a hard look. "You're kidding, right?"

"About what?" I asked.

"Well, vampires are hardly exclusive around here," he said. "That is, there's at least four other vampire-owned or operated businesses here in the metro area within five miles or so of my place."

Paige and I exchanged bewildered glances.

"You don't get out of Mableton much, do you?" he asked.

My gaze turned to stone, which appeared to make him nervous. "How did you know we're from Mableton?"

"Hey, no offense. Your mate said that," he said.

My sometimes overly-affable, chatty mate.

I suppressed a sigh and made a mental note to talk to Caleb later about that.

"I see," I said. "No offense taken."

He appeared visibly relieved.

"Do you get many vampires in here?" Paige asked.

"Nah, it's kind of cliché, if you know what I mean," he said. "Hell, we're still building our human clientele. There are two other well-established Goth bars that's our primary competition. Still, I'm hoping we'll compete better over time. I've got some ideas, but I'll need more capital before that."

Given that, he might be a relatively young vampire. Most of the older vampires I knew had accumulated reasonable sums of wealth. Conversely, perhaps he was just poor at handling money.

"Well, I hope everything works out for you," I said.

I intended to do a background check on Frankie once I returned to the estate. And a call to Alton was in order, as well.

Since Chimalma, Atlanta had fallen on my priority list. I really needed to take a larger interest in local developments.

But since the Slovene conference, developments in vampire alliances were teeming on a worldwide scale. Where would I find the time?

"I think I'd like to settle our tab now," I said. "Caleb and I need to be leaving soon."

"Um, I'm also on your tab, Red," Paige said.

I frowned at her but nodded my assent to Frankie.

"Nice to meet you, Frankie," I said, reaching out to shake his hand.

"The pleasure's all mine," he said. "You're welcome here anytime. I'll bring your tab to your table."

"I'll catch ya' later, Red," Paige said. "I still have a few more questions for Frankie."

As I walked back to our table, I noticed a dark-haired woman in a leather dress and stilettos sitting across from Caleb. Despite the loud music, my vampire hearing easily discerned part of their conversation as I drew closer.

"...she looks kind of dangerous, Caleb. Trust me, you need to be careful," the woman said.

Caleb's eyes widened at my approach and the woman turned in her chair to look up at me.

"Um, Katrina, I'd like you to meet Beth Carson. She's a local attorney," he said. "Beth, this is my ma-, I mean, girlfriend Katrina."

The woman rose from her seat to face me.

"Hello, Beth," I said, shaking her hand.

"Hi, Katrina," she said. "I was just visiting with Caleb here."

"I see that," I said coolly.

Go away.

She considered me for only a split second before taking her nearly empty drink in hand.

"Well, I better head over for a refill," she said. "It was nice chatting with you, Caleb. Nice to meet you, Katrina."

"Likewise," I replied with a forced smile.

I looked down at Caleb, who had a curious expression on his face.

"She's a local attorney," he said.

"You already said that," I said.

Sorry, but I'm not terribly interested in her right now. Tonight is all about us.

"Let's go home, shall we?" I said, fishing my credit card from my wallet.

As if on-cue, Frankie appeared with our bill in hand. I handed him my credit card and he made his way back to the bar.

"Is everything all right?" Caleb asked.

I moved to stand before him and reached down with one hand to caress my fingernails along his jawline.

"Fine, my love," I said.

Time to put some of my dominant charm to good use.

"Home?" I asked softly.

He nodded and rose from his chair, staring into my eyes with a look of desire.

Oh, yes. I like that look.

I pressed my lips against his and quickly drew a breath. He swayed slightly before breaking our lip lock to inhale some air.

I love doing that to him.

Reaching out to wrap one arm around his waist, I gently guided him through the room toward the main bar. After retrieving my credit card, we stopped by where Paige was standing.

"Had fun, kiddo," she said, hugging Caleb.

"I'll need your SUV's keys, Caleb," I said.

There's no way that you're driving after how many beers you've had, and on an empty stomach, no less.

"I'll follow you two out," Paige said.

"I need to get my cell phone from the SUV first," he said.

I pressed my lips together into a tight line as I regarded him. "So that's why you weren't returning my texts or calls."

His 'oh-shit' expression was almost amusing, except I was a little annoyed with him at the moment.

Calm down. Remember to be the 'good Dom.'

"Yeah, about that," he said.

I held up my hand and forced an agreeable expression on my face, but I could tell by the look on his face he wasn't falling for it.

"I was angry," he said with a shrug.

Oh, I do love you, but this is not a good time to let your balls drop, Caleb.

I bent down to give him a quick kiss. "Stop talking," I said. "I have far better uses for that mouth of yours tonight."

His resulting playful grin was infectious and I couldn't help but smile. Still, he wisely fell silent and simply held the door open for us as we exited.

He's learning.

Night was in full swing as we walked out to the parking lot. I followed him over to his SUV; my Audi was in the spot adjacent to his.

I used the remote to unlock his vehicle for him. He quickly got into the back of the SUV and started rummaging around for his phone.

"You okay?" Paige asked me.

"Fine, thanks," I said pleasantly. "And thanks for venturing out into the daylight to check on him."

"Sure, anytime," she said, glancing over at the SUV. "Is he okay?"

"He will be," I replied.

I'll do my utmost to make sure of that.

"Found it," he said, holding up his cell phone.

"Goober," Paige said.

"Gothanista," he said.

She appeared surprised. "Hey, who taught you that one?"

"Beth Carson did," he said.

"Who's Beth Carson?" she asked.

"Someone Caleb introduced me to tonight," I said.

I handed his keys to her. "Could I impose upon you to bring the SUV home for us?"

"Sure thing," she said. "Ethan can help me. I'll bring it by later tonight."

"Thanks, shorty," I said.

Perfect. Then I can talk to her about Caleb.

He walked over to the driver's side of my car and held the door open for me.

"Thank you, kind sir," I said.

Once I was seated, he leaned into the car to plant a firm kiss on my lips. I reached up to hold his face between my palms and followed his kiss with a passionate one of my own.

"We need to talk more often like we did tonight," I said. "We'll understand each other so much better."

He nodded. "I agree."

"Good. Now get in so I can take you to dinner," I said.

He got in and buckled up. "Dinner? I thought you said home."

"As you admitted earlier, you haven't eaten all afternoon, thanks to your impromptu drinking binge," I teased.

"It was hardly a binge," he said.

I revved the engine and whipped out of the parking lot and onto the street as The Beatles' "We Can Work It Out" played over the car's speakers.

I caught him staring at me from the passenger seat. "Oh, please. Laying it on a little thick, don't you think?"

"What?" I asked.

"Hello? The song," he said. "By the way, the 60s called…they want their vinyl LPs back; preferably unscratched."

"Hey, I like The Beatles, thank you," I said.

And yeah, I thought the song was pretty appropriate, actually.

I stuck my tongue out at him and advanced to another tune; thenewno2's "Make It Home" played.

"Oh, yeah. Much better," he said.

I rolled my eyes.

Music Nazi.

We stopped at a nearby steak house, where I ignored the odd looks from patrons and employees alike; as if they'd never seen a woman wearing Goth clothing before.

Rednecks.

I ignored them all, fully focused upon the man who'd won my heart and enchanted my world.

Everything went well until the drive back to the estate. I noticed Caleb staring out the passenger window.

"I sense you're settling into dark thoughts again," I said. "Talk to me."

"I'm an open book to you, aren't I?" he asked.

I scoffed. "Not entirely, you're not. That's why we have to talk about these things."

"I just can't help feeling that, despite really wanting you to be who you are, it's still wrong for me to want you that way," he said.

"Seriously, Caleb?" I asked. "What are you afraid of?"

Then something came to mind.

I parked in an empty parking lot and turned to him. "This is about those comments at the Slovene conference, isn't it?"

In Slovenia, he had acquired a bit of a reputation as 'that guy ruled by the two vampire women' from some of the more closed-minded humans attending the conference. A number of them were human male companions, though I heard mutterings from a few of the staff, as well.

He maintained a rueful expression but said nothing. However, I heard his heart rate increase significantly.

"I knew it," I said. "Listen, I didn't see any one of those supposedly masculine men rush forward to carry an explosives-laden briefcase across a field and throw it over a cliff before it blew up in their faces," I challenged. "Or confront a dangerous vampire with some sort of hastily-pieced-together UV light fixture. Or even battle against corrupt police officers for Dori Rousseau's honor and welfare. Those guys who were labeling you were full of testosterone-laden egos and no action, Caleb."

However, he still appeared unconvinced and I suppressed a heavy sigh.

"Okay, think about this, then. You'd never permit anyone else to treat you in the manner that I do. You wouldn't dare stand for that, would you?" I asked.

"Probably not," he said.

"Of course not; only I'm allowed to do that. Only I can give you what you need; what you desire, what fulfills you. Nobody else gets to treat you that way."

He nodded. "I understand."

"I'm not worried about whether you understand or not," I said. "I'm concerned that you just don't believe it yet."

"It's okay, Kat. I just need to work this out in my own mind, that's all," he said.

My fear was that he wouldn't.

Of course, I'm also worried that he'll end up brooding about this and I won't get any sex from him tonight.

I watched him as he once more stared out the passenger window.

I earned having good sex tonight, Caleb, and I intend to receive what's rightfully mine.

I reached over the grasped his chin between my fingertips and turned his face to look at me.

"You're no wimp, Caleb," I said firmly. "I've trained you myself. There are few men who could pick a fight with you and walk away from it. How wimpy is that?"

He looked at me with an almost juvenile visage.

"Great, the next time someone teases me about being too submissive, I'll just kick their ass," he said.

I released his chin and slipped the car back into gear. "Exactly," I said. "You have my permission. And if anybody has anything to say about that, then I'll kick their ass."

There, case closed.

His subsequent chuckling encouraged me, and I couldn't help but laugh as I whipped back out onto the street.

CHAPTER 10

Caleb

By the time Kat and I returned to the estate, I felt exhausted. I stifled a yawn as we walked through the expansive kitchen.

"I think I'll hit the shower before bed," I said.

"No bed," she said. "No sleeping allowed yet. You're gonna' take a shower and perk back up for me."

"For what? Massage? Game of chess? Maybe a movie?" I teased.

She pulled me into her arms and gazed down into my eyes in a possessive fashion. "Maybe you."

She reached down and pinched my butt.

"Hey!" I said.

"Mine," she said. "All mine."

Her hand slid down and firmly grasped my genitals with one hand. "Mine, too," she said slyly. "And I want what's mine tonight."

I kissed her hard, pressing my lips against hers and parting them with my tongue. She pressed me back against the kitchen counter, kissing me in an urgent, hungry fashion.

Her lips parted from mine and she pulled away from me so that I could see her green eyes lit up like miniature burning embers.

She's hungry or aroused...or both.

She nibbled at my neck and I felt her two fangs extend and rake against my flesh. "I'll have you tonight, my love."

Her feral tone sent a shiver down my spine. She released me and lightly kissed me on the tip of the nose. "But first, I have to make a quick phone call," she said. "Start the shower, my love. I'll join you soon."

I grinned all the way down the hallway.

My lover, my mate, my alpha vampire.

Downstairs in our sublevel master bedroom, or as I playfully called it, 'the lair', I put my iPod on shuffle on its external speaker and went to start my shower.

She joined me soon afterward, and we picked up where we left off in the kitchen.

We almost ran out of hot water.

Afterward, I wrapped a towel around my waist and went upstairs for something to drink as she finished in the bathroom.

As I downed a glass of water and leaned against the kitchen counter, I thought about the day's events, including my disagreement with Kat and the time spent at Old Skools. I wistfully recalled the memory of Paige's appearance and our time together.

Then I recalled Kat's arrival, and the very intimate discussion we had in the midst of the club. So much had surfaced about our relationship, including my own admissions to her.

She loves me so very much, and I can't live without her. But do all successful relationships constantly have to be fine-tuned or negotiated?

When I returned to our bedroom, Reeve Carney's "New for You" played softly in the background as Kat stood beyond the opposite side of the bed wearing only a sexy pair of black panties and matching bra. Her hands settled atop her hips, striking an alluring pose.

"You're simply gorgeous," I breathed.

"Come here," she said, beckoning by wriggling her index finger at me.

I started to move forward, but then stopped.

At least occasionally, I'd like to dictate terms.

"No, you come to me," I said, pointing to the spot before me.

Her eyes narrowed slightly, but she relented and slowly walked around the side of the bed toward me. It was then I noticed she was wearing an oversized pair of furry pink and white bunny slippers. There were big floppy ears extending from either side of each slipper, as well as a cute fuzzy black nose on the front.

I chuckled. "What're those all about?"

The edges of her mouth upturned slightly. "I didn't want my feet to intimidate you again."

"Oh, Kat," I said with exasperation. "I'd just like to forget all about that."

Stopping directly before me, she took my face between her soft hands and gently inclined my head upward to gaze into her emerald eyes.

She towered in front of me just like some kind of Amazon goddess, pale and beautiful with piercing eyes and a mane of flowing red hair.

And bunny slippers.

I felt truly spellbound, unable to deny her anything that she may request of me.

"What do you think about my slippers?" she asked.

I slapped her playfully on her rear using the flat of my hand, causing a loud smacking sound. Physically, she remained stationary but her eyes widened slightly in surprise.

I steeled myself for her reaction. She very slowly craned her neck downward and pressed her lips against mine in a slow, passionate kiss.

"You're just full of surprises," she said.

"A first for you?" I asked.

"Nope; my human husband, Samuel, and one other. Of course, Samuel was permitted."

"And the other?" I asked.

"I threw him through a wall," she said.

I swallowed hard.

She gave me a sly smile and softly kissed me. "Spank away to your heart's content, my love," she said. "You and only you; anytime the mood strikes you."

Grinning, I planted a firm kiss on her lips.

I was struck by a bizarre new feeling of empowerment. Something that was so simple, playful, and benign had suddenly become a power to wield over her at my discretion.

It was a heady feeling.

Slowly and deliberately, I rubbed my hand against her soft behind and patted her lightly. As I gave her another passionate kiss, I rotated my hand to the front of her abdomen and ran the tips of my fingers southward.

Her resulting sharp intake of breath was priceless.

Then a low, satisfied moan escaped her lips, and her arms encircled my waist.

"Time for you to lose the bunny slippers," I said.

She playfully flicked each of them into the air behind her even as she pressed her lips to mine.

In the blink of an eye, I felt the world tilt amidst a rush of air before finally landing on the bed, entangled in her arms and legs as my blood boiled.

Oh, pure ecstasy.

We made love with yearning and urgency, our hands and mouths searching each other's bodies. Kat's fangs had been extended on occasion, gently scraping along my skin, though never breaking it.

Then it was tender and romantic, each conveying the love that we felt for each other.

It had been simply amazing.

Later, I lay on my back in bed with Kat lying alongside me, her head against my chest and her red hair splayed across me as I massaged her neck with my fingertips. Her arm encircled my waist and one of her legs draped across both of mine, her body warm and soft against me.

This maddening, wonderful, amazing woman, who completely captivates my mind, body, and soul, is as essential to me as breathing.

My energy was spent but I felt completely fulfilled.

"You're my world," she whispered against my chest, her breath tickling my skin.

"I love you so much," I said.

She craned her head up to tenderly brush her lips against mine. "My loving mate," she said. "Sleep now, my love."

We lay together and I relished the feel of her body against mine.

The memories of the day replayed in my mind. My thoughts drifted to our conversation at the club and the subsequent intimacy that we shared.

Finally, contentment washed through me, like a gentle, peaceful wave, and I drifted off to sleep.

* * *

I awoke abruptly, lying in bed in the darkness.

"Kat?"

No response.

I reached out to the nightstand for my cell phone and tried to focus on its suddenly-glaring screen.

Almost three-thirty in the morning.

It didn't particularly worry me to find her gone. There were many nights when she would go outdoors while I slept, enjoying the escape from the gilded cage that was the estate. After all, she was largely limited to non-daylight excursions.

There was a time when I thought being relegated to the freedoms of perpetual wealth that Kat offered was something I'd never tire of. Yet, having my preferred career stripped from me, the freedom felt like banishment.

I love spending my days with Kat, but I need to get back into teaching somehow. I miss my classroom lectures and chats with students and other professors.

It was the job of a lifetime.

I massaged my eyelids with my fingertips, my mind too restless to roll over and go back to sleep.

That's when I heard raised voices and arguing coming

from upstairs.

Slipping from the bed to pull on my sweatpants and T-shirt, I turned on the lamp on my nightstand and made my way to the series of steps leading up to the first floor.

I stopped just outside the hallway to listen.

"*You're* the one who put those thoughts in his head?" Kat demanded.

"He needed someone to talk to, and yeah, I gave him my opinion," Paige shot back heatedly. "You treat him like a subordinate sometimes."

"He's my mate, and yes, I use authority when needed," Kat said. "But that somehow makes me a dominatrix to him? Or that I *emasculate* him?"

"Hey, I told him how I saw things, but if that's how he feels---" Paige snapped back.

"You programmed those words into his head, you selfish---" Kat interrupted.

"Don't even go there," Paige said. "You're such a cold bitch sometimes!"

Someone got slapped.

Then there were thuds and crashing sounds that reverberated through the walls.

Oh, hell...

I raced into the darkened hallway and saw only a blur of movement beyond the dim light in the kitchen. It looked like a dark whirlwind that bounced to and fro like a top.

I ran down the short length of hallway at them.

"Stop it!" I yelled.

Then the whirlwind struck against me, hurling me against the wall with unbelievable force, taking the wind from my lungs.

My body bounced against the wall and then back toward the blurry figures before me.

Suddenly, my body careened down the hallway and into something hard. I blinked once, just in time to glimpse an oak and glass display cabinet crashing down upon me.

My head impacted the floor with a thud, like it was being

smashed between opposing walls. I immediately saw stars dancing in circles before me.

Kat screamed so loudly that my eardrums ached. "Caleb!"

I tried to rise but I couldn't get my breath as the weight of the cabinet impeded me.

Then the cabinet's weight was instantly gone, and I heard a loud crash somewhere further away.

With effort, I drew in a breath and managed to push myself up from the floor, only to feel my head filled with splitting pain.

"Oh-no, oh-no, oh-no," Kat chanted in a frail-sounding voice.

Multiple hands reached down to pull me into a sitting position on the floor as I felt something wet dripping onto my hands.

"My love, speak to me," Kat urged.

"Oh, this is bad," Paige said in a shrill voice.

The hall light snapped on and I saw a small pool of blood forming on the floor. Only then I realized it was coming from my nose and mouth.

"S-shit," I mumbled.

The sharp pain in my head worsened, as if that were possible, and my vision blurred.

"My head," I said before darkness overcame me.

As my awareness drifted away, I heard Paige's frantic, distant-sounding voice.

"Ethan, we need you! It's Caleb; he's badly hurt!"

CHAPTER 11

Katrina

My mate, the love of my life, looked like a frail figure as he lay on the gurney before me.

The ambulance ride with Caleb was the longest of my life, despite the fact that we probably couldn't have arrived there any faster.

The entire event had been a horrible, shocking nightmare.

Normally, I felt in control of any situation, but now, I felt completely numb inside.

As I languished in the emergency room hallway just outside the examining room where Ethan and others worked to stabilize Caleb's condition, my emotions were dark and morbid as my mind raced with a jumble of thoughts.

Why hadn't I seen Caleb in the hallway? Had I been so blinded by my anger with Paige? Will he be okay? Why is it taking so long to stabilize him? Is he brain dead?

The implications of that last question filled me with horror and despair that cut me to the core of my being.

I leaned my head back against the cold wall next to me.

"Ma'am, you can't be here," a nurse said, grasping my arm.

The look that I directed at her caused her eyes to widen

in near shock.

I recognized her expression; my eyes must have flashed.

"Oh my," she muttered, her eyes locked onto mine. She quickly crossed herself, and I half expected her to thrust a cross before my face.

"*Leave me be*," I ordered in a voice so deathly quiet that I almost didn't recognize it, forcing my thoughts at her like a lightning strike.

The nurse appeared near-mesmerized and turned to wander down the hallway toward the reception desk.

"Red," Paige quietly cautioned, suddenly appearing beside me. "We're receiving unwanted attention."

With a fleeting look at the closed door leading to where Caleb was, I permitted Paige to lead me to a relatively unoccupied corner of the expansive nearby waiting room.

Another nurse approached me with a clipboard of paperwork, and I somehow managed to think clearly enough to complete the ridiculous insurance and information forms.

"You're his sister, got it?" I asked Paige, ensuring that Caleb would have family listed and present.

"Of course," she whispered, gently placing a supportive hand on my shoulder.

I listed myself as his fiancé, hoping it would grant me a modicum of access to him.

We sat beside each other for what felt like endless, painful hours; Paige never left my side.

It's my fault that he's here.

I still didn't know which one of us had harmed him during our melee.

Maybe it didn't really matter in the end. It was my fault, no matter the answer.

I had failed to protect him.

It was unforgiveable.

Numbness threatened to overwhelm me, and I hazily realized that I must've been slipping into a state of shock.

A small commotion of voices from the direction of the examining rooms brought me back to the present.

Paige's attention perked up.

"Red," she urged, grasping my arm in her small hand and half-pulling me to stand.

I had to deliberately move at human speed to avoid making a scene, revealing my preternatural speed.

It was painstakingly slow to say the least.

We no sooner made it near the doors leading into the emergency ward when Ethan appeared in his lab coat. I saw small drops of blood permeating the fabric in places.

I breathed in and immediately recognized the scent.

Caleb's blood.

His attention focused upon me with a calm expression that I somehow found infuriating under the circumstances. "Follow me," he said quietly.

We accompanied him to a small office where an orderly was eating a sandwich.

"Clear the room please," Ethan ordered in a commanding tone.

The orderly practically leapt up from his chair to exit the room, and Ethan shut the door behind him. I absently noted his authoritarian presence, so businesslike and self-assured.

Caleb was in capable hands.

"We managed to stabilize Caleb's condition somewhat, and we've rushed him upstairs for a CT scan," he said. "I can't tell for certain until I see the results, but every indication suggests that his condition is extremely critical. The X-ray image wasn't very detailed, but there's an indication he may be hemorrhaging blood on the brain."

Oh, shit.

I closed my eyes, vainly trying to wake from the nightmare that was taking place.

Paige quickly darted from the room and I heard her voice in the hallway. "Alton? It's Paige."

* * *

The sun had already risen by the time that Caleb had

been moved to a private room on the fifth floor.

That was followed by more interminable waiting.

Each minute felt like a clock ticking down to oblivion.

Time was suddenly my nemesis, gloating over me. By late afternoon, I was ready to scream as I sat at his bedside, holding his hand and staring down at his calm-looking features.

He was unconscious and hooked to a number of IVs, as well as oxygen.

I felt so damned powerless.

At least my dear friend, practically a sister, Paige, was here with me.

My dear friend, who I'd been trying to beat the shit out of only a few hours ago.

Some friend I was.

But what could I say? It was something that's happened between us from time to time over the decades. On occasion, I was angry with her; other times she was pissed off at me.

At least it was a shared experience.

We were like two competitive, slightly dysfunctional sisters. Inevitably, one got annoyed with the other enough that it occasionally came to blows.

Afterward, we made up eventually and everything would be okay again; at least, until the next eruption.

Our spats rarely got out of hand or went to extremes. And despite our occasional grievances, I loved Paige dearly.

Only this time, the person that means more to me than life itself got caught in the crossfire between us.

I took a deep, steadying breath as waves of anguish threatened to overwhelm me.

No, I'm a terrible friend and sister. And now, in the end, I'm not even a very good mate.

"I'm not good enough for you, my dear Caleb," I whispered. "I'm too dangerous for you."

Tears rolled down my cheeks, and I let them fall where they may.

The door to the room abruptly opened and, in the blink

of an eye, Paige was standing at my side, holding me and cradling my head against her stomach.

"Shh, it's going to be okay," she said.

"You don't know that," I said.

She said nothing as she continued to embrace me.

Minutes later, the door to the room opened.

"Ethan," Paige said.

I sniffled and pulled away from Paige. I gratefully accepted the tissues that she pressed into my hand and dabbed at my eyes.

Once I focused on Ethan, his eyes were tight around the edges. He held a blue patient folder in one hand, which appeared half-stuffed with paperwork and charts.

"Let's have a chat in my office, shall we?" he asked.

I frowned at him curiously. "Here's fine."

He gestured toward Caleb and pointed to his ear with one finger.

I hadn't even considered that he might be able to hear us at some level.

Ethan remained silent and somber-looking as Paige and I accompanied him to the third floor to his office.

This can't be good…

The tension level rose to such a furious height inside me that I wanted to scream.

Ethan's office was a small, spartanly furnished affair with a single, shuttered window.

He closed the door behind us and gently tapped the edge of the folder against his open palm. My eyes were drawn to it as a feeling of foreboding washed over me.

"We need to bear in mind that he already had a rather serious concussion," he said.

"Let's not rehash that," I said. "Just tell me where we are."

"The CT scan results are in," he said. "As I feared, he has a subdural hematoma, also referred to as a subdural hemorrhage."

My heart sank.

"Essentially, he has a pocket of blood gathered on the surface of his brain. In this case, it's in the area around the base of the skull near the brain stem," Ethan said.

"Well, is he going to be okay? Will it heal?" Paige asked in a tight voice.

I looked into Ethan's eyes, seeking anything hopeful or positive.

"We suspect that the bleeding is filling the area around his brain very rapidly, compressing vital tissue as is progresses," he replied. "Unless we operate immediately, Caleb's probably going to die. Even then, there's no guarantee that he'll survive the surgery."

"We can inject him with some of my blood," I said. "It will heal him."

"I considered that, as well. However, I'm afraid that's not good enough," Ethan said. "The blood needs to be carefully applied directly into the brain, near the damaged area. But too much would start the transformation process, which his body wouldn't survive in its current state. Too little, and well, he dies anyway. There's simply no precedent for this; at least, not that I know of. I don't even have any idea of how much blood to safely use for something like this."

"No," I whispered as my legs gave way and I crumpled to the floor.

Every bit of strength and courage that I embodied, every ounce of alpha female that had enabled me to confront nearly ever challenge or threat over the centuries, was suddenly spent and useless.

I'd finally confronted an insurmountable challenge.

"Red!" Paige said as she and Ethan bent down after me.

I curled up into a fetal position on the floor, crying uncontrollably; my body wracked with sobs and anguish. The pain was unbearable and I simply wanted to die.

"Shh, stop that," Paige soothed, holding onto me and brushing her fingers through my hair. "Caleb needs you now."

The door to Ethan's office opened abruptly, and I glanced up to see Alton striding confidently into the room, dressed in one of his fitted charcoal gray suits.

Tears streamed down my face. "This is all my fault. I just want to die."

"Katrina," Alton said, immediately squatting down to sweep me into his arms.

"How in the *hell* did you get here so quickly?" Paige demanded.

"You'd be surprised what I can accomplish when I need to," he said.

"As in defying all laws of time and space?" she asked incredulously.

"I was already in the States. Never mind that now. Dammit, somebody give me a status report," Alton ordered in his crisp, English accent.

* * *

Alton had reached down and pulled me into his lap like I was some overgrown child, just as he'd done only a couple of times in my past. He sat and patiently listened to everything Ethan had already revealed to Paige and me.

There had been a couple of occasions that felt like an eternity ago, when I'd been rather vulnerable in my post-human existence; Alton had been the rock that I'd needed.

My mind felt numb as I felt his arms enfold me protectively. My eyes caught Paige's as she stared back at me with a shocked expression.

I wanted to escape to someplace quiet and safe.

Moreover, I didn't care what anyone thought of me. I wrapped my arms around Alton's neck and pressed my head against his chest for the first time in centuries.

Given the hopeless circumstances, he was the only potential solace, the only remaining safe harbor, available to me.

Escape. Think about anything else.

Alton.

He was my dear friend, my former mentor, and had been the only vampire who sheltered and nurtured me when I thought all had been lost in my world. Suddenly, I felt like that same helpless, nearly broken woman he'd taken pity on over five centuries ago.

I owe everything that I've become to him. He's the reason I learned not only to adapt and survive, but to flourish. He trained me to be an alpha.

And then the renewed sense of anguish that surged back through me was once again too much to bear. There was little respite from it, even in Alton's protective embrace.

I felt irreparably broken.

"Katrina!" Ethan said, drawing me back to the present.

My eyes immediately found his.

"The recommendation and medical consensus is to proceed with the operation," Ethan said. "We have to relieve the pressure of blood around the brain."

What do I do?

"I concur," Alton said quietly.

"As do I," Ethan agreed. "But it's not my place to say. This has to be Katrina's decision."

I felt everyone's attention on me, and I glanced up at the other faces in the room.

Think, dammit. Think.

"I agree. We have to operate," I said weakly. "It's the only chance he has."

Despite sound logic, I felt as if I'd just bestowed a death sentence upon my mate and lover.

"You'll need to apply some vampire blood near the damaged brain stem area, as well," Alton said.

My head jerked up to stare him in the eyes. "You heard what Ethan said about that. It's too dangerous. We don't even know how much to use."

The corners of Alton's mouth edged upward slightly. "Indeed, you likely do not. However, I do," he said confidently. "I've learned a thing or two in eight hundred years."

I was too shocked to speak as I stared at him.

"I *can* do this, Katrina. You have to trust me," he insisted.

"I do," I mumbled, somewhat dumbstruck. "I trust you."

While I'd have gratefully embraced any far-fetched effort in order to save Caleb's life, a single spark of hope flared merely from Alton's confident tone.

It seemed as if there was nothing the nearly millennium-old vampire couldn't do.

At least, I hope so.

In fact, it was his long-distance advice to Paige over the phone last year that had enabled her to save Caleb from a near-mortal wound at the hands of a renegade vampire.

"Thank you," I whispered.

He said nothing but merely pressed his lips to my forehead in a soft kiss. With that kiss came a sliver of a chance that the heavy curtain of doom clouding my mind might lift.

With luck.

"Right then, my dear. Let's get ready to save that young scalawag of a mate of yours," he said good-naturedly into my ear, his warm breath tickling my skin.

I looked over to see Paige's tear-filled eyes staring back at me as Ethan held her in his arms.

"Now, off my lap, young lady," Alton gently said. "I have hasty phone calls to make, a hospital administrator to bribe, and a surgery to prep for. Doctor, if you would be so kind to arrange immediate introductions for me."

He half-lifted me from his lap as I struggled to stand, wiping more tears from my eyes. He spared only an additional moment to take hold of my chin between his strong fingertips.

"No more of those tears, dear lady. Caleb's going to need that alpha lover of his back again very soon," he said in an almost paternal manner.

"How can you be so certain of that after what I did to

him?" I asked.

He smiled in a completely disarming fashion.

"Never worry. He'll forgive you, Katrina. I understand that young man far better than you think," he said with an uncharacteristic wink.

I half-choked, half-chuckled back at him with a nod.

How could he be so damned chevalier?

Then, like a monarch venturing out into his kingdom, he departed the room with Ethan trailing behind him.

He's practically vampire royalty, of sorts, I suppose.

"That dude is so in control of things," Paige said.

"He's a force of nature," I said.

"No, *you're* a force of nature," she countered. "He's more like gravity on a planetary scale."

I frowned at her. "Where did you get that from?"

"The Science Channel," she said with a shrug. "One of Ethan's fixations. You can't help but pick some of that stuff up, I suppose."

I shook my head at her as she regarded me with amusement.

A fleeting split-second of quasi-normality felt almost reassuring, given the past day or so.

In fact, I craved it, drinking it up like cool water in a hot desert.

Then it was gone, passed by like a shooting star.

Paige was so dear to me, and yet, I'd been driven into such a rage that I had half-wanted to kill her the previous night.

"I'm sorry for last night," I said.

"Are you kidding?" she asked. "We've been about two decades overdue for our next big fight."

However, she regarded me sadly and then hugged me in a tight embrace. "I'm sorry, too," she said. "I should probably learn to keep my opinions about relationships to myself; particularly *yours and Caleb's.*"

I sighed. "Yeah, well, I need to try to be less bitchy and controlling, I suppose."

"Nah, our boy seems to like that sort of thing," she said. "Well, maybe not the bitchy part."

I separated from our embrace to stare down at her.

"*Hey,*" I said.

"Oops, there I go again," she said, quirking her lips together.

* * *

Daytime went and evening began again as I sat at Caleb's bedside, holding his hand in mine and whispering words of encouragement to him.

"I can't lose you, my love," I whispered in his ear, feeling every syllable resonate in my heart.

I hope he can hear me.

"You're the love of my life, the one chance I have at true happiness in centuries. I can't live without you, so you don't really have any choice in the matter."

An impromptu inspiration struck me.

"This is your alpha mate, ordering you to get well," I said in a loving, yet commanding, tone. "You will obey me, my love. I haven't given you leave to do otherwise."

Suddenly, he stirred slightly, as if returning from a deep sleep. My eyes darted to meet his, but they remained closed. And then, almost as soon as it began it was over and his body resumed its sedate state.

"You heard me," I whispered encouragingly in his ear before kissing him lightly. "I love you, and I need you, just as much as you need me."

We need each other.

Despite the rekindling of anguished feelings, I paused to reflect on the previous night's dire events.

"And this time, I'll do a far better job for you," I promised with a resolve that slowly welled from deep within me. "I'll be the alpha vampire and dedicated lover and mate that you've always dreamed of, that you deserve."

I placed a soft kiss against his cool, dry lips. Then I

reached to the small hospital table beside me and retrieved a stick of lip balm that the nurse had left, which I applied to his dry lips.

Please get well, my love. Return to me...

The door to Caleb's room opened, and I turned to see Ethan and Alton regarding me with solemn expressions. Both were dressed in blue surgical scrubs, which surprisingly seemed to suit Alton.

"It's almost time," Alton said. "They're making final preparations for us."

"We'll need to draw your blood now," Ethan said.

"How in the hell did you manage to arrange all of this?" I asked.

Alton shrugged, as if were nothing at all. "I explained that Ethan was a qualified surgeon in his own right, and that this hospital was about to become the first hospital to conduct a highly-secretive but cutting-edge experimental procedure that may revolutionize the treatment of cerebral hemorrhaging," he said.

"Ethan, you've conducted brain surgery before?" I asked.

"Yes, on a couple of occasions, actually," he said.

Wow. That's impressive.

"My man is Dr. Amazing," Paige said as she slipped past him to enter the room.

I looked at Alton. "How did you ever get the administration to approve this?"

"Well, it might have had something to do with their desire to be on the cutting edge of medicine," he said.

I noticed that Ethan, however, adopted a wry expression.

"Or it could have something to do with Mr. Rutherford's freshly-signed contract to fund the construction of a new, two-story surgical center in the namesake of the current hospital CEO," he said.

My mouth dropped open.

Alton appeared completely at ease. "Don't worry, Rutherford Enterprises will be taking quite a nice tax deferment this year."

I darted across the room to embrace him in a tight bear hug. "Thank you, Alton," I said. "I owe you."

"It's quite all right, my dear," he said. "Although you really should wait to thank me until after the surgery."

I pulled away from him to look at him sadly.

Please, don't let him doubt himself. This has to work.

"Now, now," he chastised me mildly. "If you carry on like this you're bound to wrinkle my scrubs."

I smiled despite myself.

My attention shifted to a blue-eyed, blonde-haired vampire dressed as an R.N. as she appeared in the doorway.

"We're ready in surgery, Mr. Rutherford," she said.

"And this is?" I asked.

Alton turned and gestured to the nurse. "Katrina, permit me to introduce you to Bonnie Lund," he said. "She just arrived within the hour from Boston."

"Pleased to meet you, ma'am," she said crisply.

I thought I noted a slight European accent.

"German?"

"Swiss, ma'am," she replied.

"Interestingly enough, I worked briefly with Nurse Lund at a hospital in Europe some years ago," Ethan said. "She's very accomplished at what she does."

"Thank you, Doctor," she said. "I certainly recall your good work, as well."

"Bonnie has worked for me for many years in various medical capacities, and is a fully qualified RN. She'll be assisting both with the surgery, as well as with Caleb's recovery process," Alton added.

He's already considering recovery. That's hopeful.

"If you'll please accompany me, Ms. Rawlings, I'll draw your blood for the procedure," Nurse Lund courteously said.

I nodded, but paused to place a quick kiss upon Caleb's lips before departing the room.

"I'll see you after surgery, my love," I said.

Please let the surgery be successful.

I reluctantly followed Nurse Lund from his room.

* * *

After donating a small vial of blood for the procedure, I paced around a virtually deserted waiting room just outside the surgery center. Apparently, most surgeries took place during the day, so I had the run of the place that evening, which I was actually grateful for.

Paige had left an hour or so prior to retrieve some fresh clothes for me from the estate.

"Frankly, you're beginning to smell a little stale, Red," she had teased.

Though it had been the last thing on my mind, I conceded that fresh clothes and a shower wouldn't be such a bad idea. Ethan had arranged for me to be able to use the employee showers when I was ready.

He's such a good man. I only hope that he's an equally good surgeon.

I glanced at the clock for what seemed like the millionth time.

God, this endless waiting is killing me.

As a last ditch effort at retaining my sanity, I closed my eyes and attempted to meditate.

My weary mind drifted for an indeterminate period of time upon fond memories of Caleb.

The scent of his body.

The sweet taste of his blood on my lips.

The sexual pleasures that we shared.

His laugh.

His thoughtful nature.

The love that he so freely gives to me.

My Caleb, my love.

CHAPTER 12

Katrina

"Red?"

I jolted awake, my eyes wide open.

Damn, I fell asleep!

"Hey, it's just me," Paige said, placing a supportive hand on my shoulder. "I brought your clothes. Sorry it took me somewhat longer than I'd originally planned."

"No problem," I said.

"Any word on Caleb yet?" she asked.

I shook my head.

"Hey, were you actually *asleep*?" she asked.

"Yeah," I replied.

It was a classic no-no for vampires to sleep in public; marking one of the few periods when we were highly vulnerable to attack.

"Well, you probably need it," she said. "But you should've waited until I got back. Do you want to go home and get some more rest? You can borrow my Harley."

"No, I'm fine," I said. "I don't want to risk leaving."

I didn't want him to die while I was away.

The thought of Caleb dying filled me with a fresh sense of dread.

"Why don't you go take a shower," she suggested and

handed me a small overnight bag. "I packed some clothes and other grooming items for you."

"Thanks, Paige."

I gave her a quick hug and headed for the employee locker room with bag in hand.

The hot shower felt rejuvenating and the fresh blue jeans and camisole were comfortable.

And my mood had improved somewhat as well. I felt more hopeful.

Not more than an hour after I had returned to the waiting room to sit vigil with Paige, Alton and Ethan appeared wearing neutral expressions.

"The surgery went extremely well under the circumstances," Ethan said. "Alton's careful application of blood and estimations of dosage were remarkable."

"Dr. Reynolds is too kind," Alton said. "Rather, his surgical techniques are exemplary and precise; truly impressive."

"Why, thank you," he said.

Paige slapped her forehead with the flat of her palm in exasperation. "Yes, yes, you're both amazing. Will the two of you please continue your bromance later and tell us how Caleb is!"

Ethan ushered us into a nearby empty conference room for privacy. My heart was in my throat as I waited.

"Well, he's not out of the woods yet, but I'd say his odds of recovery are very good," Ethan said.

"That's if his body doesn't attempt conversion, of course," Alton said.

I frowned and hiked my hands on top of my hips.

"What does *that* mean?" I asked. "I thought you said the surgery went well."

"Under the circumstances, it did," Ethan said. "Frankly, I'm relieved he survived the surgery; that was half the battle."

I tightly closed my eyes to regain my composure.

Time to get it together…and keep it together.

I opened my eyes and settled my attention on Ethan.

"Where do we stand?" I asked calmly.

Alton and Ethan exchanged quick glances.

"Over the next seven to ten days, Caleb's brain and the surrounding tissue will be very fragile while your vampire blood heals him," Ethan said. "However, it's also during that time that his immune system will be fighting your blood cells. If the balance isn't delicately maintained, his body either won't heal fully before the vampire blood has dissipated, or your blood will overtake his brain and instigate a vampire conversion process. If that happens, his brain tissue might not be healed enough for him to survive conversion."

I paused a moment to assimilate what he'd said.

"It's a hopeful start," I said with a nod.

"Precisely," Alton said.

"What about his concussion issues?" I asked.

Ethan rubbed his chin introspectively. "Well, if all goes well, the healing properties of your blood should take care of that for him, as well."

"That's good to know. Can I see him?" I asked.

"Not for another hour or so," Ethan said. "He's still in recovery."

"Nurse Lund is tending to him," Alton said.

I frowned. "About Nurse Lund."

"She'll stay on duty with Caleb while he's in the hospital, along with two other human nurses who I'll introduce to you very soon. Naturally, they're also employed by me," Alton said.

"The hospital has agreed to designate me as Caleb's presiding physician with the nurses reporting to me, as well," Ethan said. "In addition, I plan to stay here most of the time until he's released, just in case something comes up."

Paige hugged him and tilted her face upward to kiss him. "I'm so proud of you."

She looked at Alton. "And you, too, old man."

"Yes, thank you both so very much," I said.

"My pleasure, Katrina," Ethan said.

Alton walked over to hug me and kissed me on top of

my head. "Fear not, my dear," he said. "We'll see that young man in top form again in no time."

For the first time since the unforgettable and horrible event, I dared to embrace his optimism in whole.

And I can't wait to see Caleb again!

* * *

In Caleb's room, I sat at his bedside holding his hand in mine and patiently waiting for him to wake. He'd stirred on a number of occasions but remained unconscious.

That had gone on for hours, though it felt like days.

Nurse Lund regularly took his vitals and recorded information on his chart a number of times with the precision of a Swiss timepiece. She seemed quite accomplished at her nursing duties.

"Have you been working with Mr. Rutherford for very long?" I asked.

"Approximately seven years now," she replied.

"And what sorts of work have you done for Mr. Rutherford?"

"Medical related, for the most part. However, I'm afraid I must refer you to Mr. Rutherford for specific details, ma'am," she politely said.

"Of course," I said.

I'll be sure to ask Alton later.

Caleb mumbled something unintelligible, and I quickly leaned closer to him.

"Stop fight—," he murmured.

To Caleb, it must've looked like a veritable free-for-all between Paige and me, though I wished he'd never seen it. In truth, it'd been nothing to be worried about; we'd only been venting our frustrations on each other.

And on Caleb, in the end.

"Everything's fine now," I said soothingly.

"I'll inform Dr. Reynolds that he's rousing," Nurse Lund said, and quickly departed the room.

Caleb's eyes fluttered open slightly and he blinked a number of times. He sluggishly brought his right hand up to his face and tried raising his left arm, but it caught on his IV tube, so I reached out to steady it.

"Wha—? Where am—?" he asked.

His pulse rose significantly, so I attempted to calm him.

"It's okay, my love. You're in the hospital, but you're going to be just fine now," I reassured him.

"Kat?" he asked, squinting at me.

"I'm right here, my love," I said, holding his left hand and lightly stroking his knuckles.

My heart soared with optimism as the man I loved had finally woken up. Despite the uncertain road remaining ahead of us, it felt like my nightmare was finally coming to a close.

"I was at home and—" he struggled.

Then his eyes widened. "Fighting…you two were fighting. Then, I only remember flying…or tumbling?"

The horrific images replayed in my mind; hearing the crash and seeing his prone body on the floor, then the blood streaming out of his nose and mouth.

I barely managed to suppress a shiver over that image.

"I thought you and Paige were trying to kill each other!" he said. "How could you?"

"Caleb, please, calm down," I said, gently patting his arm.

"Don't," he said. "Don't go there. You— Your damned *Fight Club* episode flattened me."

My stomach clenched and I suddenly felt nauseous.

Oh, God, no. He hates me now.

How could I have let it happen?

Ethan and Nurse Lund hastened into the room and walked directly to Caleb's bedside.

"Well, well, our prized patient finally awakens," Ethan said.

"Ethan?" Caleb asked weakly, completely ignoring me. "What's going on? Why---"

"Everyone's just fine, Caleb," the doctor assured him.

"But let's talk about you instead. We've all been worried sick about you."

"Well," he said, and then paused and frowned as if searching for words. "I guess it's good you're in a hospital, Doc."

Despite my worry over his feelings and his condition, I rolled my eyes.

I suppose it's a hopeful sign if his humor's still intact. I missed that so much.

"Ever the comedian. I like that in a patient," Ethan said. "I'm going to examine you further, if that's all right. How are you feeling?"

Paige slipped into the room to stand next to me while Ethan examined Caleb and tested his reflexes. Her face appeared relieved as she regarded him.

"Any odd sensations?" Ethan asked.

"Tingling…some pain in the back of my head," Caleb said. "My arms and hands feel kinda' numb…my back aches. Uh, a wicked headache."

I felt so sorry for him.

And it's my fault.

I wanted to scream with rage over the unfairness of the situation. We'd only just managed to get our relationship back on track.

Now, this.

"Shape I'm in—" he said, once again seeming to struggle for words. "How bad?"

I felt too miserable to speak, and patiently looked up at Ethan to describe his condition.

"Caleb, you had some very dangerous bleeding around the base of your brain," Ethan said. "We operated to relieve the pressure and drain the unwanted fluid. Then we applied some of Katrina's blood to accelerate the healing process. Our hope is that your brain and surrounding tissue will heal over the next couple of weeks, but it's something that we'll have to monitor closely."

Caleb's features turned serious, and then he got a blank

expression on his face. I sensed he was trying to assimilate everything.

"Do you understand what I've told you?" Ethan prompted.

He looked up and slowly nodded. "Yeah, I think so."

"Good," Ethan said, gently patting his arm. "The important thing to know is you've made an excellent start. Actually, it's pretty amazing, considering the severity of your injuries."

"How long?" Caleb asked.

"We'll know more very soon," Ethan said. "Let's take things one step at a time and appreciate our small victories. I'm going to let you visit for a short time but then I want you to rest. If you need anything, just ask."

"Wait," he said weakly. "What happens next?"

Ethan considered him and then adopted a supportive expression. "Given the scope and seriousness of your injuries, we'll focus on managing your pain until the healing process advances. As with anytime that vampire blood is injected in you, your body will begin a cleansing process, so you should expect a slight fever, body aches, and maybe some chills," he said. "As to other symptoms, there may be some lingering headaches or eye strain; maybe some sporadic sensations of confusion or fleeting disorientation. Just let us know if you experience anything so that we can track it, okay?"

"Sure," he said with a tired expression.

Ethan and Nurse Lund stepped to the other side of the room, and I heard them whispering about symptom tracking and prescription regimens.

I refocused my attention fully upon my mate and reached out to lightly caress his forehead with my fingertips. He stared back at me with a searching look and frowned, as if struggling to recall something.

"I only remember bits and pieces about your fight," he said.

I stifled a sigh as everyone in the room fell silent.

"How could you? What's wrong with you two?" he

asked.

He rubbed at his forehead as if struggling to process his thoughts.

"I was *flying*, like being hit by a speeding truck and knocked into the air. I remember hitting a wall and something crashed."

A sharp pang of intense guilt surged through me, and I physically struggled not to wince at his words.

"Hey, don't dwell on that, kiddo," Paige said. "Listen, Red and I...we have a history of bickering from time to time. You know, just like two sisters having a sibling drag-out."

He continued rubbing at his forehead with a strained expression. "Yeah, well, that crap stops now. I better damn well never see that again. Do you hear me?"

I was surprised by his sudden burst of anger.

Out of the corner of my eye, Ethan quickly appeared at his bedside. "Caleb, listen to me now," he said. "It's extremely important for you to try and stay calm. We need to keep your blood pressure down for the time being, okay?"

He looked at Nurse Lund, who moved behind me to inject something into his IV drip.

"We're giving you something to help you rest, and I'm going to ask your visitors to wrap things up," Ethan said, tightlipped and glaring at Paige and me.

"I'm so sorry, kiddo," Paige said with a meaningful look at me. "We'll try to keep a lid on that from now on. Won't we, Red?"

"Of course," I said. "I'm sorry—"

I stopped, suddenly realizing that my apologies merely sounded lame.

"It's my fault, Caleb," I said. "I'm responsible for your injuries."

"Whoa, Red," Paige said.

"No, Paige. I take full responsibility," I said. "He's my mate. And it's my responsibility to make sure that it doesn't happen again."

I'll make certain of that. Or at least, I'll have to beat Paige's ass someplace remote and far away from Caleb next time.

Caleb arched one eyebrow as he stared at me. "What were you fighting about?"

Ethan inhaled a deep breath and cast a disapproving look in my direction as he shook his head negatively.

I frowned back at him and reached out to grasp Caleb's chin between my thumb and forefinger, though carefully enough not to create any discomfort.

"Nothing that isn't already resolved," I said firmly. "You don't need to be concerned by any of that now. Understood?"

For a fleeting moment, he looked somewhat affronted. Then he appeared as if something significant dawned on him, and he adopted a wary expression.

"Says who?" he asked.

I arched one eyebrow at him imperiously. "My mate won't pursue this topic further," I said. "You'll concentrate on healing and recuperating. That's the only merit-worthy concern you're charged with for the time being."

"Whatever. Just try not to kill each other while I'm asleep."

I froze, nearly in shock.

Shit. Will he ever let me live this down?

Would I even deserve for him to?

Then, I took a deep breath as I harnessed my formerly assertive resolve.

It didn't return easily.

I need to do this for him. He needs this, and I will meet his needs, no matter the cost. I love him far too much to relinquish my responsibilities to him and his well-being.

"You can be angry with me, if it pleases you. I've already said it was a horrible mistake on my part," I said.

He appeared intrigued by my admission.

"But don't you dare doubt my love for you. You are *mine*, Caleb Taylor. My love, my mate, my life," I affirmed, lightly tapping him on the tip of his nose with my index finger. "And yes, I do plan to keep you...alive and well from now on."

"Oh, brother. Way over the top," Paige mumbled under her breath.

I shot her a dirty look. *Shut up!*

She playfully stuck her tongue out at me.

However, the edges of Caleb's mouth upturned slightly, and he appeared pleased by my response.

Happily, I realized that my alpha vampire nature had once again returned and reasserted itself.

Just in time.

I noticed Ethan and Nurse Lund staring at me with a degree of amusement.

Nobody else needs to understand it. It's merely Caleb's and my special, dynamic, albeit unconventional style of relationship; something that we both seem to need...and relish.

Sensing another presence in the room, I glanced back over my shoulder to see Alton standing in the corner intently watching my exchange with Caleb.

He gave me a slight nod of approval and mouthed the words, "Very good."

I smiled back at him appreciatively.

Of anyone, Alton gets it. He seems to understand both Caleb and me all too well, in fact.

CHAPTER 13

Caleb

Being bedridden in the hospital really sucks.

The first four days of post-surgical recovery passed quickly because I slept through most of it.

That's not to say it was entirely pleasant. I had strange dreams and was plagued by fevers and body aches, not to mention headaches and repeated bouts of dizziness.

More annoying was how my vision occasionally blurred before becoming crisp again, which wreaked havoc as I tried reading or watching television.

I felt nauseous, and nothing sounded appetizing, though I was able to keep vegetable broth and crackers down.

Sleeping was definitely the preferred escape from my situation.

At least I was cared for by excellent nurses, including Nurse Lund, who insisted I call her Bonnie. She was very kind, and to my surprise, a vampire.

Despite her kindness, Bonnie was insistent about my following her instructions; almost stern at times. As such, Kat appeared to regard her with increasing appreciation and respect.

Go figure. Birds of a feather.

Browbeating aside, I was still angry with both Kat and

Paige for my present circumstances. To their credit, each went out of their way to cater to my needs and be on their best behavior; they practically walked on eggshells around me.

I realized they felt guilty about my situation.

Good.

When I woke up on the fifth day, Paige was sitting in a chair beside me reading a magazine. As usual, the blinds were shut tight, but according to the clock on the wall it was late morning.

"Mornin', kiddo" she said, continuing to read.

Before replying, I immediately realized that, aside from a headache and feeling overly warm, I felt quite different from the day before.

Somewhat better, in fact.

"You okay?" she asked.

"Sure," I said. "Although I'm hankerin' for some chocolate."

"Hankerin'?" she asked. "Well, I 'spose I could come up with something…you country bumpkin."

"Gee, thanks, *sis*," I said.

Earlier, a nurse made reference to 'my sister' making a call in the waiting room just down the hall.

"You heard about that, I see," she said.

"Anyway, I'd feel even better if I could just go home," I said. "Please help me escape. The scents in this hospital are starting to drive me crazy."

She arched an eyebrow at me.

Then I thought I smelled chicken soup and the smell of something else.

Cheese bread?

A moment later, Nurse Collins, a friendly young woman who was one of two other human nurses that reported directly to Bonnie, carried in a covered tray.

"Caleb, guess what I have for you?"

"Chicken soup and cheese bread, right?"

She frowned. "How did you know that?"

"No way," Paige said.

I glanced sidelong at her, noting the perplexed, almost wary, expression on her face.

I shrugged. "What? I practically smelled it as soon as she was at the door."

Nurse Collins quietly delivered the tray to a serving table next to my bed and promptly exited the room.

Minutes later, both Bonnie and Ethan burst into my room, followed closely by Nurse Collins.

Ethan strode directly up to my bedside.

"How are you feeling, Caleb?"

"Well, aside from a headache I feel better today. But I finally feel hungry, so I was just about to eat," I said, removing the cover to my food.

The potent surge from the scents of the food assailed my senses, causing a near-sour reaction to my stomach. I suppressed a gag reflex and quickly pushed the tray away from me.

"Man, that's powerful," I choked, turning my head away from it. "I changed my mind; not so hungry right now."

I caught a glimpse of Paige's shocked face.

"When did this start?" Ethan asked.

"When did what start?" I asked, as Nurse Collins removed the tray of food.

"Your increased sensitivity of smell?" he asked.

"Wait, earlier he said the smells in this place bothered him," Paige said.

"When did you notice that?" Ethan asked, as Bonnie stared impassively at me over his shoulder.

"I don't know," I said. "A few days ago, maybe? At least that long, I think."

I smelled the telltale scent of cherry blossoms and looked to the doorway to see Kat leaning against the door jamb, sipping from a Styrofoam cup. There was also the scent of something that whetted my appetite.

"Hey, Kat," I said. "Your eyes look better today. Get some sleep?"

At first she smiled back at me, but then her expression

turned sober as Ethan turned to stare at her.

"Everything okay here?" she asked with concern.

"Her eyes?" Ethan asked me.

"Huh? Yeah, last night before she left she had strained-looking wrinkles in the corners, and they weren't as bright looking."

Ethan turned to look back at Kat. "You can tell that all the way from here?"

"Yeah, can't you? I mean, you're the vampire, after all," I said irritably.

"Yes, I can," he said. "But you shouldn't; not from that distance."

Kat calmly moved to stand near my bedside, and the scent of her drink wafted over to me. Once again, my sense of hunger had mysteriously returned.

"Hey, can I have a sip of that? It smells really tasty," I said as my stomach growled.

"Hardly," she said. "Caleb, this is blood."

What?

Everyone was staring at me as if I'd gone insane.

My mind reeled as the realization struck me.

"Am I turning?" I asked.

I felt my heart pounding in my chest as I scanned the faces of those around me.

The only response was silence and a mix of surprised faces and blank stares.

"Schedule another CT scan immediately," Ethan said to Bonnie.

Then I felt practically ignored, invisible to everyone as they seemed to move around me in a veritable blur.

Whether I lived to be a hundred years old, I'd never forget the shocked expression on Kat's face as I was whisked away for a series of scans.

* * *

Only those who've endured a severe or prolonged illness

can understand the stress and worry of waiting on medical results—results that might determine life or death.

My entire life felt like it lay in the balance, and yet, I was left alone in a hospital bed, wondering what the next few hours would bring.

Would I die?

Would my body manage to survive a transformation into a vampire?

There were no distractions powerful enough to interrupt my seemingly endless streams of thoughts.

At first, I felt affronted for being left all alone.

Then I felt grateful.

The silence was almost soothing; or was that merely the numbness my mind felt from the anticipation?

Everyone's probably huddled in Ethan's office awaiting my test results.

Then I felt annoyed that I couldn't be there with them.

Why should they get to find out something before me? I'm the patient, after all.

I massaged my closed eyelids with my fingertips and felt weariness begin to overtake me.

My existence felt both real and imagined, all in the same moment, like something from a dream or movie.

I heard someone enter the room and my eyes snapped open.

A tall, broad shouldered man in nurse's scrubs walked over to glance at my chart that was hanging on my wall. Although he didn't look familiar, he appeared quite comfortable as he made his way over to my IV drip.

"Good afternoon, Mr. Taylor," he said cordially.

"Hi," I replied. "Who are you exactly?"

"One of your nurses," he said. "You can call me Sid, if you like."

"What's up, Sid?" I asked.

He produced a small syringe and said, "Everything's fine. I've been asked to apply a small sedative, that's all. It should help you relax."

I frowned. "I had one a little earlier."

However, he pointedly ignored me, so I lashed out with my hand.

I was surprised at how quickly I moved, though my grip felt weakened as I grasped his left wrist.

"No need to be alarmed," he said.

He dislodged my grip, so I grabbed the end of my IV needle and jerked it from my arm.

Pain lashed through my forearm and I gasped.

He grabbed me by the throat with his left hand, and I vainly pried at it.

"We'll do this the hard way—"

Though my reflexes felt sluggish, I managed to twist my body and rotate my right leg out from under my bed sheet and over the short bed railing to knee him in the ribs, though it had little effect. It felt like kneeing a side of beef.

Bonnie appeared out of nowhere, striking at his left arm with one hand while grasping him by the neck with the other.

With one swift motion, she dislodged the man's hold on me and threw him to the other side of the room where he rolled onto the floor.

Kat entered the room with a puzzled expression on her face. "What the—?"

"Intruder!" Bonnie said.

Kat instantly disappeared from the doorway, only to reappear before the fellow, who lurched up from a crouch to stand.

She slammed him back down to the floor and was upon him like a snake striking. With a slam of her fist, she knocked his head back against the floor where he lay prone.

Bonnie moved to Kat's side and bent down to pick up the small syringe.

"I'll handle this, Ms. Rawlings," she said reaching into her pocket.

She extracted her smartphone and began texting.

Kat looked at me. "Are you okay?"

"Yeah," I said. "He was trying to inject something into

me."

Though I felt somewhat groggy, I tried climbing out over the railing of the bed.

A breeze whipped by me and Kat rolled me back onto the bed, staring down into my eyes with concern.

"What *are* you doing?" she asked.

"I can't stay here," I said.

"Well, you're in no condition to be up."

I'd already figured that out for myself, but I really just wanted to get the hell out of that bed.

She pressed the flat of her hand against my chest, holding me down despite my attempts to wriggle free.

"You're persistent, I'll give you that," she said. "But you're not going anywhere."

I relented and lay still. "It's sort of amazing what I'll do to get attention from you, isn't it?"

She spared me a wan look. "As if you needed to."

A couple of curious nurses and an orderly peeked into the room, only to be pushed aside by Alton and two men wearing dark suits.

"Not sure who he is," Bonnie said. "He tried to inject Caleb with something."

I peered around Kat's body to see Alton staring back at me with a tight-lipped expression.

"Even in hospital, you're quite the troublemaker," he said.

"Uh, not my idea," I said.

He spared me a wry expression before focusing his attention upon one of the two men.

"One of you secures the perimeter door," he ordered flatly. "The other can help Nurse Lund relocate our visitor. I'll want to have a word with him."

A shiver went down my spine at Alton's cold tone.

Meanwhile, Kat very gently helped rearrange my pillows. "Are you okay, my love?" she asked, worry lines forming on her otherwise beautiful face.

I nodded. "Fine now, thanks."

She pulled the sheet and thin blanket over me as the man was removed from the room.

Alton walked to the end of my bed to face Katrina.

"Something tells me that Caleb was the likely target of the downtown snipers rather than you, Katrina," he said.

She said nothing in reply but her stony features and tight-lipped expression spoke volumes.

Alton's attention shifted to me and I could almost feel waves of power emanating from him. "Rest assured, my boy, you will not be left alone again."

"Thanks," I said.

He adopted a hopeful expression but then he looked serious again.

"You know something else, don't you?" I said. "Do you know what's happening to me?"

At first, neither Kat nor Alton said anything.

"I should let Dr. Reynolds---" he started to say.

"No, I want you to tell me," I said. "No flowery words, no double-speak. Just tell me like it is."

Alton's gaze was sober, like a judge who was preparing to render a sentence.

"You're between worlds, Caleb," he said. "Your body is teetering on a precipice, and we don't know which direction you'll ultimately fall."

Kat's features fell and a look of sadness prevailed. She reached down to take one of my hands between both of hers.

I was almost afraid to ask my next question.

"Will I turn?"

"If you do, then you'll likely die," he said. "Your brain won't be able to sustain the strain in its current state. Kat's blood may not succeed in healing your brain tissue in time for it to sustain the turning process."

I swallowed hard to relax the lump that had formed in my throat.

I didn't want to die.

But I didn't really want to be a human any longer, either.

It was as if recent events dictated that my longevity

depended upon my being a vampire; there seemed to be no other way to improve my odds for survival.

My life had become too dangerous otherwise; remaining human was no longer a viable option.

"I—I'd rather not die," I said.

I wanted to be turned.

Part of me knew that I needed to be turned.

But I had to embrace my humanity if I wanted any chance of continued…life.

Later. I can always be turned later, right?

But then, the choice wasn't really mine. My continued survival was up to my body. Or rather, it was up to my body's immune system to overcome the vampire cells that were permeating my body.

The healing blood in my body—Kat's blood—was what was trying to turn me into a vampire, even as it healed the damage to my brain.

My savior was also my damnation.

Dammit.

Kat squeezed my hand between hers supportively.

I rubbed at my forehead with my free hand.

"Fight it, my boy," Alton said.

I looked up at him. "What?"

"You're not merely a helpless pawn," he said. "Sheer willpower can accomplish things that modern medical science can't even begin to understand, much less replicate."

Willpower.

I cocked one eyebrow at him as he moved to stand next to me. He reached down to grasp my shoulder as he looked into my eyes in an almost paternal fashion.

In that moment, I felt a sense of immeasurable reassurance from him, and I wished I'd had a father like him when I was growing up.

"There's no line drawn in the sand here," he said. "This isn't your only opportunity for a transformation, you know. And it's not something to be entered into lightly. There are accommodations that can make the transition much more bearable, and we haven't prepared any of that yet."

Accommodations?

"And besides, we have so much more left to accomplish before then," he said. "Think upon that."

Okay, that sounded pretty cryptic.

Then, without another word or before I could query him further, he turned and quietly exited the room without even looking back.

Kat sighed. I looked into her sharp green eyes.

"What?"

"Don't even ask me what he meant by that," she said with a shrug. "He certainly hasn't consulted with me on the matter."

While I was willing to bet that annoyed her in no small way, frankly, I was too exhausted to contemplate the matter further.

I lay back against my pillows feeling wearier than I recalled in a long time; my mind felt both hazy and tired.

Kat sat on the edge of my bed, gently caressing her soft cool fingertips across my forehead.

I closed my eyes and soon felt myself drifting off to sleep.

"Rest well, my love," I heard her whisper.

* * *

It was late morning on the sixth day following my surgery that Ethan, Kat, Alton, and Paige gathered around me for a discussion. The mood in the room seemed ominous to me, though Ethan offered me a reassuring expression. And while I considered him to be a sincere person, I wondered if it was more a practiced response than genuine optimism.

"Well, let's have it, doctor," Alton said.

Paige closed the door to the room and Kat moved to stand next to me, reaching out to hold my right hand between both of hers.

"Caleb, I realize you've already spoken with Alton about the gist of things," Ethan said. "Based upon previous extensive studies, it's readily known that a vampire's conversion process, commonly referred to as the turning, occurs first in the area surrounding brain stem."

"I don't suppose I could read the white papers on that," I quipped.

Ethan smiled. "Those might be hard to come by."

Kat arched her brow at me.

I shrugged. What could I say? Levity was sort of a defense mechanism for me.

"As conversion centers near the brain stem, the direct application of Katrina's blood in that region during your operation was a delicate process. We placed blood close to where it would most ideally stimulate efficient healing of the damaged areas while hoping to avoid the conversion process," Ethan explained.

"So the vampire cells are currently converting my brain tissue?" I asked.

"They're attempting to," he said. "Fortunately, you have a strong immune system and we've been injecting you with some of the strongest antibiotics available, so the vampire cells are being hampered. However, we're at a stage where the vampire cells may be gaining the upper hand."

I wondered if anyone else in the room found it ironic that my hope of survival involved overcoming Kat's blood and its attempt to overwhelm me.

I half expected Paige to say, *I warned you Kat might consume you in the end.*

As those odd thoughts and symbolisms floated through my mind, Kat perched on the edge of my bed and enfolded me in her arms.

"What now?" I asked, looking up at Ethan.

His attention reverted from me to Alton, who nodded.

"At this point, there's not much more that we can do but wait," he said. "But if things progress negatively, we don't want to draw any undue attention here in the hospital. Already, the episode with your attacker risked undesirable exposure."

"Who was Sid, anyway?" I asked.

"Sid?" Paige asked.

"He said his name was Sid," I said.

"Sidney Darzoli was a midrate assassin who won't be troubling us any longer," Alton said. "And soon, neither will those who sent him."

"Agreed," Kat said.

Ethan cleared his throat. "As I was saying, Caleb, I think that it's time to discharge you. There's very little else we can do here that I can't provide you at home, and you'll probably feel more comfortable there."

A sense of uneasiness pervaded in me.

"So, there's nothing more we can do except wait?" I asked.

"I'm afraid so," Ethan said. "Although we'll have around the clock nursing assistance for you, and I'll be available at any time, if needed."

My eyes scanned the faces in the room, each looking somber and quiet.

"We'll make you very comfortable, my love," Kat said in a tight voice. "You won't want for anything."

A lump formed in my throat. I felt like a patient being placed on hospice.

Alton walked over to me and placed a firm hand on my shoulder. "We're not giving up on you, Caleb. And to be brutally honest, we're not sending you home to die," he insisted, gazing down upon me with a self-assured expression. "We merely need the privacy of somewhere discreet, and the estate meets both yours and our needs quite nicely. Understood?"

To be brutally honest…

Alton had always shot straight with me when using our secret phrase. It was our agreement, of sorts.

It was a matter of honor.

I nodded in silent response, more than ever determined not to give up my life without one hell of a fight.

CHAPTER 14

Katrina

How much pain can one woman endure in five hundred years?

Despite my best efforts, my nerves were frayed.

Caleb had been home at the estate for three days, though his condition seemed to be worsening.

I didn't know what else I could do but wait, as well as try to be positive and support him emotionally.

I felt so damned helpless once again; powerless to affect his condition.

For all my strength, skills, and experience, I could do nothing.

If not for our houseguests, I'd probably be a nervous wreck.

Bonnie Lund was one hell of a nurse for a vampire. I really didn't expect that, but I genuinely appreciated it.

Alton had commandeered our dining room, turning it into some sort of impromptu command center. Between his three large displays and no less than three notebook computers, he barely had room to place his tea mug.

Alton's personal vampire assistant, Marla Kendrick, had arrived last evening. I welcomed her arrival to help ride shotgun over Alton, and Caleb was particularly fond of her.

The amazing Ms. Kendrick was a force unto her own as

she effortlessly made due in her limited environment. She efficiently used a discreet amount of space in Caleb's study, leaving notably ample space for her own teacup.

Only English vampires would still drink so much tea after being turned. It probably rivaled their intake of blood.

I spent most of my time watching over Caleb as he lay in our bed, often sitting and watching him sleep as the minutes ticked by.

Sometimes I read and other times I meditated.

Either way, I felt as if I was trapped in a sort of purgatory, stuck between heaven and hell.

So, I waited.

Ethan had been absolutely wonderful. He stopped by frequently to check in on Caleb; only I had the odd sense that it was as much for me as for him.

He was such a kind vampire, truly surprising in a refreshing and reassuring way.

Bonnie Lund stayed with us, as well. Her assistance was likewise immeasurable and welcome.

That filled our guest rooms to capacity.

Of course, Paige had taken up partial residence in the estate; splitting her time between our estate and the home she shared with Ethan across town. I think her motorcycle trips to and fro helped to distract her.

There were no less than three plainclothes guards on the grounds at all times; two humans and a vampire during the day, and three vampires at night. Fortunately, they had hotel accommodations off-site in either Mableton or Atlanta proper.

"How is he?" Ethan asked in a whisper.

I looked up to see him and Page approaching the bedside where Caleb was sound asleep.

"The same," I said. "He seems feverish more of the time, and he complains of being hot, achy, tired, and generally nauseous. He's barely keeping vegetable-based foods and fluids down now."

His revulsion to animal-based food or liquid was a telltale

sign that we were losing our battle to keep him human.

I was fearful of the inevitable outcome.

He won't survive a conversion in his physical state.

And I can't live without him.

"Are you sure his brain's not healed enough yet?" I asked, grasping at hope.

Ethan regarded me patiently. "The odds improve ever slightly with each day his conversion is delayed, but I seriously doubt it."

I shook my head as Paige placed a supportive hand on my shoulder.

"With the vampire blood trying to convert his cells, his body is battling just to remain human," Ethan said. "And there's limited energy for his body's normal human healing processes."

I can tell he's growing weaker every day.

"He walked around the house a little bit today," I said.

"Yeah, I practically had to chase him back into bed before he fell over," Paige said with a snicker.

Caleb stirred slightly and then fell back into a deep sleep.

"He's seems so determined to fight it," I said. "Even when he wants conversion so badly."

He's very brave.

"Still, with each passing day there's hope," Ethan said. "We can't forget that."

I wanted to believe him, but I feared otherwise.

* * *

I envied Alton.

He seemed in constant motion, blissfully distracted with things both mundane and arcane: exchanging numerous phone calls, working with Marla on various tasks and projects, and typing like a madman on the array of computers before him.

He'd been chatting with me about the state of vampire politics abroad, though I hardly remembered a word of it.

My mind was firmly set upon the love of my life.

"Will Caleb survive?" I asked yet again.

Alton remained silent as he reached out for his mug of hot tea. It seemed to take forever for him to drink from that mug.

"Alton?" I asked.

He sat the mug down and stared into my eyes. "I honestly don't know, Katrina. Heaven knows, I genuinely hope so."

His voice was thick with sincerity in a manner that pulled at my heart. I felt my eyes moisten.

"You need a distraction," he said. "Something to pass the time."

"Like what?" I asked. "And if you say 'make a cup of tea' I'll scream."

I certainly could use a good scream.

And then, perhaps a cup of tea.

"I know who hired Caleb's hospital assassin," Alton said.

Now that's a worthy distraction.

"Who?" I asked.

"Raul Balefor is the head of the Balefor clan, residing in the ancient city of Merida, Spain. He was yet another strong ally of the late Baldar Dubravko."

My mind raced with both anger and scorn, and I wanted to leap from my chair for the first plane bound for Europe.

"Never heard of him, not that it matters," I said. "I'll see to him personally."

I'll crush him.

"I thought you might feel that way," he said with a weary tone.

I looked at him sharply. "And just how else am I supposed to feel?"

"I realize you're upset, Katrina, but perhaps you could wait long enough for my insights before you run off on a killing spree."

I folded my arms before me and glared daggers at him.

"Thank you," he said in that unnervingly patient manner of his. "Balefor's merely one of many vampires who's aligned themselves together."

"What sort of Alliance?" I asked. "I thought Hakizimana said there were merely numerous parties who opposed the Slovene conference. I don't recall any mention of an alliance."

He nodded. "Indeed. They've either organized far more quickly than we have, or they've been far more secretive than I gave them credit for."

"It's hard to believe they could've out-organized you following the conference," I said.

"I've been working rather aggressively on my own alliance in the short time since the conference, if I do say so myself," he said. "That was one of the reasons I was already here stateside when Paige called me about Caleb's condition."

Caleb.

"And how are your efforts coming along?" I asked, though more to distract myself again.

"Quite well, actually," he said.

Alton was many things, but a braggart wasn't one of them. He was one of the most capable and charismatic vampire leaders on the planet, in fact.

"But not as well as our opposition," he said.

"Then they've been organized for a time," I said.

"Yes, it would seem they have," he said. "Recall that few if any of us were expected to have survived that briefcase bomb at the conference. After further consideration, I suspect they would've initiated large scale actions internationally by now had the bombing not been thwarted by Caleb."

I nodded. "These attempts against Caleb must be a revenge vendetta; a message to others not to interfere. You suggested that might happen before we ever left Slovenia."

He shrugged. "On that matter, I'm sorry to have been correct."

A bitter realization struck me. "And that means they're probably not going to stop."

"Perhaps," he said. "But perhaps not, if we act properly."

I wondered what hope for success I had if I boarded a plane for Europe.

One vengeful vampire against who knows how many aligned opponents? That's a daunting prospect, even for me.

"You're contemplating the odds, aren't you?" he asked.

I looked up, startled.

"What can I say? I know how you think, Katrina," he said.

"Perhaps," I said cryptically.

"Well, you can forget about it," he said. "We're in this together, you know. Caleb is likewise dear to me, but it goes well beyond him now."

"Far beyond Caleb?" I asked, arching my brow.

"We've reached a potentially dire crossroad in the vampire world," he said. "I've seen this in our future for some time, actually. That's why I pushed so hard to form the Slovene conference.

"Regrettably, I greatly underestimated how quickly we've arrived at this pivotal moment. I ran out of time. Perhaps if I'd started a decade ago," he said.

I frowned. "All right, you're late. Now please tell me you have some grand plan in mind."

His eyebrows rose. "It is rather grand, of sorts; certainly ambitious."

The tone in his reply reminded me of a gambler whose bluff had been called.

"Go on," I said, though part of me wished I hadn't.

"The arms are fair, when the intent of bearing them is just," he said.

"Where's that from?"

"Henry IV."

"And why are you quoting Shakespeare?"

For some strange reason, I suddenly felt very cold.

"For the first time in a nearly three hundred years, House Rutherford is preparing for war," he said. "I'm raising an army, as well as a coalition of willing partners among our kind. Some have already declared an allegiance to the venture; not surprisingly, many of them were potential victims of the recent Slovene summit bombing attempt."

I stared back at my friend and former mentor with

disbelief. My only experience with one of Alton's wars was not long after I'd been turned, and Alton had taken me in under his wing to train and mentor.

Given my lack of experience, I'd taken very little part in sorties as a young vampire; though Alton had taken me on a few minor excursions as part of my training. Most of my experience came later when I ventured out on my own.

"That's what you've been busying yourself with these past few days?" I asked.

He shrugged. "I've been running the scenarios, weighing the odds and options of diplomacy."

He stared at me with a piercing, questioning look.

"And now you want to know if I'll join you?" I asked. "At a time like this? With Caleb on death's doorstep?"

He cast a sardonic look at me. "I know the timing's very poor, but I have a feeling you'll join with me."

I frowned at him.

"If Caleb dies, you're going to want to lash out at something or someone. And I'd rather it not be me," he said. "But if Caleb lives, you'll want to protect him from continued adversaries."

"And, of course, the best defense is a good offense," I said.

"Precisely."

He may be correct. Yet, it's another distraction to draw me further away from Caleb…if he survives.

"But, Caleb---"

"Rest assured, he would be well taken care of during your absences," he said.

That's something, I suppose.

If he lives.

I fought to repress such thoughts.

"It's been a long time since I followed you into battle, though never a wholesale war," I said. "It was only ever minor skirmishes."

"Good times," he said fondly.

Seriously?

His expression sobered as I stared at him.

"However, this time I won't be on the front lines as often," he said. "In this venture, my primary role will be strategic; battle planning, raising forces and organizing resources, securing funds, and negotiating alliances and treaties. Though, rest assured, I'll make appearances from time to time as needed."

I frowned. "Then who's leading this grand army of yours?"

He arched a brow. "Hopefully, you will."

I was stunned. "*Me?*"

"You've come a long way since the fledgling young alpha that I trained," he said. "Now you're one of the most feared vampires of our kind."

I stared back at him incredulously. "How could you dare ask me something like that at a time like this?"

"Fate doesn't wait to do our bidding. And you had to know that something like this was coming, Katrina. With Caleb squarely in the center of a targeting reticle, surely you realize you're going to have to go on the offensive eventually," he said.

I considered that for a moment.

Finally, I nodded. "True enough, I suppose. Caleb's long-term safety depends upon an elimination of the outstanding threats."

"Exactly," he said. "Caleb's and your enemies are also mine, so why not lead the army that can eliminate them. Our objectives are the same, my dear. Be my General."

My mind raced with possibilities and calculations.

"Caleb is my concern, first and foremost," I emphasized.

Alton nodded. "I understand," he said. "I would do no less for Dori, as well."

I quietly considered the merits of his proposal.

No matter the justification or benefits, Caleb's not going to like this.

However, I realized that where his safety was concerned, he may just have to learn to live with my decisions. They were in his best interest, after all.

"What army?" I asked. "The last I was aware of, you only had two dozen or so vampires at your disposal."

"Once I realized diplomacy was unlikely, I immediately began reaching out to those who were near-victims at the conference," Alton said. "The ranks of my forces have nearly tripled since then; and those are merely the ones who've passed extensive background checks and security evaluations. That doesn't include the allies, and their available resources, that had already flocked to my banner even before the conference ended."

"I can't imagine it's going to be easy trying to take the lead with so many," I said. "What makes you think the others will all defer to you?"

"Admittedly, I have a lot of negotiating left to do on that front. Still, I'm no fool to think that I can fight our opponents on my own. However, with a willing global coalition, many more things are possible."

Well, he's certainly thought this through. He's always been a master of command and logistics, not to mention one of the world's premiere diplomats.

"What about the human race?" I asked. "Don't you think someone's going to notice if the vampire world erupts into open warfare?"

"I'm still mulling that matter over," he hedged.

He doesn't know.

If humanity was drawn into this, and vampires were exposed, there'd be hell to pay; it might even be a sort of apocalypse for both sides.

I hastily considered my options, though I'd already labored over the prospects of maintaining my own support system around Caleb. Certainly, I knew I could rely upon Paige, Ethan, and maybe even Devon Archibald for assistance.

Devon was a tall, imposing figure of a vampire; a former rival who had tried to make a meal of Caleb at a remote wildlife reserve. Now he was a member of our little clan, and someone who I looked to for patrolling the territories I lay claim to.

Those days seemed like a lifetime away.

Unfortunately, as Alton already said himself, I had little if any hope of going it alone.

Caleb and I made powerful enemies from our Slovene exploits.

I almost wished we'd never gone.

Still, Alton needed me, didn't he?

And now, he needs me again.

"Katrina?" Alton asked, breaking me from my reverie.

"Very well. Define the expectations, and latitude, of my role as your general," I said.

His enthusiastic smile had the likeness of a cat that had just cornered its next meal.

"Careful," I warned.

Any further and you'll drool all over yourself.

He quickly adopted a more reserved expression and cleared his throat slightly.

"Use our forces as you see fit, including protecting Caleb. Just ensure that our common objectives are addressed, and any decisions will be yours. I only ask that you first consult me on major initiatives so I can advise you, as well as coordinate resources and allies," he said.

"I answer exclusively to you?" I asked.

"Absolutely," he said. "I'd have it no other way."

"And you believe others will follow me, having no track record to draw upon with most of them?" I asked.

He scoffed. "Oh, do be serious, Katrina," he said. "Everyone, including the enemy, knows of your reputation; which, I might add, was only bolstered by your time in Slovenia. As I said, you're considered one of the deadliest vampires in the world today."

Some reputation.

"Caleb's not going to be very happy about this," I said.

"Caleb's going to have things to occupy his time," Alton said.

Oh, really?

"I don't suppose you'd care to share those things with

me?"

"We're talking right now, aren't we?"

I sighed.

"I'll want occasional time with him," I said. "Guaranteed visitations and what not."

My God, this sounds like custody proceedings.

"And you'll have time at your discretion," Alton said. "I have a second-in-command already picked out who can assist you, pending your approval, of course. He can certainly stand in for you during your time with Caleb."

Well, that's something, at least.

"Caleb's going to hate me for this," I muttered.

"Nonsense," he said. "That boy loves you like no other. The sun rises and sets on you."

I like that thought.

"He'd hate you calling him a boy. He's quite a man, you know," I said. "Paige already refers to him as 'our boy' and I think it annoys him to no end."

Alton wanly smiled. "Yes, well, it's meant as an affectionate title. Besides, he's only twenty-seven to my eight-hundred-plus. I could be his grandfather many times over."

"Bite your tongue," I admonished. "I'm over five hundred, and I'm not about to think of myself as his ancestor many times over. Besides, the same could be said for you and Dori, I might add. How gross and creepy would that be?"

Alton blanched. "Too true. Let's stop right there."

Courting younger beings definitely has its challenges.

Maybe that's why we vampires so often stick to our own kind.

"If things go well with Caleb's recovery, I need to figure out how to explain all of this to him," I said, massaging my temples with my fingertips.

It's amazing how much tension I seem to still endure as an eternal being.

"Don't worry," Alton said. "I have an idea."

I stared at my friend and former mentor suspiciously.

What do you have up your sleeve now?

"But let's focus on his condition for now, shall we?" Alton

asked. "The next day or so will be telling, I think."

I ground my teeth as a renewed wave of dread threatened to overwhelm me.

CHAPTER 15

Caleb

I think I'm dying.

At least I was at home among people who loved me.

I'd come close to death once before, lying on the dining room floor after Kat had nearly drained me of blood to heal her body following Chimalma's attack.

To save Kat's life…

I remember how the strength had waned in my body on that fateful day, just as it had been doing over the past couple of days.

It was a strange, ominous feeling, like the Grim Reaper was trickling my energy away bit by little bit.

My body ached as I took a deep breath and let it out slowly.

I didn't want to die yet. There were too many things left that I wanted to do.

Too many things I wanted to share with Kat.

I didn't want to believe what Alton or Ethan kept saying. Instead, I kept hoping my body would strengthen as Kat's vampire blood permeated my body, my brain.

Most likely, I was wrong.

That really sucked.

Harnessing sheer willpower, I steeled myself for the pain

to run through my body as I sat up on the edge of the bed.

Well, I'm not giving up. Death's going to have to rip me from existence if he wants me.

After a trip to the bathroom, I slowly climbed the short set of stairs leading up to the first floor. I heard a movie playing in the theater room down the hall, as well as the distant sounds of Alton and Kat's voices at the back of the house, though I couldn't quite make out what they were talking about.

I smelled the scent of cookie dough wafting down the hallway from the kitchen.

There was still a dent in the sheetrock where my body impacted the wall.

My vision blurred slightly as I braced my hand against the wall until it cleared again. Then I saw minute dust particles floating in the air around me, just like miniature snowflakes.

We need a maid.

My senses had been sharpened by the vampire cells transforming my body, though the effects kept phasing in and out. If only I could survive the rest of the transition.

What other wonders might I experience?

Life was full of wonders, if we only looked for them.

I slowly walked to the sitting room at the front of the house. The bright halo at the top of the closed curtains suggested it was still daytime.

I walked to the windows and parted the curtains slightly.

The thin fingers of late afternoon light filtering between the blades of the blinds felt like fire against my arms and hands, and I flinched from the discomfort.

I stepped back, nearly losing my balance, but soft hands grasping my upper arms quickly steadied me.

"Careful, Caleb," Bonnie Lund said. "We cautioned you that sunlight might be uncomfortable."

"I had to see for myself," I said.

She released her grip on my arms. "Well, I made some chocolate chip cookies for you, if you're interested. Ms.

Rawlings said they're your favorite."

"Oh, they most certainly are."

I felt like I was a child again, waiting to eat Mom's cookies. She'd been a great baker, my mother.

"Well, come have some when you're ready," she said.

"Thanks," I said, fleetingly wondering if I could keep one down.

I watched her leave the room and then sat on the edge of the nearby sofa to catch my breath. I rubbed at my forehead to wipe the sheen of sweat from my skin despite the chills that coursed through my body.

Dammit, I feel miserable.

Staring at the closed curtains, I recalled how much I loved the sunshine, how it felt like a warm blanket enveloping me.

I missed the sunlight.

Was that how vampires felt after a time?

I supposed I could get used to that. Of course, merely surviving through what I was enduring would make almost any other challenge or sacrifice pale by comparison.

I reflected upon all the important people in my life who I loved so dearly. Since being home from the hospital I had received regular phone calls from Dori, Aiden Henderson who was my human friend from the Slovene conference, and even Maddy Baker, another wonderful human I befriended in Slovenia.

Even Devon Archibald had driven from nearby Marietta just to check in with me personally. We'd visited in the front room, in fact.

Devon turned out to be a really great guy. He's someone I consider a friend now.

We'd had a pleasant chat, though I found it hard to concentrate on any given topic for very long.

Before leaving, he had looked upon me with a hopeful expression. "Caleb, I know you feel very poorly right now, but never give up hope. The world can look differently with the dawning of each new day."

"Sure," I'd said to him.

"*Give me my robe, put on my crown; I have Immortal Dawn in me,*" he said.

"You've been reading Shakespeare again, haven't you?" I had asked him.

He had merely shrugged. "Antony and Cleopatra."

Thinking back upon his visit, I hoped he was right about that quote.

I wondered if that visit would mark the last time I ever saw him.

With a degree of effort, I stood up using a pair of wobbly legs that felt nearly ready to give out from beneath me.

The way I'm feeling, I'll probably not see another sunrise.

A wave of sadness crashed over me at that realization.

I need to spend as much time with Kat as possible.

Unsteady legs carried me from the room, and I grasped onto the bannister at the foot of the stairs to balance myself.

I looked up to the second floor as an eerie epiphany struck; an idea I knew neither Kat nor anyone else was going to approve of.

Though admittedly desperate, what did I have to lose?

Maybe nothing.

Maybe everything.

All that might await me was a few fleeting days, or even hours, of life spent lying in bed like an invalid, wasting away to nothingness.

My mother wasted away from cancer.

I don't want to go out like that.

Not like that.

I half-considered going to spend time with Kat. But then, she'd probably know something was on my mind.

It was nearly impossible to hide my thoughts, much less my emotions, from her.

But what if this was my only chance to say…goodbye?

God, how I love her.

I'd told her that just earlier in the day, in fact.

My legs felt as if they were going to give out from beneath me. A ripping pain coursed through my head like a knife.

I'm nearly out of time. I can feel it.

Kat, please forgive me.

Grasping the bannister, I laboriously climbed each stair step, often pausing to catch my breath. It felt like an eternity before I finally reached the top landing.

Slowly and using the wall to lean against, I made my way into the west-facing bedroom that had been assigned to Bonnie.

I staggered inside as quietly as I could, hoping nobody heard me downstairs.

I closed the bedroom door behind me.

With pain coursing through my body, barely able to get my legs to move, I willed my body toward the heavy curtains before the window.

I parted the curtains, and despite the closed blinds, the skin across my face, arms, and hands tingled furiously.

Reaching out to the pull cord for the blinds, I paused for only a moment.

Kat, I'll love you forever.

Mustering the remaining strength in my upper body, I yanked upon the cord. The blinds rose upward and blinding light burned into my eyes and across my skin.

I wanted to scream and barely managed to contain the pain coursing through my head as I gritted my teeth.

My body shook and trembled and the combined explosion of fire and electricity roared through my head and down my spine.

I felt myself falling backward, as if into an endless chasm, but I maintained a death grip onto the cord as if it was my lifeline to sheer existence.

Something crashed to the floor.

I bounced on something soft but my body continued to burn.

Acid flowed in my veins!

I tried to scream but had no breath in my lungs. Gasping for air but finding none, my chest felt like it was imploding in on itself.

Writhing in agony, my heartbeat pounded in my ears until it sounded like thunder. I thought my head was exploding!

Then it stopped.

Faint ringing formed in my ears, distantly at first, and then built to a high-pitched crescendo.

A great white light formed before me, and I felt myself being drawn toward it.

My body no longer felt pain; I felt strangely numb and comfortable.

I was finally at peace.

Blissful.

I wish you were here, Kat.

I love you...

CHAPTER 16

Katrina

"Close the shutters!" Bonnie screamed from somewhere upstairs.

Almost by instinct, and despite the shock I felt from the shrill impact of her voice, I rushed to the nearest wall-mounted security console to activate the estate's reinforced emergency shutter system.

Immediately, heavy metal barriers locked into place before all exterior doors and windows, sealing the estate's most vulnerable access points.

Alton had already rushed upstairs, but I heard him shout, "Katrina!"

I raced upstairs, pushing my strength to its limits. Within seconds, I stood in the doorway to the upstairs bedroom where Bonnie was giving CPR to…Caleb!

I rushed to the bedside to see a bluish pallor on his face, which sent a cold stab of pain into my heart.

Oh, God, no…

Then I noticed that his arms, hands, and neck looked reddened, almost burnt.

With a single, wane gasp, I heard his heartbeat; irregular at first, then more rhythmic.

I gasped, realizing that I, too, had stopped breathing for

those brief moments.

"What happened? How did he get up here?" I demanded.

"Hush," Bonnie said as she held his wrist and placed her ear against his neck and then to his chest.

I waited as precious seconds ticked by.

She checked his pupils with a small penlight, and then sat upright on the edge of the bed. Marla stood to one side of her, an uncustomary expression of shock on her face.

"Ethan, we need you here now," Alton spoke into his mobile phone.

My mind felt numb as I stared into Bonnie's eyes, her expression one of shock. Alton's continued dialogue was quickly drowned out by my own desperate musings about what had just happened to Caleb.

Why wasn't he rousing?

"I found him basked in sunlight from the open window, and he wasn't breathing," Bonnie said. "The sunlight was too intense for me, so the shutters were faster..."

"You did the right thing," I said. "How is he?"

She shrugged. "We won't know until Dr. Reynolds gets here, but at least he's breathing on his own."

It seemed as if she was masking something further.

"Tell me," I said.

"He's not waking, so I'm a little worried about brain damage," she said.

That was almost too painful to contemplate after having just restored his heartbeat and breathing.

"I understand," I managed to say, though it sounded like some else's voice rather than my own.

Alton's dire expression conjured similar volumes of dread in me.

"Can you open the access to the doors of the house?" he asked.

"Yes, I'll take care of that," I said.

"I need to inform the two guards outside about what's happened," he said, turning to leave.

I was numb inside as I made my way to the nearest security panel.

* * *

Ethan and Paige arrived by motorcycle in what must've been record-setting time. Paige looked on the verge of tears as we watched Ethan examine Caleb. Together, he and Bonnie were able to perform some basic reflex tests so one could feel for muscle reaction while the other watched eye movement and listened for changes in heartbeat.

I thought Caleb stirred at one point, but Ethan discounted it as a breathing-related anomaly.

"Coma?" Alton asked.

I'd been too afraid to ask that.

"Perhaps," Ethan said. "But it's not a deep one, if it is a coma."

A faint glimmer of relief attempted to foster itself in the back of my mind.

That's when I noticed that Caleb's arms no longer appeared as red as they had earlier. And though his face looked pale, at least it was better than its former bluish hue.

I can't lose him.

I can't bear it.

"What the hell was he thinking?" Paige asked.

"I can't say for certain," Ethan said. "But it might've been ingenious, if not poorly executed."

My eyes locked onto the good doctor's. "What?"

"You think he was trying to neutralize the vampire cells?" Alton asked.

I stared at him as if he were insane.

"It makes sense at one level," Ethan said. "He was still half-human, so he may have gambled it would give his white blood cells a better chance if they didn't have to fight the vampire cells."

He was killing the part of me that was killing him?

Oh, I'm desperately going to need therapy after this.

"That was rash," I said.

"He's an idiot," Paige said, though she was furiously rubbing at her eyes with her knuckles.

"He was dying anyway," Alton said. "There was little to lose."

I glared at him. "Well, that was a convenient omission on your part; you never shared that opinion with me."

"I said I hoped he'd survive," Alton said. "And that was absolutely the truth."

Maybe I merely wanted the opportunity to focus my anger at someone or something, but I had a hard time stomaching his nuanced explanation.

"But why won't he wake up?" Paige asked.

"Possibly shock," Ethan said. "His body might be resetting itself. We should know more in the next twenty-four hours."

"Are you sure it's not brain damage?" I asked.

"I think we restored his breathing quickly enough," Bonnie said. "I heard a commotion upstairs from the kitchen, and I was at the door in a matter of seconds. It was less than a minute later when I was able to give him CPR."

"I concur," Ethan said. "There likely wasn't enough time for significant brain damage to set in."

"But what about his brain injury?" I asked.

"Somehow, I think we're okay there," Ethan said.

"You're not sure, though, are you?" Paige asked. "Shouldn't we get him to the hospital or something?"

"I'd rather not move him, for now," Ethan said. "But no, it's difficult to be certain about a diagnosis in these circumstances, especially in this early stage."

"So, we wait? For how long then?" I asked.

"As I said, let's give things twenty-four hours," he said. "Then we'll reassess."

More waiting.

Shit.

This is going to be the death of me.

The emotional strain in my body felt nearly unbearable.

I realized, of course, that I'd gladly trade places with Caleb, the love of my life, if only I could rest assured he'd survive.

CHAPTER 17

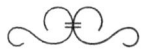

Caleb

Self-awareness.

I am me. I am here.

Then I heard faint voices of those I care most about, the people I love.

They sounded like they were at the end of a long tunnel in the distance.

What happened?

Where am I?

A nothingness of numbness and haziness; not disconcerting, but more like a peaceful blanket.

If this was heaven, I was sorely disappointed.

Where are the clouds and harp music?

Wait, I remember the sunlight.

It burned so much.

I wondered what I might do next, though part of me didn't care. The nothingness was soothing and oddly reassuring.

I could stay here forever, compared to where I was before.

Time had no meaning; though I occasionally heard what I thought were the distant whispers of voices.

I floated and floated in a comforting sea of sheer

weightlessness.

* * *

"Caleb?" someone asked.

It was…Ethan.

Then bright light, like standing before a spotlight; it engulfed my nothingness, though there was no heat accompanying it.

Sensations of feeling and physical awareness assailed my senses all at once; smells and sounds tingled across my skin.

My eyes fluttered. I felt them.

My first sight was bright green eyes staring back at me. The scent of cherry blossoms permeated the air.

Kat.

"I missed you," I said, though my voice sounded hoarse and not quite my own.

"Welcome back, my love," she said softly.

Oh, how I missed her.

My eyes scanned the room from where I lay on the bed. Ethan looked down at me from behind Kat.

The air was filled with a series of swishing sounds, each followed by the appearances of Paige, Alton, Marla, and Bonnie, each looking down at me with expressions of relief or wonder.

My friends. My loved ones.

I missed them all.

* * *

Days passed quickly, during which time I basked in the warm affections and attentions by those around me, though occasionally laced with moments of disapproval over the fateful decision that brought me to this point.

Kat was particularly a dichotomy of both love and a degree of wrath, so torn in her emotions over what had happened. Thankfully, the moments of love outweighed those of her ire.

She told me that she understood my decision, but I didn't have to be a mind reader to realize she was profoundly hurt by my abrupt decision. A rare bout of tears on her part emphasized that point.

It made me feel rather selfish.

To my credit, I apologized profusely while hugging her to me, all the while at a loss to know exactly the best thing so say or do.

So, I quietly held her for a time. Honestly, I think it may have done as much for me as it did for her.

At least, I hoped so.

Paige gave me an earful, though Ethan and Alton were surprisingly accepting. Following her initial rant, Paige had conceded, "Well, I'll be damned. Our boy came up with a cure for early onset vampirism."

Kat had groaned at that.

I endured it all in stride, merely happy to have returned to 'the living'…and as a human, no less.

For approximately a week, my every need was catered to by vampires; certainly a memorable experience worth savoring.

Despite the strength that only slowly rebuilt in my body, I suddenly found that being human felt pretty damned good by comparison; though I missed the enhanced senses of smell, hearing, and sight that I had briefly enjoyed.

Still, little of my transitional time spent between worlds garnered similar appreciation.

It had been miserable, painful and debilitating.

I never wanted to go through that again.

Fortunately, my appetite returned with a vengeance, and my aversion to cooked meats quickly dissipated. I even enjoyed a fresh batch of chocolate chip cookies Bonnie made for me.

"I should make you eat the stale original batch instead," she had teased with an arched brow.

I adored her.

As soon as I was able to walk, I was taken to the hospital for a series brain and body scans.

Fortunately, each resulted in favorable assessments, which pleased me to no end. Essentially, my brain was healing and the remaining vampire cells in my body were progressively dissipating, destroyed by my body's immune system.

I still experienced fleeting moments of blurriness, some body aches, and dizziness, but Ethan assured me it was relatively normal for my circumstances.

"Will I recover fully, doc?" I asked.

"I'm encouraged to think so," he said.

It was as close to definitive as I could get from him, but it was better than nothing, given my condition.

I spent the evening of the Fourth of July watching the downtown Atlanta fireworks from the vantage point our front yard, arm-in-arm with Kat and surrounded by my friends, including Devon Archibald.

I still hadn't got used to the guards on the property, though I appreciated their presence, given all that had happened recently.

* * *

Within ten days of waking from my coma-like state, Alton and Marla made plans to return to London in the coming week or so. Bonnie Lund said her time with us was also preparing to end.

"Dr. Reynolds is confident you'll be fine on your own, with his and Kat's supervision, of course," she said.

It saddened me to see her leave, though I was more than pleased to be feeling better with each passing day. I'd grown fond of Bonnie in the short time I'd been around her.

"I'll miss you," I said, embracing her in a warm hug. "Nobody makes cookies like you, you know. But don't tell Kat I said that."

"I'll keep in touch, Caleb," she assured me. "Don't take

this the wrong way, but I hope you'll not need my services again anytime soon. Nevertheless, I'll be here if needed."

"Thanks," I said. "And I feel the same way, actually. I'd prefer if this were a one-time event."

Bonnie left the following day.

Another week passed, and I was already strong enough for moderate exercising. My body felt debilitated, and I was anxious to regain my strength and stamina. It also helped to pass the time.

I was growing restless.

Marla left within the week for London, and Alton said he'd only be staying for a few more days.

"How can I repay you for saving my life?" I asked him, once we had a moment alone together.

"Saving? I nearly cost you your life," he said.

"I'd have died at the hospital, according to what Paige told me," I said. "You gave me a chance, at least."

He reached out to pat me on the shoulder in a paternal manner. "You're here. That's all that matters now."

He refused to say anything further on the matter.

However, I soon discovered that Kat hadn't been so fortunate.

One evening following dinner, I sat in our dining room, still serving as makeshift operations center for Alton, and alternated exasperated looks with him and Kat.

"Why does Kat have to go to London?" I demanded. "The debt is mine to repay, not hers."

"The debt was mine, not yours," Kat said sternly.

"Stop with all this talk of debts," Alton said. "It's pure nonsense. I need Katrina's assistance with matters of imminent gravity, nothing more."

"I'm going, too," I said.

"No," both Kat and Alton said simultaneously, each pausing to stare at the other.

Just great, denied in stereo.

"It's too dangerous," Kat said.

"I concur," Alton said.

I ignored him for the moment.

"I'll be safer with you in London," I said, staring at Kat.

"I don't want you there. It's too dangerous and you'll only distract me, Caleb," she said flatly.

Her words stabbed into my chest like a hot knife.

She doesn't want me there?

I stared back at her incredulously. How could she say something like that to me?

I just practically returned from the near dead, for God's sake.

She reached out for my hand but I jerked it free from her grip.

"Don't," I said.

I don't want you there…

If she didn't want me there…well, that changed matters entirely.

Fine!

I stormed from the room, slamming shut the French doors to the dining room as I left.

"Caleb!" she called.

Pointedly ignoring her, I made for the nearest exit.

I caught Paige's surprised look from where she stood in the kitchen as I barreled for the door leading out onto the back patio. I snatched my iPod and ear buds from a small table near the door as I darted outside.

Practically stomping my feet in anger, I proceeded through the backyard and into the night as I jammed the ear buds into place.

Seconds later, The Dresden Dolls' "The Kill" blared in my ears.

I glanced over my shoulder and caught a glimpse of one of the suit-clad vampires following me.

Great, one of the goons is shadowing me.

I was determined to get as far as I could before my 'safety zone' was deemed to be exceeded.

My thoughts were jumbled and my anger coursed through me in waves. Before I knew it, I was passing through the neighborhood park, past the bench where Kat had revealed her vampire secret to me last fall.

It seemed like a lifetime ago.

"Dammit."

I ran my fingers through my hair in frustration.

What the hell am I supposed to do now that my mate doesn't want me around?

CHAPTER 18

Katrina

Caleb's shoulders were squared and stiff as I watched him march away.

We'd only just welcomed him from the brink of oblivion, and he was already angry with me...yet again.

Once again, I'd said something that he took totally wrong, eliciting another heated reaction from him.

With practice, I could learn to be more diplomatic with him.

I need to try better, I suppose.

Being abrupt with others was another one of my less than charming attributes. It was no wonder I've had such a checkered past with relationships.

Of course, that tidbit of self-actualization hardly helped me at the present.

Personal faults aside, I was somewhat surprised he hadn't permitted me time to explain further.

I rose to pursue my wayward mate, only to feel Alton's grip tighten around my arm.

"Let him go, Katrina," he said.

I frowned and jerked my arm from his grasp with more force than I'd intended. "Why should I? I need to reason with him."

He spared me one of his more patient-looking

expressions, which I merely found infuriating.

"Give the young man time to cool off," he said.

"He's acting like a spoiled teenager," I said.

"Careful there," he cautioned. "I remember cradling a grown woman in my arms not so long ago."

"I was grief-stricken, thank you very much," I responded.

An arched brow was his only response.

I rolled my eyes, though I suppose he made a good point.

"He'll come around when he's ready," he added.

I hitched my hands atop my hips. "Oh, really? And just when did you become so well versed in all things Caleb?"

One of the French doors opened and I looked up to see Paige staring at me curiously.

"What the hell was that all about?" she asked. "Our boy looked like a road rage poster child."

I closed my eyes and massaged my fingertips against my eyelids, not really interested in explaining things to her at that moment.

"Caleb won't be accompanying us to London," Alton said. "He didn't take the news well."

"Gee, do ya' think?" she quipped.

"He'll be fine once we help him understand the dangers and implications involved," Alton said.

"Don't worry, I'll smooth things over with him," I said.

Paige quirked her lips and looked at each of us.

"You know, when it comes to the soft sell, you two really suck," she said.

I frowned at her sarcastic admonition.

However, she made an excellent point, I suppose.

"I can assure you we have things well in hand," Alton said. "He'll cool off soon enough and then we can rationally discuss the matter."

She scoffed and stared at me in a penetrating fashion. "I'll talk to him."

"And tell him what?" I asked.

"What any friend would," she replied. "What he needs to hear."

She sped away toward the living room.

I sighed. Paige always seemed to have a colorful way with Caleb that I desperately envied at times. It was yet another aspect I needed to improve upon if I wanted to smooth the path between him and me moving forward.

However, I hoped her advice to him was intended to be helpful versus obstructive. Sometimes she had her own agenda, or at least her own angle on other peoples agendas.

Unfortunately, I wouldn't know which for certain until afterward.

Flip a coin.

I loved Caleb so dearly, and I only wanted what was in his best interest.

In the end, I could only hope he also realized that, over and above his sense of frustration.

CHAPTER 19

Caleb

At such a brisk pace it didn't take me long to traverse the length of the park and make my way out to the addition's central road leading to the entrance.

A few minutes later, I walked through the addition's main exit gate and along the asphalt county road. I glanced back over my shoulder long enough to see my vampire escort following me while talking on his mobile phone.

I could practically imagine the conversation: *Subject in sight, headquarters. Awaiting further orders.*

Oh, well. Everyone needs a job, right?

Hell, I wished I still had one.

I let that thought slide and appreciated the fact I was alive and relatively well.

Count my blessings.

One of the nice aspects of the surrounding area was the relatively rural feel of things. The Pine Valley addition was the only one of its kind, amidst large expanses of virgin land, and some acreage that hosted cattle.

On a normal evening, I'd probably have found it quite soothing.

However, my thoughts returned to my anger over being left behind; once again, when things appeared even remotely dangerous. It made me feel like some helpless invalid needing to be coddled and sheltered.

Kat's words echoed in my mind.

I don't want you there, Caleb.

That was the real heart of the problem.

I couldn't force her to want me.

"Crap."

I lost track of time as I walked. A car passed by and I half expected it to be Kat coming to retrieve me. However, the regal looking Lexus merely sped down the road until I lost sight of its tail lights in the distance.

I'd made it a lot further than I'd anticipated.

A slight breeze kicked up and the woodsy scent from a nearby copse of pines assailed my nose.

How many more scents am I missing that a vampire would've been able to detect?

If only I were a vampire then Kat would let me go with her to London.

But the way things had been going lately, I had no idea if I'd ever be turned.

What if she didn't want me in a forever sort of way?

A lump formed in my throat as that notion plagued my imagination.

Rejection was one of the worst feelings in the world.

I think I'd almost rather be dead.

Had I died once before when I visited that state of nothingness? Was that the afterlife?

A raccoon burst from the trees to my right, startling me. It raced past me, skittering across the road to disappear into the night.

I removed my ear buds, staring into the treeline and listening closely for anything unusual.

A slight breeze shuffled the pine limbs together in a restless fashion. I heard an owl hoot in the distance but little else.

The snaps of breaking twigs sounded and I warily turned to confront whatever was there.

I spared a look back toward where my vampire escort had been only minutes prior, but he was nowhere to be seen.

Paige appeared out of the treeline, brushing a stray leaf from her short hair.

"Stupid raccoon," she said. "He gave away my position."

"Where's my persistent tail?" I asked.

"On your persistent little ass, silly," she said with a smirk.

"Oh, fun-ny," I said.

She shrugged. "I sent him back home."

"What're you doing here? Did Kat send you or something?" I asked.

"You and your whiny indignation can dry up, Miss Prissy Pants," she said.

I gave her a dirty look.

"So, are we walking or just standing around here all night?" she asked.

I shrugged and resumed my trek along the road.

"Babysitting me tonight?" I asked.

"Nah," she said.

"Spying?"

"Nope. Big sister tonight," she said, brushing her shoulder against mine with a slight shove.

I couldn't help but smile.

My century-old, way-shorter-than-me big sister.

We walked in silence for a time. While I hadn't been craving company, it felt somewhat comforting to share my walk with her.

"You looked pretty angst-ridden back there, kiddo," she said.

She had a way of reading me in a manner that was sometimes even keener than Kat.

"Yeah," I said. "Heavy thoughts, I suppose."

Problems with my relationship type of thoughts.

"She's merely concerned for your safety," she said. "In a smothering kind of well-intentioned but I'm-the-bitchy-boss sort of way, that is."

I nodded. She had Kat pegged. But then, she'd known

Kat for most of her vampire lifetime.

"She drives me crazy sometimes," I agreed.

"Yeah, well, in case you hadn't already noticed, you seem to know how to push her buttons, too."

I looked over at her and saw the satisfied expression on her face.

Yeah. Maybe I do after all.

"I just need to figure out which button to push to get her to let me go to London with her," I said.

She chuckled. "Good luck with that."

"She doesn't have the right to make that decision for me," I said. "I should be able to make some demands, just like she can."

She fell eerily silent.

"You really don't want to go there, sport," she finally said. "Neither of you do."

"Why not?"

"Because one or both of you will say something you may regret for years to come," she said. "And that doesn't help either of you in the end. One of you needs to take the high road on this and give in to the other."

She made a sobering point, one I pondered at length as we walked.

Who'll blink first, Kat or me?

I felt as if I was the one always giving in to her demands. But then, was that merely the downside of courting an alpha female?

Furthermore, would she ever give in, or stubbornly pull us both over the emotional cliff just to make a point? Who's more suicidal?

Then again, I'd been the one to risk oblivion by getting blasted with sunlight over a week ago.

I sighed with exasperation.

Tonight's not my night for gambling, it seems.

"You sigh just like a steam engine pulling into a station," Paige said. "Or maybe a teenage girl."

I cast a dark sidelong look at her.

"Hey, it's your sigh. I'm just sayin'," she said.

I jammed my hands into my jeans pockets and glowered at the road ahead.

Teenage girl, indeed.

Maybe a break was exactly what both Kat and I needed to gain some perspective on our relationship.

Who knew? Maybe she'd grow to miss me.

And perhaps this 'teenage girl' needs to mature some more.

If so, then why did that last thought generate such a sour feeling in the pit of my stomach?

Crap. I'm so damned tired of feeling insecure.

The time had come for me to take charge of my life for a change; time to realize my independence.

Hell, after what I just went through, it's my golden opportunity to have a new lease on life.

I pondered my options for a time.

"Maybe I'll go back to college," I said.

Paige reached out in a blur of movement to grasp my upper arm, halting our walk.

"*You're* giving in?" she asked in a surprised tone.

I frowned. "Why not? You said one of us needed to take the high road."

She slowly blinked. "Yeah, but I meant her."

I shrugged. "Sur-prise," I chimed.

I continued my walk down the road, leaving her standing in what appeared to be a state of shock.

I'm going to do it. It's time for a change of scene, and maybe a chance to get my bearings in life.

It's time for me to embrace my recently recovered human life.

She appeared beside me again amidst a swish of air. "Are you sure you know what you're doing?"

"Not really," I said. "But then, that's the wonder of it, isn't it? I'm sure as hell going to find out one way or another."

She regarded me with a quizzical expression.

"Besides, I just might need this more than I originally

thought," I said, looking up the road to study an approaching car.

After the vehicle passed us, I glanced over at her and noted she was frowning, appearing to be deep in thought.

"A penny for your thoughts?"

"Not for sale right now," she said.

I let it slide.

As we walked on in silence, I was happy that she'd shown up.

In fact, the earlier wave of anger that had welled inside of me had already begun to dissipate.

However, she remained silent for quite some time as we walked together.

Finally, I stopped to catch my breath. Even at only a brisk walking pace, my body had gotten winded.

It was probably going to take quite some time for my body to be back in its former shape.

"We'd better head back now," she said softly.

The subdued sounds of the night enveloped us on the way back to the addition. I hadn't realized how far we'd walked; our return seeming to take forever. But then, maybe that was due to the somber mood that we'd both fallen into.

Either way, I was pleased once we finally passed through the addition's main gate. As we drew closer to home, Paige looked up sharply and stared into the trees bordering the neighborhood park, placing her hand on my arm to halt our progress.

She cocked her head slightly to one angle, as if listening to something in the distance.

"What is it?" I asked. "Did you hear something?"

"Singing," she said.

Singing?

She looked up at me with a solemn expression. "Go through the park. I think there's somebody waiting for you."

"Who? Kat?" I asked.

"I'll see you back at the house," she said, before turning to walk down the street.

What's gotten into her?

* * *

As I topped the small incline and stepped over the short, ornamental wooden-railed fence bordering the park, I caught sight of a lone figure sitting on a bench.

Kat's long red hair was unmistakable in the glow from a nearby light pole.

Her last words to me before I went on my walk echoed in my mind.

I don't want you there, Caleb.

"Here goes round two," I muttered.

As I traversed the short distance to Kat, she maintained a blank stare ahead of her.

"This isn't round two," she said.

A wave of embarrassment washed over me.

"Sorry. Figure of speech," I said, taking a seat beside her on the cool bench.

"Hm," she said neutrally.

"Listen, there's no need to rehash our squabble," I said. "I get it…you don't want me."

She moved in a blur, slamming both hands against the back of the bench on either side of my body, her face mere inches from mine, her green eyes brightly aglow with emotion.

To say that startled me was an understatement of epic proportion. She'd definitely captured my complete attention.

"I knew it. I knew that's what you were thinking when you stormed away. Let's get something straight right now. I never meant I didn't want you," she said. "I said I didn't want you *accompanying me to London*. There's a difference."

I heard what she said, but it had still made me feel as unwanted as when she'd said it the first time.

"Understood?" she asked.

"Yes."

"Good," she said, maintaining her steely gaze into my

eyes. "Don't ever think I don't want you. I *always* want you."

I felt the intensity building between us as her eyes bore into mine. It was as if she was staring into my soul, laid bare before her. It nearly terrified me.

"Now that I've got you back from near-death, I want you even more," she said. "With every fiber in my body."

She abruptly looked away. "Whether that's safe or not is another thing entirely. I won't willingly place you in dangerous situations. Though considering your most recent injury, being anywhere near me would seem to qualify as a dangerous situation."

"Stop," I said. "Don't say that. I don't see it that way, so neither should you."

She looked at me with a hard expression. Then her eyes softened a bit. She leaned against me, pressing her soft lips against mine to impart a long, deliberate kiss.

As I blinked, her lips separated from mine and she reverted to her initial position, calmly sitting beside me while staring out into the night.

Despite her subdued manner, my heart raced. She could be so unpredictable sometimes, particularly when angry or upset.

"I don't mean to unnerve you," she said, as if reading my thoughts. "But you evoke such strong emotions in me, from passion to frustration."

Her revelation was definitely a two-way street.

After a moment, I extended my arm across the top of the bench, encircling her shoulders.

A peace offering.

She shifted her body to nestle closer to me and placed her hand on my thigh.

Seeming much less agitated, she turned to gaze into my eyes in alluring fashion. "I love you."

Such a simple declaration, and yet, so meaningful.

"I love you, too," I said.

Our lips met in a warm, lingering kiss.

So addictive; I could kiss on her forever and a day.

Then her lips were gone, and she reverted to staring ahead of her into the darkness beyond.

At least the mood between us had lightened considerably, and it was nice just to sit together with her in my embrace, two people appreciating each other's company.

This is how it should be between us. These are the moments I cherish with her.

"I wish we could go somewhere together, free from life's troubles," I said. "And our disagreements."

She took a deep breath and let it out slowly. "Me, too."

I listened to crickets chirping and the sounds of rustling leaves from the warm evening breeze.

"Paige said she heard singing," I said. "Yours?"

She nodded.

Kat didn't often sing in my presence, though I'd occasionally overheard her voice as she accompanied music playing over her computer speakers. In truth, for someone who claimed to be nothing more than nature's worst predator, she had a mesmerizing voice.

"Will you sing it again for me?" I asked.

She paused, and after a moment of silence, began to sing in a lilting voice; the words sounded Gaelic and pretty, though somewhat sorrowful.

Her song pierced the quiet around us, softly adding to the night's soundtrack.

After a few fleeting stanzas, she stopped.

"That was beautiful," I said, grasping her hand in mine. "What was it?"

"It's called "Eibhlín a Rún," she replied. "It's an Irish love song that's even older than I am; something I learned as a little girl."

She explained that it was about a young maiden named Eibhlín (Eileen or Ellen in English) Kavanagh who was betrothed to a man she didn't love. Then, instead of going through with the marriage, she secretly eloped with the man who was the true love of her life so they could enjoy a life of happiness together.

"Please don't tell me you're betrothed to another," I said.

"I'm betrothed to duty," she said in a somewhat bitter sounding tone. "Though you're the one I want to elope with."

Duty.

I pondered that for a moment.

"Duty to Alton?" I asked.

"Yes."

I thought so.

"So, how about we simply run away and live out the rest of our lives together happily ever after instead?" I asked.

"If only," she said. "I'd prefer that, actually."

Yeah. Me, too.

"You really do have a beautiful voice, Kat," I said. "You should sing around me more often."

A sad smile formed on her face. "You're very kind, my love," she said. "I used to sing to my children, and then occasionally around Samuel. I stopped singing after they died."

"Why?"

She gave a wistful sigh. "Because the lights in my human life were extinguished, and then life as a vampire was filled with more darkness than light."

I nodded, though I had virtually no experience to draw upon by comparison.

"Can't I become a light in your life?"

She stared back at me, her green eyes glistening in the lamp light above us.

"My love, you already are," she said. "You're the reason I was singing tonight."

That meant the world to me.

I squeezed her hand in mine and she returned the gesture. Then I lifted her hand to gently brush my lips across her soft skin.

"Come on. Let's go find Alton," I said. "I've come to a decision tonight, but I want both of you to hear it together."

Her arched brow held a silent question, though she said

nothing as we walked hand in hand toward the estate.

* * *

We found Alton sitting at the dining room table furiously typing on one of his laptop keyboards. I noticed that he'd already packed away the large monitors.

He looked up with a curious expression as Kat and I took seats at the table.

"Have a pleasant walk, my boy?" he asked.

"Yeah, it's just what I needed, thanks. I cleared my head and did some thinking," I said. "In fact, I've come to a decision."

"Indeed?" he asked, deftly closing the lid of his laptop and neatly folding his slender fingers atop the case before him. "Do tell."

Why did I suddenly feel as if I was sitting down for a discussion with a parent?

Kat reached out to take my hand in hers beneath the table. Despite her neutral expression, I could almost feel the tension coming off of her in waves.

Why's she so tense?

"I've decided to go back to college this fall," I said. "I want to pursue a PhD in history so I can teach again. With positions being so scarce, I need every edge to compete."

I looked over at Kat to see an unmistakable expression of relief on her face, and she squeezed my hand supportively.

Well, at least one of us seems wholly pleased.

In truth, I was still warming to the idea. I'd much rather accompany Kat to London, but I realized it would likely lead to more conflicts between us; just the kinds of emotional tension we hardly needed. It seemed like things kept piling atop one another with us lately, each issue adding to an increasingly unbearable weight.

Eventually, something was bound to break our relationship in half, and I couldn't bear the thought of that happening.

I mean, how many challenges could one relationship withstand anyway?

"I, for one, applaud your decision," Alton said.

"And I support your decision, as well, my love," Kat added.

Okay, this is way too easy.

I felt I'd made a logical decision, though I hoped I wouldn't soon regret it.

"Have you given any thought to which college you'll apply to?" Alton asked.

Why did I feel like I was talking to my parents all of the sudden?

Memories of having the same topic of discussion with my mom so many years ago flooded over me. I'd selected Georgia State University back then.

"Not in depth," I said. "Maybe Georgia State again. I liked the faculty there, and they have a strong history department. A lot of it will depend upon program availability, I suppose. It's only July, but that's still really late in the summer to be applying for the fall semester, especially PhD programs."

And funding. I'll definitely have to look into some student loan programs.

"A reasonable choice, I suppose," Alton said.

I frowned at him.

Just what did he mean by that?

"Given my late start, I need to start applying immediately," I said.

Kat squeezed my hand. "I'm sure there's still time to apply."

Out of the corner of my eye, I caught a glimpse of someone appearing near the open French doors.

Paige.

"Yes?" Alton asked.

Her blue eyes locked onto mine. "Sorry to interrupt the meeting," she said, stuffing her hands into her front jeans pockets. "I'd like to talk to Caleb for a minute."

I glanced at Kat, who released my hand and nodded.

"Certainly. We'll speak more on this later. Perhaps tomorrow, in fact," Alton said. "He's all yours for now."

I couldn't imagine what Paige needed to talk to me about but the set look to her eyes concerned me.

* * *

I followed Paige through the house and out through the front door. She finally stopped at the driveway where she leaned against the side of her car.

"What's up?" I asked.

"So, we're going to college, then," she said.

My eyebrows shot upward. "Whoa. Just what do you mean by *we*?"

She gestured back toward the house. "I overheard what you said in there. You know Red's not letting you go alone."

That much was probably true.

"Paige, I don't even know where I'll end up at," I said. "I haven't even been accepted anywhere. Hell, for all I know I could end up in Alaska or worse."

"So be it. Alaska wouldn't be so bad," she said. "It's practically dark there for half the year. I'd have one hell of a social life without all the damn sunlight. It's night for twenty hours a day during the winter."

"Well, maybe," I said.

"But absolutely no summer classes," she said. "We'd come home every May, no matter what."

She was so unbelievably cute sometimes.

I simply adored her.

Then something else occurred to me.

"Now what's the matter?" she asked.

"I can't separate you from Ethan like that. You've only just met," I said. "It wouldn't be fair to either of you. I mean, he's only just relocated to Atlanta to be with you."

"True," she said. "But he can always fly up to see me on weekends. And then there's all those semester breaks. They still do that, right?"

I laughed. "Of course they do."

However, her plan didn't exactly sound like a formula for potential success with Ethan.

But then, considering my situation with Kat, I was hardly an authority on sound vampire relationships.

"I'd feel a lot better if you talked to Ethan about this first," I said.

"I already did," she said.

I frowned. "How's that? I just got through telling Alton and Kat—"

She removed a smart phone from her back pocket and wiggled it before my face. "Hey, ever hear of a smart phone? They're pretty handy," she teased. "You should get one soon and ditch that ancient flip phone of yours."

I stared at her blankly.

"Hello? You mentioned college while we were out for a walk, Sherlock," she said.

Oh, yeah.

"You're going to need way more brain power if you expect to do well in college," she said, tapping my forehead with her fingertip.

"Shut up," I groaned, swatting at her finger and meeting only empty air.

"Anyway, Ethan approved the idea," she said. "He said he's spending a lot of time at the hospital establishing his practice, which might take months. In fact, he said he's been worried about neglecting me. And he understands I'm your surrogate vampire. I'm duty-bound."

I looked at her sharply.

Again with all this talk about duty?

"What?" she asked, narrowing her eyes.

"I don't know about this, Paige," I said.

"Aw, listen kiddo, this'll be good for both of us," she said, reaching up to place her soft palm against the side of my face. "And, unlike some, I'm not about to abandon you. I'm here for you, tiger."

Her palm felt warm and comforting against my skin, but

what she said bothered me.

"Paige, nobody's abandoning me," I said.

"I'm just sayin'," she said softly. "And you can damn well bet I'll be there to call you out when your bullshit meter pegs."

"Lucky me," I muttered.

She instantly withdrew her hand and popped me on the back of the head with the flat of her palm.

"Hey!"

"It pegs so frequently, you see," she said.

"Oh, brother."

"It's settled then," she said, pulling me into a tight embrace. "If you're going to college, I'm going with you. Otherwise, who knows what kind of trouble you'd get yourself into? You're practically a magnet for chaos."

I wrapped my arms around her and considered the situation. I had to admit it was an intriguing prospect at the very least.

"That's a physics concept from one of Ethan's documentaries," she said. "You're bound to learn about it in college."

I chuckled.

Things were happening so fast. Hell, I'd only just settled on the idea an hour or so ago.

Still, the vision of Paige on a college campus tickled me.

"*You're* going to college," I said. "As in, actually taking classes?"

She pulled free from our embrace and planted her fists atop her hips. "Hey, don't be such a doubter. I've gone to college before, you know."

That definitely ranked as one of the day's biggest revelations.

"I see. And precisely what did you major in?"

"Sex Ed," she said with a grin. "I made straight *A's*!"

CHAPTER 20

Caleb

I put off the remainder of my discussion with Alton and Kat concerning my plans to return to college until I could do some research. Of course, they spent hours in closed-door sessions in our dining room together, pouring over printouts and looking at laptop screens, so it wasn't hard.

I suspected they were formulating their plans for Kat in London.

I still felt put out that she didn't want me to accompany her. Nevertheless, I understood the nature of her objections, and I was willing to respect her perspective; for the time being, at least.

What I would've given to be able to listen in a little bit on their deliberations. Some of their interactions appeared intense, which worried me somewhat.

They looked like two generals planning a war.

I tried not to dwell on that analogy at length.

Instead, I spent most of my time in the small library that Kat and I had converted into my office scouring university websites for prospective history post-graduate level PhD programs.

Somehow I had the feeling each of them would grill me on details and particulars as if it were some finely-tuned mission.

It's the 'two generals' analogy all over again.

As was my luck, I was paired with the world's most detail-oriented and meticulous vampires.

Speaking of details, there were many variables to compare and consider, including tuition costs and financial assistance—likely student loan eligibility in my case—as well as application periods that were still open to me, given my late start.

In fact, I'd had a difficult time sleeping the night before because my mind felt overwhelmed by the details.

By mid-morning, I'd narrowed my selections to a handful of colleges, foremost of which was Georgia State University, my alma mater for my former undergraduate and graduate degrees. At least GSU was closer to home; not that Kat would necessarily be around when I visited.

I sighed over that realization.

While I liked living in the estate, it could be a pretty lonely place for me alone. Not that I dreaded living alone; it was just much cozier in an apartment rather than an expansive, empty mansion.

Wait. Does our estate qualify as a mansion?

"Busy?" asked Kat.

I jolted in my chair and abruptly looked up from my laptop with a frown. "I hate it when you sneak up on me like that."

She shrugged, leaning against the door jamb with her arms casually folded before her. "It's a vampire thing."

"Right," I said.

"And you could've closed the door."

I gave her a weary-looking expression.

"Never mind. Let's finish our chat about college," she said, turning to walk away.

"But—" I barely managed before she disappeared from view.

I helplessly looked down at the various stacks of printouts covering my small desk.

Did I have everything I needed for an in-depth discussion?

"Oh, what the hell," I said, gathering up my research and grabbing my laptop. "It'll have to do."

In the dining room, I couldn't help but notice the mildly amused expressions on Alton's and Kat's faces as I sat down, arranging my stacked paperwork before me.

"You brought a script?" Alton asked.

"Funny," I said. "Really. I'm laughing on the inside."

"Somebody's feeling a little grumpy this morning," Kat said.

I started to counter with something sarcastic, but Alton quickly interjected, "Why don't you share with us what you have there, dear boy?"

"Um, sure," I said.

I spent the next twenty minutes describing my efforts, finishing with the names of five colleges I had in mind, including the University of Idaho, the University of Oklahoma, the University of North Dakota, and of course, Georgia State University.

They politely listened and appeared interested, occasionally nodding at points, all of which assuaged my earlier feelings of aggravation.

By the end of my presentation, I felt much better about the quality of my research and my evaluation process.

"You said you picked five colleges, but you only named four," Kat said.

"Oh, yeah," I said. "The University of Alaska in Anchorage; the tuition's not that bad, actually."

"Anchorage?" she asked with a frown.

"Yeah, kind of surprising, right?"

"I have a suspicion as to who may have suggested that one," Alton said.

Kat glanced at him and then stared at me in a penetrating fashion, though I quickly broke eye contact with her and looked at Alton.

"Well, I'm actually torn between Georgia State and

Oklahoma," I said.

Alton thoughtfully tapped his chin. "Reasonable selections," he said. "Both are rather folksy places, aren't they?"

"Folksy?" I asked.

"However, I'd like you to consider an additional option," he said.

"Oh? Such as?"

"There's a wonderful campus in New Haven, Connecticut," he said.

"A college in New Haven?" I asked.

"Yale," he said.

My mouth dropped open in shock.

Oh, that New Haven college.

I traded looks with each of them, shaking my head.

"No way," I said.

"Why not?" he asked. "Did you even consider Yale?"

"No, I'm pretty sure I didn't."

"Caleb, if this is about tuition…" Kat said, reaching out to grasp my forearm.

"Of course, it's about tuition," I said, pulling away from her. "But that's just for starters. And before you say anything else, no, you're absolutely not paying my tuition."

"Caleb," she said gently, placing a supportive hand on my shoulder.

"No," I said firmly.

"Young man," Alton began authoritatively. "You shouldn't discount things out of hand. Please try to bear an open mind."

I laughed aloud. "Seriously, no."

He arched one brow, instantly projecting an imperious expression.

I've upset the king, it would seem.

"Yale has one of the finest History and Renaissance Studies programs in the States," he said. "Besides, the city of New Haven isn't currently declared by any vampires. It's neutral territory, which is far less complicated for us. You should at least consider Yale."

"Alton, you just don't get it, do you? They probably wouldn't even respond to my email," I said. "I'm a veritable nobody; no connections, no society background. Hell, I don't even qualify for a minority preference of any kind. I'm a WASP with no angle."

I looked over at Kat to see her wearing a perfectly livid expression.

"You are *not* a 'nobody', " she emphatically stated.

"Indeed," Alton said.

I took a deep breath and let it out slowly. "Well, I am as far as they're concerned."

There it was. It was hardly self-depreciating to point out the truth.

"If that were so, then why are you scheduled to meet with their Dean of History tomorrow night?" he asked.

My mind took a couple of seconds to process what he'd just said.

"What?" I asked. "How's that?"

He sat back in his chair, a satisfied expression adorning his face. "It would seem that, despite your protestations, you do indeed have valuable connections."

I was dumbfounded.

Me? Yale?

"But tuition," I said.

"Again, you have options you haven't yet considered," he said. "We can discuss that tomorrow evening after we see how your meeting with Dean Eddings goes."

"Dean Eddings. Tomorrow night," I parroted.

"Precisely at 8 o'clock. Our flight departs at five. We'll be flying on Sunset Air, of course," he said.

"You and me?"

"And Katrina, naturally," he said.

I looked at Kat, who maintained a neutral expression.

"Naturally," I said.

Somehow, I should've known she'd want to accompany us.

Still, she *was* my mate, after all.

"You should have more than enough time to review Yale's website, familiarize yourself with the campus, and pack. Now, if you'll please excuse Katrina and me, we have some additional pressing business to attend to," he said.

Pressing business?

His attention returned to some paperwork before him, and I rose from my chair in a state of semi-fugue.

My gaze shifted to Kat, who appeared to be struggling at containing a smile. She even winked at me.

I'd barely reached the closed French doors to leave when Alton prompted, "Oh, and Caleb, please do pack a suit. You can leave your stylish concert T-shirts at home this trip."

I looked back over my shoulder at him with a withering expression, only to be met with amused expressions on both their faces.

"Why, thank you for the fashion advice," I said. "Ralph Lauren?"

"Well, if you don't own Tom Ford, I suppose Lauren will suffice," he said.

I rolled my eyes.

Tom Ford?

I wished.

Fashion snob.

* * *

The flight to New Haven had been a direct charter flight via Sunset Air, an international carrier that was vampire-owned. It operated a dual fleet; one fleet catering to traditional human patrons and the other catering to their sunlight-sensitive clientele.

Their vampire-centric fleet consisted of exclusive, regal aircraft sporting individual cabins, likely nicer than many hotel rooms.

It was simply amazing; decadent comfort at its best.

Most surprising, however, had been an unexpected gift

from Kat that awaited me in the cabin; a tailor-fitted black Versace suit, complete with crisp white silk blend shirt and black silk tie.

"How did you manage this on short notice?" I asked.

She shrugged, as if it were nothing.

"It's not Tom Ford, but it should do quite well," she said. "You look amazing, nonetheless."

She'd been correct about the suit, of course. As soon as I put it on, I felt like a million dollars, a facet that immensely boosted my self-confidence going into the meeting with Dean Eddings.

Alton never explained how he managed to secure the meeting. I wondered, not for the first time, if there was anything he couldn't do or arrange.

Of course, he couldn't make my meeting go well. That much was left up to me.

Yale? Never in a million years.

On the limousine ride to the campus, Kat discreetly whispered in my ear, "Just be yourself, my love, and you'll charm everyone's socks off. You certainly did mine."

Lusty thoughts accompanied her revelation as I appreciated her silver silk dress; her cleavage tantalizingly displayed her dress' plunging neckline. Her hair was pinned up in a particularly elegant and alluring fashion.

She kissed me while slowly tracing my calf with the sharp heel tip of her stilettoes, sending a shiver down my spine.

Kat easily drove me to heights of desire most of the time, but that night I found her to be particularly tempting. I wanted to have her right there in the back of the limo, only I was certain that Alton wouldn't have appreciated the display.

Dr. Harry Eddings was a distinguished looking, gray-haired gentleman who appeared to be in his mid- to late-sixties. He looked every bit like a dean, and spoke in a precise cadence of speech, as if each word were measured and presented just for that moment.

Halfway through our meeting, though I definitely thought of it more as an interview, things seemed to be going quite well, and I began to wonder why I'd felt so hesitant.

Then a pointed question froze me in my tracks.

"Mr. Taylor, our program is highly competitive to be accepted into, much less on such short notice. In particular, I rarely grant such meetings as this after hours. In truth, I'm only here per an impromptu request from our president," he said. "Given that, what unique and valuable qualities do you bring to the table that not only enrich our school's fine heritage but advance the study of history? In essence, what makes you worthy of being a Yale man?"

My breath caught in my throat, and I thought my brain might cease its operation entirely.

I swallowed hard and forced my mind back into action. The passing seconds felt like hours as I struggled to formulate a viable response.

"Through my personal life experiences, I bring an entirely fresh perspective on the world around us," I said. "One that I doubt many students, if any, could claim."

One of his eyebrows arched and he regarded me with a sincere-looking air of curiosity.

Oh, shit. How do I follow up on that with specifics?

I'll be killed if I reveal any vampire-specific details to him whatsoever.

It was at that moment I believed my interview was destined for complete and utter failure.

Better failure than death, right?

"That's a decidedly vague, yet tempting, answer, Mr. Taylor," he responded. "Despite our short time together, between the information in your file and our meeting this evening, I sense you're quite an intelligent, competent young man in your own right. However, to be quite honest, we're currently at a full complement of students in our post-graduate programs."

My heart sank.

"Perhaps if you—"

A knock at the door behind me interrupted Dr. Eddings. He frowned and rose from his chair.

I heard his office door open but I couldn't see who it was. I was still reeling from what he'd told me.

Still, at least I had tried my best. I hoped Kat and Alton wouldn't be too disappointed in me after all the trouble they'd gone to.

"I do apologize for the interruption, Dr. Eddings, but you simply must meet my guest," said a gentleman behind me.

"President Yarborough," said Eddings. "Um, yes, please do come in. I was just interviewing a prospective student; the one you'd asked me about, in fact."

"I assure you, we'll only take a moment," said Yarborough. "Dr. Eddings, permit me to introduce you to Mr. Alton Rutherford, President and CEO of Rutherford Enterprises. He's come all the way from London to invest in our college. In fact, he has some amazing news to share with you."

My eyes nearly popped from their sockets as I peered around the side of the high-backed reading chair I was sitting in.

"Dr. Eddings, a pleasure to meet you," Alton offered in typically charming fashion.

"Mr. Rutherford, the pleasure is all mine," replied Eddings.

"Your books on eighteenth century Quaker culture are quite impressive," Alton said.

"Why, thank you," Eddings said.

"I'm particularly intrigued by a member of your faculty, Dr. Samuel Gowan," Alton said. "His research into American and European Enlightenment figures is renowned. I attended one of his guest lectures at Cambridge some years ago; quite impressive, really."

"We're very proud of Dr. Gowan; he's one of our most competent and devoted professors," Eddings said. "He lives for his research."

Alton appeared pleased. "Good to hear that. Speaking of research, I was just chatting with your president at the foundation dinner about an investment I'd like to make on behalf of your history department," he said. "I understand you're developing a fund toward a new museum of history on Yale's campus?"

"What? Oh, yes, the project's a labor of love of mine, but we're only fifteen percent funded at this point," said Eddings. "I suspect we're years away from construction. There's a master list of strategic foundation priorities, you see, and the museum is closer to the bottom of that list. Hopefully, I'll live long enough to see its completion."

"Indeed?" Alton asked, strolling into the office as if he owned the place.

He casually glanced down at me.

"Why, Caleb," he said. "Are you still here? I thought you'd been interviewed already."

"No, I---"

"Well, I won't interrupt you for long," he said, quickly returning his attention to President Yarborough and Dr. Eddings.

"You know this young man?" Eddings asked.

"Why, yes, he's my nephew," Alton replied.

"Your nephew?" Eddings asked. "But I thought his name was Taylor."

"Oh, I'm from his mother's side," Alton said.

"Ah," Eddings said.

"Now, Dr. Eddings, you mentioned your museum's funding level. Well, I'm particularly passionate about history myself; one might say I'm a student of it, in fact."

I had to grin over that.

"Nevertheless, I've been so impressed by this university and your memorable career here in particular, that I'd be interested in seeing the construction come to fruition," Alton said.

"Oh, well, that's most kind of you, Mr. Rutherford," Eddings said. "I'm certain that any donation would be welcome."

"Specifically, I'm willing to fund the remaining balance

for construction," Alton said.

I watched the shocked expression on Eddings' face. "Full construction?"

Alton shrugged. "Absolutely, and with a wing dedicated to your years of fine service here, I should think. It could serve as a repository for much of your research and artifacts surrounding Puritan culture."

As Dr. Eddings ran his hand over his mouth and looked at Yarborough, I almost thought he was going to pass out. My gaze shifted back to Alton, who had a satisfied looking expression on his face; one that I'd seen a number of times before on Kat, in fact.

It was the look of a predator that just captured its prey.

"Oh, my," Eddings said. "Mr. Rutherford, not only would your offer be immensely generous, it would be singularly amazing."

"I'm pleased to hear that. We can finalize the details of my donation in the near future with your foundation's director," Alton said. "I do apologize for interrupting your meeting. Shall we go now, Dr. Yarborough?"

"Certainly, Mr. Rutherford," Yarborough said. "Good evening, Dr. Eddings."

Alton shook the dean's hand.

"My pleasure, Dr. Eddings," Alton said, and then quickly led the president from the office.

Dean Eddings lingered at the door for a moment before closing it fully and returning to his seat across from me.

He momentarily stared across the room with a distant look in his eyes, appearing almost lost, and then returned his attention to me.

"Mr. Taylor, your uncle is quite an interesting man," he said. "Remarkable even."

Then he paused, appearing to fall into some sort of deeply reflective mood. He looked at me again and rubbed his chin with his fingertips.

"Where were we?" he asked.

I swallowed to relieve the tightness in my throat.

"You were telling me about how your program is full already," I said, struggling not to wince from having to say it aloud.

"Oh, yes," he said. "Well…"

I rose from my chair and extended my hand to him. "Thank you, Dr. Eddings, for taking the time to meet with me. It's been a sincere pleasure," I said.

He rose, shook my hand, and said, "Yes, well, welcome to Yale and the program, Mr. Taylor."

I felt my mouth gaping open.

"I'm sorry, I thought you said---"

"Ranking and placement is often viewed rigidly at the university. Fortunately, we deans have some discretionary latitude available to us. With one so deserving as you, we can always make room for one more," Eddings said.

He must've noticed my perplexed expression.

"You'll learn that's simply how some things are done here at Yale, Mr. Taylor; just as it is in the real world outside these hallowed halls."

"Er, thank you, Dr. Eddings," I said, still somewhat numb from the swift turn of events.

"Your uncle appears to be a very savvy man," he said. "It's nice to meet men like you and him; both passionate about history, as well as focused upon what they want in life. Please convey my best wishes and appreciation to him, won't you?"

If you only knew…

"Yes, sir, I certainly will."

I was still in a near-stupor as he escorted me to the building's entrance and held the door open for me.

"My staff will email you with additional placement information and program registration details, and the admissions office should contact you in the next day or so regarding your initial enrollment," he said. "Good night, Mr. Taylor, and once again, congratulations."

Moments later, I found myself standing alone outside in the cool night air, taking a deep breath to attempt to clear my head.

Unbelievable.

I only walked a short distance along a lonely sidewalk when I heard a momentary rapid click of heels, and then Kat was suddenly standing before me.

"Well, how did it go?" she asked excitedly.

I opened my mouth to speak but nothing came out.

She looked down at me expectantly.

"I'm in," I finally managed to say.

She enveloped me in her arms, nearly squeezing the breath from my lungs.

"I'm so very proud of you, my love," she said.

"Really, it was nothing," I said dryly.

Nothing I did, anyway.

CHAPTER 21

Caleb

We boarded a return flight to Atlanta later that night. Apparently, Alton had exclusive chartering of our plane, which must've cost a small fortune.

There seemed to be a lot of small fortunes being spent on my behalf lately.

While I settled in with Kat in our cabin, Alton was still outside the aircraft and hadn't yet boarded the flight.

She reached out to grasp my hand in hers, and then leaned over to kiss me. Her stiletto clad foot once again lightly traversed up my left leg.

"Are you excited about going to Yale?" she asked with a glint in her eyes.

I grinned. "Who wouldn't be?"

She turned as the cabin door opened to reveal Alton, still looking amazing in his fitted designer suit.

"We've taken on an impromptu passenger who'll be staying on for Miami after we deplane in Atlanta," he said.

"Really? Anyone we know?" Kat asked.

"Hm, I think you've met," he said. "Does Sabira ring a bell?"

"Sabira?" she said. "Yes, she was an Arabic vampire from the Slovene conference."

She looked at me with an inquiring expression. "I'd like to go say hello, if that's okay with you."

I shrugged. "Sure."

She exited the cabin as Alton settled into the free seat on the opposite end of our short row of four.

My thoughts immediately jumped to my meeting with Dr. Eddings. After a moment, I rose and moved to the empty seat beside Alton's.

"You're welcome, my boy," he said with an easy smile.

I blinked and stared into his hazel eyes. "Why?"

He frowned slightly. "Why, what?"

"Why did you do this, Alton? Why go to all this trouble for *me*? You purchased a museum just to get me into Yale. You've spent a small fortune flying us here and back to Atlanta," I said.

"Don't you think yourself worthy of going to Yale?" he asked, cocking his head to one side with a quizzical expression.

"Yes—I mean, no; not at such a high cost," I stammered. "They—the students—are way out of my league."

His eyes flashed bright hazel and he laughed.

A second later, his eyes narrowed and his features hardened. "So, the poor, abused boy from Columbus, Ohio, doesn't think he deserves to be at Yale? Is that right?" he demanded. "You're from humble roots and that makes you more stupid and worthless than all of the snot-nosed rich kids; those favored sons and daughters of powerful CEOs, senators, and congressmen?"

"Stop it!" I shot back. "Don't go there."

"No, you stop it. You've been beaten down so much in your past you've bought into the ridiculous rhetoric, dogma, and stupidity of fools," he said. "You're already twice as intelligent, capable, and worthy than half of the spoiled, foolishly entailed students in Yale, yet you're your own worst enemy.

"Consider that many of your soon-to-be fellow students

are steeped in pretention, primarily gracing those halls because of whom they know or where they came from. I know you can best most of them in so many ways, if you merely assert yourself and try."

My jaw muscles tightened.

"You listen to me, right now, and you listen well, my son," he said, power virtually emanating from him in waves. "I'm from a time when power was inherited, usually from the pampered and the favored. I'm also from a time when a good man with a strong arm who can swing a sword and comport himself with honor is worth ten times his weight in gold.

"I'll stake my life and limb on just one honorable peasant's boy over a hundred grovelers, manipulators, and political sycophants…every—single—time. Give me ten humble, ethical, sincere souls and I can build a kingdom; give me a hundred and I can rule an entire nation.

"Do you want to know who I see when I look into your eyes; when I divine the depths of your soul? You're one of those sons of so-called commoners who could lead an army and be worthy of it; who could be king, and be worthy of a crown," he said.

His hands darted out to grasp the sides of my head between his strong fingers. "You may not believe me now, but relatively soon those things I said are going to become self-evident to you, even if I have to flay the world bare and then set fire to parts of it to prove it to you. I'm going to *make* you see the truth, and then you'll believe; because once you do, you'll be nearly unstoppable."

I felt awed; completely speechless.

"When I purchased a hospital wing to be able to perform life-saving surgery on you, you were worth it then. When I purchase a museum to give you a fair opportunity that you should by all rights have access to in the first place, you're worth it. When you discover your tuition to be prepaid at Yale, you're worth it.

"In all the things I have done for you or may do for you in the future, you'll accept both my grace and my gifts as I deem them so, and you *will* be worthy of them. Do you understand me?"

I was speechless. Nobody had ever said anything like that to me before.

I tried to nod my head but his grip precluded it.

"But I—I could never repay you for all your generosity," I said.

"Oh, you will, son. You most certainly will," he said. "You'll bear the weight of all those who'll look down upon you when they deem you unworthy. You'll excel in your studies, and believe me, I'll be watching closely to see that you do. You'll act in good character, even when you see an easier, less noble path before you. You'll shine when the darkness falls upon you. You'll hone your skills and you'll harness your courage, and you'll do it, not only because I demand it, but because it's who you are, deep down inside where it counts most.

"And finally, I'll speak to things I've seen and heard recently between you and Katrina. When a certain, red-haired woman lays her heart, soul, and body at your feet, you'll accept her, honor her, and cherish her; because she has deemed you to be worthy of her, and you will move heaven and earth to prove that she's chosen well. Am I understood?"

Immediately, Kat's visage appeared in my mind's eye, even as Alton's words echoed in my mind.

I didn't know what else to say except, "Yes. I'll do those things, as well."

"Good," he said. "It appears there's hope for you yet."

He inhaled a breath and let it out slowly, and released me. Then he patted my cheek with his open palm.

"Thank you, Alton," I said, nearly dazed.

"You're welcome, dear boy," he said. "Now remember what I've said and ruminate upon it."

I stared at him as he once more sat back in his seat as though nothing extraordinary had just transpired between us.

I felt stunned; my world had just been rocked, long-held illusions cracking around their raw edges.

That was something entirely new for me.

Then something ironic that he'd said struck me.

"You know, it's not easy at times when that same red-haired woman demands to be the alpha in the relationship," I said.

His look of amusement spoke volumes. "True. Therefore, you may instead find yourself being the one at her feet, but if you do the other things I said, things will be splendid between you."

"Charming," I said dryly.

It just stands to reason, I suppose.

"Don't worry, I know you have it in you," he said. "So few men do, actually. In truth, it makes you stand out even taller among others."

"Short of stature, large in character," I said wistfully.

He chuckled. "Yes, something like that."

"Alton?"

"Hm?"

"Why Yale?"

"There's a number of perfectly logical reasons, actually," he said. "However, there's one in particular that supersedes the others. Don't worry, when the time is right, you'll discover why. Actually, I think you'll be quite intrigued.

"For now, accept that as far as seeking an academic position, the prestige of hailing from Yale has quite an impact on prospective employers, even today. Then there's the advantage of having you closer to the east coast, making travel between there and London easier," he said.

I conceded the logic of each.

"But enough of that; let's focus on getting you settled and through the thesis selection process for your dissertation, shall we?"

He was right, of course. There were a host of things needing to be addressed in the near future.

I looked sidelong at him with a curious expression.

"This evening, you introduced yourself to Dr. Eddings as my uncle," I said.

"It made matters so much easier to negotiate," he said.

I did my best to repress a growing look of surprise. "So, are you adopting me?"

He regarded me with an amused expression, and my eyebrows rose in silent query.

"You could say that. We're family in every way that matters now," he said. "And I suppose you may call me Uncle Alton if you like. For all intents and purposes, I declared that this evening out of need, if not for equal reasons of sentiment."

I smiled. "Thanks, uncle."

It was a thoughtful gesture on his part, and I marveled over the novelty of once again having a family to be a member of, even if it wasn't by birth.

Who could ask for more?

The satisfied expression on his face was likewise unmistakable.

The cabin door abruptly opened and Kat stepped inside. As soon as she closed the door and turned around, she frowned at us.

"You two look rather suspicious. Did I miss something important?" she asked.

"Hardly," Alton said as he gazed into my eyes. "We were merely discussing my expectations for my nephew, Caleb, now that he's been accepted into Yale."

"*Nephew?*" she asked, her gaze alternating between us like a tennis match.

* * *

Alton ordered a chilled bottle of champagne for us on the flight. Between the spirits and the late hour, by time we landed back in Atlanta, I was feeling both relieved and decidedly relaxed.

However, I still marveled over all that had taken place in the span of only a few hours. My life was in a whirlwind.

Ethan and Paige met us as we exited the plane; Paige

jumping up and down with a big grin on her face. She rushed up to wrap me in her arms as soon as I cleared the exit area.

"Congrats, kiddo!" she said. "You must've made a kick-butt impression."

"Well—" I said, sparing a glance at Alton, who gave me a hard look. "Actually, yeah, I charmed the hell out of 'em."

He nodded with a look of approval.

"Well done, Caleb," Ethan offered with a warm smile, shaking my hand while Paige still clung to me. "The best of congratulations to you."

"Woo-hoo, we're going to Yale!" Paige exclaimed, parting from our embrace.

We?

My own smile faded somewhat as I looked at Kat with concern. Paige's enthusiasm waned as she spied my subdued mood.

"What's wrong?" she asked. "We're going to Yale, right?"

"We're certainly going to New Haven together," I said.

"Paige, Caleb will be enrolling at Yale," Alton said. "And you are indeed going to college, as well."

She frowned and folded her arms before her. "Just what the hell do you mean by that, exactly?"

"Don't worry, you'll be right next door practically," I said in a supportive tone.

She looked at me and then back at Alton with a perplexed expression.

"Gateway Community College, to be precise," Alton said. "I estimated their general studies degree would be ideal for you. Such curriculums are broadly transferrable."

"What!" she asked incredulously. "What a load of crap! So, I'm not smart enough for Yale or something?"

I nearly winced from her tone, though Kat was trying to repress a smirk.

I gave her a disapproving look.

Evil, evil, Kat.

"I need your schedule to be more flexible, which

wouldn't be the case as a Yale freshman undergraduate. We can discuss this further back at the estate," Alton said.

"Community college, my ass," Paige said.

I moved to stand before her, grasping her by the upper arms. "Listen, you don't have to do this, you know. I'd understand, and I'll be fine."

She took a firm hold of my tie, pulling my face closer to hers. "Don't even go there, twerp."

My eyebrows rose.

"Listen, I'm still going with you. I just didn't expect this little twist, that's all. Some people aren't willing to share their plans ahead of time," she said, peering around me to glare at Alton.

"And I'm still very proud of you," she said, letting go of my tie and straightening it. "You look all snappy and dapper in your chick-magnet of a suit, too."

I beamed with pride. "Thanks."

"Shall we go?" Alton suggested.

Ethan wrapped his arm around Paige's slender shoulders. "Hey, either way, I'm still dating a college student."

She snickered and draped one arm around his waist. "Yes, you are, you cradle robber."

As Kat took my hand in hers, I couldn't help thinking that each of our lives was drastically about to change.

* * *

Alton left for London two days after my debut visit to Yale. Before he left for the airport, and following what appeared through the dining room's French doors to be a serious discussion between him and Katrina, he took me aside.

"Remember what we discussed on the plane," he said. "And I'm just a phone call away if you need me."

"Thank you for that," I said. "For everything."

I embraced him in a hug, which he returned in kind.

I felt very proud at that moment.

The feelings lasted for days after Alton returned to London.

Time flew, and before I knew it, it was July 17th; my birthday.

My twenty-seventh birthday.

Frankly, I wanted to ignore the occasion entirely, though I doubted that was likely to happen.

I gazed into the mirror, seeing the same face in the bathroom mirror I'd seen the day before, and yet, I was another year closer to thirty that morning.

I wasn't sure exactly what it was I expected at twenty-seven, but I couldn't have guessed a year ago that it would've involved having a vampire mate, or even realizing the existence of vampires, for that matter.

A year ago, I'd been preparing to start my first full-time position as a professor at a small Atlanta-based community college. And yet, barely a year into it, I'd been laid off due to the poor economy and Draconian budget cuts.

Now I was once again preparing for my return to college, only once again as a student.

Yale, no less; courtesy of the world's most generous vampires…who aren't supposed to exist.

"What a crazy-ass life," I muttered.

I rubbed the shaving cream across my face and picked up my safety razor.

Kat made breakfast for me, and fortunately didn't try to give me any more birthday gifts. The SUV in the garage was more than enough for me.

Alton had sent me a regal-looking birthday card that arrived via express courier service. Inside, he wrote:

Caleb,

My gift to you is your tuition, fees, and any associated expenses toward the completion of your degree at Yale. Make excellent use of your time, and make me proud.

Best wishes for a happy birthday.

Warm Regards,
"Uncle" Alton

I recalled our intense dialogue on the flight from New Haven, as well as both the declarations made and expectations given.

I frowned for a moment.

I'll do my best to honor both.

Kat politely asked to read Alton's card. She glanced over it, smiled, and handed it back to me.

"You're okay with this whole uncle-thing, right?" I asked. "It's not actually real, after all."

"I have no objection, and it's more real than you think. In fact, congratulations are in order," she said. "It's not uncommon for childless lords from his time to adopt aspiring young men into his family; particularly those deemed of high merit. And, call me biased, but I happen to find you of impeccably high merit."

I nodded, though something in the back of my mind wondered if there were more to it than that.

Even so, she didn't revisit the topic again.

The remainder of my special day was spent at home with her sharing quality time together.

Time was precious as the clock ticked down toward the fall semester, so I relished any time with her I could.

Of course, that evening, Ethan and Paige came over to visit. And, as I both half-expected and half-feared, they brought gifts.

He gave me a practical and much-needed backpack, which was fortunately made from good old heavy-duty canvas rather than something less durable. However, inside the backpack was an Amazon gift card of a sizable amount.

"*To pick up any last-minute items that need toting in your backpack,*" he wrote in my card.

I took the high road and thanked him, despite the fact

he'd been way too generous.

Then I got a little worried over Paige's gleeful expression as I jiggled the wrapped box she handed me.

Inside was the latest generation of Apple's iPad tablet, which was something I'd been wanting for some time, but hadn't gotten around to getting.

"The perfect gift for the nerdy reader in your life," she said with a squeal before giving me a bear hug.

I chuckled. "Aww, thanks, Paige. This is great!"

"I think you can even subscribe to your favorite porn magazine on it, too," she said in a conspiratorial tone.

My eyes shot wide open and I looked over at Kat, who appeared completely surprised.

"Hey, we've talked about his before," I said. "Remember, there are actually no 'real' porn subscriptions for me."

Kat strode over to me and placed a sharp fingernail beneath my chin as her emerald eyes gazed into mine. "Good. Let's see that you keep it that way while you're away at college, or else your dominatrix-mate *won't* be very happy."

I swallowed hard. "Got it."

"Excellent," she said, removing her finger.

Close call.

I glanced over to see Ethan and Paige barely containing their amusement, and I felt my cheeks burning.

"Great, no porn for Caleb. Now that that's settled, how about we all go out to dinner?" Paige asked in a perky tone. "Birthday boy gets to pick the place!"

Later that night, after they dropped us off at the estate, Kat pulled out all the sexual stops and showed me why I had no need to consider pornography in my future.

We shared an amazing, passionate, and memorable experience together.

That was my twenty-seventh birthday in a nutshell, and decidedly the best birthday in my life.

The final two weeks of July were spent preparing, packing, and completing final details for Kat and me; me heading to Connecticut and her relocating to London.

Relocating.

Just the thought of being separated from her generated both anxiety and sadness. Suddenly, all of the fortitude I'd mustered had dissipated.

I don't know if I can do this.

The excitement of attending Yale was palpable, but, in the end, I'd much rather have gone with Kat to London. Surely, I'd be able to enroll at one of Britain's colleges, even with Alton's assistance, if needed.

In retrospect, Kat and I hadn't been separated for any length of time since she and Alton had pursued the renegade vampire, Chimalma, across the country.

That had only lasted for approximately a week, and it nearly drove me crazy.

I must be an obsessive relationship addict or something.

Maybe our time apart will be a formative experience.

Inhaling a deep breath, I returned to setting out some more clothes for packing. We were scheduled to depart Atlanta in two more days, and keeping busy was the best way to avoid dwelling on my anxiety.

Once I arrived at Yale, staying busy would likely be the last of my worries. Completing a PhD program seemed, by far, the biggest challenge of my academic experiences.

I slowly scanned the master bedroom that we shared, vowing I'd return someday to pick up where we had left off.

Someday.

Yet, I felt a growing sense of foreboding that things were about to change in profound ways; that life was changing forever, never to return to what once was.

That unsettled me more than I'd admit to anyone.

At least Paige would be there with me.

Paige.

Then another realization struck me.

Paige and Ethan will be separated, as well; and it's all because of me.

A wave of guilt flowed through me. Leaving an array of

clothes strewn across our bed, I went upstairs, grabbed the keys to my SUV, and headed toward the garage.

I felt compelled to do something while there was still time.

* * *

After parking my SUV, a gift I was certain to miss in my absence, I made my way into Atlanta's regional hospital and headed for the administrative offices.

Soon, I sat in a rather uncomfortable waiting chair in a bland-looking hallway.

I never liked being in hospitals; even less now given my recent experiences.

"Caleb? Is everything okay?" Ethan asked.

As usual, he looked like some sort of Hollywood actor who portrayed a doctor on television.

Damn, some people have all the luck.

"Me? Yeah, I'm fine," I replied. "I hoped we could chat, if you have a spare moment."

"Sure," he said with a welcoming smile. "Let's go upstairs to my office."

As we walked down the hallway, a few stray beams of afternoon sunlight crept in through parted blinds on a window to our right, but he neatly raised his clipboard he was carrying to shield his face as he sped past it.

Still, I heard a split-second long sizzling sound and noticed him absently rub his hand as we resumed our walk down the hallway toward the elevators.

Impressive. He's probably practiced for all sorts of awkward daytime circumstances over the years.

I noticed how nurses and doctors alike spared him a greeting or admiring look as we passed them.

He'd really fit in with everyone since his arrival.

Upon entering his small office, he said, "Have a seat."

I sat in the nearest guest chair and he rolled a small wheeled-stool to sit down before me, regarding me with a reassuring expression.

Not for the first time, I marveled at the amazing bedside manner he had.

"What can I do for my favorite repeat patient? Do you have a sudden case of pre-Yale jitters?" he asked, placing his clipboard atop his desk.

"Funny," I said. "Actually, I should've taken the time to talk with you about this before now, so I apologize for that. But I'm hoping you're one of those 'better late than never' kinds of guys."

"Okay," he said, frowning slightly. "Now I'm intrigued."

I rubbed my palms across the thighs of my jeans. "I'm feeling a little guilty about Paige accompanying me to Connecticut."

"Ah, but she's your surrogate vampire, and Katrina is needed in London," he said. "It only makes sense, logistically. You do have an uncanny tendency to attract trouble."

I quirked my lips. "Busted."

His responding chuckle was encouraging.

The memory of Kat bestowing the rarely used title and responsibility of surrogate vampire to Paige made me smile. I was both honored and pleased that Paige sincerely seemed to relish the role. She did such an excellent job of protecting and supporting me during Kat's infrequent absences.

However, managing the interpersonal challenges from two vampires that frequently got on each other's nerves could sometimes feel a bit overwhelming.

"Listen, the initial stages of a relationship are the most formative, and yet, I'm depriving you and Paige of that important time," I said. "It feels wrong and selfish of me. But there's still time to— Well, you know, I could always ask Kat to find someone else to take Paige's place or something. Maybe Devon?"

Our conversation felt much more awkward than when I'd practiced it in my head on the way there. Part of me really wanted for Paige to accompany me, but the nobler part of me resisted.

"Caleb, listen to me," he said. "I know how important Paige is to you, as well as how important you are to her. She cares for you very deeply, and I'm okay with that."

I carefully considered my next words.

"Ethan, I want you to know you can trust me to do the right thing," I said.

His eyebrows rose.

"I know that. As long as the two of you don't get locked in a vault together, you'll both be just fine," he said.

I felt heat rise in my cheeks. In truth, I still felt periodic bouts of shame over what had transpired in the Slovene hotel vault between her and me; not just on behalf of Ethan, but also for Kat.

I should feel even more ashamed for really enjoying it.

"You're half-right about that," I said sheepishly.

He knew about our confinement, but probably not about the heated emotions exchanged between us inside that vault.

However, he gave me a reassuring look. "I'm *fully* right about that. Paige told me everything; the blood, the kiss. Everything."

I felt the color drain from my face.

"Oh," I said.

"But I'm okay with it," he said. "It was unusual circumstances, and she and I hadn't formed the bond that we're forming now."

"Listen, I *really* want to see things work out between you and her," I said with more emphasis than I'd planned. "And I don't want to be a source of additional strain in that area."

"Ah," he said, as the corners of his mouth upturned slightly.

"This amuses you?" I asked with a frown.

He leaned forward, grasped my shoulder with one hand, and looked into my eyes with a compassionate expression.

"Listen to me, Caleb," he said. "You've been so supportive of us from the very start; hell, you introduced us, and I appreciate that immensely. But whether she and I either succeed or fail, it'll be because of the two of us, our commitment to each other, and our ability to confront and overcome conflicts or challenges. It's no different than between you and Katrina. What will be, will be."

He paused, as if in reflection. "You know, I haven't told you this, but the moment I met you at the Slovene conference I knew you were someone special," he said. "I've found you to be an honest and honorable person, and I can't imagine anyone I'd trust more to support the important lady in my life during my absence than you."

I felt both relieved and humbled, and I swallowed to ease the tension that had formed in my throat.

Wow, this guy's amazing.

"Thank you," I said. "You're very kind and extremely understanding, Ethan."

"Think nothing of it. And don't worry, I've got quite a bit to keep me busy here while you're both away," he said. "And, just so you know, I plan to come to visit as frequently as possible. In truth, this situation will provide some helpful pacing for Paige and me. It'd be really easy to rush into things with her."

"She's wildfire in a bottle, isn't she?" I asked.

He sat back and laughed. "Precisely. Explosive, passionate, and occasionally too hot to handle; but that's definitely part of her allure, and I adore her."

I grinned.

Yep, that's Paige.

He rose from his seat.

"I appreciate you coming by to visit with me; it's yet another reason why I respect you so much, Caleb," he said.

I stood and extended my hand to shake his.

"Call me if you need anything at all, okay?" he asked. "I'll be there for both of you."

"Thanks, Ethan," I said. "You don't know how happy and grateful I am to hear you say that."

His cell phone beeped, and he swept it into his hand with a flourish, gazing down at the screen.

"Anything wrong?" I asked.

"Just a text. It appears I have an impromptu surgical assist to prepare for this afternoon, as well as two patients waiting to see me," he said. "You see? Boredom simply isn't an issue around here."

He smiled warmly and accompanied me to the elevators.

As I walked through the parking lot, I felt greatly relieved about some of the things that'd been weighing upon me.

Maybe the prospects of Yale didn't loom as large on the horizon as it did an hour ago.

I can do this.

JAZ PRIMO

Part II

New Haven

CHAPTER 22

Caleb

In amazing time, Kat had secured a relatively spacious three-story colonial style home in New Haven, conveniently located just a few blocks east of the Yale campus. It was prime real estate, to say the least.

Despite the darkness outside, the exterior lighting was ample enough to discern that the house had been well maintained. The white bannisters accenting the covered front porch was charmingly rustic looking.

My new home appeared to be one of the nicest houses on the block, in fact.

While the design was of an older architecture, which I was impressed by on a purely historical level, there'd been a remarkable amount of remodeling done on the inside to modernize it with all of the latest amenities and décor.

To say the entire effort must've cost a fortune would've been an understatement.

"Really nice, but kinda' pricey, I bet," I said to Kat.

She arched her brow at me. "This is your second home of sorts, and likely will be for some time, so I want you to be comfortable here. Besides, it needs to be fully functional for a vampire's needs."

That meant the basement had been converted to a

veritable shelter-like condition, complete with reinforced doors and blocked windows.

In addition, the third floor, which had essentially been an oversized attic, had been remodeled into a storage room and small bedroom with half bathroom.

There were already three regular-sized bedrooms on the second floor and a master suite.

"Expecting company?" I asked during my initial walk-thru with her.

"Well, the master suite is yours, as well as mine when I visit. Paige can have her pick of one of the second floor bedrooms, and that leaves three bedrooms in the house for guests and staff."

"Staff?" I asked with a sharp look at her.

"Security, maids, whichever," she said.

"I have Paige for security, thank you," I said.

She cast one of her best dominatrix-esque stares at me. "Security is whomever I dictate as such for you."

I rolled my eyes and proceeded on our tour of the house. There was even a small den on the first floor, just beyond the living room.

While not nearly as spacious as our estate in Atlanta, it was nevertheless roomy enough for our needs. Besides, I'd be home for holidays and the summer, so it was really just a spring and fall home.

I never imagined having a second home before. If my old college friends could see me now…

I considered that for a moment.

Yeah, they'd probably tease the crap out of me.

I walked into the attached single car garage, which was the plainest-looking facet of the property.

"I'll let Paige select a vehicle for you two," Kat said. "She can at least pay for that much."

"This is a great location; we're walking distance to the main campus, actually. And I'll be able to hang a bicycle on that far wall," I said, pointing. "Of course, I also noticed there's a bus stop just on the corner. Wasn't that at Lincoln and Trumbull?"

She nodded. "I think so."

I turned to wrap my arms around her waist and pulled her close against me. "Thank you for arranging all of this on short notice," I said. "I love it. And I love you."

I placed a warm kiss on her lips, which she responded to in kind.

"I hope you enjoy living here while you're in college," she said.

"I'd enjoy it better if you were here, too," I said.

She sighed. "I know. I'm sorry, but Alton needs me in London."

"Sure. But I'm already worrying about you," I said.

She'd explained to me that Alton wanted her to serve as a leader for his forces. The idea of a vampire army, complete with a cadre of humans, was a bit larger scale than I would've expected.

The fact that the world was being divvied up between two large opposing vampire factions wasn't very encouraging, either.

Frankly, the entire scenario sounded like the latest script for some blockbuster Hollywood film. The words 'dangerous' and 'lethal' both factored into my vision, as well.

Suddenly, I felt very protective and possessive of her.

"Promise me you'll visit as much as possible," I said. "Or, I could come to London periodically."

She hugged me tighter in her embrace. "Of course, I'll try. But we're going to be busier than you think, and time will pass very quickly for both of us. And I'll call you, and we could video chat over your computer."

A brief wave of melancholy washed over me.

I didn't want to be separated from her for very long. And the thought of possibly losing her in the growing conflict was harder than I could bear.

"Be safe," I said. "Come back to me."

"It'll be my number one priority," she said.

Paige abruptly appeared in the garage, startling me. "Hey,

you smoochers, break it up. A big truck just pulled up outside with new furniture, and I don't have a clue where most of this stuff goes."

That was pretty much the extent of my quality time with Kat before she left for London.

She left via taxi the next evening, though not before the arrival of a tall, dark-haired man of Asian lineage earlier that evening.

Paige and I stood in the living room as the man stepped through the front door, nodding deferentially to Kat.

"Caleb, this is Roman Lee," Kat said. "He's an ex-Navy SEAL who's been employed by Alton for a number of years. He's also your new bodyguard."

I politely shook hands with him, sizing him up and noting his firm handshake.

"Hello, Caleb," he said. "Pleased to meet you and I look forward to getting to know you better over the next few days."

Paige exchanged introductions with him as I gave Kat a hard look.

She arched her eyebrows and mouthed, be nice.

"I'll give you a quick tour of the house and you can select one of the available bedrooms for yourself," Kat said.

He selected the solitary one with the three quarter bath that had been recently renovated on the third floor. Kat later said he told her he wanted to make his stay as unobtrusive as possible.

I hoped he felt that way when he was shadowing me everywhere.

This time, a daylight-friendly goon to watch over me.

Later, I walked arm in arm with Kat to the taxi that was parked in the street before the house.

"I'll miss you," I told her.

"I'll miss you more," she responded.

We shared a lingering kiss, followed by some smaller ones as the driver loaded her two suitcases into the trunk.

"He's on a meter, you know," Paige called from the

front porch.

Kat and I both gave her a dirty look and shared a final kiss. I held the taxi's door open for her.

Then I leaned inside and kissed her again.

"I love you," I said.

"I love you, too," she said with a flash of her green eyes.

Then I watched the taxi drive away until it turned the corner at Trumbull and was gone.

I miss her already.

Paige was savvy enough not to say a word as I quietly ascended the short set of porch stairs and stepped inside the house.

*   *   *

The next week was spent busily preparing for my classes, including reading a number of books that were prerequisite readings. Fortunately, I was able to download all of them onto my new iPad.

I also met with the professor who was recently assigned by Dr. Eddings to be my dissertation chair and research advisor, Professor Samuel Gowan.

Dr. Gowan was a pleasant-natured man in his mid-fifties who seemed to have an affinity for bow ties. His attire reminded me of something out of the *Nutty Professor's* wardrobe, in fact.

He asked that I consider my interests for a dissertation topic, and meet again with him in a couple of weeks.

Kat had been correct in that the days went by like a speeding train. I was so preoccupied that I rarely noticed Roman following me around. Often, I lost sight of him altogether.

Stealthy guy.

Roman and I got along nicely, and Paige and he seemed to have hit it off well enough, as well. As I suspected, he took his primary orders from Kat, but Paige had the ability to issue local directives to him.

The current arrangement was he was on duty beginning at sunrise, and Paige took over at sunset.

Imagine that.

On campus, I made a few new acquaintances early on, thanks primarily to a fellow history graduate student named Trey Baker. He majored in Middle Ages History and was actively advised by Dr. Gowan.

Gowan was Trey's dissertation chairperson, and had been his master's thesis chair, as well.

Small world.

Trey introduced me to a group of his friends who frequented a local coffee café during the day called Witches Brew on Grove Street near the main campus.

During the evenings, my new acquaintances liked to hang out at either a bar called Yalehoos over on Crown Street, or a pub called Prime Time on Chapel Street. Within a couple of weeks, I'd visited all three places and it was hard to pick my favorite.

To my happy surprise, New Haven was a great town to socialize in.

Of course, Paige had already figured that out. She'd bribed Roman on a couple of occasions to hang around me during those evenings so she could go 'investigating the area.'

In actuality, it was carousing time for her. She quickly established social contacts at the nearby community college.

Oh well, I figured she deserved distractions as much as anybody.

At first, it was almost painful to be away from Kat. Following my recovery from the nearly lethal events surrounding my quasi-turning, my time with her had taken on renewed emphasis in my mind.

Our daily phone calls and computer-based video chats felt essential for me to cope with her absence.

However, over the period of about a month, our video chats and phone calls were less and less frequent; we moved to intermittent texting in conjunction with a phone call most nights before I went to sleep.

However, what really bothered me was that, while she and I easily discussed my experiences in New Haven, she was less forthcoming with details of her activities in London.

I only hoped she was being as careful as she promised she was.

But then, very gradually, I got used to it. My coping mechanism was to throw myself further into my studies; not a hard task given the high standards and aggressive curriculums that Yale hosted.

A helpful aspect to Roman was his regimented approach to exercise. Every morning, we'd jog over to Yale's athletic center and work out.

Somehow Alton had managed not only to receive a permit for Roman to carry concealed weapons on campus; he'd arranged Roman's guest privileges on campus for the duration of my time at the university.

Honestly, Alton was nearly magical at times.

Typically, after workouts, Roman and I jogged back home, where my full day of classes and assignments took over.

That became my busy routine life; at least, for a time.

CHAPTER 23

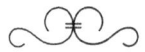

Caleb

As I sat in Witches Brew with a double espresso to kick-start my morning, I received a text from Alton asking me to check my email.

He'd sent a message to me recommending a topic for my dissertation; specifically, an early evolutionary biologist named Dr. Oliver Simonson. Based upon the brief information included in Alton's message, Simonson, who was born in 1854, assisted his father in Union hospitals during the American Civil War where he gained an interest in phlebotomy.

Sounds boring.

I replied to Alton, politely thanking him for his assistance, and stating I was looking for something more dynamic.

Minutes later, instead of an email reply, I received a text message on my phone that said, *Not a suggestion, nephew. Simonson is your topic.*

"What!"

My surroundings grew quiet and I noticed everyone in the place was staring at me.

"Sorry, weird text," I said, shaking my phone to and fro in the air while slouching into my chair.

A text from Roman appeared on my cell phone asking, *Ok?*

I'd forgotten he was sitting on the other side of the café from me.

I replied, *Yes, thx.*

Then I replied to Alton's annoying text with, *Fine, uncle bossypants. IF prof oks.*

A quick reply from him was, *He will.*

I only narrowly avoided cursing aloud.

Oh, this is going to suck rocks!

As Mother Mother's "Little Pistol" played over the café speaker system, a shadow fell across my table and I looked up as a cute brunette stood in the café entrance, intently surveying the room.

She looked at me twice before scanning the room again.

"Is there a Caleb?" she asked aloud to nobody in particular.

A number of people muttered negative responses before I raised my hand and said, "I'm *the* Caleb."

She smiled broadly and walked over to my table.

"Listen, I'm a friend of Trey's, and he said to meet him here. He said he was supposed to meet someone named Caleb," she said. "So, I think I must've beaten him here, and---"

"Got it," I said. "Have a seat."

"Chance," she introduced herself while holding out her hand toward me. "Chance Noble."

I stood to shake her hand and pulled out a chair next to mine for her.

"Nice to meet you, Chance," I said. "Um, so you're a big gambler, maybe?"

She scowled. "You're hilarious, but I've heard that one before. Actually, my dad's more of a gambler than me. I'm just the college student in our family."

"Yale?" I asked.

"Yep, freshman year," she said. "Marketing and management major."

230

"Yeah, there's no gambling involved there," I said.

She wrinkled her nose at me. "It's not gambling if I'm professionally trained and credited."

I nodded. "Well, carry on, then."

Moments later, Trey walked into the café, his lanky frame hoisting an overly-full looking backpack over one shoulder.

"Hey, Chance, you must've run over here," he said. "Hi, Caleb."

"I was already on campus when you called," she said.

"Man, do I need some caffeine," Trey said as he dropped his pack onto the floor and headed for the main counter.

"Me, too," Chance said, quickly joining him.

I watched both of them for a few seconds.

I like her.

My thoughts immediately shifted to ruminating over what had suddenly become my mandated dissertation subject.

What the hell's so interesting about Oliver Simonson?

I realized it was finally time to put my research skills to good use.

* * *

As I researched background information on the mysterious Dr. Simonson, I felt like I was being pulled in too many directions at once.

I had three courses to divide my attentions, each of them requiring papers and further readings. Two were seminar classes on orals and prospectus preparations to help me prepare my dissertation development and defense processes.

Academics aside, my thoughts frequently shifted to Kat and what she was up to.

In addition, Paige and Roman were charged with my self-defense training regimen; largely knife combat skills. Although I found it somewhat ironic that all I carried with me was a small Swiss Army knife.

Not even James Bond could probably kill somebody with that!

Besides, I needed skills with weapons I could fight vampires with. Maybe I was just growing paranoid, but the world seemed to be teeming with vampires, and one day Roman and Paige might not be so handy when I needed them.

Finally, and perhaps more importantly, I wanted to pursue some semblance of a social life just to unwind from the stresses of my other diversions.

Fortunately, my newfound collegial acquaintances were excellent social outlets. Granted, most of us were grad students, except for Chance and an engineering major named Anthony Hess, both freshmen undergraduates.

On Friday evening, Paige received a visit from Ethan, so Roman and I decided to abandon the house to them.

I was jealous that Paige got to see her partner while I had to make do with phone calls and occasional video conferences.

Roman and I made our way to Yalehoos, though he spaced our entrances long enough that it didn't look like we'd arrived together. Once inside, I found Trey and a group of his friends surrounding a large table.

They invited me to join them, and soon the beer was flowing in heavy order.

Everyone appeared to be having a great time, including Roman, who discreetly sat over at the bar talking up a blonde bartender.

Trey was telling scandalous stories to the group about his time as a pool lifeguard at an exclusive addition over the summer.

"Then one day these really hot-looking babes show up and started sunbathing topless," Trey said. "So, after a few beers in the hot sun, things got pretty crazy---"

"Whoa, Trey," Chance interrupted. "Um, not interested in your pervy exploits."

"Agreed," said Lillian, an English Lit grad student. "If I want that crap I'll watch old Baywatch reruns."

"Aww, c'mon, ladies," Trey said. "Wait; they did topless

scenes on that show?"

Chance flicked beer at him off her fingertips.

"Hey!"

Anthony laughed and leaned over to me. "I wish I had any wild stories to tell. My brother and I spend our time having *exciting* debates with my dad over innovations in light bulbs and batteries."

"Light bulbs and batteries?" I asked.

"Yeah, my older brother, Gregory, works at Benton Technologies in their R & D department. They're a big defense contractor," he said. "Anyway, my dad's one of the high-level execs, and he's hoping I'll join him and Gregory there after college. But it sounds kinda' lame."

"Well, take it from an out of work history professor, any full-time job is a good job in this economy," I said sourly.

"Yeah, but light bulbs and batteries?" he asked. "Gregory spends his days trying to improve the strength of small flashlight batteries. Boring. I mean, I'd rather design the next space shuttle or something."

"Even shuttles need batteries," I said. "And lights."

"True," he said.

I considered that the prospects of Antony receiving a high-paying engineering job were a hell of a lot better than me landing a teaching job again.

Still, that's why I'm at Yale.

I looked up at the neon lit clock near the bar's entrance and took a swig of my beer.

Then an idea completely off the wall hit me.

Whoa. What if?

I leaned back over to Anthony. "Hey, any chance you could arrange a phone call between me and your brother?"

He shrugged. "Yeah, sure. I'll give you his cell number and you can call him. What's up? You thinkin' about a career change?"

"Actually, I'd like to ask him about a special project I have in mind," I said.

Later that night as we said our goodbyes outside the bar,

I noticed two shady-looking guys standing across the parking lot watching us.

What seemed odd was, despite the cool night air, they both looked like they were sweating profusely.

About that time, Roman exited the bar behind us and stepped out into the parking lot while gazing at the two men that'd caught my attention.

They quickly turned and walked away, and Roman caught up with me as I walked home alone.

"Those two men in the parking lot looked sorta' weird," I said.

"Yeah," he agreed. "It was probably nothing, but I'll keep an eye out for them. Let me know if you see them again."

* * *

Before sunrise on Sunday morning, Ethan had left to return to Atlanta, and Paige seemed much more relaxed after his brief visit.

That morning, with Roman in tow, I made a special trip to Yale's Center for Science and Social Science Information on Prospect Street to do some research. It was an impressive facility hosting state of the art technology and a vast collection of both printed and electronic resources. It definitely dwarfed anything I'd seen during my time at Georgia State.

I delved into my research with a vengeance, and quickly lost track of time. Although sometime before noon, Roman convinced me to stop briefly for something to eat.

After we ate, I made a quick phone call to Anthony's brother, Gregory, about the idea I had in the bar Saturday night.

To my pleasant surprise, it went really well. He liked the idea for my experiment and promised to follow up with some additional information in the near future.

Roman and I returned to the center, and by late

afternoon, I had a better idea of how to proceed with my research.

It was past six o'clock when Roman appeared at my side. "Sorry to interrupt you, Caleb, but Paige wants us back at the house ASAP."

"Now?" I asked.

He shrugged. "That's what she said."

We'd barely walked through the front door when Paige appeared from out of nowhere directly before me.

"What the hell have you been doing all day, mister?" she asked.

"Hey, you know I was doing research," I told her.

"Well, you completely blew me off for your hand-to-hand training," she said.

"Geez, what's got you so spun up? Did Ethan's visit wear off already?"

She gave me a really cross look. "Well, snarkety-snark-snark. Never mind that, sassy. Why haven't you returned any of my texts this afternoon?" she demanded. "I had to call Roman just to get your attention."

"God, what are you, my Mom now?" I shot back; removing my old cell phone from its holder and flipping open the lid.

As was the case so often recently, the battery was dead.

"Crap. And I only made one phone call this afternoon," I said. "This thing's been running dry faster and faster over the past few weeks."

As she snatched the phone from my hand, I saw Roman making a discreet exit upstairs.

Lucky bastard.

"They probably don't even make batteries for these anymore. Honestly, grandpa, how old is this stupid relic?" she asked. "I mean, I know you're a history buff and all but there's no reason to carry around a piece of junk like this."

I gave her my best 'go to hell' look.

"And who still carries a flip phone around? I don't think you can even get Internet access on this model," she said.

"You need a smartphone like mine, or at the very least something built in the past decade."

"My iPad has Internet access through a provider," I said. "Besides, smartphones are still kinda' expensive. I only need a phone to make phone calls, and maybe a text now and again."

Her resulting deadpan stare was slightly unnerving.

"What?" I asked.

She casually flipped open my cell phone and flicked at the screen with the tip of her finger. The ensuing cracking sound sent a shiver down my spine.

I grabbed the phone from her.

"What did you do!" I demanded, examining the shattered display.

"Looks like your old cell phone broke, kiddo," she said in a matter-of-fact tone. "We'd better go get you a new one."

"You broke my friggin' phone!" I said. "You're such an *ass* sometimes!"

I was furious as she zipped around the living room in a flurry of movement. The next thing I knew my leather jacket was draped over my head.

"C'mon, the sun just set. Let's bring you into the twenty-first century, old timer," she said.

We left Roman at home and she drove us to a nearby AT&T store in her new cherry red BMW convertible.

"Stop moping," she said. "You're gonna' thank me for this later."

"Whatever. And when do I get to drive the car?" I asked.

"Ha. Never," she responded, pulling into the parking lot.

We browsed the selection of phones until a sales associate named Len assisted us.

"I just need the lowest end---" I started to say.

"He needs the latest Apple iPhone; whichever model has the most memory and preferably in black," Paige interrupted. "Oh, and be sure to add the maximum text and data plan, unlimited, if possible."

I tried to get a word in edgewise, but she interrupted me again.

"Let's see…accessories…he'll need two chargers, a belt carrier, and ear buds. Also, he'll be closing his current account and merging onto his fiancée's plan," she said sweetly.

My eyes bugged out and I pulled at the sleeve of her leather jacket.

"Paige. Fiancée?"

"Red'll be fine with it," she told me.

She swatted at my hand and cast a movie star worthy smile at the associate, who pointedly ignored me. He appeared much happier at being the center of her attentions.

"I'm only too happy to help. I need to enter this into the system and I'll be right back with you," Len said, clearly smitten with her. "Would you like bottled water or maybe a soda while you wait?"

"Sure, I'd love one," she said with a gleam in her eyes.

Len hurried away on his mission as I scanned the store and then stared at Paige.

"They give bottled water and soda away here?" I asked.

"Who knows," she said with a slight shrug. "Nice staff here, though."

"And what's with putting me on Kat's plan?" I asked.

"Aw, keep your shirt on," she said. "She'll be so flattered she won't even think twice."

Great; yet another facet of my independence absorbed into the vampire collective.

Bottled water was quickly provided to Paige by the young man, though I noticed I wasn't asked about one.

Oh, brother, the effect she has on people sometimes…

We wandered around the store, and I paused to gaze outside through the storefront glass. Under the glow of a street lamp on the other side of the boulevard, I caught sight of one of the pasty-faced men I'd seen outside the bar the other night.

The man was exiting a small shop while talking on his cell phone, and he appeared agitated.

"There's one of those guys," I said.

I looked around, only to see Paige on the other side of the room.

"Paige," I called.

She frowned and quickly made her way over to me, but once I looked back outside, the guy was nowhere to be seen.

"What?" she asked.

"It's one of those guys Roman and I saw outside the bar last night," I said. "He came out of that shop over there."

"Did you see where he went?"

"No, I was *trying* to get your attention."

We were interrupted by Len's nervous-sounding voice over at the main counter. He was talking on the phone to someone.

"The manager? Oh, yes, ma'am. Wha---? Right away, ma'am," he said in a concerned tone.

He immediately sought out the manager. "Mr. Spalding? This lady, Ms. Rawlings, asked to speak with you."

"What's the matter, Kevin?" the manager asked, taking the phone from him.

"Oh, this should be fun," Paige murmured.

I frowned.

"Hello, Ms. Rawlings, I presume? I'm Glen Spalding, the manager, and we're trying—" he said, glancing in our direction. "Why, yes, he's standing directly across the room from me, along with a short, blonde-haired young lady... Oh, yes? Well, this is highly irregular; we typically require the account holder's signature and—"

Glen's eyes widened and he almost came to stand at quasi-attention as his grip visibly tightened around the handset. "Yes, ma'am, I understand entirely, but— No, there's no need to contact the district office. Surely we can— Oh, yes, a fax request with a copy of your ID would be more than fine, I'm sure," he stammered. "I do apologize for the inconvenience, Ms. Rawlings. We'll have this ready for him immediately."

"I knew I'd love this," Paige said with snicker.

I jabbed her in the ribs with my index finger.

"Troublemaker."

"Stop poking me," she said, swatting at my hand.

The manager's facial expression appeared strained, as if he'd rather be anywhere else but on the phone at that moment.

"Ms. Rawlings, would you like to speak with your fiancé?" he asked. "Oh, no, I merely— Yes, ma'am, I'm right on it; this should take only a few minutes. Thank you, Ms. Rawlings."

The man swallowed hard as he hung up the phone and sharply glanced in the direction of our associate.

"Len, gather the merchandise *right now*," he snapped. "I'll enter this myself."

"Kat didn't want to talk to me," I said, feeling somewhat disappointed.

"Ah, she was probably just busy," Paige said. "But did you see that guy's face? Priceless!"

I gave her a withering look.

Less than twenty minutes later, I walked out with Apple's newest smartphone and a bagful of accessories.

I sent my first text to Kat: *Luv U. Thanks bunches, Kat.*

She quickly replied: *Anytime, my love :)*

I felt somewhat better about the entire affair; that was, until I got home and had to manually program my phone with all my old contacts information. My phone had been too outdated for their transfer process.

It was a real pain, to say the least.

CHAPTER 24

Caleb

A few days passed before I heard back from Gregory Hess.

I was pleased that he thought my idea had merit, though the prospective costs of pursuing the project further were higher than I'd expected.

Unfortunately, I needed additional resources that were way outside the capacity of my personal savings account.

I didn't dare call Kat; she'd ask too many questions, and might even try to talk me out of the venture. And there was no way I'd ask Paige for money.

However, there was the unexpected investment from my Slovenia trip that Alton invested.

I stepped out onto the front porch and dialed my new smartphone.

"Hello, dear boy," Alton answered. "Is everything okay?"

"Oh, absolutely. Everything's fine," I said. "I'm calling to ask a favor of you, but first, I need to ask if we can keep this just between us for now."

There was a silent pause.

"That's a tall order, given how sensitive Katrina is regarding your activities," he said in a guarded tone.

"Uh, yeah. Well, I'm concerned that, if my idea doesn't

work out, she might be disappointed in me."

"Then perhaps you should reconsider your options," he said.

I winced. "Alton, *to be brutally honest*, I really need your support for this to work. I need for you to liquidate some— well, most—of my funds that you're managing."

"Whatever for?" he asked. "Those funds are intended for securing your financial future."

"Yes, I know, but I'm examining some potentially ground-breaking research on a subject of personal interest," I said vaguely. "I've researched this, and I have it on very reliable authority that my venture has a high prospect for success."

"Is this a profit-making venture of some sort?" he asked.

This is so much harder than I imagined it would be.

"I suppose there's the potential for that," I said. "However, this would actually be more of a beneficial step forward for me personally. It would mean a great deal to me to pursue this."

Seconds passed as I waited with crossed fingers.

Why do I feel like I'm begging my dad for money?

Hell, my real rat-bastard of a father wouldn't even have had a dime to offer me after spending it on booze.

Stop. Don't think about him.

Just as I was ready to give up hope, Alton said, "Very well, Caleb. I trust your instincts on this, but I hope you're approaching this carefully and with a high degree of scrutiny."

"Thanks, uncle," I said, enjoying the use of that word. "I am. And this means a lot to me."

"You're welcome," he said. "I hope all goes well. Let me know where you'd like the funds transferred to, and I'll see to it."

"Oh, and about Kat?" I asked.

"For now, we'll keep this between us," he said.

I let out a breath I didn't realize I'd been holding.

"Thanks, Alton," I replied.

We visited a short time longer about my research into

Oliver Simonson's background, but he failed to reveal why it was so important for me to use him as the focus for my dissertation.

An unimaginable amount of work went into a dissertation, and I challenged how little information might be available on Simonson to justify the effort. However, rather than be deterred, his enthusiasm for everything seemed to increase slightly.

This fellow better be worth all my research efforts.

After I got off the phone, I scheduled a meeting with Professor Gowan for that Friday afternoon to discuss the matter further. However, I had a suspicious feeling that Alton had already laid the groundwork for the project.

Before I knew it, the week had passed and it was Friday. By the end of my meeting with Gowan that afternoon, he'd asked me to write up an official proposal for him.

Just great, that had to be the fastest dissertation subject selection in Yale's history!

Throughout the weekend and the following week, I was a complete grouch. The weekend came and went without a call from Kat, though a text to Alton resulted in his assurances that all was well. He said that she was merely extremely busy.

Too busy for me?

By Tuesday, the brief fifteen-minute chat she and I had that afternoon seemed like little more than a token gesture.

At least I knew she was okay.

Meanwhile, my life was a boring repetition of exercising or training, reading, writing, attending classes, and generally drowning in my own self-pity.

Wednesday evening, after Roman went off duty and left the house for an evening out, I crashed on the couch with a bowl of popcorn to watch a horror movie festival on the super-sized television mounted on the wall.

Just as Freddy Krueger was about to nab another victim, Paige grabbed my shoulders from behind and I lurched forward, flinging popcorn everywhere.

"You turd!" I shouted.

I grabbed her by one arm and her upper body and pulled her over the back of the couch to land beside me.

She laughed and her hands darted to my ribs. I nearly went crazy as she tickled me, flailing around and vainly trying to push her away.

"Stop it!" I yelled.

In a last ditch effort before losing my breath entirely, I flipped her body with one arm and tried to pin her body against the couch cushions.

She abruptly stopped tickling me, our faces only inches apart, and she stared at me in a penetrating fashion.

Her blue eyes were beautiful.

In that moment, I felt drawn to her, and I smelled the scent of bubblegum as I felt her warm breath against my face.

Maybe it was the adrenaline, but a wave of desire rushed through my body as I stared into her eyes. I felt one of her hands slowly creep up my back while the other encircled the back of my head.

That's when her face started moving closer to mine.

Danger!

I lurched backward out of her grasp, even as she rolled off the couch away from me.

"Yeah, uh, better get this mess cleaned up," she stammered, looking anywhere around the room except at me.

"Yep, I'll get a trash bag," I said, quickly retreating to the kitchen.

I paused long enough to send a quick text message to Ethan. *Hey, Ethan. Paige misses you 2 much. Try a surprise visit soon. Take care.*

I took a deep breath and a few swigs from a fresh cold beer out of the fridge before returning to the living room with the trash bag.

As I walked into the room, I noticed her slipping her phone into her back pocket.

We both avoided looking at each other while picking up popcorn from the floor.

What the hell was I thinking?
Sheesh, I miss Kat.

* * *

While on campus that Friday morning, I ran into Chance, well, by chance. Just as I was enjoying a nice chat with her in the commons outside, I was interrupted by a text message from Roman.

Two targets nearby. Enter nearest bldg and wait.

I diplomatically told her that I had to get going.

I didn't want any innocents getting hurt on my account.

"No problem. Hey, how would you like to get together at a place called Carlucci's Restaurant?" she asked. "It's over on Wooster Street."

I shrugged. "Sure, sounds like fun."

"Great, be there around 8 p.m.," she said. "See you then."

"Later," I said as I walked away.

"Oh, and ask for Chance's table," she said.

I nodded and quickly entered the nearest building; the Yale University Art Gallery.

Within ten minutes, Roman appeared with a concerned expression on his face.

"What happened?" I asked.

He shrugged. "Both those guys took off in different directions as soon as you entered the building."

"Did you get a good look at them?"

"Just a glimpse," he said. "Couple of pasty-faced thugs."

"Pasty-faced?" I asked.

"Yeah, well, they're not vampires, being outside in the daylight like they were," he said. "But they were mighty white."

"Maybe the two guys we saw outside the bar that night?" I asked.

He shrugged. "Could've been, but I can't say for certain."

That evening, I went to Carlucci's, though not without Paige for an escort.

"You want to be my plus-one?" I asked.

"Are you kidding? What sister wants to hang around with his brother and all his nerdy friends?" she asked.

"Angelina Jolie did with her brother," I said.

She adopted a sour expression. "Ew, let's not go there. I'll wait around out here. Text me if something suspicious happens. I'll text you now and again, just to check in."

I went inside and asked for Chance's table, and I was a little surprised when I was led to a candlelit table for two.

Chance looked up with a smile. "You made it."

I sat down and looked around. "I thought we were meeting the gang here."

"Nope, just you and me tonight," she said.

Warning bells went off in my head all at once.

"You know, Chance, I should tell you I'm in a committed relationship," I said. "Katrina and I are a couple."

"Oh sure," she said. "No pressure. I just thought it'd be cool to get to know each other better."

I nodded. "Sure, no problem."

I didn't want to sound rude, but I wasn't on the market, so to speak. At least I'd made my relationship with Kat clear to her.

At first, we visited about typical things, such as her college classes and professors. Then the topic of family came up, and I told her that my parents had both passed away; carefully avoiding any details.

"So, what about your family? Do you have any brothers or sisters?" I asked.

She shook her head. "I'm an only child," she said. "My mom's a former fashion model who's now a full-time shopaholic. She even posed for Vogue for a time."

"And your dad?" I asked.

She shrugged as she picked at her salad. "Dad's always on the go; business ventures and deal-making are his thing."

"When we first met, you said something about your dad

being the gambler in the family," I said.

"Oh, yeah," she said. "Well, when he's not turning a business deal, he likes a good horse race or casino."

"Is that how you got the name Chance?"

"Actually, Chance was my mom's idea," she said. "She said she wasn't sure if she could conceive children due to an operation she had when she was younger. I was the 'chance' they had to have a baby."

"Cute," I said. "So, your dad's not a bookie or anything, then?"

"Dad? Nah, he just likes the thrill of gambling," she said. "I mean, he's not in any debt or anything. In fact, he comes out on top more often than not. No, he's all about building the company or investing in the next new venture. But, much like his gambling hobby, he's been pretty successful overall."

Enviable.

"I'm not much of a gambler, myself," she added.

"Me either," I said. "Although I won a hundred dollars once playing the Georgia Lottery."

"Ha! I bet the IRS was knocking on your door," she said.

"Yeah, well, that's my only big win," I said. "So, I bet your parents are really proud to have a daughter who's going to Yale."

She appeared reflective. "Mom's very proud, but dad wanted me to go to the University of Pennsylvania instead. We're from Philly and he wanted me closer to home. He's so overprotective. Mom's more of a 'go see the world' kind of person."

"I guess that makes sense. You're their only child, after all," I said.

I almost made the mistake of telling her I was an only child too, but I caught myself.

"Sometimes I wished I had a brother or sister," she said. "At least you have a sister."

"Yep, Paige and I are quite a pair," I said.

If you only knew.

"And your girlfriend, you mentioned she's in Europe?"

she asked.

"Kat's doing some corporate consulting over there," I said.

"What kind of consulting?" she asked.

"Um, strategic planning and restructuring," I said. "Stuff like that."

"I'm sure you miss her very much," she said with a penetrating look on her face.

"Oh, absolutely," I said. "I can't wait until we're able to see each other again. Hopefully, sometime soon."

Fortunately, the conversation turned to less sensitive topics after that.

In the end, the food was great and we had a good time talking. Chance seemed really sweet, in fact.

We said goodbye outside the restaurant, and she offered to give me a ride home, but I politely declined, which must've seemed strange given the cold dampness and a brisk northerly breeze that evening.

"Nice night for a walk," I said.

"Yeah, if you're a vampire," she said.

My eyes locked onto hers and I tried my best to sound clever. "Or a werewolf?"

"Exactly," she said. "Zombies don't care, either."

I watched her walk to her car, no less than a silver Lexus sport coupe that looked almost new.

I whistled. "Whoa, what a car."

After making my way through the parking lot and out onto the sidewalk, I heard rapid footsteps behind me.

I turned just in time to see Paige fall in step beside me.

"You sure the car is all you were whistling at?" she asked with an edge to her voice.

"What? You're kidding, right?"

"I'm just askin'," she said.

"Yeah, right," I said. "As if she's any comparison to Kat."

"Yeah, well, I've got my eye on her," she cautioned. "And hey, what's with the cozy little table for two? I thought you said you were meeting 'some people' here."

I gave her a cross sidelong glance. "Hey, don't make this about me. I thought I was meeting a group, too, you know. She said it was a get together."

"Mm-hm," she said.

I scoffed aloud. "Come on, I wasn't going to be rude. And I told her right off that I was in a committed relationship."

"You want to know what I think?" she asked.

"No," I said.

She flicked at the edge of my ear with her finger.

"Ow!"

"I think spoiled little rich girl doesn't care about that," she said.

"She never said she was rich," I said.

I don't know why I suddenly felt so defensive.

"A jobless freshman driving a *Lexus sports car*?" she asked.

I gave her a sharp look. "I'm pretty sure I never told you she was jobless. Are you spying on me and my friends now?"

"I'm your surrogate vampire, kiddo," she said. "Of course I *spy* on you...and around you...and on those around you. You have a tendency to get into a lot of trouble on your own, you know."

I shrugged. "Whatever."

"Now, *you*; you're a freakin' full-time job," she said. "I don't even have time to study."

"Yeah, right," I said. "As if you study anyway."

"Good point, professor nerdo," she said. "Speaking of which, would you mind writing a short history essay for me? Nothing fancy; I don't use a lot of big words."

"Oh, sure," I said. "*Not!*"

"Well, snarkety-snark-snark-snarkety-snark," she chimed.

"Way too many snarks in there," I said.

"Nah," she disagreed. "I'm a vision of perfect snarkiness."

"Stop saying snark!" I complained. "What's with all the

snarking lately?"

"People love my snarking," she said. "And pick up the pace, slowpoke, I've got a stupid history paper to write when we get home."

Holy crap, Paige drives me crazy sometimes.

Then I smiled.

But I adore her.

As we walked home, I tried not to think too hard about Chance. Still, she'd surprised me a little bit with the impromptu dinner for two.

Damn, between Roman and vampires, they're making me paranoid.

* * *

By late Saturday afternoon, I felt worn out from a long day of writing papers for classes and engaging in an extra session of combat training with both Paige and Roman. However, my mood improved somewhat following a long video chat with Kat.

On Saturday evening, I met a group of my friends at Prime Time, a popular pub with the college crowd over on Temple Street. It felt soothing just to unwind over a few beers.

Following some early challenging weeks at Yale, I grew more comfortable immersing myself into the college scene again, though I had to admit I felt a lot older than I'd remembered from my days at Georgia State.

Felt? Hell, I am a lot older.

Yet, despite my age differences, for perhaps the first time since my arrival I was finally starting to feel settled about being in New Haven.

Even Roman had grown on me.

I glanced up to see Paige confidently striding through the pub, acting like she owned the place.

In the short time we'd been hanging out there, she'd managed to catch the eye of most men, and some women, who frequented the place.

She was a social creature of historic proportions.

"Hey, there's a hot piece," Joshua said to Anthony with a grin as Paige caught his eye.

I noticed Paige's telltale smirk as she glanced over at our table while swaying to Django Django's "Default."

"Serve me up for some of that," responded Anthony.

Trey shook his head at me. "You gonna' tell 'em about her, or should I?"

I shrugged.

"*Hello*, and thanks for talking about women like we're menu items," Lillian said to Joshua.

"Yeah, you two are such pigs," Olivia added, giving both Joshua and Anthony a sour look. "What're you, like fifteen?"

Olivia was a fellow grad student and a regular in our group. I admired her boldness in never hesitating to call us out when she felt the need.

Despite that, everyone at our table watched as Paige danced over to our table in alluring fashion.

Wow, I've seen professional dancers perform with a helluva' lot less skill than Paige does.

Then I recalled that she'd been a dancer before she became a vampire.

In the 1920s, no less; a flapper girl.

"Howdy, study hounds," Paige said, flashing a Hollywood worthy smile.

"Hey there," Joshua said with a self-assured grin. "I'm Joshua."

Lillian and Olivia both groaned, resulting in a massive blush from the young man.

"Everyone, this is my sister, Paige," I said.

The resulting shocked faces around the table were priceless.

"No way," Olivia said. "We've seen her in here like a dozen times, Taylor, and you've never thought to mention that before?"

"She's a *freshman* over at Gateway Community College," I

said.

Paige gave me a withering look.

However, I was more interested in the wide-eyed looks that continued around our table.

Unlike the others, Chance frowned. "*You're* Paige?"

"In the flesh, little chicky," Paige said with an elaborate flourish of her hand.

"Seriously, Caleb? She's your *sister*?" Anthony asked.

Paige winked at him before focusing her full attention upon me. "Brother, are you ever in trouble," she said with a wicked-looking expression.

Wasting no time, she reached down to snatch my glass of beer and took a long swig that nearly drained it.

She returned my near-empty glass to the table with a thump, and leaned down close to my ear and whispered, "Snarkety-snark."

"Again with the snarking?" I asked.

"Thanks for the drink, *brother*," she said, her hot breath against my ear. "Although you're probably going to need it more than I did, tiger."

I frowned.

But before I could inquire further, she offered a slight wave to everyone and danced her way over to the other side of the bar where a couple of fellows were playing pool.

Trey looked at me with an astonished expression. "Dude, my sister never does that with me."

"She's more of a half-sister, really," I said.

"What was that all about?" Olivia asked.

"Aw, you never know with her," I said. "I think she's in an awnry mood tonight."

The truth was I was curious about Paige's behavior, as well.

I signaled to a passing waitress for a fresh beer and fielded a host of questions about Paige from Trey, Joshua, and Anthony.

"Guys, she seeing somebody," I said.

"Like somebody here in New Haven?" Joshua asked.

"No, Ethan's a doctor back in Atlanta," I said. "We're only here in New Haven for spring and fall semesters."

"A doctor? She dates a *doctor*?" Chance asked.

"Yeah, why?" I asked, as our waitress delivered fresh drinks to our table.

I noticed that even Olivia stared at Chance with a curious expression.

"Hey, sorry, no offense. Just asking," Chance said defensively.

I took a swig of my fresh beer.

That's when I saw one of those guys from the parking lot outside of Yalehoos standing near the bar. He glanced over at our table a couple of times before engaging the bartender in conversation.

I looked over at Paige to get her attention, but she was busy playing pool with some people on the other side of the main room.

However, when I looked back at the bar, the fellow was gone. I scanned the room twice but didn't see him anywhere.

Not for the first time, it seemed as if there was something familiar-looking about the guy, but I couldn't quite place it.

"Caleb?" asked Trey. "Man, everything okay?"

Everyone at our table had ceased talking and was staring at me.

"What? Yeah, I'm good," I said. "Did I miss something?"

"Yeah," said Anthony. "I was trying to get your attention. My brother said he should have something for you in the next couple of weeks or so."

"Really? That's great," I said.

Wow, that was fast. Maybe that's a good sign my idea was a viable one.

"What something? Is it a secret project sort-of-something?" Trey asked.

"Nah, just a small something," I said. "More of an experiment, really."

Thankfully, Anthony let the topic drop and the conversation returned to various professors that were either liked or avoided.

As The Black Keys' "Howlin' for You" began to play, I looked around the room again, hoping to catch a glimpse of the fellow I'd seen earlier.

My breath caught in my throat as Kat stood just inside the entry area, scanning the room like a predator selecting her next prey.

She looked so sexy in a fitted dress and black leather boots, and I felt intense desire rush through my body at the sight of her.

But there was something different about her too; something harder, edgier than when I'd last seen her.

Her eyes flashed bright green as they settled upon me and she slowly made her way to our table.

She stopped directly beside my chair and I started to get up, but she held up her hand in a halting motion. Then she bent down to kiss me warmly on the lips.

"Surprise," she whispered.

Despite my surprise, I felt a renewed rush of desire wash over me.

She stood beside me scanning the faces of my tablemates. Everyone's eyes were locked upon her, including the ladies present.

"Everybody, I'm proud to introduce you to my girlfriend, Katrina," I said.

I fumbled for a title, almost referring to her as my mate; that would've generated a lot of odd looks and questions.

Kat gave the cutest half-wave. "Hi, everyone."

At first everybody remained silent. Then they muttered various polite greetings.

I was so shocked; I didn't know what else to say. I was just overwhelmed with joy to see her.

And I wanted to have sex with her right there on the spot.

"To be honest, we all started to wonder if you were real

or not," Chance said.

"Oh, I'm quite real," Kat said while appearing to closely study Chance.

"Way real," Trey muttered.

"Twin revelations, and all in one night," Chance said. "Imagine the odds."

I narrowed my eyes at her.

"Well, it was nice to meet each of you," Kat said, though her eyes lingered on Chance briefly before sweeping back to me.

She reached out with one hand to caress the side of my cheek with her fingernails while staring down into my eyes. "Honey, I'm home," she said.

Then she turned and walked toward the exit.

She's leaving?

I started to say something, but words failed me.

It was as if I was nailed to my chair as I watched her exit.

"Is it just me, or is it hot in here?" Anthony asked.

Chance looked at me with a really peculiar expression and then watched Katrina walk away.

Paige stepped into my field of vision with a tight-lipped expression and motioned with a jerk of her head toward the exit.

Thankfully, my brain finally kicked into gear again.

"Gotta' run," I said while scrambling up from my chair and fumbling with my wallet to fish out some money for my drinks.

"Jesus, Taylor," Lillian said. "I'm straight and I'm going to beat you to the door!"

"Just go!" Olivia exclaimed, shooing her hands in my direction.

I grabbed my leather jacket and practically tripped over Trey's chair as I bounded for the exit.

"Told ya'," Paige said as I bolted past her. "Snarkety-snark!"

Once I made it outside the pub, I scanned the parking lot, but didn't see Kat anywhere.

I rushed out toward the street and looked up and down both lengths of the sidewalk. Again, no Kat.

It took a second to get my bearings, and then I walked at a fast pace down the sidewalk along Temple Street toward Trumbull in the direction of our house, located on Lincoln.

As I approached Trumbull, a figure appeared out of the shadows nearby.

I quickly turned to confront the person.

It was Kat.

She slyly smiled. "Miss me?"

I reached out to pull her against me, crushing my lips against hers in a passionate kiss.

Time seemed suspended as I held her tightly in my arms, kissing her.

"I missed you so much," I said between kisses.

"I missed you too, my love," she said.

She gave me another kiss before separating from me slightly. Reaching down to take my hand in hers, we briskly walked together in the direction of the house.

I scarcely recalled the distance from the front door to our bedroom. Mere seconds after I kicked the bedroom door closed, our clothes were shed.

Soon, our bodies were intertwined on the bed together amidst a flurry of passionate kisses.

Then time stood still.

CHAPTER 25

Caleb

When I awoke, one of Kat's legs and arms were lazily draped across my body, and she was eerily still.

I got the distinct impression she was asleep, in fact.

However, as soon as I moved slightly, she lifted her head up from the pillow; her sharp eyes targeting mine.

"Good morning, my love," she said.

"Sleeping?" I asked.

"Dozing," she said, and then softly kissed me.

"I'm so happy you're here," I told her.

"And I'm happy you're happy," she said. "By the expression on your face last night, I definitely surprised you."

I chuckled. "You could say that."

She gave me a quick kiss on the lips.

"We've got a lot to catch up on," she said. "But first, I'd like to know more about these two men who you've been running into around town."

I repressed a sigh. *Security-related talk already?*

"They seemed really odd. I wish I had more to tell you," I said. "You may want to speak to Roman."

"I already did," she said. "But I will again."

"So, how are things in London?" I asked.

"Oh, you know, just boring vampire politics," she said.

"But I didn't come all the way here for vampire shop talk. I'm on holiday."

"You're even beginning to sound British," I said.

While it was amazing to have her lying next to me, it bothered me she wouldn't talk about what was going on overseas. And I knew better than most that vampire politics were rarely boring; usually deadly.

"I was originally English, you know," she said.

She lay her head back down and began nuzzling my neck, which tickled slightly.

"Well, as much as I'd like to stay, I better get up. I've got class in little over an hour," I said, stifling a yawn.

Her fangs extended against the skin of my neck.

"Not quite," she said. "I haven't finished with you yet."

I froze. "I see somebody's feeling particularly feral this morning."

Her soft lips sealed against my neck and I felt her silky tongue press to my skin. The telltale feeling of numbness quickly formed around the affected area.

Moments later, she made a pleasurable sound, almost a growl, and I felt a dull sensation as her fangs extended into me.

Soon, I heard the suckling sounds of her drinking from me as she caressed her fingernails across my chest.

She hadn't taken blood from me since before I arrived in New Haven.

I lay back, closed my eyes, and drifted on a sea of soothing contentment.

This was something of myself that I could freely offer her; something to convey my love and commitment to her.

Later, after a quick shower, I went downstairs, and caught a glimpse of Kat perched on a stool at the breakfast counter conversing with Paige with a very serious expression on her face; hard and stony.

Kat often confided things in Paige; things she didn't want me having any part in. It only made my curiosity about events in London all the more pointed.

However, she quickly noticed my presence and her expression transformed into a welcoming, pleasant visage.

After a quick kiss and a promise from her not to leave town abruptly without saying goodbye, I headed to class with Roman in tow.

My mood was vastly improved from recent weeks, and the day seemed to pass more quickly than normal.

For once, life felt more as it should.

It was the closest I had felt to normal, and happy, in quite some time.

Kat only stayed for three days, but they were three absolutely enjoyable days. It was how I would've preferred my entire experience in New Haven and Yale to be.

It felt complete.

However, at the end of those three days, Kat left for the airport and her absence once again felt stark to me.

My life in New Haven felt incomplete yet again.

Still, I had needed the quality time with her, however brief.

I think she felt the same, too.

During her brief stay, I noted occasions where she seemed stoic and guarded.

I sensed that her time in London was changing her, and I hoped it wouldn't be for the worse.

As with so many things, time would tell.

* * *

The days seemed to drag on after Kat left. I was also dismayed that, despite her assurances before her departure, she didn't stay in regular contact with me for very long.

Oh, I received an occasional text now and again, but our phone calls were infrequent. It wasn't uncommon to go many days in a row without actually talking to her.

That bothered me.

About three weeks after Kat left, I received a box from Benton Technologies. It was from Anthony's brother,

Gregory.

A simple handwritten note left inside the box said:

Caleb,

I hope you like the prototypes I shipped to you. This was a lot of fun and a real challenge. There are still some things we need to iron out, but let me know what you think.
Then we'll know where to go from here...

Gregory

I unpacked the box's contents with the excitement of a child on Christmas morning. Within minutes, I was giddy with enthusiasm.

Gregory, you rock, my friend.

However, I kept silent about it for the time being; at least until I felt the time was right. Besides, there were still those issues left to work out that Gregory had alluded to; topics I discussed at length with him during the following week.

* * *

Two weeks later, early on a Thursday evening, Roman and I had no sooner walked through the front door at the house when, to my surprise, I saw Alton sitting at the kitchen counter talking to Paige.

"Alton?" I asked.

"Caleb, Mr. Lee," he said rising to stand.

"Mr. Rutherford," Roman said with a nod.

"Roman, Paige tells me you've been doing an admirable job here," Alton said.

"Thank you. My pleasure to be of service, sir," he replied.

"I appreciate that very much. Why don't you take the rest of the evening off?" Alton said. "Caleb and I are going to spend some time together."

"Yes, sir," Roman said. "Thank you, sir."

Wasting no time, like a soldier who'd been dismissed, he quickly proceeded upstairs.

"I'm glad I could surprise you, dear boy," Alton said, focusing his attention upon me.

"Oh, I've learned you're always full of surprises," I said.

Paige laughed aloud and Alton gave her a disparaging look.

"Is Kat here, too?" I asked.

"She's still in London, I'm afraid," he replied.

Something in the way he said that didn't sound particularly settling.

"Is she okay? Has something happened?" I asked, a feeling of dread rising in my chest.

"She's fine," he said with a casual wave of his hand. "But let's you and I take a walk. There are some things we need to discuss."

Paige maintained a neutral expression as my sense of curiosity increased.

It was a cool evening; the air was crisp and held the nostalgic scent of burned wood from nearby fireplaces.

We walked down Trumbull, chatting about how the weather compared between New Haven in London. As we strolled onto Yale's campus, the glow from streetlights overhead brought the rich colors of fall leaves to life around us.

Yale hosted such beautiful campus grounds.

We stopped to sit on a wooden bench in the midst of the beautiful, park-like area. Alton casually folded his arms before him and stared across the grounds.

"So, what brings you to town?" I asked. "London's a bit far away for a quick trip just to see me."

"True enough, I suppose. As it happens, I was on the east coast on other business, so I thought it would be nice to drop in and say hello," he said.

"I'm glad. It's always good to see you, Alton," I said.

His arm extended across the back of the bench behind

my shoulders. "I do enjoy our chats, Caleb. I wish I could visit more frequently."

I studied his features as he stared directly ahead of him.

"How's college coming along?" he asked.

"Great. I'm settling in here, and I like my doctoral program so far; although you insisted upon a particularly challenging subject for my dissertation."

"Do you need some assistance getting started?" he asked.

"Like I said, it's challenging but nothing I can't handle," I said.

"Good, good," he pleasantly said. "I never doubted your potential for success."

"I'd like to know why him; why Oliver Simonson?" I asked.

"First, tell me what you've learned about him so far," he said.

I explained that research materials still hadn't fully arrived from the interlibrary loan process. However, I was able to discover that Simonson worked alongside his father in Union hospitals during the American Civil War where he became interested in phlebotomy.

"I'm not sure why he found blood so interesting," I said.

"Ah, more to the point, the Ancient Art of Bloodletting," Alton said.

What?

"I still haven't researched phlebotomy yet," I said.

"Sorry, spoiler," he said. "Do go on."

"Well, Simonson completed advanced medical degrees from the University of Pennsylvania School of Medicine, and then traveled to Europe to study under leading physicians," I said. "So far, it all seems kinda' unremarkable."

"Do you recall when we flew to New Haven for your meeting with Dean Eddings?" Alton asked.

"How could I forget?" I countered.

"Do you remember what I said to Eddings about Professor Gowan?" he asked.

Why does everything have to be so cryptic with Alton? Couldn't he just tell me straight out and be done with it?

I searched my memory. "I don't know; something about the Enlightenment period, I think."

"Correct," he said. "Dr. Gowan specializes in the American and European Enlightenment period. At one of his lectures that I attended, he spoke about the early scientific contributions of Dr. Hugh Simonson, Oliver's father, as an Enlightenment figure and his early medical research into human diseases."

"Okay, so why aren't I studying Hugh instead of Oliver?" I asked.

"Because Oliver took some of his father's research and advanced it in remarkable ways for the late 1800s," Alton said. "And I believe there's much there worthy of delving into. You've only reached the tip of the iceberg."

"Look, you apparently already know way more about this than I do," I said. "Why don't you do the research?"

"Because you need a dissertation topic; one that hasn't been overdone again and again. You need something unique," he said. "And frankly, I don't have the spare time to delve further. I need someone like you, someone who has a sharp mind and enjoys historical research, to find out what I need to know more about."

"Okay, that all makes sense, I suppose," I said. "Then why didn't you just tell me that to begin with?"

He turned to look at me. "Because I needed to see if you had an aptitude for this sort of thing, dear boy."

I stared at him.

"And you do," he said. "So, carry on with that, and call me from time to time on your progress."

"I could simply email you," I said.

"I'd rather you didn't," he said. "It's not terribly secure, and I'd rather that prying eyes were kept at bay for now."

That seemed strange. Who would even care about some obscure physician from the 1800s?

"So, this is why you flew out to see me?" I asked.

"Can't an uncle stop by to visit his nephew from time to

time when he's on the same continent?" he asked.

I shrugged. "Of course."

Then an important topic triggered in my mind; one that I'd given a great deal of thought to in recent weeks.

"I hope you realize how very grateful I am to you for all of this; even more than that, actually. I mean, I know Kat's paying for my room and board, but it's you that's paid for my education here, as well as practically assured my acceptance into the program."

He used his arm across my shoulders to pull me into a momentary hug, our shoulders pressing against each other. "You're quite welcome, dear boy. I'm just happy to be of assistance."

"Still, my time here serves a dual purpose for you, doesn't it?"

He sharply glanced at me. "Really? How so?"

"You need Kat to handle things in Europe for you, though I still have no specifics what those *things* might be. And you realize she's less likely to help unless I'm safely preoccupied elsewhere," I said.

I watched as the corners of his mouth upturned slightly. "You're a very perceptive young man," he said. "However, my motives are not entirely calculated. I do want to assist in your endeavor to regain a professorial position, and your being here is an important part of that goal."

That's nice to know.

"But you're also correct; Katrina was more agreeable to assisting me once you were busy with college. Suffice to say, this serves each of us in useful ways in the end," he said.

We sat in silence for a few minutes.

"There's something else I'd like to talk to you about," he said.

"Okay."

"I've noticed Katrina has been burying herself in her endeavors, which I appreciate for the most part," he said. "But I'm growing concerned. How are the two of you getting along? It must be difficult for you, being so displaced from each other at length."

"Funny you should mention that," I said. "I noticed she became awfully distant after her last visit here. At first, I thought she was just busy, but I'm starting to wonder…"

"Yes?" he asked as he stared into my eyes.

"Well, this is probably just me being overly sensitive," I said. "It's like she's pulling away from me or something."

"Ah," he said, maintaining what I could only describe as a poker face.

"When she was here a few weeks ago, I caught moments, glimpses really, when she seemed sort of colder, more distant," I said.

It was hard to put into words, but I'd definitely felt it.

"I thought perhaps that was the case," he said.

"What? So, you've noticed something?" I asked.

"Marla picked up on first, actually," he said. "But once I took more notice, I had to concur."

Okay, that really bothered me.

"What do you mean?" I asked.

"She's overworking herself, I think," he said. "I need her to be at her sharpest, but she can't do that if she's obsessing. It's dangerous, in fact."

"Okay, now you're worrying me. What can we do about it?"

He appeared introspective, almost thoughtful, as he stared back at me. "How do you feel about coming to London?"

Wasn't that what I asked to do in the first place back in Atlanta?

"I've mentioned that, but she either changes the subject or says 'maybe sometime later' or asks me to be patient a little bit longer," I said. "It sort of pisses me off."

He arched one of his eyebrows at me, almost similar to the way Kat did at times.

I nearly laughed over the similarity. "It's really starting to bother me."

"Colleges still have periodic breaks, don't they?" he asked in an odd tone, as if it were the most foreign of topics to him.

"Yeah. Fall break's coming up next week, in fact," I said. "It only lasts four days, though."

"That should be sufficient," he said. "I'll make some arrangements for you and Paige to fly over."

"That's great," I said. "But Kat---"

"Let's keep this as a surprise between you, me, and Paige, shall we?"

I frowned. Kat hated surprises.

"Are you sure?" I asked.

"Don't worry, I'll handle the details, as well as any repercussions," he assured me.

He knows her all too well, I see.

"Thanks, uncle," I said.

I was growing fond of my new title for him. Regardless of the self-proclaimed nature of it, I relished the opportunity for having at least a semblance of family ties again.

"Think nothing of it, nephew," he said, sitting back against the bench.

I also felt better about the plans for the London trip by the minute.

Alton's awesome, and I can't wait to see Kat again.

"So, how long are you in town?" I asked.

"Just for this evening, I'm afraid," he replied. "My flight leaves just after midnight."

Then he rose to stand. "It's a nice campus, Yale. But you would've enjoyed Oxford, too, I think."

I rolled my eyes. "Oh, please. Don't even go there."

Imagine me at Oxford. Don't students have to wear some kind of uniforms there?

Lame.

As we continued our walk, two attractive young women jogged past us.

"Although I can see obvious advantages to being here, as well," he said.

"Uh, yeah," I agreed.

"Have you eaten this evening?" he asked.

"Not yet."

"Come on, I'll buy you dinner," he offered. "You look like you could use a meal, and I noticed a nice Italian bistro not far from here."

"What about the heavy garlic smell?" I asked.

"I'll endure on your behalf," he said.

That's a considerable concession from a vampire.

I texted Paige with an update on our plans as we walked to the restaurant, a place named Sapori d'Italia near the corner of Chapel and College.

The food and service were excellent, and I appreciated the time with Alton.

In particular, I enjoyed the stories he discreetly shared from his experiences in feudal England.

If only Kat could've been there with us, the experience would've felt complete.

I missed her terribly.

Her absence aside, it was a wonderful evening spent with my quasi-adopted uncle.

Despite everything, life is really good sometimes.

Part III

London and Back

CHAPTER 26

Caleb

Our Sunset Air charter flight touched down in London on a Thursday morning, my first day of fall break. I had slept relatively soundly on the flight over, though I felt tired once we landed.

Despite Kat's reticence about surprises, I looked forward to her reaction when she finally saw me. Not only was I was anxious to see her, but maybe I'd discover why she'd acted so distant toward me recently.

Alton arranged for two vampires to meet us at the terminal, as well as a shiny limousine to pick us up. As we rode through the city, my cell phone rang.

It was uncle Alton.

"Welcome, my boy," he said. "How was your flight?"

"Just great, thanks," I said. "The limo's awesome, too, thank you."

"And Mr. Moneybags *finally* sprung for satellite radio, I see," Paige said loudly. "Snarkety-snark."

I gave her a wan look.

"What was that last bit about?" he asked.

"Oh, she's all about snarking lately," I said.

She stuck her tongue out at me.

"Snarking?" he asked.

"It's like—oh, never mind," I said.

"Ah, today's faddish colloquialisms. I'll simply ignore her, what say?" he asked. "I instructed the driver to take you to a pub where Katrina checks in frequently. With luck, you won't have to wait long before she arrives."

"Got it," I said.

"Oh, we *love* pubs," Paige said.

"Eavesdropper," I said.

"Uh, *vampire hearing*," she said, pointing her finger at her ear.

"Rude," I said.

I heard Alton chuckle over the phone. "At any rate, I'll have your luggage delivered to the hotel. I hope you have a nice time while you're in London," he said. "And I'll attempt to keep Kat's agenda clear while you're visiting. You could both do with a break."

"Thanks, Alton. I sincerely appreciate it," I said.

Paige's hand darted out and grabbed my phone from me.

"Oh, and I'll be sure to have a nice time too, thank you," she said.

She listened to his retort with a smirk. Then her jaw dropped. "*On call?* Hey, I need a break, too, you know."

I watched with amusement as she rolled her eyes and shook her head back and forth in disgust.

"Oh, whatever, you old fuddy-duddy," she said, clicking off the phone and tossing it back to me.

"Richie Rich gets what Richie Rich wants, I suppose," she said.

"Well, snarkety-snark-snar---" I began.

"Oh, can it, twerp," she said. "I'm all snarked out tonight."

"Maximum snarkage exceeded?" I asked with narrowed eyes.

She swatted at my body with a flurry of slaps, so I slapped back at her until we both spontaneously agreed to a cease-slap.

Before long, our limousine pulled up before a pub called

the Red Griffin. It had an Old World appearance about it, complete with its own hallmark banner suspended from a pole above the entrance; a gold painted griffin on a red background.

"Hey, what a cool-looking place," I said.

"Yeah, well, if it's Alton's, I'm sure its way more Ye' Olde than yee-haw," she said.

As soon as we crossed the threshold, I could tell the place had character. The interior was decorated in rich wood paneling, old style lighting, polished oak tables, and a combination of open-styled seating in the main area and enclosed booths along one wall. The central fixture was a long span of polished wood bar lined with stools.

The walls were lined with old photos of people, places, cityscapes, and events. Old wooden casks and barrels sat atop periodic wall partitions, adding to the rustic setting.

The place appeared busy with patrons who barely looked up at us as we entered.

"Wow," I said.

I'd been in pubs on my first visit to London, but I'd never seen any place quite the Red Griffin before.

Paige's cell phone rang and she glanced down at it.

"Gotta' take this," she said. "I'll be back."

She quickly exited the pub to stand out on the sidewalk.

When I turned back around, a tall man with wavy red hair who appeared to be in his mid- to late-thirties stepped up to greet me.

"Hello, guv'nor," he said. "Please do come in."

"Thanks."

He frowned. "Have we met somewhere before?"

"Nope, don't think so," I said. "Just got into town, in fact."

He gestured grandly with his arm in a welcoming fashion. "Well, welcome to the Red Griffin."

"Nice," I said. "I love the place."

"And so you should," he said. "We've got the finest taps in London. I'm your host, Gavyn."

I reached out to shake his hand. "Caleb."

"Nice to meet you, Caleb," he said, frowning slightly. "Won't you come in and have a seat."

I sat down at the nearest unoccupied table.

"You look thirsty, Caleb. What can I get you?" he asked.

"How about a pint of something local?" I asked.

"I've got just the thing," he said.

He quickly returned with a frothy-topped mug of beer.

"Looks good, thanks," I said.

A series of hoots and hollers sounded from a small room separated by a set of frosted glass doors to my left, and I looked up with interest.

"It sounds like there's where the party's at," I said.

"Ah, do you like a bit of sport then, Caleb?" he asked.

"Me? Um, sure, from time to time," I said.

He motioned for me to stand and led me into the room where a group of men and women were gathered around a game of dice. Stacks of currency were on a small table and everyone seemed to be holding varying sized wads of bills.

A man with a scraggly beard threw some dice, followed closely by a series of groans and moans.

"Sorry, Duffin, no Jimmie Hicks from the sticks for you tonight," said a gentleman wearing an elaborate vest who appeared to be presiding over the game.

Laughter ensued.

"Oh, bollocks," the man said before taking a swig of his beer.

"Craps?" I asked.

"Oh, do you like a game of hazard?" Gavyn asked. "Care to give it a try?"

The players gathered around the table looked at me with amused expressions.

"Here now, is he a Yank?" one woman asked.

"Leave him be. Let the lucky young man try his hand," said one old guy with a gleam in his eye.

Paige appeared in the doorway and her eyes widened. "Caleb, can't I turn my back for a minute on you?"

I watched Gavyn's amused expression slowly dissipate as he looked at Paige. "Wait a minute. You, I know."

She smirked. "You should. I beat your ass at cards the last time I was here."

Gavyn's gaze shifted from Paige back to me and he frowned. "What did you say you're name was, young man?"

"Caleb," I said. "Caleb Taylor."

"Taylor…Caleb Taylor," he repeated.

"As in Mr. Katrina," Paige said with a sly expression.

Everyone in the room fell silent, and Gavyn ran his pale right palm across his face. "Oh, bloody hell. *That* Caleb Taylor."

"Seriously, how hard would it be to post a photo of him around here?" she asked.

He quickly ushered me from the room. "C'mon Caleb, you don't want to mess about in here. It's a bit too dodgy, for you, my lad."

"Dodgy?" I asked.

"So, did you get those issues all sorted out with Ye' Olde Gambling Commission?" Paige asked.

"Now, now, no jesting about such things," Gavyn said. "Let's all go have a nice chat out in the main room."

Moments later, we were all sitting at a cozy-looking private booth in the main area, just around the corner from the main bar.

"Like a little something to eat maybe?" Gavyn asked. "Perhaps a nice hot cottage pie?"

"Mm, sounds good," I said.

"Think big, Gavyn," she said. "He eats like a horse."

He winked and caught the attention of a passing waitress and placed my order.

"So glad to finally meet you, Caleb. I've heard quite a bit about you," Gavyn said. "Though I confess, I didn't realize you were coming."

"It's kind of on the QT for Miss You-Know-Who," Paige said with an arched brow.

"Ah, I see. No matter," he said. "Your secret's safe with

me. I better pass the word about that, in fact."

He disappeared and I turned to Paige. "Who is he?"

"Oh, he and Alton go back a ways," she said in off-handed fashion. "Drink your beer and relax."

Later, Gavyn returned to deliver a piping hot cottage pie, as well as a glass of beer for Paige.

It tasted amazing.

As I ate, the place filled up with people, including a sizable contingent of vampires.

"This must be the vamp hangout, of sorts," I said.

"You could say that," Paige said.

I supposed that even vampires needed a place to hang out with their own kind.

"Hey, who called you earlier?" I asked.

"Ethan," she said in a forlorn tone.

"What's wrong?"

"I was trying to get him to join us in London, but he had to assist on a last-minute surgery," she said, leaning her cheek against the palm of her hand. "It seems that ever since you had your little brain surgery episode, suddenly every doctor wants him assisting on their surgeries."

I felt bad for her. "Sorry."

She sighed. "Aw, don't be. You were worth it, I suppose."

I took another bite of tasty cottage pie.

"You owe me, though," she said.

I frowned. "Whadda' mean by that?"

"Don't chew with your mouth full," she said.

Suddenly, the formerly boisterous conversations in the room fell to a hush.

Paige cocked her head to one side and motioned to me with her forefinger to her lips.

"It's her," she mouthed silently.

I strained my ears to listen in.

"Well, General, welcome back," Gavyn said. "Fine evening, isn't it?"

"Gavyn," Kat said in a formal tone. "Anything to

report?"

"Indeed. I must say, you're quite the popular topic around here this evening," he said jovially. "Oh, and someone would like to schedule an impromptu meeting with you, as well."

"Really?" she asked flatly. "Who?"

"Mysterious fellow, really," he replied in a subdued tone, though I was still barely able to hear him. "I'd watch myself with that one."

"Where?" she asked.

Damn, she sounds absolutely lethal.

I didn't hear anything else but Paige adopted a wry expression.

Then I caught a blur of movement out of the corner of my eye.

My mouth dropped open and I froze in place as my eyes fell upon Kat, garbed in black and wearing a designer leather trench coat. Her long red hair was pulled back into a single tight ponytail and her eyes were hooded-looking, just like a predator waiting to strike.

As soon as she targeted her sharp eyes upon me, her face also shone complete surprise.

"Hey, Red," Paige said.

"Shorty," Kat said as she fluidly removed her trench coat, her gaze never leaving mine.

A vampire wearing an old style bartender's outfit stepped forward to quietly retrieve Kat's coat from her.

I took in the fitted black Lycra pants and knee-high leather boots she wore and arousal rushed through my body like adrenaline.

Oh. My. God.

She looked drop-dead-super-sexy dangerous.

"Ah, surprises abound tonight, I see," she said with narrowed eyes as she undid the buttons of her leather vest to reveal a fitted knit shirt beneath.

"Well, I'm just gonna' give you two kids some space," Paige said, scooting out of the booth and taking her beer with her.

Kat wasted no time and launched herself toward me, bodily pushing me further into the booth with her momentum. As my back pressed to the wall, her lips crashed against mine in a hungry fashion.

I reached up, cupping the back of her head in my palm and pulling her into my kiss.

It felt amazing to once more feel her lips and body pressed against mine.

I missed her so much!

From the moan that sounded from deep in her throat, I suspected she felt the same.

Upon parting lips to catch my breath, her eyes bore into mine with a near-feral intensity.

"Oh, how I've missed you," she breathed.

Her words made my heart soar even as another surge of carnal desire threatened to overcome me.

"You, too," I said, staring into her eyes.

Her body pressed against me and she planted a hard kiss as I reached out to pull her to me. We shared a series of passionate kisses, heedless of our surroundings.

Suddenly, the many weeks of sleeping alone, of reaching over during the middle of the night to find a cold empty space in the bed beside me culminated in me all at once. Her protracted absence was over; she was finally in my arms again.

Her lips felt like a piece of heaven, heightening the arousal in my body to frustrating levels.

"Somebody's glad to see me," she murmured into our kiss.

"You have no idea," I said.

"Oh yes, I do," she said.

"Nice look," I said when our lips parted again.

"I probably look like a really mean dominatrix right now," she said.

"I'm good with that," I said.

"I thought you didn't want a dominatrix," she said.

"I lied," I said.

"Such a bad boy for lying," she murmured. "I'll have to see to that later."

I was almost in a frenzy to have sex with her.

As I reached out to her and ran my hands down her sides to rest them upon her waist, I felt a number of hard objects pressed against her body.

I looked down and held open her leather vest to see that there were a series of knife hilts and throwing stars sheathed inside.

"Quite an arsenal you have there," I said.

She took my hands in hers and forced a pleasant expression. "Nothing more than tools of the trade."

"You look like one sexy superhero in that outfit," I said.

"Super heroine," she corrected, lightly tapping me on the tip of my nose with her fingertip. "Though I'm hardly headed for Marvel Comics stardom after what I've been up to."

"Surely, not a villain," I said.

"That's a matter of perspective, I suppose," she said.

I frowned as Gavyn abruptly stepped into the center of the pub.

"Attention, everyone. The General's taking a bit of personal time, if you know what I mean," he announced in a mock-discreet voice, to which many chuckled. "So, first round's on the house."

Cheers flowed through the pub as people flowed toward the bar to collect their unexpected reward.

"Gavyn's certainly a charismatic fellow," I said. "I like him a lot."

"He's a character," she agreed. "And one of the best around, for sure."

The pub suddenly seemed alive again with bodies moving to and fro through the place, drinking and conversing.

Once again, Gavyn appeared in the middle of the room with beer in hand and loudly cleared his throat.

The room quickly fell silent.

"A toast to the General and her mate," he called out.

"The General and her mate!" yelled everyone in unison.

"May God rest the poor man's soul!" shouted one woman from the back of the room.

Hoots and barks of laughter erupted throughout. Even Kat giggled in uncharacteristic fashion and turned to look behind her as I grinned from ear to ear.

"Oh, get off with you now," she chastised good-naturedly in a booming voice.

Another round of laughter permeated the room as she returned her attention to me. She looked much more relaxed than a few minutes prior.

The din of conversations quickly renewed throughout the establishment.

"Well, you certainly have a way of brightening the mood in a crowd, don't you?" she asked.

"Me? Something tells me they're glad to see you happy," I said. "You didn't look particularly pleased to see me when you peeked around into my booth."

She shrugged. "I'm happy to see you, though I asked you not to come here."

That bothered me.

Moments later, Gavyn appeared around the corner to place two cold glasses of beer onto our table with a thump. "Here are your first rounds."

"Thanks, Gavyn," Kat said.

"To your health, mum," he replied and disappeared.

We each took a swig of beer, our eyes never straying from each other's.

"You look absolutely amazing," I told her, unable to take my eyes from her. "It's so great to see you."

"You, as well. Although, you've lost weight," she said with a frown, reaching out to squeeze my sides until it tickled.

"I'm fine," I countered, gently grasping her wrists in my hands.

She glanced at my half-eaten cottage pie. "You need to finish that while it's warm. You obviously need it," she said reproachfully.

"You're mothering me," I warned.

She scooted away from me just enough to permit me access to my plate. Then she wrapped her arm around my shoulders.

"I can't stop touching you," she whispered.

"I hope you never do," I said.

She kissed me on the cheek. "Though a surprise, it's wonderful to see you. But what're you doing here? Is everything okay at college?"

"I missed you and wanted to surprise you. And besides, it's fall break," I said between bites of food.

"Is it already?" she asked, her expression suddenly distant-looking. "The days and nights have passed in a blur."

"To me, it's felt like an eternity since you left," I said.

"My loving Caleb," she whispered reverently.

She bent down to press her soft lips to my forehead in a lingering kiss. Then she sat beside me, silently watching me eat for a time.

"How long are you planning to stay?" she asked.

"I'd like to stay forever," I said.

She adopted a wan smile. "Ah, but you have classes to finish, and I believe, a dissertation to continue working on."

"True enough," I said. "In that case, I suppose I'll only be here for about three days."

"We'll have to make them memorable then," she whispered, rubbing her hand suggestively along my thigh.

"Can you spare time for me?" I asked.

"I'll make time," she said.

That's all I could ask. Hopefully, Alton would help out with that just as he promised.

I finished the remainder of my meal and took another swig of cold beer, which tasted great.

We conversed at length about my classes and how my research was proceeding.

"It may not be teaching, but I'm really enjoying being back at college," I said. "Now, tell me more about what's

JAZ PRIMO

been going on around here."

Her eyes momentarily scanned the room around her. "We can talk more about that later," she said. "Suffice to say I've definitely been busy."

"Relatively safe and nonviolent business, I hope?"

She ran her fingernails down the back of my neck, evoking a shiver that traveled down my spine.

"Everything's fine, my love. Nothing you need concern yourself with," she said simply.

I frowned. "Now I'm concerned...General."

She grasped my chin in her hand and rotated my face to meet hers.

"You aren't to call me that, Caleb," she said firmly, her green eyes almost steely-looking. "That's a term used by my subordinates. I'm your mate and your lover, not your general."

Whoa, she turned awfully alpha on me all of the sudden.

"Okay," I said. "Although I did feel somewhat subordinate just then."

She released my chin with a sigh and caressed the side of my face with her soft fingertips. "I didn't mean to sound so harsh," she offered in a gentler tone. "You'll have to excuse me. I'm not used to displaying my softer side around here."

She kissed me on the lips warmly, to which I responded.

I decided not to press the matter.

Once again, the pub grew eerily silent, and Kat peered around the corner of the booth to catch a view of the entrance, her free hand pressing me further back into the booth in protective fashion.

My alpha heroine in action.

She relaxed as Alton walked through the room greeting people left and right until he arrived at our booth.

"Well, Caleb, I see you found the place all right," he greeted.

"Hard to get lost. Your driver dropped us off right out front, after all," I said.

"Just so. I do apologize for not accompanying you, but I

had an important matter to attend to," he said with a pointed look at Kat. "I trust you were surprised by your mate's visit?"

"You have no idea," she said. "Do I have *you* to thank for this?"

"Well, it was a combined effort, but I was happy to facilitate matters on your behalf," he said.

"You could've mentioned it," she said with a slight edge to her voice.

Gavyn appeared amidst a rustling of air to stand before Alton. "Evening, sir," he said crisply. "I have a table ready upstairs, if you're interested."

"Yes, thanks ever so much, Gavyn," Alton replied.

We followed Gavyn around the periphery of the bar to a circular staircase with polished oak railing.

I grabbed Paige by the crook of her arm as I passed where she was chatting with a couple of vampires.

"Hey, what's up?" she asked, falling in alongside me.

CHAPTER 27

Caleb

Upstairs was a smaller, less occupied area with small booths along two sides and a large oak table in the center of the room.

"Please, be seated," Gavyn said, holding a chair for Paige while I did the same for Kat.

After he sat down at the table, Gavyn snapped his fingers loudly.

A waitress quickly appeared at the top of the stairs, and he pointed to our table and made a circular motion with his finger.

Soon, fresh glasses of beer were brought up to us.

"To your good health," he offered, raising his glass.

Following the toast, I said, "This is a wonderful pub you have here. And the cottage pie was excellent, thank you."

"You're quite welcome, Caleb," he said.

"My apologies for not being here to conduct a proper introduction, Gavyn," Alton said.

"Oh, and isn't that a fine how do you do?" he said. "But I managed ever-so-awkwardly on my own, thank you.

"The young man crossed my threshold and I thought he was just another wayward American tourist. Just arrived, he said," Gavyn recited, sounding much like an old-time storyteller sitting around a campfire. "Oh, really, I say, introducing myself like the silly git I am. Caleb, he says his name is. That name sounds familiar, I think to myself. But then, there's a lot of Caleb's in the world, aren't there?

"I welcome him in and serve a beer. Then he hears the commotion in the parlor room, so I show him around. *'Oh, is that a game of dice?'* he asks. Why, yes, sir, and why not try your hand at some games of chance, I offer; fool I am. My memory doesn't kick in until a few minutes later, naturally, when this attractive blonde bird next to me wanders in to seek out her charge. Now, her, I've seen before, I said."

Gavyn gestured grandly in my direction. "Then I'm realizing it's nothing short of the General's mate that I have before me. And to think, I offered him a dodgy game of hazard!"

There were chuckles around the table over that.

I looked at Gavyn, but then my eyes were once more captured by the vision of Kat before me.

She's so captivating; I just can't take my eyes off her.

I wanted her so badly at that moment. I literally craved taking her by the hand and off to the nearest bed.

Her eyes widened upon noting my intense scrutiny. She reached underneath the table to hold my hand as she fondly gazed back at me.

"There, there, Gavyn. Don't be too hard on yourself," Alton said. "You'd never met him, and he has a way with social engineering. He'll overwhelm you with politeness and courtesy."

I gave him a wan look. "Whatever."

"Well, Sir Osborn, what do you think of our Caleb thus far?" Alton asked.

My eyes darted to Alton.

Sir Osborn?

The charismatic man who I knew as Gavyn regarded me at length and pursed his lips as if in deep thought.

"Quite a promising young lad, really. Certainly squire material, M'Lord," he said in a serious tone, in stark contrast to his previous lighthearted tone and demeanor.

M'Lord?

The edges of Alton's mouth upturned slightly. "Indeed?"

"Quite right, M'Lord," Osborn said soberly. "Of that, I'm confident. Excellent bearing in this one."

I looked at Kat, who was watching me with a partially amused expression.

"Caleb, permit me to formally introduce you to Sir Gavyn Osborn, owner of this fine establishment and honorable Knight of the Realm," Alton announced in a grand tone of voice.

My gaze shifted to Osborn, who nodded his head in a suddenly regal fashion.

"If you'll permit me; *former* Knight of the Realm, M'Lord," he corrected.

"Gavyn has been my most trusted knight since 1202," Alton continued warmly. "And a true friend. In addition, he's one of the most accomplished swordsmen I've ever known."

"Most gracious. And an honor it's been to serve, I assure you, M'Lord," Osborn said.

I stared back at Gavyn Osborn with awe.

Wow. An actual knight from medieval times.

A medieval vampire knight.

"And, Gavyn, if it pleases you, sir," he said to Alton. "I've mentioned time again that I gave up on stuffy titles hundreds of years ago."

"If it pleases *me*? You still throw M'Lord around at me all of the time, though, don't you?" Alton countered.

"Well, that's quite different, isn't it? I mean, you being a Scottish duke; regal bearing, and all, no less," Gavyn teased, returning to his previous off-handed tone.

"Former duke," Alton corrected.

"Once a duke, always a duke, I say," Gavyn argued.

"And I suppose Saint George slayed a dragon," Alton said.

"Well, a large lizard, surely, M'Lord," the former knight countered.

I laughed aloud.

Alton groaned. "Oh, bother."

Gavyn grinned and glanced around the table. Then he stood and reached out to shake my hand.

"A pleasure to meet you, Caleb. Now if you'll excuse me, I have a pub to tend."

I stood to shake his hand and thanked him once again for a delicious meal and his kind hospitality.

"My pleasure. And please do visit again while you're here in London. In fact, consider it your safe haven," he said meaningfully. "I often dreamed of owning a pub. This place is like my second home, and as such, you're welcome any time."

"I will, thank you," I replied.

"M'Lord," he said to Alton with an exaggerated bow and a flourish of his hand before him.

"Oh, do go on," Alton said with a dismissive wave. "I'll be in touch soon, Gavyn."

He waved his hand in the air in a series of elaborate flourishes with a chuckle as he walked away.

"What a remarkable man," I said.

"He's one of the best," Alton said. "Just like Katrina."

Kat warmly smiled over the compliment.

"So, Alton, Scottish duke, eh?" Paige asked. "Why don't we ever see you in a kilt?"

"What the devil for?" he asked.

She adopted a mischievous expression. "You could pull it off. I mean, you really do have such regal bearing," she said. "You're like Lord Grantham from *Downton Abbey*. Or more likely *Macbeth*."

"*Macbeth*? Don't you even start, young lady, or I'll take you across my knee right here and now," he warned.

"Well, I never," she said.

"Sure you have," Kat said dryly. "And recently, I'd wager."

Paige crossed her arms and stuck out her tongue at her. "Ethan hasn't visited me in some time, I'll have you know."

"TMI," I said.

Then I frowned. "Wait, *you* watch *Downton Abbey*?"

Paige shrugged. "There was a marathon on cable recently and I was bored. It was a lark."

Alton cleared his throat. "Now, about Caleb's stay during the next few days," he said. "Katrina, you're to take a respite while he's here with us. You're officially on holiday."

"There are a couple of loose ends to tend to that we discussed this morning, though they shouldn't take long," she said.

I wondered what those might be, though I doubted that she'd actually tell me.

"Hm. Quite right. Well, after those, then," he said. "Shall I drop Caleb off at the hotel?"

"Oh, no," I immediately spoke up. "It's a nice night for a walk, and surely we can catch the Tube."

"Katrina?" Alton asked.

She considered me at length. "All right, I suppose we can do that," she said. "Paige can accompany us, as well."

"I can?" Paige asked, catching Kat's stare. "Oh, yeah, on call. Sure I can."

"I'd better get back," Alton said.

As I said goodbye to him, I noticed Kat discreetly passing two sheathed combat knives to Paige, who slipped them into the back of her jeans, neatly concealed by her leather jacket.

"Merely precautions, Caleb," Alton said in a low voice. "Since the Slovene conference, things have become quite interesting here in London, to say the least. I want you to be careful and observe any limitations that we prescribe for you during your stay. Understood?"

I nodded with a frown, wondering what sort of 'interesting' things had been happening in London.

"Excellent," he said, patting me lightly on the shoulder. "Nothing to worry about, I assure you."

Maybe I can somehow convince Kat to fill me in about it later.

As I held Kat's coat for her and slipped into my leather

jacket, I also noted that four other vampires were readying themselves to leave.

As the seven of us walked out into the night, it occurred to me that this wasn't going to be just some intimate stroll back to the hotel.

Two of the vampire escorts walked across the street and mirrored our progress, scanning the area as they walked. The other two escorts followed a few steps behind us.

"So, you have an entourage now," I said, holding Kat's hand.

"Very funny," she said. "They're quiet, when needed. One of the vampires behind us, Thom Rowley, assists me with field communiques."

I looked behind me at our escorts and one of the men nodded and reached up to tip an imaginary hat in gentlemanly fashion.

I nodded back at him.

We walked for a block, and I noticed there was very little traffic and only an occasional pedestrian in the area for mid-evening. The businesses and shops all seemed to have closed for the day, leaving only the street lamps for illumination.

The sound of a cell phone ringing almost startled me, and I glanced behind me.

"Are you sure? Now?" Rowley asked.

He quickly stepped forward and handed the phone to Katrina. "Mum, it's the office," he said.

She reduced our pace a bit while listening to the person on the other end.

"Yes. However, this is well ahead of our original schedule," she said flatly. "Fine. We're relatively close so we'll escort her."

She handed the phone back to Rowley.

"What is it?" I asked.

She frowned and appeared contemplative. "Someone's requesting asylum from Baldar Dubravko's former organization. Vampires jump ship from time to time, but lately it's been a near exodus."

The vampire who I'd killed with his own briefcase bomb back during the Slovene conference hadn't seemed like someone I'd enjoy working for either.

"You trust them when they do that?" I asked.

"Trust is earned," she said. "But we provide them with an opportunity if we detect sincerity."

"What if they don't seem sincere?" I asked.

She didn't answer my question.

"We'd agreed upon a specific date for her safe transfer, but our central office said she's afraid she's under surveillance and wants it to be tonight. Now, in fact," Kat said while motioning to the vampires across the street.

She drew everyone into the nearest alleyway.

"Inia Sabine's transfer to us is happening right now," she said. "We'll provide safe escort. Threats are unknown, though she claims she's being followed. We're closest, so we'll convey her back to the Red Griffin."

"What about your mate?" one of the vampires asked.

"I don't like it, but there's no time," she said with a hard look at me. "He'll accompany us. Paige and Lamport are charged with his protection. Let's move."

I was in near-awe as she quickly assessed the situation and confidently issued orders to everyone.

She really did seem like a general.

She spared me a reassuring look, but I sensed that it bothered her to have me along at all.

I'm not helpless, and I'm surrounded by vampires.

"Paige is in charge," she emphatically stated to me. "And remain as silent as possible, please."

I nodded and she lightly ran her fingertips across my cheek.

Once again, two vampires from our group headed to the opposite side of the street while Rowley stepped up beside Kat. Paige and the remaining vampire fell in alongside me.

We walked at a brisk pace on a circuitous route through the city. I was certainly seeing the 'city behind the city' as we made our way; the side of London that few, if any, tourists or visitors saw.

The streets seemed darker and the alleys more ominous than where we had just come from. A number of the passersby and bystanders loitering around the vicinity weren't particularly savory-looking, in my opinion.

Steam rolled out of an alley that we passed and I thought I saw a dim set of yellow eyes peering at me from out of the fog.

I tried to bring it to Paige's attention, but she raised her finger to her lips and ushered me forward by pressing her hand to the small of my back.

In the distance, I saw a petite-looking brunette wearing a trench coat standing along a brick wall just up ahead at the next intersection.

Kat motioned with her hand at us, and Paige grasped my upper arm to halt our progress. The two vampires across the street slowed but continued walking to their end of the street.

Meanwhile, Kat and Rowley briskly walked toward the woman.

As I stared at her, a set of hands reached out from inside the building she stood next to and pulled her inside.

"Help!" she yelled.

Kat and Rowley moved like lightning to aid the woman, and I quickly lost the ability to visually track their progress.

Rapid gunfire sounded to my right, and I saw two vampires emerge from the alleyway across the street with guns blazing. Paige yanked me into the alley beside us and tossed me behind a nearby dumpster.

"Stay!" she ordered.

Before I could say a word, combat knives appeared in her hands and she charged from the alley amidst a gust of air.

Lamport produced a pistol and held a long-bladed combat knife in his other hand. He stood in a combat stance, constantly scanning the entrance.

As an afterthought, I reached into my jacket pocket to grip the metal casing of one of the prototypes that Gregory Hess had sent to me.

I extracted it and held it at the ready beside me.

While I hoped it might prove useful, I was likewise afraid to find out firsthand.

From somewhere deeper into the dark alley, I heard the sound of hard-soled shoes slapping against pavement, as if people had dropped in from above.

Lamport swiveled just in time to fire two rounds before a blade slammed into his shoulder. His pistol clanked harmlessly to the concrete.

He and another vampire were quickly engaged in hand-to-hand fighting, slamming against the nearby brick wall with a dull thud.

I reached over to grab the fallen pistol, but a foot swiftly kicked it farther down the alley.

Looking up, I stared into the face of a pale-complexioned and angry-looking vampire.

"Trophies abound tonight!" he said.

CHAPTER 28

Caleb

The vampire snarled as a knife blade glinted above me, and I instinctively clicked on my device.

Amidst a blinding white light, a vampire's angry-looking features quickly turned to horror as his skin sizzled before me.

He screamed in pain and his hands flew to his face as he staggered backward from me.

I wanted to do something more offensive in nature, but I was weaponless—essentially helpless.

The vampire recovered slightly, and I brandished the light before me. He shielded his face with one arm while lunging forward and lashing out at me with his knife.

Something whizzed in front of me and the vampire screamed as a throwing star imbedded in his wrist.

I heard rapid boot steps and a loud flapping noise above me, and I managed to glance up just in time to see a figure in a black leather trench coat sailing over me.

The figure practically ran up against the brick wall next to me as a lengthy glinting blade flashed in the darkness, beheading the vampire before me. That's about the time I noticed a long, red ponytail draped down the figure's back.

Kat!

She kicked the other attacking vampire away from Lamport, who sagged against the wall with a gasp.

Another flash of her blade attracted my attention before it was thrust into the opposing vampire's chest.

In one fluid motion, she withdrew her blade while swift-kicking his body to the pavement.

She spun with her back to me, both of her boots clicked against the concrete, and she peered back at me in with a surprised expression, her emerald eyes practically blazing brightly.

For a moment, I was half-stunned, and I marveled at what I'd just seen.

Time seemed suspended as we stared back at each other, though most of her face was shielded by her coat.

Fortunately, I had the presence of mind to click my device back off.

"Are you okay?" she asked in a rough voice.

I nodded, still too astonished to speak.

She wiped her blade against the prone body before her, sheathed her blade inside her boot, and moved over to where Lamport was slumped against the wall.

"I'm sorry, General," he rasped.

She placed a hand on his shoulder. "Are you critical?"

He shook his head slightly. "Nah. Healing now."

She patted him on his good shoulder as Paige appeared in the entrance to the alley.

"We're good out there now," Paige said. "Inia's secure."

Then her expression darkened. "Hey, what the hell happened here?"

"Later," Kat growled from deep in her throat, and turned her attention back to me.

Oh, please don't get into another fight with Paige.

She walked over to grasp me by the shoulders, relief evident on her face.

My mind still reeled from what had she'd just done. I knew she was an experienced fighter, but that was like something out of *The Matrix*.

"You're way-over-the-top amazing," I whispered.

She took a deep breath and let it out as a relieved expression washed over her. Then, her eyes focused upon the metal tube I still held in my hand.

"What is that?" she asked, holding her open palm before me.

I handed the device to her and she carefully examined it.

"Watch out, it—"

She motioned for silence and flicked the light on against the opposite wall.

Gasping, she quickly extinguished it. "Where did you get this?"

I shrugged. "It's sort of serendipity, really…"

* * *

No more than ten minutes following the ambush, a panel van flanked by two black SUVs pulled up nearby.

As dead vampire bodies were moved into the panel van, the remainder of us were quickly ushered into the SUVs. I accompanied Kat and the vampire named Inia in one of the vehicles.

We were quickly transported back to the Red Griffin.

After Kat spoke briefly with Gavyn and remanded Inia to his custody, one of the SUVs transported her, Paige, and me to the Summit Towers Hotel where we had stayed during our spring vacation to London.

The hotel was a fifteen-story luxury hotel adjacent to the high-rise office building that hosted Alton's central business offices and his penthouse.

By the time we arrived around eleven-thirty that night, the lobby was relatively devoid of guests or other social activity.

Kat and Paige appeared tight-lipped and seemed rather distant as we entered the lobby. Somehow, I had the impression that emotions were still running high from the events in the alley.

Given the tension that practically permeated the space between each of us, I found it difficult to appreciate our arrival.

Perhaps it had been the overly-long flight or the recent adrenaline-laced events, but aggravation quickly overtook me, and I took each of them by the hand and strode in the direction of a nearby empty conference room.

"Where---" Kat began.

"Just follow me," I said.

I closed the set of double doors behind us and turned my back to face the two most beloved women in my life.

I felt quite put out, and for emphasis, I hiked my hands atop my hips.

"All right. You both listen to me, right now," I said. "I don't want any hard feelings or arguments between you two. Everything worked out okay in the end tonight, so let's just count our blessings.

"You're going to patch this up between you right now. And if I even get a hint that you two have fought, I'm getting on the next damned plane out of here and I won't look back. Got it?"

Both women started to open their mouths simultaneously.

"And before either of you get indignant, I'll remind you that I *earned* the right to demand this of you. Both of you are scary-as-hell dangerous, and I don't think I'd survive trying to break up another fight between you," I said.

Both of them fell silent and stared me.

Kat looked completely mortified, while Paige's expression turned to one of utter regret.

"Thank you for your help tonight, Paige," Kat said quietly. "You did what you thought was most appropriate."

Paige nodded and swallowed. "I'm sorry for leaving our boy, Red," she said. "I'd thought that he was going to be fine, and your vampires were in a really tight position at the time. I probably should've stayed with him and sent Lamport instead. I won't let that happen again."

Kat nodded. "I understand that now. And thank you. I just worry---"

"Yeah, I know," she interrupted.

I looked up at each of them in turn, and felt satisfied that I'd made my point.

Then Paige lurched at me and gave me a bear-like hug. "I'm sorry, kiddo. I love you."

Returning her hug in kind, I patted her on the back. "It's okay. Love you, too, Paige."

This is way better.

Afterward, I said nothing, but merely opened the doors to the conference room and headed across the marble-floored lobby toward the elevator.

I heard two sets of footsteps close behind.

"I think I'm heading to the bar for a drink before I go upstairs," Paige said.

"Nite, Blondie," Kat said.

"Nite, Red."

As I neared the main counter, a pretty young woman hurried toward me.

"Excuse me. Mr. Taylor, I presume?" she asked. "I received a call a few minutes ago that you were coming. This is the keycard to your suite."

The woman turned to call out to Paige. "Ms. Turner, here is your suite keycard, as well. I hope that both of you enjoy your stay with us."

Then she returned to the main desk.

"Sleep well and mind your Dom, tiger," Paige said, and headed in the direction of the bar.

Oh, don't even go there.

"Whatever," I said.

I proceeded to the elevator and felt the presence of Kat at my back. Her hands touched my shoulders and began lightly massaging them.

Oh, that feels simply amazing right now.

"A Dom who also massages," she mused. "You're one lucky guy."

"Mm," I moaned, completely smitten with that idea and how wonderful her fingers felt as they kneaded at my muscles.

Most of all, it was a relief to feel safe once again, and finally arrive at the hotel.

God, I'm beat.

We stepped inside the elevator, and as soon as the doors closed, I looked up at her; she was gazing down at me with adoration.

"I love you so much," she said.

She enveloped me in her arms in a manner that made me instantly feel both loved and secure.

"Please don't be angry with me over what happened earlier," she said.

"Sure," I said. "But it'll cost you a kiss."

Her eyes flashed bright green and her soft lips pressed against mine in a passionate kiss.

In contrast to my body's recent sense of exhaustion, a surge of passion erupted in me. I returned her kisses with a hungry intensity as she pinned my body against the wall of the elevator.

The elevator doors opened, but I gave it little attention.

I was heedless of time as my recent feelings of desire, worry, and love were communicated through our lips.

She parted from our kiss and stared into my eyes. "I'm suddenly very happy you're here."

"Me, too," I agreed. "And did I mention you look smokin' hot in that outfit?"

"Once or twice as a matter of fact," she said. "I like what this outfit evokes in you."

"Of course, you'll look even hotter once you're out of it," I said.

"Play your cards right, and you might get to find out," she said.

"You wouldn't be playing hard to get, would you?" I asked.

She chuckled and unwound her arms from around me. I

took her by the hand and turned to depart the elevator.

That's when I noticed two suit-clad vampires, a man and a woman, standing in the hallway observing us with wide-eyed expressions.

I felt the heat immediately rise in my cheeks as I realized the spectacle they must've just seen, or worse yet, heard.

"Welcome back, General," the fellow said. "Everything's clear here."

At first, the woman stared at me with intrigue. Then a look of subtle amusement formed on her lips.

"General," she said.

Kat released my hand and wrapped her arm around my shoulders possessively, once more in command of her surroundings…and of me.

"Mr. Schaffer, Ms. Devereux, this is my mate, Caleb Taylor," she said.

Both nodded and greeted me in unison. "Mr. Taylor."

"Hi," I said with a slight wave of my hand. "Nice to meet you."

"Good evening to you both," Kat said.

She swept me in a tight semi-circle, nearly causing me to stagger, and guided me toward the suite at the end of the hallway.

"My mate looks particularly cute when he blushes," she whispered.

Behind us, I heard Devereux stifle a laugh.

Oh, brother. Kat's really pulling out the stops tonight.

"Kat," I whispered, to which she affectionately squeezed my shoulder.

* * *

Kat shrugged out of her trench coat and took my jacket to hang them both up in the small coat closet near the door.

"Welcome home," she said.

I gazed around the suite's spacious and rich-looking interior. It appeared very much like the one we'd stayed in at the other end of the hallway in the spring, except with an opposing view of the city.

I noticed the place failed to look particularly well-lived in.

Her arms wrapped around me from behind, trapping my arms to my sides, and she kissed me on the cheek.

"Something the matter?" she asked.

"I'd hardly know you were staying here," I said. "It looks like we just arrived."

She sighed. "Well, I don't spend a lot of time here," she said. "Frankly, it's not as enjoyable without you."

I turned around in her arms to face her, or rather, looked directly into her sternum.

Man, she's even taller in those boots.

I craned my neck to look up at her, and she gazed down with an amused expression.

"You've lost weight and height, my love," she teased.

"Oh, so funny," I said.

She kissed me on the tip of my nose and then pressed her lips against mine in a deep, long kiss that nearly drew the breath from my lungs.

My heart soared with passion and love for the woman holding me in her arms. She was, by far, the most wonderful, amazing lover I could've been blessed with.

On top of that, she was ravishing.

"You're absolutely gorgeous," I said. "No, you're stunning."

And I love you.

The endearing look she bestowed upon me was award-winning; it reflected heartfelt, raw emotion.

She pressed her lips against mine, and we shared another long, passionate kiss.

My pulse raced as my body hungered for hers.

Before I knew it, we were undressing each other. Clothing fell around us as we kissed our way back to the bedroom.

Then we fell onto the bed, laughing.

The passion we shared felt magical, and time seemed suspended.

* * *

When I awoke, it was morning, and I was alone in bed.
She's gone already?

I suspected that Kat must've been called to some important duty. After last night, I sensed that her command role was central to everything that seemed to be going on in Alton's world.

Reaching up, I felt at my neck where she'd partaken in my blood after sharing the most wonderful sex in recent memory.

I felt no welts, so I was confident there'd be no visible marks; her saliva typically healed everything nicely.

All that remained was a slight telltale sensitive spot just beneath the skin. But even that would probably abate by later that day.

It was strange, but I actually relished sharing my blood with her; it was something decidedly unique and intimate I could offer of myself.

The bedroom curtains were open and I noticed it was cloudy and bleary-looking outside, though the UV-protective coating on the window made it look much darker outside than it actually was.

Ahh, London and its clouds.

Still, I felt very happy to be here. It was far better to be in the same city with Kat rather than half the world and an ocean away.

I could spend every waking minute with her.

She was like an addiction to me. Maybe I was obsessed, but I didn't care. All I wanted was to have her in my daily life; everything else seemed negotiable.

I stretched and glimpsed a note on the nightstand, held in place by my prototype flashlight that was standing upright like a candle. The note was in Kat's handwriting.

My Love,

I adored watching you sleep last night, and I hope you slept well.

When you're up and around, Alton would like to meet with you in his office. Please use the underground passageway. And please bring your new toy with you.

Love,
Dom-Kat

I smiled as I lay the note aside.

My loving Dom-Kat.

If that made me her Sub, then I couldn't imagine being happier as anything else.

At least until Paige razzed my ass about it endlessly.

Then something about her note triggered in my mind.

Wait a minute. Toy?

I rolled out of bed and stretched. A glance at my watch revealed I'd slept away most of the morning already.

I didn't want to keep anyone waiting on me, so I immediately went to shave and get dressed.

CHAPTER 29

Caleb

Twenty minutes later, I grabbed my leather jacket and walked out the door to find two sets of suit-wearing vampires staring at me.

One of them, a dark-haired and youthful-looking male, said, "Good morning, Mr. Rawlings."

Rawlings? Really?

Resisting the urge to roll my eyes, I stared at him.

"Good morning, Mister—?"

"Kempf, sir," he replied.

"Kempf," I said, and continued my walk to the elevator.

The other male vampire gave me a courteous nod and then glared over at his partner. "Good morning, *Mr. Taylor*," he said with emphasis on my last name. "I'm Adamo."

I looked at him with approval. "Good morning, Mr. Adamo. You, I like."

He grinned. "Kempf's relatively new to our group, as well as rather aloof."

I glanced back over my shoulder at Kempf, whose crestfallen face may have paled even further than his vampire features normally dictated. "I see."

"My apologies, Mr. Taylor," he said. "It was a slip of the tongue, I assure you."

"Yeah, be sure and tell that to the General, Kempf," Adamo muttered with a chuckle and a wink at me.

Yeah, I definitely liked Adamo.

"No harm, Kempf," I said, heading toward the elevator.

Adamo fell into step behind me and I turned to frown at him.

"I'm to accompany you, sir," he said. "General's orders, you understand."

Oh, Kat. So protective…

I nodded and the two of us took the elevator to the lobby.

"Not planning on going outdoors, I hope," he prompted.

"Nope, the tunnel leading next door to Alton's—Mr. Rutherford's—office," I replied.

"Very good, sir," he said.

Alton had ordered the construction of the underground passageway prior to our visit in the spring. It connected the hotel to his office building, of which he owned both.

Minutes later, we arrived at Alton's upper-floor offices. Just as I recalled from our last visit, the offices were staffed almost entirely by vampires.

"I'll just wait here for you, sir," Adamo said, taking a seat in a chair in the small waiting area near the elevator.

I nodded to him and proceeded down the carpeted hallway, past offices that hummed with the sounds of a typical office setting: typing, phone calls, and shuffling of paperwork.

"Caleb!" Marla Kendrick exclaimed with a bright smile. "It's so good to see you again."

Alton's assistant looked ever the consummate professional in her crisp gray suit. I hadn't seen her since my surgical recovery during the summer.

"Hi, Marla," I said warmly. "You're a sight for sore eyes, too."

She hugged me in a warm embrace with one arm while holding a stack of files in the other. Marla was definitely one of my favorites.

"Mr. Rutherford mentioned that you arrived last night.

Would you believe he didn't even tell me you were coming?"

That was surprising; Marla was usually in on everything Alton was up to.

"It gave me such a fright when I heard about the attack you were involved in last night," she said.

Various individuals peered out from their offices to stare at us with curious expressions.

"Yeah, pretty scary. But I'm fine, really," I said.

"You look healthy enough, but it looks like you've lost some more weight since I last saw you," she observed with a frown as she gently squeezed my bicep through my jacket. "No, this simply will not do."

Was there a conspiracy around here regarding my weight or something?

"Oh, not you, too," I said.

Between her Dutch accent and the manner in which she arched an eyebrow at me in an all-too-familiar fashion, she pulled off quite a stern headmistress impersonation; or, given her green eyes, perhaps just a blonde-haired Kat.

"Come," she said, ushering me toward a set of large oak-finished double doors. "I'll announce you. Ms. Rawlings is in with Mr. Rutherford, and they'll want to see you straight away."

She knocked at Alton's office door and entered.

"Mr. Rutherford, please forgive me, but we have an impromptu celebrity visitor and he'd like to meet with you," she said in a serious tone.

"Celebrity?" Alton asked incredulously.

Marla motioned to me and I slipped past her to enter the palatial office. Kat and Alton's curious expressions were priceless until they realized it was only me.

"Oh, Marla, honestly," Alton said with near-exasperation.

She winked and closed the door behind me.

Despite the regal-looking office décor and a breathtaking view of London's business district, my eyes were immediately drawn to Kat.

She looked absolutely beautiful with her hair down and

wearing a leather skirt and sweater.

"Good morning, young man," Alton said, dressed impeccably in his Armani suit. "Nearly good afternoon, in fact."

I embraced Kat and we exchanged a quick kiss.

"Good morning, Dom-Kat," I teased.

"I thought you'd like that. Did you sleep well, my love?" she asked, staring down into my eyes.

"Yep, though a bit longer than I'd planned," I said. "I didn't come all this way to see you, only to sleep the time away."

She frowned. "Stop that. You had an exhausting flight, followed by a nearly fatal evening. You needed the sleep."

"I'll consider myself properly admonished," I said.

"Not until I say so, you won't," she said with a smoldering look as her fingertips caressed the side of my face.

The arousal that flooded through me at that moment was palpable, and I felt the heat rise in my cheeks.

Turning quickly to Alton, I shook his hand as he regarded me with an amused expression.

"Katrina mentioned you have something to show me," he said.

"Oh, yes," I said, withdrawing the device from my jacket pocket and handing it to him.

He examined the plain-looking metal tube, turning it over in his hand. "So, this is what your grand experiment netted. Quite a small result for over half a million pound investment, wouldn't you say?"

My mouth dropped open and I heard a small gasp from Kat.

Half a million pounds? No way!

"Ohmygosh, that's a helluva' lot more than I thought it would end up being," I said.

Kat regarded me with a disapproving look. "You came up with this idea?" she asked. "And why, exactly, didn't you come to me about this instead of him?"

Her rebuke almost stung, and I suppressed a wince.

Aw, crap.

"Well, I—I," was all I managed to say.

"Now, now, Katrina," Alton interrupted, placing the flashlight on his desk. "The young man wanted to fund it himself, in fact, because he was hesitant to ask you for the capital. He only called upon me because only I have direct access to the investment trust account that we set aside for him."

That is, my former, and now completely dissolved, trust fund.

Kat's expression softened a bit, but she still looked injured over the matter. I carefully reached out to hold her right hand in both of mine, gently massaging it between my fingers.

She silently stared back at me. "I see," she finally said. "Though it hurts you didn't have enough faith that I'd support your venture."

"You've already done too much for me as it is," I said.

Her eyes glistened at that.

Oh, please don't cry.

"Listen, I'm sorry," I said. "I really wasn't trying to hurt you, much less insult you."

I brought her hand to my lips and reverently kissed it.

"The boy meant well," Alton said. "And I was overseeing his efforts."

She took a deep breath and let it out. "Alton, a moment with my mate, if you please," she said coolly.

The two of them shared a silent exchange.

"Very well. I'll be right outside," he said.

He calmly exited the office to the hallway beyond, pulling the door closed behind him.

She stepped closer to tower before me, gazing down at me with a neutral expression.

Her green eyes were nearly piercing as I stared up into them, and I sensed a strong, commanding influence that felt simultaneously intimidating and slightly arousing.

"Harboring secrets from me is not within your purview as my mate," she said.

"But I---"

Her eyes narrowed. "I will not have it," she emphasized.

My heartbeat pounded.

"No more secrets. Understood?" she asked.

I nodded and swallowed hard, momentarily speechless over the aura she projected.

Then her expression softened. It felt like a roiling storm had passed as she lightly stroked my cheek with her fingertips.

Okay, this is a lot better. Yet...

"Love and trust go hand in hand," she said. "I'll give you every bit of both that I'm capable of, but I will not spare calling you out, when necessary."

Who is this woman towering before me?

"Now, kiss me," she said.

My eyes never left hers as I stepped up to her and craned my neck to offer my lips, which she met with a long, passionate kiss.

"Now, do again...only better," she insisted.

I smiled, and initiated a passion-filled kiss of my own. Her arms encircled me and pulled my body against hers, garnering a powerful surge of arousal within me as my pulse raced.

When our lips parted, the edges of her mouth upturned slightly. "That'll do."

I was gobsmacked.

"Who are you?" I asked.

"I'm who you want...and who you need," she said simply.

I stared back at her blankly.

"Surely you understand yourself, my love? After our chat in the club, I know I finally do," she said. "As I promised, I'll do my utmost to fulfill the key role you need and desire. In fact, I relish it."

I blinked.

Our conversation that night in the Goth club quickly resurfaced in my mind.

She reached up, using both hands to lightly run her fingertips down the sides of my face and all the way down my neck in a manner that elicited a shiver through my body.

"Remember to be true to yourself and embrace it, just as I embrace you," she said. "And to hell with what anyone else thinks."

She kissed me softly, affectionately.

"I'm your mate," she said. "I'm not trying to rule you, or smother you, or demean you, or take away your independence. I'm only trying to protect you and fulfill you…"

She looked down into my eyes with affection, and I nearly dropped to my knees.

I will do absolutely anything for you.

I felt virtually rooted to the floor in awe as her words slowly sank into the depths of my mind.

"You're so endearing-looking right now," she said. "Which is in stark contrast to how I'm feeling about you."

She gave me a smoldering look. "I want to do some really wicked things to you right now."

My breath caught in my throat and the muscles in my body tensed with anticipation.

Oh, I want that, too.

"Nothing that'd hurt," I said.

"Only if you want it to," she said in a husky-sounding voice.

Her eyes drilled into mine with a predatory, hungry look that made my blood burn for her. She reached out to slowly scratch the tips of her fingernails down the back of my neck.

Her touch sent erotic chills down my spine, and I closed my eyes. Then, I felt her lips against mine and she breathed in as our lips locked, momentarily drawing the air from my lungs.

It felt like pure ecstasy.

The seal of our kiss broke just in time for me to take in a large breath of air, refreshing my senses.

"I love you so damned much," I said with all of the fiber in my being.

She appeared quite pleased over that. "And I'll love you forever."

She tapped me lightly on the end of the nose with her forefinger. "Now, what are we going to cease?"

"Secrets," I whispered.

"Good boy," she said with an endearing expression. "Don't forget."

She spared me a reassuring look and walked over to open the door to the office as I stood speechless.

"I sincerely appreciate your patience, Alton. I believe we're done for now," she said simply.

For now? Oh, please let this meeting end very soon.

I peered out of the corner of my eye at Alton, who observed me with a partially amused expression.

He walked over to his desk and picked up the flashlight again, as if there'd been no earlier interruption.

Kat watched me with a self-assured expression. She winked at me as I regarded her with an imploring look.

She knows exactly what she's doing to me. I feel like I'm about to explode right now.

"Better now? Good," Alton said. "About this new invention of yours…"

With great difficulty, I fought to focus my mind and return my attention to him.

"Um, you might want to be careful with that," I said, holding up my hand.

Ignoring me, he turned it away from him and activated the power button. The light blared out from one end and he quickly switched it off.

"Odds-bodkins, that is powerful," he said, handing it back to me. "Mere proximity to the beam makes it almost too painful for me to hold."

"The batteries are specially engineered for high output. However, that limits the battery life to a few minutes, at best," I said. "At least they're rechargeable. And I was thinking perhaps we could have some more manufactured. You know, maybe a few for both me and Dori?"

Alton nodded. "Absolutely. Capitol idea, actually."

I was quickly reminded of an unfortunate funding matter,

given the revelation about the initial development costs.

"Although I'm sure not much, if anything, is left in my investment fund," I said.

"I'll cover his costs," Kat said.

Alton held his hand up at her as he stared at me.

"My dear boy," he said. "You've paid for none of this. Consider it part of the Rutherford research and development process."

I hadn't expected that.

"Really?"

"I've funded your little experiment since the very start, Caleb," he said. "I've happily discovered that you have a promising instinct; one I'm willing to grant some latitude to."

He stared directly at Kat. "An instinct I believe others should embrace and not discount out of hand, wouldn't you agree, Katrina?"

She looked at him, then at me, and finally, back at him. "Oh-so-subtle, my old mentor," she said irritably.

Then she looked at me with a searching expression. "However, I'm willing to concede that your assessment may have merit where a specific human is concerned."

I mouthed the words: *Your human.*

She smiled. "I'm willing to grant him some degree of latitude; within reason, of course."

That seemed like quite a victory, of sorts.

Maybe she'll begin to trust my observations a bit more.

"No need for either of you to worry. I'm funding the production orders for additional units for Caleb and Dori; and perhaps for special human agents in my employ," Alton said before his gaze settled upon me. "Don't forget, you're family. You're a Rutherford now."

I felt very gratified to hear that.

Then I withdrew a smaller version from my jacket's interior pocket. "Oh, and it comes in penlight, as well," I said, holding it up.

Kat and Alton looked at the item in my hand, and then exchanged glances.

"I should've known," he said.

I offered him my best smug look.

"Here," he said, while handing me back the larger version. "You may yet need this."

"I should hope not," Kat countered darkly.

A light knock sounded at the door, and we all turned toward it.

"Come," Alton said.

The door opened to reveal Ms. Kendrick, who wore an apologetic expression. "I'm sorry to interrupt your conference," she said. "But one of our field agents, Mr. Thomas, requires a consultation with the General. Oh, and Ms. Turner, as well."

"I'll be right back," Kat said.

She quickly departed the office, pulling the door closed behind her.

I watched her leave, and wondered what Paige was up to. I hadn't heard from her since we arrived at the hotel last night.

I turned to Alton, who appeared circumspect as he quietly regarded me.

"Nephew, while you and Katrina were having your earlier exchange, I couldn't help but overhear part of your conversation through the door. So, please pardon my boldness, but would you mind if I offered you a small piece of advice?" he asked.

I shook my head, though part of me felt embarrassed that he'd overhead anything that she and I had discussed. "I suppose."

He walked over to me and placed a supportive hand on my shoulder.

"I recognize that expression on your face, but there's nothing for you to feel ashamed about. A vampire-human mating is very unique to each coupling," he said. "There's no template; there's no model. There are only two unique personalities trying to make the near-impossible plausible. Do you understand?"

I nodded.

314

Okay. Where's he going with this?

"Please remember this if you remember nothing else," he said. "Yours and Katrina's dynamic are your own. Whatever that may be, if it's right for you both, then that's what it should be."

I considered his words for a few moments.

...if it's right for you both, then that's what it should be.

"All right," I said. "But that's easier said than done."

He regarded me with a sober expression. "Look, to be brutally honest, the two of you seem to complete key components that each needs from the other. You're essentially mutually nurturing. And that, I believe, is why your future together is hopeful. But that's only true if you're both willing to embrace it honestly within yourselves."

"To thine own self be true?" I asked.

He arched one brow. "Indeed. Shakespeare was no idiot, Caleb."

"Thanks, Alton," I said. "I value your counsel."

"My boy, you're more than welcome," he said. "This may sound rather odd, but despite your seemingly unconventional pairing, it's undeniable; you and Katrina are very much in love, and you're envied by a number of vampires and humans alike in my midst."

Okay, that's a revelation in and of itself.

I smiled at the same moment that my stomach growled, almost like a lion's roar.

"Have you eaten today?" he asked.

"What? No, not yet," I answered.

"Shame on you," he said.

"Really, it's no big deal—"

The door abruptly opened we both fell silent and turned to see Kat returning. My attention was immediately drawn to the small wooden box she carried.

She hiked her free hand atop her hip and frowned. "You both appear oddly guilty of something," she said. "What were the two of you just discussing?"

"Oh, this and that," Alton said.

"Guy talk," I said with a shrug.

She regarded me with an amused expression as she walked across the office toward me.

"I suppose I'll allow it," she said, lightly running her fingernails down the back of my neck. "I'm no tyrant, after all."

"Oh, please," Alton said.

"I was speaking to Caleb," she said.

"Oh," he said. "Well then, do carry on."

I looked at Kat with a wide-eyed expression as she regarded me with a wicked grin.

I fear I'm at the mercy of some new kind of alpha-vampire now.

And, oh, how I relished the prospect.

CHAPTER 30

Caleb

Before we exited Alton's office, he reminded Kat that she was officially on holiday, and he encouraged us to take in the sights in London. He also recommended a fine French restaurant for us to try that evening called Paris Revisité.

"Come," Kat said.

"Where to?" I asked. "Maybe back to our suite?"

The feelings for her that had overtaken me in Alton's office were still vivid in my mind…and body.

She gave me a sly look. "Patience. Wait for it."

Now, there's a real challenge!

"Bye, Marla," I said, passing her office.

"Take care, Caleb," she said. "And please eat more."

I halted to peek into her office and gave her a sour look.

"Be *nice*," she said with an arched brow. "Or I'll have a word with you-know-who."

I shook my head at her and then hurried to catch up with Kat, who appeared amused.

"General," Adamo stood and greeted Kat as we approached the elevator.

She frowned. "Where's Kempf?"

"Guarding your suite, mum," he said, stifling an amused expression.

"Is something the matter?" she asked.

"Oh, nothing at all, General," he replied soberly. "Kempf greeted *Mr. Rawlings* quite nicely this morning."

At first, she had a blank expression. Then, her eyes widened and she looked at me sympathetically. "Oh, dear."

I gritted my teeth. "No harm done."

"I'm sure between the two of us we can keep an eye on *Mr. Taylor*," she said to Adamo.

"Certainly, General," he said, sober-faced. "I corrected Kempf already."

My stomach growled loudly, and both vampires looked at me.

I felt my face flush.

"Haven't you eaten anything yet?" Kat asked with a suspicious look.

Not her, too.

"Did Alton say something to you?" I asked.

"No," she said. "Why?"

"Oh, no reason."

The silence lasted only a couple of seconds.

"Well?" she asked.

I sighed.

"No, not yet," I said. "When I woke up, I thought I needed to get to Alton's as soon as possible. Half of the day had practically passed, you know."

Her displeased expression spoke volumes.

Jeez, it's no big deal. I can always grab a sandwich somewhere.

"You've lost a lot of weight," she said. "Is this your way of acting out against me for depositing you at Yale?"

What? Are you kidding?

I lost some weight. No big deal.

"I won't even dignify that with a response," I said.

When the elevator finally arrived, I followed her inside. Adamo also entered and stood facing the doors.

"I'm concerned, that's all," she said, wrapping her arm supportively around my shoulders. "Are you at least still taking the daily vitamin supplements we agreed on?"

"Mothering again," I warned. "But yes, I am."

"And did you bring them to London with you?"

Aw, crap.

"Um, forgot them, actually."

I stared straight ahead into Adamo's back but nevertheless saw her staring sidelong at me in my peripheral vision.

She actually growled at me.

"So, what's in the box?" I asked, attempting to divert her angst.

"You'll see," she said evenly. "And please try to take better care of yourself. You're the only you I have."

Just great. I hope I'm not in the doghouse with her again.

We stopped at the tenth floor which provided me with a hint as to where we were headed.

My suspicions were confirmed as we approached the doors to one of the nicer restaurants on that side of London, Shakespeare's.

Naturally, it was one of Alton's diversified companies. We'd eaten there with him in the spring during my first London visit.

Adamo held the door open for us, and we walked into a plush-looking entryway with a large, airy dining area beyond. The place was already bustling with the lunch crowd with an assortment of men and women in suits or other fine attire.

I glanced down at my casual pants and Oxford shirt.

Well, it beats the jeans I had on the last time I was here.

The maître d', Mr. Gibbons, a middle-aged man wearing a finely tailored black suit, stepped forward to greet us.

"Ms. Rawlings, Mr. Taylor, how good to see you both again," he said. "May I have the pleasure of seating you?"

"Please," Kat said. "If you have something available, that is."

The man appeared almost shocked.

"Oh, Ms. Rawlings, please," he said. "A discreet seating, perhaps?"

"That would be marvelous," she said.

He led us to a small private dining area along the far side of the restaurant that was separated from the main dining area by a set of French doors.

"The Rutherford Room," Mr. Gibbons announced grandly.

"Of course," Kat said.

Adamo took up a position outside the doors as Kat and I followed Gibbons inside.

"This is new, right?" I asked, appreciating the elegantly decorated table that seated ten.

"Added only a month or so after your spring visit," Gibbons replied. "Please note the marvelous view of London. And, of course, it's specially adapted for our more discerning clientele."

Secret code for vampires.

I gazed outside at a spectacular view, made safe for daytime vampire viewing via the coated glass.

Kat immediately went to a seat at one end of the table that permitted her a view of the city while also seeing the entrance to the room.

I held her chair and took a seat facing the window.

Within minutes, our places had been set and drinks and fresh-baked bread were brought out for us. I ordered the Beef Wellington while Kat ordered a fruit and cheese assortment. A fine bottle of chardonnay was brought to our table soon afterward.

"I ordered something high calorie, high protein, and even fattening," I said. "Truce?"

Kat stared at me in a manner that was almost unnerving. "Fine for now. But I want to see more meat on your bones in the near future."

I winked at her, and after a moment, she smiled back.

It was the perfect setting for us, and I felt very happy to be there with her. Fortunately for me, her recent displeasure with me seemed to have abated.

Once the wait staff left and we were alone, I looked at the small box sitting on the table to her right.

"So, as for the box," I said.

She adopted an amused expression. "You're very curious about that, aren't you?"

I shrugged.

"Clear a spot," she said.

I moved my plate and she placed the box before me.

"It's a gift," she said. "From Paige and me, and with Alton's blessing."

Okay, now I'm really curious.

"Go ahead," she said. "Open it."

I snapped open two small brass clasps and slowly lifted the lid.

Oh, wow.

Nestled into red felt were two small combat knives with matching black leather sheaths.

I looked up at her and she was grinning back at me.

"Take them out and see if you like the weight and feel of them," she said. "We had them specially balanced for throwing, though you and I have yet to train on that. Paige delivered them just before we left Alton's office earlier."

So that's what you were called out of Alton's office for.

I removed one of the knives and it immediately felt comfortable in my hand. The weight was light and easy to wield, and as I raked my thumb across the dual-sided blade, I found it to be lethally sharp.

"We wanted to wait for a special occasion to give them to you, but after last night, Paige and I agreed we simply couldn't wait," she said. "Your clever gadgets may be excellent for defensive action, but you need to be able to follow up with a killing strike."

I looked up sharply at her. "Killing vampires?"

"Or anyone else that attacks you," she said.

"Got it," I said.

She stared into my eyes in a penetrating fashion. "Listen closely to me, Caleb," she said. "Don't get a false sense of security from carrying these. If possible, you're to withdraw to safety when threatened; at least to the safety of those protecting you. However, if you're forced to fight, you're to kill anyone facing you, whether vampire or human. Rely upon the training you've been given; let it be fluid and automatic. Don't think; react. But most of all, if forced to fight, don't struggle merely to wound, don't falter... *kill*."

I must kill?

It was an odd edict to accept. But, like the vampire in the alley the previous night, I'd been an intended victim in their minds.

A dead victim.

"Do you understand?" she asked.

I swallowed and nodded.

I've killed a human and a vampire before.

Although that was using a briefcase bomb, and not entirely by design.

I can do this.

"What will you do if you have to?"

My eyes widened. "Kill."

"Good. Very soon, I'll instruct you in how to conceal them, and Paige will continue your training when you return home," she said. "In fact, Roman will be of excellent assistance, as well."

"Yeah, but these are illegal to carry around," I said.

"Perhaps in some settings and locations, but they'll do you no good unless you carry them," she said. "Obviously, you'll need to be careful to watch out for screening centers and metal detectors. However, Alton or I can work to address any issues that might arise from them being discovered on you, legal or otherwise. I simply can't risk you being killed or injured from lack of protection.

"There was a time not so long ago when I wanted to be the only person who could protect you. I wanted you to be dependent upon me for that," she said wistfully. "Unfortunately, it's a luxury I can no longer afford. And, with things the way they are now, I can't even be there if I wanted to, so the risk is too great."

I reached out to grasp her hand in mine. "Kat, I'll always

need you," I said staring into her eyes.

She glanced back down at the knives. "I'm glad you like them," she said. "Though it seems like such a dark gift to give a mate."

"No, they're incredible," I said. "And I appreciate your faith in my training and abilities to use them properly."

"Still, you'll continue to train regularly," she said, more as an imperative than an acknowledgement.

"Certainly," I said.

This is excellent; though I'll need to be careful carrying these around with me.

"You'll need to always use Sunset Air when you travel, so you can store them in your luggage," she said. "Alton has made arrangements with the company to ensure you can travel using their VIP-vampire fleet, whether you're accompanied by a vampire or not."

"Cool," I said.

Sunset Air is the best flying experience I could imagine.

"Though, for the most part, I expect for you to have a vampire escort with you as a general rule," she said. "Is that understood?"

"What? Oh, of course," I replied. "I'm not planning on gallivanting all over the world by myself or anything."

"Good. See that you don't," she said. "I don't take disobedience very well lately."

Uh, oh. She's gone all Dom on me all of a sudden.

What's happened to her in recent months?

Then, her mood lightened again, and she casually sipped her wine.

"Now, put your toys away and let's enjoy our day together," she said. "I thought we might see some sights via the Tube until it turns dark. Then we can try that French restaurant this evening."

I still hadn't forgotten our interaction in Alton's office.

"And some quality time in our hotel suite, perhaps?" I suggested. "We'll need to stow these away before we go out, right?"

Her sly look appeared deliciously amorous. "Oh, I intend to see to that, and to you, my love."

She squeezed my hand in hers and gazed into my eyes in a penetrating fashion.

Oh, how I do love her.

After a wonderful lunch of Beef Wellington, my hunger for food was more than satiated. However, there was one hunger still remaining, or as I preferred to think of it—dessert.

We returned to our suite, where I deposited my gift on the nightstand on my side of the bed.

Kat looked at me inquisitively. "Are we done here?"

"I don't know. Can I get you anything?" I asked. "Coffee? Tea? Me?"

She scowled and launched herself at me, practically colliding with me in the blink of an eye, passionately pressing her lips to mine.

Her actions immediately pushed the erotic buttons inside me, and I pulled her to me, communicating my heated desire through my own kisses.

She was what I craved most at that moment.

I caressed my hand across her thigh and continued my track upward underneath her leather skirt. Then I continued until my fingers lightly found their desired destination.

She moaned with pleasure, which only heightened my excitement. Parting from our kiss, she cupped my face between her hands.

"Oh, Caleb," she purred. "You've grown so adept at this."

"All for you," I whispered.

She pulled me against her body and permitted me to steer us to the edge of the bed where we fell upon the mattress together with a bounce.

Dessert is served.

* * *

I felt amazing by the time we left our suite.

We used the underground Tube access and rode the shuttle to the Holborn station.

Kat led us to a maintenance area where she produced an odd-looking key to unlock a large metal door. From there, we accessed an obviously abandoned portion of the Tube, where we traveled by foot through a creepy-looking and dimly-lit section.

My previous experiences inside the tunnels hadn't been very enjoyable. However, I felt more than safe with her present and Adamo in tow.

"Where are we?" I asked.

"This is part of the British Museum Tube station," she said.

"I haven't seen this place in forever," Adamo said from behind us.

"This is part of the London Underground's Central Line that was closed in the 1930s," she continued.

I was very impressed. "This is cool."

"I thought you might say that, my beloved historian," she said. "Alton was helpful in acquiring a key for us."

Of course; Alton can arrange most anything, I think.

We proceeded upstairs into the British Museum, along the Great Russell Road.

Ah, this is the kind of quality time with Kat I was hoping for.

The interior of the museum was a visual spectacle, divided into sections by category and period. Each section had its own distinct architecture and style, and the artifacts on display were a historian's dream.

For a time, everything felt perfect.

However, eventually my mind wandered, and my thoughts were drawn to recent events.

"What is it, my love?" Kat asked, squeezing my hand to get my attention.

"Things have happened so fast since spring, and not entirely for the best," I said.

She held my hand and looked at me with concern.

Glancing around the area, she motioned to Adamo and guided me into a small room containing old paintings and memorabilia.

"Talk to me," she said.

"Sometimes I feel like I've been drawn into a twister. First, a host of vampires from around the world were seeking us out after the whole Chimalma crisis," I said. "Then there was the international intrigue surrounding the Slovene conference and our nearly-fatal ending. Now, you're in charge of Alton's army, and there's no end in sight that I can see."

She adopted a sympathetic expression, though I detected a sense of sadness reflected in her eyes.

"Please, my love, you must have faith," she said. "Faith in me and faith in Alton. There'll be an end to this, one way or the other."

Although I wanted it all to end sooner than later, I didn't like the potentially dire implications in her prediction.

But then, maybe I was just being overly dramatic.

"What *is* Alton's end game?" I asked.

She took a deep breath and glanced up to see Adamo standing in the doorway to the room.

"The way Alton and I see it, there are two equally-acceptable ends to what we're trying to accomplish," she said. "Either we use strength to deter continued violence among our kind, or we eradicate the major threats. Hopefully, if we're able to eliminate the preeminent hostiles, the smaller threats will fall in line. If not, they should be easy to remove."

I had to admit that it all seemed very straightforward.

"I just want all of this to go away," I said. "I just want for us to be together; for our only concern to be mundane and silly; like running out of milk in the morning, debating our next vacation destination, or trying to talk Paige out of one of her harebrained schemes. I want to get back to some semblance of 'normality' or something a lot like it."

She wrapped her arms around me and affectionately kissed my forehead. In turn, I wrapped my arms around her waist and held her close.

"I know, my love," she said. "I want to get back to that, too. But please trust me when I say we will someday; and sooner than you think if I have anything to say about it."

I chuckled.

"You do. You're the General," I said. "You have an army at your disposal, after all."

One that, according to Paige, is growing larger every day.

She sighed. "So it would seem."

I loved the simple moment we were sharing; just me holding her and her holding me. I breathed in the sweet fragrance of cherry blossoms, a scent that'll always be associated with the woman I love.

Moments like this is what I want more than anything; an endless lifetime of this.

"My dear, sweet, beloved Caleb," she whispered. "Come, we should try to at least walk through a few more of the exhibits. It won't be long until sundown, and we can walk outside for a time before dinner."

I reluctantly parted from our embrace and craned my neck to gaze up into her eyes.

"You have the most beautiful eyes," I said.

She smiled and bent down to kiss me warmly.

"Come on, you little charmer," she said.

We enjoyed walking through more of the museum together and then exited streetside into the London night with Adamo trailing a discreet distance.

* * *

My remaining time in London passed enjoyably and uneventfully, though very quickly. Dori even made a quick journey from Paris to visit.

She, Alton, Kat, Paige, and I all went out to dinner together. Then we all went to the Red Griffin and celebrated until well after three in the morning.

It was wonderful. We were like one big happy family out on the town together.

Then before I realized it, the days passed and it was suddenly time for Paige and me to return to New Haven.

I actually dreaded it.

Alton must've sensed my hesitation because he took me aside on my final morning in London as Kat attended a brief, impromptu meeting with a couple of vampires.

"We're only a phone call away, my boy," he said. "And there's so much waiting for you when you return to Yale. Time will pass quickly, and before you know it, the holidays will be upon us."

I frowned. "You don't celebrate Thanksgiving here, do you?"

"No," he replied while thoughtfully tapping his forefinger against his lips. "Although I suppose we'll have to start. We can fly over to you, or you can come here. Either way, I'll arrange for a proper meal. Let me know which you prefer, and I'll see to it."

I grinned and reached out to shake his hand. "Thanks, uncle."

He shook my hand, and then pulled me into an paternal embrace. "No thanks needed; it's what families do, dear boy."

Kat accompanied us to the airport in Alton's limousine, and I didn't want to let go of her as we embraced each other in the boarding area.

"Stay safe, my love," she said. "And call me as soon as you land."

"I will," I said. "I love you."

"I love you more," she said.

I pulled away from her. "Hey! No fair."

"Gotcha'," she said with a satisfied expression.

She initiated a passionate kiss.

"Okay, okay, break it up, Bella and Edward. We've got a plane to catch," Paige interrupted, suddenly standing next to me. "Oh, and just for clarification, you're actually Bella, Caleb."

"Oh, *shut up*," I said.

"Yes, shorty, please do shut up," Kat agreed.

"Well, snarkey-snark-snark," she said with a snicker.

"Oh, no," I said. "The snark is back."

"That's right," Paige said. "And you two just got served big-time in a snark attack."

"Good luck on your flight back," Kat said with a wry expression.

"Thanks, I think I'll need it," I said.

Paige grabbed her carry-on luggage and stuck her tongue out at us.

CHAPTER 31

Caleb

Once Paige and I returned to New Haven, time did pass as quickly as Alton said it would.

The days flew by and I fell back into my routine of classes, research, and diversions with friends when I had some spare time, typically on weekends.

However, on the third Friday night following our London trip, my social plans had to be cancelled.

It was a shut in night for me.

Roman was sick upstairs with the flu, though Paige kindly injected some of her diluted blood to help speed his recovery. Even with that, he was still going to be recovering for most of the weekend.

I'd planned to go out to a group dinner and movie with friends, but Paige was feeling stir crazy and needed some quality time out clubbing.

She left as soon as the sun set, in fact.

So, I took the high road to avoid creating a scene and decided to stay home. At the very least, I could check in on Roman and see if he needed anything.

To be honest, it had felt like a hectic week between classes and continued research into the somewhat elusive background of the mysterious Dr. Oliver Simonson.

Using Yale's library services helped a lot, particularly their intercollegiate materials loaning agreement. Through them, I requested some rare editions of books that Simonson had either written or been cited in regarding his research surrounding Phlebotomy and his insights into the studies that later became known as evolutionary biology.

Needless to say, I had a lot more reading in my future.

Suddenly, a night of movie watching and popcorn sounded especially relaxing.

The only problem with my plan was the discovery of only a meager handful of popcorn kernels remaining in the house.

I cursed under my breath and told Roman I needed to go up the street to the nearest convenience store.

"Not alone," he insisted before sneezing repeatedly, followed by a bout of coughing.

"C'mon, it's just up at the corner," I said. "It's highly public and I'll be twenty minutes, tops."

"Take your knives," he said. "And nobody says anything to Paige; it's between us."

"Got it," I said with a nod.

"Hey," he called as I made it halfway down the steps from the third floor. "More cough drops!"

"Done!" I said.

See? I'm handy as all get-out tonight.

Using the advice Kat had provided, I slipped one of my knives in the small of my back underneath my leather jacket and the other one I strapped to my calf, grip downward and concealed by the cuff of my jeans.

There was a cold north wind that night, so I zipped up my jacket and walked briskly to Trumbull, and headed west a short distance to Whitney Avenue. Then it was a quick walk from there to the Haven Sent Mart.

I quickly found what I needed and walked toward the checkout. As I rounded the aisle, a pensive-looking man wearing dark clothing stood at the main register and asked for a pack of cigarettes.

The guy kept looking around him and nervously placing a hand in his jacket pocket.

The young woman at the register appeared wary and glanced over at me.

Was the guy preparing to rob the place?

Kat and Paige had always lectured to me to pay attention to my surroundings and think ahead over possible scenarios.

I didn't see anyone else nearby, though I remembered an old lady in the medicine aisle at the back of the store.

Get ready.

I stepped toward the register, acting nonchalant, but unzipped my jacket and started to reach to the small of my back to seek the hilt of my knife.

The guy noticed me approaching him and he turned to look at me.

We stared back at each other for a few seconds, and I kept thinking, *be ready for whatever he does.*

Combat techniques started flowing through my head like clockwork, and I tried to relax my body so I could move faster.

Then the fellow said, "Uh, I don't think I have my wallet. Just forget about it."

Then he quickly made his way to the exit.

My heart felt like it was beating a mile a minute as I let out a breath I'd been holding and placed my items onto the counter.

The cashier—her nametag said Cathy—looked relieved, too. "That guy was giving off a real bad vibe."

"Yeah," I said. "Maybe you shouldn't be working alone here tonight."

She shrugged. "One of the assistant managers had a flat tire, so he's not here yet."

I texted Roman and then visited for a few minutes more with Cathy until I noticed an older gentleman enter the mart.

"Finally made it, Cathy," he said. "Thanks for covering things for me."

Never a dull moment in my life.

"Hey, thanks a lot," Cathy said to me as I started to leave.

"Glad to help," I said.

I was relieved nothing actually happened, but I'd felt reassured about my state of readiness.

It was at that moment I fully appreciated the value of mental conditioning as much as practicing combat techniques.

I zipped up my jacket against the cold wind and rounded the corner onto Trumbull. For some reason, a shiver went down my spine.

I turned to look back over my shoulder and noticed those two thuggish-looking guys who I'd periodically seen around town; they were following behind me.

They were closer than I'd ever been to them, and that's when I took notice of their pasty-white faces. Despite the cold air, they both looked like they were sweating; almost as feverish-looking as Roman had been.

One of them had dark hair and the other fellow had a burr cut, and both looked to be around my age, maybe a little younger.

Why was there something so familiar-looking about them?

That's when it occurred to me that I'd seen those telltale symptoms before…back when I was transforming from human to vampire.

My own face had appeared quite similar.

Given the occasional traffic driving by, it wasn't as if I felt alone, but I didn't necessarily feel exactly safe, either.

A sense of aggravation and irritation bubbled up inside me. I was so tired of these two popping up to and fro on a whim.

I turned to confront them. "Who the hell are you guys, anyway?"

Rather than answer, they both rushed forward with a quick burst of speed that caught me off guard. They knocked me off of the sidewalk and into a dense line of ornamental trees.

Stupidly, I held onto my plastic bag of items, but successfully kept my balance with a pivot and spin of my body.

Each of them grabbed one of my arms and half-hauled me up to the doorway of an old building that we were in front of. That's when I managed to drop my grocery bag.

One of the guys kicked the rickety door open as I struggled to free myself. Then they threw me inside.

I rolled just as I'd been taught and recovered into a crouching position. It was so dark inside I could barely make out where they were both standing.

"Whose vampires you runnin' with?" one of them asked.

"What?" I demanded.

"You heard him, asshole, which clan you with?" the other man asked.

I just stared at them.

Clan?

"Let's beat it outta' him," the first one said.

Don't wait for them!

I lunged forward at the one that was closer, but the other fellow moved quickly to my left and slammed his fist into my ribs.

Spinning away from his punching side, I used my body's momentum and caught him in the solar plexus with my fist.

It felt like I hit a solid side of beef.

He swung at my head, and I managed to duck and pivot out of the swing, but the other guy was already trying to foot sweep me.

Damn, they're fast!

I barely managed to avoid falling and used my left hand to right my balance while reaching back to retrieve the combat knife hidden beneath my jacket.

The blade came free as I spun around with it in my hand. My arm made a neat arc and the blade imbedded firmly into the dark-haired fellow's chest.

The look of shock on his face must've matched my own, and everything seemed to freeze in time for a split second.

He gasped, as if out of breath, and staggered backward with his hands around the blade's hilt until he impacted the sheetrock wall behind him.

The other man rushed forward and began pummeling me about the head and gut almost simultaneously. I only managed to fend off a few of his blows as a series of pains erupted wherever they impacted me.

I saw stars on two different occasions before feeling myself falling backward.

My body impacted the floor with great force along with a huge wave of pain that coursed through my body, nearly taking the breath from my lungs.

Before I could roll up off the floor, my assailant was upon me, punching me over and over again.

His strength was ferocious.

I managed to bring my right knee up between me and his body, and kicked him away from me.

Reaching down to the cuff of my jeans on my right leg, I fumbled to grasp the hilt of my other combat knife.

I heard an angry roar and the guy was atop me again, raining a hail of punches down upon me.

My left hand reached into my jacket and grabbed at something—anything—I could use against him.

I felt one my small flashlights, which I activated and jammed toward his face.

To my surprise, he yelled out and held his right hand up before his face as his left fist shot out at me, catching me in the forehead.

My brain felt numb as I desperately sliced my knife upward in an arc at him.

I heard a gurgling sound coming from him as he teetered away from me.

I managed to make out his pale hands grabbing at his throat as he staggered to get up and then fell back onto the floor.

Everything had happened so fast that I was still reeling from shock and couldn't think straight.

I fought to understand what had just happened.

Flashlight? Why the flashlight?

The man's reaction didn't make sense.

I felt as if I was fighting to keep from blacking out as pain permeated my body. My head throbbed horribly even as my heartbeat was hammering in my ears.

I struggled in vain to get up but finally lay back onto the floor, listening to the sound of thunder somewhere nearby as I fumbled around for my cell phone.

…must've fallen out of my pocket during the fight.

Then I realized neither of the men was moving anymore; both had fallen strangely silent.

I thought I heard the distant sound of my cell phone, but it seemed so surreal I thought I might be hallucinating.

Then the sound of wind and rain outside, coupled with my ragged breathing, were the only noises around me.

Time felt suspended as I lay on the floor in a painful, winded state trying to recover enough to move again.

"Caleb!" yelled Paige's frantic voice seemingly from out of nowhere.

"What?" I asked, suddenly foggy-brained.

Then I felt her hands patting me over, which only exacerbated the pain my body was in.

"Are you injured?" she asked in a frantic voice.

"Ouch, stop, stop, yes," I said, trying to catch my breath. "I got the hell beat outta' me."

"What the freak happened?" she asked. "Who are these guys?"

"Vam-somethings," was all I managed to say in my addled state of mind.

"Vampires?" she asked. "You're not making sense, these guys smell like…no way."

"How did you find—?" I asked.

"Tracked your cell phone," she said. "Found it outside."

I felt a swish of air by me and heard the sound of rapid scuffling across the room and back.

"They're both dead, Caleb," she said. "Wait, I've seen

those knives—aw crap, did you kill them?"

"No choice," I mumbled.

"Okay, okay, we gotta' get you outta' here and then clean the scene," she said.

I coughed and then groaned as a sharp pain traveled through my ribs.

"Paige? Caleb?" asked Roman's raspy-sounding voice.

A beam from a flashlight swept the room and I vaguely made out the two bloody bodies in the room that had been my attackers.

"Oh, shit," I said, suddenly realizing I'd actually killed them.

Wait, Paige already said that…

"Roman, help me," Paige said. "We've got to get Caleb home and then take care of this…"

I tried to push myself up from the floor as intense pain coursed through my chest and abdomen. Lightning flashed through the open doorway, and I looked down at the blood-covered combat knife I was still holding.

That's the last thing I remember before seeing stars and then the world went black around me.

CHAPTER 32

Caleb

The next thing I remember, I woke in my bed with Paige sitting beside me. She caressed my face with her cool, soft fingertips and smiled down at me.

"Feeling better?" she asked.

As soon as I shifted where I lay, my body was filled with pain, and it was only slightly more bearable than not; certainly not as bad as I'd felt that night.

"What time—what day is it?" I asked, feeling confused and slightly disoriented.

"Saturday," she said. "You've been mostly unconscious since we brought you home last night."

She told me that she and Roman managed to dispose of the bodies, using her car to transport them outside of town once they got me safely home.

"You were pretty out of it, but we had to take care of things while we could," she said.

She also said they set fire to the abandoned building to mask forensic evidence.

She examined me at length and we both felt comfortable that nothing was broken, although my torso and head had already formed some ugly bruises.

I mostly slept for the remainder of the day.

When I awoke that evening, I felt as if I was in a semi-lucid state. At first my vision was slightly blurry, but then it focused and I recognized Kat sitting by my bedside.

I felt a wave of relief at seeing her. However, I still felt numb inside and half-asleep.

"Hello, my love," she said.

"What time?" I asked.

"It's Saturday still; almost eleven at night," she said. "Alton and I arrived as soon as we could. Ethan's here already, too. He's downstairs with Paige, but he wants to examine you further."

I took in a deep, pain-laden breath and let it out.

"S-sure," I said.

"How do you feel?" she asked softly, running her fingertips lightly across my face, just as Paige had done.

It tickled, but felt oh-so-very-soothing.

"Numb," I replied.

It was the word of the day for me; yet, so very appropriate. My mind felt clouded and hazy.

"Mild shock," she said.

"I kill---"

"I know. Paige told me about the two men," she interrupted me.

I killed two men last night.

Wait, there was something else.

"Not men," I said.

"Shh, rest now," she said, caressing the skin on my right arm with her fingertips.

A pleasant wave of tingling superseded the pain I was feeling.

"I've corrupted you, haven't I?" she asked. "I've gone too far this time, equipping you to contend with circumstances that you never should've been confronted with."

"No, you haven't," I said. "If you hadn't...well, I'd probably be dead right now."

I heard her sharp intake of breath.

"You know, most people go their entire lives without killing anybody," she said. "You deserved that sort of life. A life where you never had to worry about vampires, good or evil, or people stalking or preying upon you just because of who you love or are affiliated with.

"You deserve a life of peace and harmony with someone whose only contention might be that you forgot to pick up eggs on the way home from some mundane job," she said in a sad tone of voice.

"That doesn't matter anymore," I said, trying to keep the bitterness out of my voice.

I don't even know if what she described was even a possible reality anymore.

Was it really ever for me?

My childhood had started out pretty screwed up. *Would I have had any real possibility of making it to adulthood had a lovely, yet suicidal, vampire not intervened on my behalf?*

"What does matter, then?" she asked, searching my eyes as if seeking some hidden secret of the ages.

For me, no matter what I'd experienced since childhood, or since being reunited with Kat, there was only one reality that mattered.

"I love you," I said. "That's all that really matters to me."

She took my face in her hands and gently pressed her lips to mine, kissing me with tenderness and affection.

"Oh, my dear, sweet Caleb," she whispered. "I love you now and forever."

Ethan and Alton peered over her shoulder at me. Ethan wore a concerned look, but Alton's expression was different.

He smiled down at me; he looked proud.

That's when something fully solidified in my mind.

I had killed before; explosives thrown at a vehicle, only to have two living beings blown to bits, remnants of their carcasses aflame on the asphalt.

But what had just happened was so different.

"It felt so…personal," I whispered.

Kat frowned at me. "What?"

Alton squatted next to me and placed his warm hand on my forehead. "I know," he said soothingly.

"But it was more than that," I said.

"Yes?" he asked.

"It happened so fast. And much of it was automatic; like my body was replaying a memory," I said. "But it was awkward...erratic. Then it seemed so *easy* when it finally happened."

The tightness that immediately formed in my throat and chest spoke volumes of my shock over that simple realization.

"What you experienced, that's how it often happens, my boy," Alton reassured me.

"It shouldn't feel that easy," I whispered.

"Oh, but it should," he said. "It must, or none of us would be able to do it effectively. Your life depends upon it."

"My enemy too, though," I said.

"Yes, only you must be better than them," he said.

Yes, Alton had to be correct about that. To think anything less would seem foolish otherwise.

"Let me have a look at him," Ethan said.

Kat and Alton stepped back for Ethan to have access to me.

Fortunately, he said I should recover fine, and that he didn't think there was any neurological damage to be concerned about based upon his examination. He said I was likely in a state of mild shock, which should pass.

Additionally, as was done in Slovenia, he injected small amounts of Kat's blood beneath my skin to boost the healing of injuries. Then Kat topically applied her saliva to my cuts and bruises.

The numbing effects felt wonderful, in fact.

Later, she and I were once again alone; she lie facing me in bed, running her fingers through my hair.

"Who were those guys?" I asked.

"Alton's examining their cell phones. Rest assured, my love, we'll find out who those men were, as well as who they worked for," she said.

"Good," I said.

"And someone's got hell to pay," she said.

I had no doubt of it, in fact.

"One more thing," I said.

"Yes?" she asked.

"Please don't be angry with Roman," I said. "None of this was his fault."

"He shouldn't have let you go alone," she said in a displeased tone of voice.

I felt her body tense against mine.

"He was sick, and I was only going up the street a short distance," I said. "And Paige needed time to herself, as well. Who could've imagined any of it?"

She remained silent.

I reached out to place my hand to her cheek. "Please."

"Very well," she said. "As you wish, my love."

Despite the pain of moving, I shifted my body to be able to kiss her on the lips.

"Thank you," I said.

"In the future, you must learn to be more careful and honor the protections I put in place for you, my love, because I simply can't risk losing you," she said. "Promise me."

"I promise," I said.

I couldn't imagine not having her in my life either. I only hoped she was being as careful in London as I was supposed to be.

Then a warm feeling flowed through me, momentarily cutting through the fugue in my mind, simply knowing that she loved me so.

That's when I knew that my brain needed to wake up from its half-slumber. I needed to formulate cogent thoughts again.

"What now?" I asked.

In response, she moved to the other side of the bed and spooned alongside me, literally curling her body around me in a protective fashion. Her arm encircled my waist and she placed a warm palm against my bare chest.

She was coiled like a viper ready to strike, and yet, I felt as if I was nestled in the midst of the strongest fortress.

"Rest now, my love," she said. "Sleep and recuperate. And later, when you wake, we'll speak about such things."

Moments later, she lifted her arm and caressed my forehead and the side of my face with her fingernails as we lay together in silence. The warmth of her body permeated into me, and I gradually began to feel comfortable again.

I felt safe once more.

The soothing sensations of her ministrations lulled me into a kind of blissful disconnect from the world around me.

Time seemed to cease.

And eventually, I peacefully drifted off to sleep.

ABOUT THE AUTHOR

Jaz Primo: Delving into flights of fancy and realms of imagination; eagerly sharing with you.

Jaz takes great pleasure in sharing his creative visions. He's a history aficionado, "pun-master", and all-around fan of vampires. He authors paranormal romance, urban fantasy, and young adult literature, and has enjoyed a fulfilling background and career in higher education, including teaching U.S. History classes during evenings. Jaz lives in the Great American Midwest.

You can easily find Jaz Primo online at the following locations:

Website: http://jazprimo.com

Twitter: @jazprimo

Sunrise at Sunset: Revamped
Sunset Vampire Series, Book 1
(Second Edition)
by Jaz Primo

The Sunset Vampire Series achieved Third Place in the Reviewer's Choice Award for Best Paranormal Series of 2012 (Paranormal Romance Guild).

This new, second edition of the original, has new never-seen-before material, *Revamped* includes a forward by Jaz explaining how this version improves over the original. Additional bonus material includes a new bonus chapter that bridges events between the first novel and the sequel, *A Bloody London Sunset*.

When is a bloodthirsty predator the best protection against a psychotic killer?
When the predator is both a vampire...and the woman you love.

Caleb is bravely overcoming a dark past while having no memory of the beautiful vampire that saved him. Despite a promise to stay away, Katrina is compelled to return to him.
However, a vengeful rival from her past has dire plans for both of them.

Available in trade paperback and all major eBook formats!

Go to http://jazprimo.com/books for purchasing links!

Winner of the Paranormal Romance Guild's Reviewer's Choice Award for Best Young Adult Novel of 2012!

Gwen Reaper
A Young Adult Paranormal Romance
by Jaz Primo

Boy meets beautiful and mysterious, yet reclusive, girl who harbors a potentially-lethal secret.

"A thing of beauty is a joy forever: its loveliness increases; it will never pass into nothingness." John Keats, English romantic poet.
I never thought that my first exposure to real beauty would be tinged with the threat of oblivion...
~ ~ ~ ~ ~
When high school junior Scott Blackstone is forced to move from his childhood home in Springfield, Illinois to small-town Custer, South Dakota, he expects nothing less than to languish in complete disappointment. Instead, he discovers a beautiful and mysterious seventeen-year-old girl named Gwen, who captivates him from his initial, adrenaline-laced sight of her on the shores of Stockade Lake. Scott's pursuit of the elusive Gwen sweeps him into the midst of a potentially lethal family heritage that was birthed in hope, only to be passed into a legacy of guilt and death.

Scott engages in a journey of discovery, tinged with both angst and danger. Like many dire legends throughout history, he is unprepared for the untimely revelation that both love and despair are often two sides of the same coin.

Gwen Reaper
(A Young Adult Paranormal Romance)
is available in trade paperback and all
major eBook formats!

Go to http://jazprimo.com/books for purchasing links!

A Bloody London Sunset
Sunset Vampire Series, Book 2
by Jaz Primo

In *A Bloody London Sunset*, a timid spirit rises to assert himself, a forbidden love sparks, and a forgotten past threatens to topple the power of love.

Katrina Rawlings is a vampire who has finally rediscovered happiness for the first time in centuries. But unwanted complications erupt with a vengeance. Decisions of necessity combined with dark memories from a forgotten past threaten her relationship with the love of her life. When a sacrifice must be made, can she endure her decision?

Caleb Taylor's life is finally back on track. He has rebounded from a near mortal injury, both physically and emotionally. Yet, his reality is shaken by the suggestion of a betrayal of trust from the woman he loves. Can the power of love overcome the power of a lie?

Paige Turner is a century old vampire who fearlessly revels in a simple existence pursuing blood, dancing, and sex. Simple needs, and all met in the same manner: hot, fast, and without regrets. But a spontaneous visit leads to heartfelt sacrifice, and unexpected complications strike fear to the core of her soul. Will she survive the revelations?

In the exciting second novel in the Sunset Vampire Series, a trust is betrayed, bonds of friendship are strained, relationships may end, and a tenuous neutrality among the world's vampire population is threatened. With stakes so high, some will not survive A Bloody London Sunset!

Go to http://jazprimo.com/books for purchasing links!

Summit at Sunset
Sunset Vampire Series, Book 3
by Jaz Primo

Does the fate of one innocent human soul outweigh the needs of the entire vampire race?
The third, and most exciting, novel in the *Sunset Vampire Series* has finally arrived!

Powerful vampire Katrina Rawlings and her human mate, Caleb Taylor, are once more drawn into dangerous circumstances. Representatives of the most powerful and influential vampires from around the world converge upon a scenic mountain retreat located in Slovenia's Upper Bohinj Valley for a summit of historic proportion. Mystery leads to treachery, and events quickly spiral out of control. With the fates of both vampires and humans in jeopardy, Katrina desperately struggles to reconcile the balance of worldwide vampire power against honoring her commitment to the love of her life. Unwilling to be rendered helpless, Caleb initiates a desperate gamble that leads to a mortal decision. Meanwhile, the sexy and sassy vampire, Paige Turner, spearheads her own mission involving both surprising revelations of heart and grave circumstances for those around her.

In *Summit at Sunset*, unlikely alliances will be sought, eternal bonds of friendship will be tested, unrequited love will be unleashed, blood will be shed, and one pivotal person's fate will collide with destiny.

Available in trade paperback and all major eBook formats!

Go to http://jazprimo.com/books for purchasing links!

Wicked Sunset
Sunset Vampire Series, Book 4
by Jaz Primo

A Quick Note from Jaz:

Now that you've finished reading Wicked Sunset, would you please post a quick recommendation for my Sunset Vampire Series on your website, blog, or Facebook page to help spread the word about my works to others? How about a quick tweet or share my novel cover images on Pinterest?

While you're online, please post a quick review on Goodreads.com, Amazon, Barnes & Noble, Shelfari.com, or any other book review outlets available on the web.

Thanks so much for your kind support and assistance!

All the best,
Jaz Primo

Sunset Rising
Sunset Vampire Series, Book 5
by Jaz Primo

In *Sunset Rising*, the exciting fifth installment in Jaz Primo's Sunset Vampire series, life is the ultimate prize in a race against time.

Vowing retribution, Katrina tenaciously seeks out those behind the attack against Caleb, whose research to unravel a centuries old mystery attracts both unexpected competition and mortal danger.

Paige's conflicted feelings erupt, altering the lives of those she loves and leaving emotional disaster in her wake.

Battle lines are drawn as the vampire world's fiercest beings choose sides, rendering those undecided few as hotly contested spoils in a growing war.

In *Sunset Rising*, all bets are off!

Keep an eye out for book #5, Sunset Rising, coming out in late 2014!

www.ingramcontent.com/pod-product-compliance
Lightning Source LLC
Chambersburg PA
CBHW060155260626
47160CB00001B/282